The
ELOQUENCE
of the DEAD

Conor Brady

NEW ISLAND

THE ELOQUENCE OF THE DEAD
First published 2013
by New Island
2 Brookside
Dundrum Road
Dublin 14

www.newisland.ie

PRINT ISBN: 978-1-84840-299-7
EPUB ISBN: 978-1-84840-300-0
MOBI ISBN: 978-1-84840-301-7

British Library Cataloguing Data. A CIP catalogue record for this book is
available from the British Library.

Typeset by JVR Creative India
Cover design by Nina Lyons.
Printed in Sweden by ScandBook AB

10 9 8 7 6 5 4 3 2 1

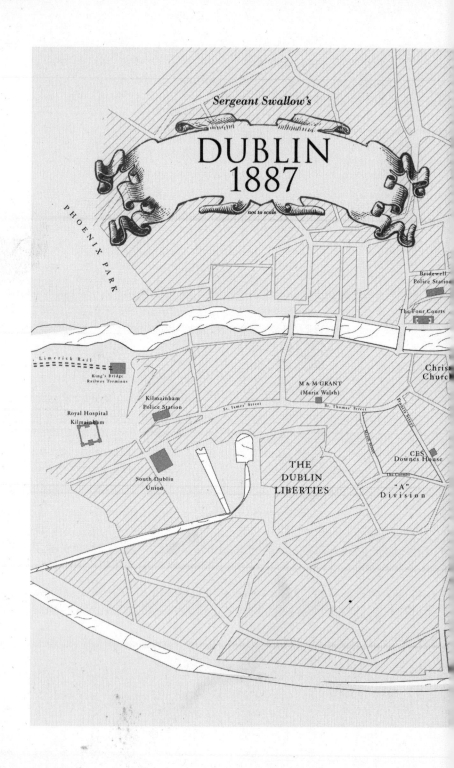

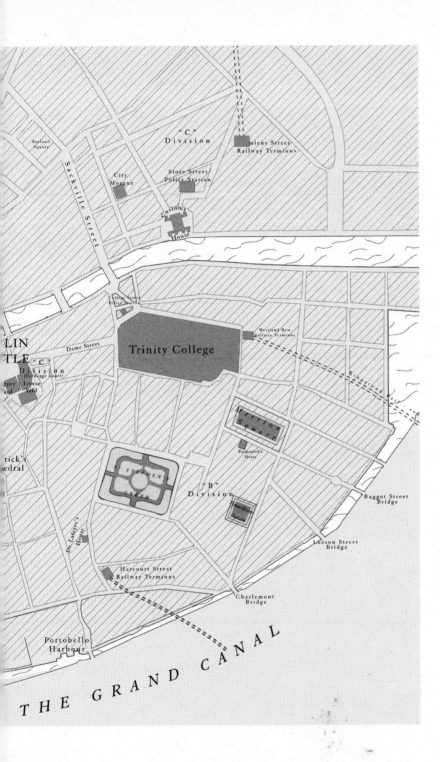

Rutland
Square

"C"
Division

miens Street
Railway Terminus

City
Morgue

Store Street
Police Station

Sackville Street

Custom's
House

LIN
TLE

"C"
Division
(the Lower Court)

Dame Street

Trinity College

Westland Row
Railway Terminus

Kingstown Rail—

per
d

Lower
ard

trick's
edral

Merrion
Square

Fitzpatrick's
House

STEPHEN
GREEN

Dr. Lafeyre's
House

"B"
Division

Baggot Street
Bridge

Leeson Street
Bridge

Harcourt Street
Railway Terminus

Charlemont
Bridge

Portobello
Harbour

THE GRAND CANAL

Acknowledgements

After learning of Detective Sergeant Joe Swallow's investigations in *A June of Ordinary Murders*, innumerable friends and readers came forward with ideas about how a policeman's conflicted role in 1880s Dublin might be further developed. Indeed, there were suggestions as to how he might secure his coveted promotion. There was even advice about his love life.

Some of this has made its way into *The Eloquence of the Dead*. I am very thankful. And I am thankful to everyone who has found Swallow's adventures and vicissitudes sufficiently engaging to have come back to read more.

I am grateful again to Eoin Purcell and the team at New Island Books for their encouragement and enthusiasm. Justin Corfield has been a challenging and meticulous editor. Who else would have known that from 1884, the London Underground Station at Tower Hill wasn't actually called Tower Hill? Gráinne Killeen did tremendous work on publicity for *A June of Ordinary Murders* and I know she has similar plans for Joe Swallow's second flight.

I would also like to acknowledge the many wonderful organisers and enthusiasts behind the arts and literary events that now so enrich life around Ireland. I was flattered and delighted to have been invited to so many of these over the past 18 months to read or to talk about Joe Swallow and the murky nineteenth-century world of Dublin Castle's G-Division.

Finally, I would like as ever to acknowledge the love and forbearance of my family while I have been time-travelling back to Victorian Dublin. Their patience and support have been untiring, and I am both fortunate and thankful.

Conor Brady
Dublin
September 2013

Prologue

In the morning, she knew, the officials and the clerks would come. They would arrive at the house, perched on their rattling traps and half-bred horses. In her mind's eye she could see them, advancing past the now abandoned gate lodge and along the avenue.

They would gather in typical disorder around the sweep of the granite steps outside. The bolder ones would stare insolently through the windows. Some of them would already show the signs of drink.

There would be rain. She had known since girlhood how to interpret every combination of cloud and wind and light that came across the mountains from the west to Mount Gessel.

She could sense it with the softening of the air, a faint tang of salt and oil and dampness. It would be the penetrating, grey rain that could roll in off the Atlantic in any season and settle on the Galway countryside like a blanket.

They would mill about the forecourt, stoat-like, strutting their little authority. They would affect politeness, deference. They would nod obsequiously, as they had to generations of Gessels. They would call her 'Yer Ladyship,' or 'Lady Margaret,' as in the past, but now in a tone that conveyed their new confidence and their contempt.

Some of the tenants, impatient to be masters of their acres, would probably come too, muttering in their Gaelic, cursing her and her kind. And it would be made legal. She would be gone. The deeds of transfer were drawn up. The last boundary maps were signed off. The cheque was in the solicitor's office in the town.

It was her late husband's cousin, Richard Gessel, who had finally persuaded her to get out. Sir Richard was a rising star, she had been told, in Prime Minister Salisbury's staff, and he had the inside track on things.

'Lord Salisbury's government are agreed that the way to pacify Ireland is to give it back to the Irish, field by field, farm by farm,' he had told her when he visited Mount Gessel in the springtime.

'If you sign up early you'll very likely get the best price. And if we're put out of government, a new administration might not be as generous to the Irish landlords,' he warned.

She would step out the front door at 10 o'clock, and she would surrender the key to the solicitor's clerk. At precisely the same hour, in the town, another clerk would cross the street from the lawyer's office and deposit the government cheque with the local agent of the Bank of Ireland. In two days, the money would be safely in her account in London.

Christ, she would be glad to be out of it.

If the early generations of Gessels lived well out of the place, she had seen little of it. After her husband's death, all she could remember was misery, bills, pressure from creditors and battles with rot and damp to keep the house from falling down.

Nobody could say that she had not done her bit. Or that the Gessels had been bad landlords. Forty years ago, when the Great Famine, as they were now calling it in the newspapers, devastated the countryside, did they not do their best for the people? A great cauldron of soup was made ready every day in the yard. She had helped prepare it herself, and taken charge of its distribution to the starving, silent wretches who staggered in from the fields and the roadways to have its nourishment.

They had dropped some rents in the bad years when others had refused to do so. In Mayo and Roscommon, she knew, some landlords had actually raised them. In the end, of course, when there were no rents coming in, there had to be evictions. Most of the families had gone to America, as far as she knew. No doubt, they were better off there.

It would be a relief to have money; to be able to pay her way; to meet old friends without worrying about the cost of lunch; to be able to travel, perhaps to Switzerland, for sun or to take the mountain air; to end her time, perhaps in a good hotel on the Sussex Coast or even in the south of France.

She walked through the rooms for what would be the last time. Some of the best furniture had been sold to stave off creditors, but there were still a few good paintings in the gallery. Most of the silver, marked with the Gessel family arms, was still in the dining-room. There were the display cases of ancient coins brought back from Italy and Greece by her late husband's grand uncle. Now these would go too, to be auctioned or sold by the government agent before the house was boarded up or torn down.

Margaret Gessel was beyond caring.

Six months ago, the Land Leaguers or some of their friends had burned the stables. The screaming of the horses as they perished in their stalls had pierced the granite walls of the house. The following night, the constables on protection duty outside had shot and wounded two locals – would-be incendiaries, they said – at the back of the house.

The District Inspector implored her to go to Galway to stay at a hotel for a while in order to let things settle. He had instructions from his superiors, who had in turn been contacted by Sir Richard at the Prime Minister's office in London, to afford her maximum protection. But, he explained, there was only so much he could do with the limited man-power at his disposal.

When a fellow landowner told her in the hotel dining-room that he was going to take up the scheme put forward by Lord Salisbury's govern-ment, she decided it was time to follow Richard's advice. The next day, she ordered her solicitor to negotiate a deal for the sale of Mount Gessel under the new tenant-purchase programme.

She went into the empty ballroom. One of the few happy memories she had of the house was of parties here. Now there were only ghosts. The chandeliers were long gone; the mirrors carried off to be auctioned. The fire mantle of polished Carrara marble was blocked with timber against the winter draughts.

She crossed to one of the bay windows and drew down the steel bar from the heavy wooden shutters. The first of the rain was falling, light drops against the glass, but there was sufficient moonlight to see the sweep of the estate across the fields.

Out there on the open sward, Gessel ancestors had drilled their militiamen before leading them off to fight Bonaparte, in Spain and at Waterloo. In happier times, the East Galway hunt would meet on the forecourt between the house and the meadow. For a moment, she believed she could still hear the jingle of harness, laughter, the yelping of the hounds as they moved out along the avenue.

She could make out the dim sheen of the lake, where generations of Gessel children had skated on the winter ice or swum in the heat of summer. She followed the curve of the avenue along which her husband had brought her as a young bride to become the new – and the last – mistress of the house. He had died young, a long time ago. Nobody around the district seemed to remember him any more. Sometimes now she even had difficulty in trying to recall his face.

It was more than 20 years since their son, the only child of their union, had driven away down the same avenue. She could see the boy still, turning to wave as he left for India, travelling to a forgotten war from which he never returned.

Beyond the boundary wall, towards the village, she could see the faint outline of the parish church that the Gessel family had endowed after they were granted the land by William and Mary almost two centuries ago.

She could still hear the drone of successive preachers as she sat, bored, in the front pew, reading and rereading the memorial plaques on the walls, proclaiming the gallantry of long dead Gessel soldiers and the virtues of their mothers, wives and sisters.

The ground over there by the churchyard was latticed with Gessel bones; fathers, mothers, soldiers, farmers, maiden aunts and strange uncles, babies that failed to thrive, grandparents who lived to ripe old age, children who fell victim to mishap or disease, young wives who died in childbirth.

To hell with them all, she thought bitterly. They all had their time, and they were better times than hers. She was leaving them to a country gone to savagery and disorder, where property could neither be maintained nor made safe, where demagogues and agitators ruled public life, encouraged by a subversive press and tolerated by a spineless government.

Now the rain was spattering on the window, obscuring any view. To hell with them, to hell with the crumbling house, the interminably demanding land, the devious, brutal people, the whole cursed place. She had held on at Mount Gessel for longer than anyone could have reasonably demanded. Everyone of substance, everyone she knew, from the Shannon to the sea, was cutting their losses and getting out.

To hell with Ireland.

THURSDAY SEPTEMBER 29TH, 1887

ONE

News of the murder of Ambrose Pollock at his pawn shop on Lamb Alley travelled swiftly through the Liberties.

His killing especially alarmed the shopkeepers and dealers. But there was nobody in Dublin of whom it could be said that they mourned him. And if ever he had a friend or anyone to speak warmly of him, nobody could remember who that might have been.

It was the brutal and mysterious circumstances in which he died that impacted mostly on the public consciousness, causing fear and anxiety to spread abroad in the city over the dry, shortening days of late September.

The Commissioner of the Metropolitan Police, Sir David Harrel, did not attempt to deny that the murder of the pawnbroker and furniture dealer should have come to light sooner.

When the Assistant Under-Secretary for Security at the Castle, Howard Smith Berry, sought an explanation for the delay, the head of the detective office at Exchange Court, John Mallon, insisted that there had been nothing in the intelligence reports to suggest the imminence of any unusual criminal activity.

But Smith Berry's personal security advisor, Major Nigel Kelly, was not persuaded. The word around the Castle was that the irascible ex-soldier from Belfast had given warnings about the laxity of the police in general, and the detective branch in particular.

Earlier, when the city Medical Examiner, Dr Harry Lafeyre, was called up to examine the body, its state of decomposition told him that the man had been dead for many days.

That the crime of murder could remain so long undetected on the flank of the Liberties, a stone's throw from gates of Dublin Castle itself, was a serious failure of policing at a time when the administration desperately needed to show that it had the upper hand against crime and disorder.

The significance of various recent occurrences at Pollock's only became apparent after Sergeant Stephen Doolan from Kevin Street police station had forced the back door of the shop earlier that morning.

The pawn shop and furniture dealer's frontage faced across Cornmarket to the two churches, located side by side, both named in honour of St Audoen.

Dubliners were untroubled by this oddity of double nomenclature. One was Roman Catholic. The other, the older, was Church of Ireland. It was only fair, citizens argued reasonably, for both religious traditions to keep a partial claim on the peripatetic little Norman saint who had protected the city's walls since the reign of King John.

Neighbours and customers reckoned that Ambrose Pollock was probably 60. His sister Phoebe with whom he operated the business was younger, perhaps 40. One side of the premises was occupied by a warehouse in which were stored the furniture that Ambrose bought and sold. In the trade, it was said that anything good that came into Pollock's was sold on to the more lucrative London markets.

Brother and sister lived on two floors above the pawn shop. The greater volume of Pollock's pawn business was drawn from the maze of poor streets, courts and alleys that stretched away towards The Coombe and the great, sprawling workhouse known as the South Dublin Union. But with the reputation of never refusing to make an offer on goods, however little that offer might be, it drew trade from across most of the poor, miserable areas of the city.

Phoebe dealt with customers in the pawn shop from behind a brass grille, while Ambrose monitored transactions though a half-frosted window from the back office. If he thought that she required direction on the price of any item brought in for pawn, he would rap sharply on the glass, then she would leave the counter and retreat to the back office to have his decision. It was Ambrose who determined charges, values and prices.

A grimy window with three pawnbroker's spheres suspended overhead advertised Pollock's to those with business on the main thoroughfare. But the entrance to the shop was around the corner on Lamb Alley.

Thus, while the pawn shop had a high visibility on the bustling commercial street, the entrance on the laneway enabled customers to come and go discreetly.

This was supposed to place a particular obligation upon patrolling constables of the A-Division. Officers walking the beats that touched on Cornmarket or High Street were to proceed through Lamb Alley to satisfy themselves that the premises of the pawnbrokers was secure. They were to note any unusual persons that might be encountered in the vicinity and to record anything that was irregular.

It was to emerge in the aftermath of Ambrose Pollock's murder that these requirements had been allowed to fall into desuetude. Careless beat men no longer diverted into the alley, preferring to shorten their tour by continuing directly through Cornmarket. In reality, the premises were rarely checked. No intelligence was gathered on persons coming to it or going from it. Had it been otherwise, it is likely that the pawnbroker's brutal murder would have been discovered more quickly.

A few days earlier, a young constable had just ascended the Forty Steps from the Liffey embankment to the curtilage wall of the older St Audoen's. As he reached the street, he saw a closed car turning into Lamb Alley. It bore the trade livery of Findlater's, Dublin's most select grocers and wine merchants.

The policeman's curiosity was aroused. None of the residents of Lamb Alley or its environs would be in the way of ordering their provisions from Findlater's.

He crossed High Street, and turned into the alley. The deliveryman had drawn his vehicle to a halt outside the pawn shop entrance. The constable saw the driver's helper open the doors of the car and drag an open basket to the tailboard. He balanced it briefly to adjust his grip and then hauled it through Pollock's door.

The constable stepped across the alley and grinned up at the driver.

'Things must be bad when the gentry are poppin' their groceries into the pawn shop.'

The man laughed.

'Ah, you've the wrong end of it. It's an order from the woman of the house. Mind you, she must be plannin' a good dinner and a fair sup of refreshment too.'

He winked, and raised his hand to his mouth, mimicking a drinking gesture.

The helper exited the shop and resumed his seat on the car. The deliveryman flicked the reins and moved off.

The policeman knew that Phoebe Pollock was not a woman who would send for expensive food and drink to be delivered to her door. Perhaps it was stolen property. Perhaps he had let the Findlater's car depart too quickly. He pushed Pollock's door and stepped into the shop.

Phoebe sat behind the counter as usual.

'Is everythin' all right, Ma'am?'

Phoebe Pollock smiled. The constable thought that when she smiled he could see the remnants of a once attractive woman. Behind her, in the back office, he could see her brother's head and shoulders outlined through the frosted glass.

'Why wouldn't it be, Constable?'

'I saw some unusual deliveries just comin' in the door. You were expectin' them?'

'That was just some groceries I needed.' She gestured airily at the shelves and display cabinets around her. 'Everything here is grand, as you can see for yourself.'

The policeman returned to his beat. Why should he worry if people decided to spend their money in shops that charged double the prices they might pay in their own neighbourhood?

Later, at the station canteen, he joked about the incident. But he did not report it in the occurrence book. It was a negligence that was to cost him a reprimand and a deduction from pay.

On the following Wednesday, just before midnight, another more experienced beat officer had an unusual encounter a short distance from the pawn shop.

Some policemen disliked the beat section past the gates of old St Audeon's. It was said that the place was haunted by a long-dead vicar whose malevolent ghost disliked human company. It was also a favourite dumping spot for nightsoil from the nearby tenements, where a dry privy might be shared by up to 100 people. The shit stank in the summer, and oozed across the pavement in the wet of winter.

So the constable had crossed High Street to take up an observation point in a shop door.

A slight, respectably dressed woman was crossing the street, picking her way over the cobbles. Even allowing for the uneven surface, her step seemed unsteady.

When she reached the pavement, he recognised Phoebe Pollock. She seemed to sway slightly on her feet as he approached.

'Good night, Miss Pollock.'

In the street light, he could see that she was focusing with difficulty. She made a little shuffling step and put one hand out to the lamppost for support. The constable realised that Phoebe Pollock was drunk.

'The footpath there is terrible broken and uneven,' he said tactfully. 'You'll be makin' for home, Miss. Sure, I'll walk down that way with you.'

She reeked of alcohol, but she produced a key from her bag and after some fumbling managed to find the keyhole. She muttered a thank you and made her way inside. The policeman retreated to the corner of Lamb Alley, and watched the house until he saw a faint glow illuminate one of the upper rooms.

Later, he entered the incident in the occurrence book, noting Phoebe Pollock's name and address and the time of their encounter.

Sergeant Stephen Doolan saw the entry the following morning when he went through the night patrol reports in the sergeants' office. He crossed the corridor to the day room, where the morning shift of constables was preparing to parade.

'Who's on the first beat through High Street and Cornmarket?'

'That's me, Skipper,' a constable put his hand up. 'What's on your mind?'

'Get along up to Pollock's. As soon as they open the door, go in and have a word to make sure everything is all right. One of the lads on the night shift found Phoebe Pollock the worse for wear out on the street at midnight.'

Every policeman knew the Pollock's reputation as eccentrics who kept to themselves, but some older people in the district recalled when Phoebe was a pretty young woman, full of life, with many friends in the neighbouring houses and streets of Dublin's Liberties.

There were chuckles and hoots across the parade room.

'Jesus, she must have robbed the shop to be out spendin' money on drink.'

'Ould Ambrose wouldn't approve. That fella has his first communion money – if he ever made a first communion.'

'Sure them two is as tight as a frog's hole. And that's watertight.'

Later, the constable positioned himself at the junction of Lamb Alley and Cornmarket. Ordinarily, he knew, the shop would open between 9 o'clock and 9.30. But the hour came and went. At 10 o'clock, when the officer tried the door, he found it still locked. He walked back to peer through the window facing Cornmarket, but he could see no movement inside. At 10.30, when there was still no sign of life, he decided it was time to report to Kevin Street.

Twenty minutes later, Doolan took two men in from their beats and borrowed a ladder and a crowbar from the hardware shop on High Street. One of the beat men leaned the ladder against the back wall of Pollock's. With an agility that belied his bulk, the bearded sergeant climbed over and dropped down into the small yard. The constable followed.

When the back door resisted the impact of their combined weight, Doolan jemmied the crowbar between the lock and the receiver, then he pulled hard on the metal bar. The wood splintered above and below the lock. They shouldered their way through.

They were hit by the unmistakable, cloying smell of death. Doolan drew a handkerchief from his pocket and clamped it across his mouth and nose.

It was only a few paces to the shop floor. There was no sign of Phoebe Pollock, but Doolan noticed that the high stool on which she was usually perched was now lying sideways on the floor.

His square of flannel did nothing to alleviate the smell. As he crossed to the counter with its brass railing, he could see Ambrose Pollock's outline through the half-frosted glass window, seated as usual in the back office. The pawnbroker was in his customary chair with his back to the door, his head inclined at a slight angle towards the desk with its ledgers and account books.

But Ambrose Pollock was not at work. The back of his head was a dark mess. Shards of broken skull protruded through matted grey hair. When Doolan walked around the desk, he saw that the face and hands were a mottled black. A pool of crusted bodily fluid, agitated by the wriggling and heaving of white maggots, gathered where the dead man's feet rested on the boards.

Doolan retreated across the shop to where the door exited to Lamb Alley and flung it open. He half-gagged, drawing the clean, fresh air from the street deep into his lungs.

The startled constable waiting in the alley placed a concerned hand on the senior man's heaving shoulder.

'Are y'all right, Sergeant? What's after happenin'?'

'Go down to Exchange Court and tell them to have the G-men up here fast. And get them to send for Doctor Lafeyre. There's been murder done.'

TWO

Joe Swallow deeply resented the fact that he had to wheel and deal over the duty rosters to get the free time for his painting class.

Regulations stipulated that leave was 'subject to the exigencies of the service.' With the G-Division fully stretched in surveillance and protection duties since Queen Victoria's jubilee in the summer, there was little or no flexibility in the application of the rules.

The jubilee had passed off without serious incident, in spite of rumours and threats. It had been all that the authorities had wished it to be. A celebration of Britain's might and majesty, of industry and progress, of military power and civic enlightenment. A full one quarter of the globe was marked out in red, ruled over now for half a century by this small, rather plump little woman as Queen and Empress.

Ireland, however, remained the troublesome child of the worldwide British family. Even though the government had pumped money into schools, infirmaries, harbours and roads in the aftermath of the famine, the Irish were not content. The tenants on the farms, led by the one-armed agitator, Michael Davitt, were making impossible demands. Reduced rents, security of tenure and now outright ownership of the land. Each night brought reports of burnings, shootings and attacks from over the country. Meanwhile, the charismatic Charles Stewart Parnell was driving the campaign for Irish Home Rule, effectively aiming to separate Ireland from the Kingdom.

The police had intelligence about dynamiters and assassins, poised to strike as the actual jubilee celebrations took place in June. But a combination of harassment and skilful use of the Coercion Act by the police forces ensured that Dublin remained a relatively safe enclave in a country racked by agitation.

The plainclothes elite of the Dublin Metropolitan Police were housed at Exchange Court, huddled in against the dark, northern flank of Dublin Castle. The G-men dealt with both 'special' or political crime and 'ordinary' crime. They provided armed protection for the key officials in the Castle administration, the Chief Secretary, the Under-Secretary and their senior aides. They were also the administration's eyes and ears, watching over the activities of the myriad groups and individuals across the city that might constitute a threat to security.

'A half day to go to a feckin' paintin' class? Are ye serious, Swalla'?'

Detective Inspector Maurice 'Duck' Boyle was master of the Exchange Court rosters. Every week he contrived to skive a full day off police work proper, retreating to the warmth of the inspectors' office to labour over the production of a duty timetable for the G-Division.

He threw his pencil on the desk in exasperation.

'The city's plagued be Fenians, land grabbers and dynamiters. There's so-called intellectuals and fellas talkin' t'each other in feckin' Gaelic so we won't understand them. There's a new crowd of throublemakers now settin' up some sort o' spiritual debatin' club.'

He leaned back in his chair and joined his hands across his corpulent belly.

'Apart from that there's the fuckin' criminals. Scuts, gougers, knackers. The Vanucchi gang is out robbin' houses in Donnybrook. And you want time to go to a paintin' class. Jesus, how am I supposed to cover that?'

'I don't want you to cover anything,' Swallow answered testily. 'Just give me the bloody Thursday half day and put me down for the night shifts. It's a fair bargain.'

It was more than fair, he knew. Every night G-Division was stretched, watching meetings and gatherings across the city. There was any number of extremists out to break with England. There were land leaguers trying to mobilise action against the big estates. Demagogues harangued crowds at street corners and in halls. American–Irish veterans from the Civil War delivered inflammatory orations at public meetings, promising dollars and guns.

'You need all the men you can get for the night shifts,' he told Boyle. 'I'll do more than my share if you fix me up for the half day like I'm asking.'

He ended up taking on five consecutive nights on the escort and protection detail.

Senior Castle officials were under twenty-four-hour guard since the assassination five years previously in the Phoenix Park of the Chief Secretary, Lord Frederick Cavendish and the Under-Secretary, Henry Burke, by the Invincibles.

Swallow had been part of the investigating team that tracked down five of the extremists. He watched them hang at Kilmainham for their crime.

On a human level and as fellow Irishmen he felt pity for them, pathetic, misused pawns, sacrificed by men who were clever enough to keep their distance when there was killing to be done.

He understood their convoluted motivation too, after long nights of conversation with the condemned men in their cells at Kilmainham jail. There was no love of England in his childhood home in County Kildare. His own grandfather had joined the pikemen in the rising of '98. But violence was futile, he believed. More had been achieved for Ireland by the pacifist emancipator, Daniel O'Connell, he reckoned, than by all the hotheads who had led others to their doom in half-cracked plots and rebellions.

The threat level against the senior figures in the administration was as high as ever. The Chief Secretary, Arthur Balfour, had earned the soubriquet of 'Bloody Balfour' for his strong law-and-order policies. The new Under-Secretary, Joseph West Ridgeway, lately arrived from military command in Afghanistan, was equally deemed a hate figure by the extremists.

G-men were also assigned to provide protection for the Irish parliamentary leader, Charles Stewart Parnell. Swallow disliked the detail, but it was a means to an end.

The early hours with Parnell usually passed quickly. The acclaimed leader of Irish nationalism would be on the move each evening, attending official functions and public events. But once he returned to his house at Fitzwilliam Square, the night was tedious. Swallow and the other armed detective on the detail kept watch through the long hours from the shadow of the park's overhanging trees.

Officially, the G-men were on protection duty. But it was well understood that the detail was simultaneously a surveillance.

The G-men had learned to interpret the movements of the household, noting and recording arrivals and departures. Parnell's political lieutenants often stayed late, and were sometimes accommodated in the house. So too, the G-men noted, did Mrs Katharine O'Shea, the wife of

Captain Willie O'Shea, formerly Member of Parliament for Clare. The fact that Parnell and Mrs O'Shea had been lovers for several years was common knowledge among the G-men.

At the end of the shift, the details recorded in the G-men's notebooks would be copied into the intelligence register at Exchange Court. Swallow was uncomfortable with the espionage. As an Irishman, he recognised Parnell as the greatest leader of his country since Daniel O'Connell, but it added to his tally of hours worked just the same.

It had been Lily Grant's idea that he should enrol in the water-colours class that she ran at the Metropolitan School of Art on Thursdays when her teaching schedule at Alexandra College left her free.

Her suggestion had been floated in happier days; before Swallow's relationship with her older sister, Maria Walsh, had cooled. He had since vacated his lodgings above Maria's public house on Thomas Street where his romance with his one-time landlady had developed.

If anyone had asked him if he loved Maria he would have said yes. But even that surprised him still. Until he knew her, love had never really flowered in his badly ordered life, defined initially by excess of alcohol and later by job ambition. She had helped him to find self-respect, to accept that he was valued not just as an efficient police officer but as a man. But in spite of that, when the time had come to make a full commitment, he had baulked.

Yes, he could say he loved Maria. With equal certainty he could say that he disliked her sister.

The two sisters were as unalike in character as chalk and cheese. Grant's public house had come down for three generations through the female line. As the elder daughter, it was natural that Maria would take over the business. But it also suited her sociable, outgoing temperament. Lily was born to thrive in the starchy, formal atmosphere of a college for young ladies.

'You have a natural talent with the brush. But you're still lost in some basic techniques, an amateur really,' she had told him haughtily.

But her distain and his dislike for her did not deter him from enrolling in her class. At forty, he had been a late starter, even though he had been a constant sketcher in his childhood in rural Kildare. He had discovered pleasure and satisfaction in his new pastime while growing more disillusioned in his job.

He acknowledged grudgingly that she was right about his techniques. He was clumsy in mixing primary pigments, and he invariably saturated the paper when he tried to apply a wash.

The unhappy parting with Maria put further strain on relations between teacher and student. There was the added complication that Lily Grant was engaged to Swallow's friend, Harry Lafeyre, the Dublin City Medical Examiner. He did not envy Harry Lafeyre the prospect of a life with Lily Grant.

With typical brashness, she had addressed the issues head-on.

'The fact that you and Maria have gone your separate ways is no reason why you shouldn't persevere with your painting,' she told him. 'If you enrol for my course, we'll just have to rise above any unpleasantness that may persist.'

Shortly after Stephen Doolan had broken through the back door of the pawn shop on Lamb Alley to discover the body of Ambrose Pollock, Swallow was in Lily's class, dipping his brush in and out of his palette to finish a Dublin Bay seascape

Katherine Greenberg had been painting beside him since the start of the class. The young Jewish woman was probably the most talented member of the group, Swallow reckoned. Now the class was finishing. She rose from her easel, moved behind him and looked over his shoulder.

'You have a lovely view of Howth Head there, Mr Swallow. And you have the cloud cap in a wonderfully deep blue.'

He was unwilling to admit that the nimbo stratus he had created over Dublin bay was the random outcome of mixing too much indigo with insufficient water.

'That's what I like about the sea,' he answered. 'It changes all the time. So you can paint it in any colour you want.'

He hoped he sounded convincing.

He glanced at Katherine's easel. She had completed her still life; red and green fruit in a silver bowl with a fluted decanter standing beside it. She had depicted the two vessels on a brocaded cloth, falling in heavy folds from a tabletop. The backdrop showed a furnished room with a high mantle in black marble.

'That's very good. Is it from the imagination or did you set up the scene?'

'Oh, I wouldn't rely on my imagination,' she laughed. 'It wouldn't retain the detail. So I set up the model at home. I borrowed the bowl and the jug from the shop and I stole the fruit from the housekeeper.'

Ephram Greenberg's shop on Capel Street was one of the city's best known dealerships in antique silver and gold. The Greenbergs had traded there in precious metals, rare coins, fine paintings and classical statuary for decades.

'You'd be best not to tell me about any crimes you've committed, Miss Greenberg' he said cryptically. 'I'd be in trouble with your father if it turned out that I hadn't taken appropriate action against a thief.'

'I think I can get away with a couple of apples,' she laughed again. 'He relies on me a lot to run the business now. He never really got his strength or his spirit back after my mother died.'

Swallow knew the Greenbergs since his days as a young beat constable at the Bridewell.

Katherine had her mother's dark features and hair, deep brown eyes and a slight tendency to weight. Unusually for a Jewish girl in the Dublin community, Swallow knew, she had not married. Swallow reckoned that she was probably around thirty by now.

'Yes, I know they were a very united couple.'

'Mind you, he wouldn't take it well if I forgot to put the silver back where I found it. They're both George III, you know, Irish, very rare,' she said jokingly.

For a brief moment she dropped a hand, lightly touching Swallow's shoulder as she pointed to the bowl and decanter in her picture.

Lily Grant saw the touch as she came across the classroom. Her sharp eyes ran over the pictures set up on the semi-circle of easels. She stopped beside them.

'I hope I'm not interrupting anything.'

The edge to her voice was sufficient to convey her disapproval of their bantering.

'I'm going to see Mrs Walsh – Maria – for lunch,' she told Swallow. 'You'd be welcome to join us, if you like.'

He picked up the tone. It irked him that Lily should presume to intervene in his conversation with Katherine.

'Actually, you did interrupt. I had asked Miss Greenberg how she had composed the scene for her still life.'

Lily gave a little sniff.

'I see.'

'As to lunch, thank you, but no,' he told her. 'I'll have to make do with the canteen at the Castle.'

He knew that even though Lily was under no illusions as to how he felt about her, she wanted a restoration of good relations between himself and her elder sister.

Maria had put in five years of widowhood before he had come into her life. Over time, their relationship developed. First, there was friendship, then physical intimacy. Swallow had not led a sheltered life in that respect. Twenty years as a policeman in the city had put him in the way of female comfort more often than he wanted to remember. He could still recall the perfumes of the whore-houses where he had roistered in his alcohol-fuelled student days. But with Maria it had been unlike anything he had known heretofore. He felt a part of her, drawn in completely into a union of the flesh and the spirit that he had never known before.

Soon there was talk of a future together. But when Swallow felt that Maria was pressuring him to a decision, he hesitated.

Matters had come to a head during the investigation of the Chapelizod Gate murders earlier in the year. He had unwittingly placed the two sisters in danger. Maria had been implacably angry. Against a backdrop of tension and recrimination, he had vacated his lodgings at Grant's. For more than a month now he had rented a small house at Heytesbury Street, off the South Circular Road, with his sister Harriet.

He told himself that he had stepped back, not walked away. The relationship was not dead. Maria had made no attempt to rent the room to anyone else after he left. He came to visit the bar a couple of times since then, but he made no attempt to stay. She made no effort to persuade him to do so.

For a moment, he thought that Lily was going to retaliate. Instead, she smiled coldly.

'Maria asked if you and Harriet would be free to come to dinner on Sunday. Harry and I will be there. Maybe Harriet might like to bring a friend as well. I gather she has a widening social circle.'

He was not ready yet to engage in any serious discussion with Maria. But Sunday dinner accompanied by his sister might be as good a way as any to break the ice. Maria and Harriet got on well. He sometimes believed that Maria's relationship with his sister was warmer than it was with her own.

'I don't expect to be working,' he said without enthusiasm. 'So I'll be there. Please extend my thanks.'

Lily eyed Katherine. 'You'll understand, Miss Greenberg, that Mr Swallow and my sister, Mrs Walsh, are close friends.'

The message was clear. There was to be no dallying with a man who was still in Maria's life, however tentatively. But Katherine Greenberg was not to be put down so easily. The dark eyes flashed in annoyance.

'And you'll understand, Miss Grant, that Mr Swallow and I have known each other since my childhood.'

Lily smiled with exaggerated sweetness and turned to leave the classroom.

'Well, Miss Greenberg, I had no idea. That must have been such a very long time ago.'

THREE

Although he estimated that the pawnbroker had been dead for at least a week, Dr Henry Lafeyre could say with reasonable certainty what had killed him.

'Broken like an egg,' he told Detective Inspector 'Duck' Boyle after a brief examination of the back of Ambrose Pollock's skull. A two-pound iron weight on the floor, stippled with dried blood, seemed a likely candidate as the murder weapon.

'He was hit where he sat.' Lafeyre pointed to the blood-splashed papers on the desk. 'You can see the spattering there.'

Two lengths of rope encircled the dead man's chest, fixing him to the back of the chair. The wrists were tied in front with a thin rope. Another was looped and knotted around the ankles. Anyone looking through the frosted glass from the shop would have seen Ambrose Pollock in his usual sitting position with his ledgers and account books.

Boyle was the senior officer on duty at Exchange Court when the breathless constable dispatched by Stephen Doolan turned in to make his report.

It was unwelcome news. 'Duck' Boyle had brought the avoidance of crime work to an art form. On this occasion, he had no option but to respond. He sighed and put down the sheaf of duty rosters on which he had been happily idling.

'Swann… Feore,' he barked at two young G-men ploughing through their own paperwork at their desks.

'On ye'er pins. There's a murder above at Lamb Alley.'

Paradoxically, the corpulent Boyle was glad of the fresh late September air after the dankness of the detective office. G-men invariably grumbled that they were housed in the unhealthiest part of the Castle. The complaint was not unfounded, and it was reflected in a high incidence of respiratory illnesses among the detectives.

'Duck' Boyle had earned his soubriquet from the curious, waddling gait that caused his posterior to swing from side to side as he walked. But he kept up with Swann and Feore, covering the quarter mile along Lord Edward Street and past Christ Church to Lamb Alley in what he saw as a respectable ten minutes.

Assailed by the odours from inside the pawn shop, he had waited outside for the arrival of the Medical Examiner and the police photographer.

Dr Harry Lafeyre caught the stink the moment he stepped out of his brougham carriage. He took the stopper from a small bottle of scented salts, put it to his nose and inhaled deeply. Then he handed it to Boyle.

'Have a sniff of that, Inspector. You won't imagine you're in a rose garden, but it'll help.'

Curious onlookers had gathered from the nearby tenement houses and street stalls. Shawled women and ragged children. Idle men in worn-out clothes and old, broken boots. Any excitement was welcome in lives lived out in crowded tenements with poor nutrition and primitive sanitation. They were being kept at a distance from the entrance by half a dozen constables. Lafeyre heard his own name being spoken as someone in the crowd identified him.

Stephen Doolan met him at the door.

'One man dead in there, Doctor. Ambrose Pollock. He's the owner. The sister who runs the place with him is gone missing. We've searched from top to bottom.'

Boyle and Doolan led him to the back office.

Even at midday, the light was dim, just sufficient for Lafeyre to take in the essentials of the scene. After a visual examination of the body, he gestured to the bloodied iron weight on the floor close to the dead man's feet.

'That would have done the deed easily enough, without needing too much force.'

'And light enough to be wielded by a woman,' Doolan observed. 'But the woman isn't here. She's away, isn't she?'

He had checked for any signs of a forced entry on the ground floor. When he found none, he opened two of the windows facing into the yard in an effort to vent the odour.

Then he went through every room, moving upward floor by floor. The smell was fractionally diluted as he climbed higher, but he kept his handkerchief clamped over his nose and mouth.

The parlour on the first floor was littered with empty bottles – port, sherry, gin and whiskey. An oval table was covered with dirty plates and pots, fragments of food, bones and what might have been chicken carcasses. The smell of organic rot contested with the stench from the floor below. When he stepped into the room, a platoon of small brown creatures scurried away under the ends of the curtains.

Two rooms with peeling wallpaper on the top floor functioned as sleeping quarters. A pair of boots and a hanging tweed suit signalled that the first was used by Ambrose Pollock. An unmade bed, strewn with female clothing told Doolan that the second room was Phoebe's. There were more bottles on the floor and on the washstand.

But there was no trace of Phoebe Pollock.

When Lafeyre had finished, examiner and policemen stepped gratefully out of the office into the fresh air of the back yard.

'She must have taken off early this morning,' Doolan said. 'The house is clear and there's no sign of a break in. A beat man found her on the street late last night, full of drink. That's why we wanted to check out the state of things here this morning.'

'Duck' Boyle smoothed his beard and then clasped his hands across his waistcoat.

'I believe that I can put up what's called a hypothesis,' he said solemnly. 'This woman done a runner. She musta' brained him for some reason unknown and then took to the drink over a number o' days.'

He paused. 'It would be me further hypothesis – it's a Greek word be the way – that she propped him up so the clients would think he was workin' away as normal. Then she takes to orderin' in as much food and drink as she could handle until eventually she legs it outta here, knowin' that the game was up.'

'It looks that way all right, Inspector,' Doolan said cautiously. 'But in case it isn't an inside job, we'll need to circulate a warning around the area.'

'That's what we'd want t'avoid,' Boyle said impatiently. 'We don't want to be frightenin' the lives outta the citizenry. It's a simple case that a madwoman's after killin' her own brother. I hope I'm clear on that.'

Lafeyre and Doolan nodded in unison, seeking to convey their shared appreciation of Boyle's deductive capacities.

Detective Tony Swann appeared at the back door.

'The tills are empty here in the shop. She must have taken whatever cash there was.'

Boyle smirked. 'There y'are now. What did I tell yiz?'

'She'd have been driven out by the stink sooner or later anyway,' Doolan said after an awkward interval. 'I wonder why she did it. What happened between them?'

'Should you send for a priest... or a minister?' Lafeyre inquired.

Doolan shook his head. 'I don't believe Ambrose Pollock had any religion at all. If he did, he didn't take it very seriously. I wouldn't trouble any holy man for him.'

'Well, you have to locate Miss Pollock one way or another. In the meantime, we'll have the photographer make a record of what's to be seen here. And I'll arrange for an ambulance to take what's left of her brother to the morgue for a post mortem.'

'We'll notify the special posts on the railways and the sea packets in case she tries to leave the city,' Doolan said. 'I'll get a description out on the ABC.'

The ABC police telegraph system had been installed after the Phoenix Park murders. It enabled messages to be diffused simultaneously across the city's network of more than thirty stations.

'Yer right, Sergeant,' Boyle slapped a pudgy fist into the palm of his other hand. 'We'll dhraw a net of steel aroun' Dublin city and in that net we'll surely catch Phoebe Pollock, the fish we want.'

FOUR

Swallow rinsed his brushes, and closed down his colour box. The sea-scape was quite dry by now, so he could put it safely in his portfolio. As he came down the staircase, making for the front entrance of the school, he found himself in step with Katherine Greenberg. He held the door for her.

'I think I upset Miss Grant,' she said as they stepped into Thomas Street. 'I certainly didn't intend to. Do you think I should apologise?'

Swallow snorted impatiently.

'You needn't be so sensitive. If anything, you're the one who's due the apology. She thinks she should be protective of me. You see, I had been… how shall I put it… keeping company with her elder sister, Mrs Walsh. She's a widow. She owns a business just up the street. I had accommodation there for a time before I moved on. '

'Ah, now I understand,' she laughed. 'She's looking after her sister's interests and she saw me as some sort of a threat. You'll have to explain to her that I've known you since I was – what – ten? And anyway, a Jewish woman and a gentile policeman of a certain age wouldn't seem a likely partnership, would they?'

A certain age? That hit him. He hoped his face did not betray what he felt.

He was not that old. He was fit and active. A match for any man of her own age. Maybe more so. And she was not so very young herself at this stage.

He avoided giving an answer.

'If you're going back to Capel Street I'll walk that way with you. I'm due back at the Castle for 2 o'clock.'

They turned into John's Lane, passing Power's model distillery. White banners of steam were rising from the ventilators of the still house. The air was sweet from the carpets of grain spread out across the drying floors. Somewhere under the scent of the grain there was the sharper tang of malt. It was said that up to 1,000 men were at work in John's Lane at any hour of the day or night.

'You're a detective sergeant now,' she said. 'I've seen your name in the newspapers.'

They stopped on the pavement to allow two of the distillery's drays to lumber out through high gates into the cobbled street.

'That's right. You won't read many happy stories about me in the papers.'

'Do you enjoy it?'

Swallow had not expected the direct question, even though it was one he found he was increasingly asking himself.

His boss at G-Division, the legendary John Mallon, had marked his career cards earlier in the year. If he stayed in G-Division he was unlikely to move beyond his present rank. His Roman Catholic religion was against him for a start. His inclination to challenge authority did not help either.

'Go and make a decent woman of Mrs Walsh,' Mallon told him. 'You can draw your pension and run the business with her. Or go for promotion in the uniformed ranks. Religion and politics won't block you there, at least not to the same degree.'

If he were truthful, he knew, he would say that he was boiling with rage. He worked his guts out on the job. He took risks for it. And he was better at it than most of those who had moved ahead of him in rank.

'I don't enjoy it as much as I used to,' he told her. 'I've been at it a long time. I won't deny it can be very satisfying when you manage put a committed criminal out of the way. But it's a hard life.'

'Is it dangerous? We read of terrible things happening around the country with evictions and shootings and burnings.'

Oddly, that was a question he rarely asked himself. Two unarmed policemen had been shot at Essex Gate, not half a mile from Dublin Castle. One died and the other was permanently invalided. There had been other casualties in the city since, but none fatal. G-men were always armed on duty, and many chose to carry their Bulldog Webley revolvers off duty as well.

He considered his answer.

'Things haven't been too bad for the city police. The Royal Irish Constabulary in the countryside have been taking the brunt of it. Most of my work is investigating crime or doing protection duty around the city.'

They followed the descent of St Augustine Street towards the river and turned into Bridge Street.

'I remember you telling me when I was a young girl that you started off in life to be doctor,' she said, 'but you became a policeman.'

'I did.' He heard the bitter edge to his own voice. 'I drank my way out of medical school.'

'I can see that you regret it,' she said. 'I'm sorry.'

'Nobody's fault but my own. My parents worked hard to see me educated. I threw it back in their faces.'

'Are they still living?'

'My mother is. She's not young, but she runs the family business down in Kildare. A public house and grocery at a crossroads called Newcroft. The usual business in rural Ireland, I suppose.'

'Do you remember you told my father that he should think about medicine for me? You told him they were training women to be doctors in England and that soon they'd be doing it here too.'

'Advice is easily given,' he said ruefully. 'You've heard the expression "do not as I do but as I say." I'm not a great example. But you didn't follow my advice anyway.'

They came to the river at Usher's Quay, crossed to the pavement beside the Liffey wall and turned downriver.

The water had been sucked out into the bay by the ebbing tide. It was black and viscous where the channel ran between oozing mud banks. Across the river, Swallow could distantly see a gaggle of barristers gathered on the steps of the Four Courts. Their black robes and white wigs put him in mind of a flock of wagtails.

'No, I didn't. My father would have been very willing to see me educated to be a doctor,' she said. 'It would have been a great distinction for a family that started here in Dublin with nothing. But I like the business. I enjoy it and I think I'm good at it.'

A skein of geese flew past them above the water, honking to each other, following the river's line to the sea.

'And are you happy to operate the business there with your father, or have you ever thought of spreading your wings to see a bit of the world?'

She gazed after the birds as they made their way along the water course.

'Jewish people are often thought of as wanderers,' she said after a moment. 'But when we find a place that gives security and comfort, we're much like anybody else. We stay where we're content. And I've seen a bit of the world, London, Paris, Berlin. I worked in the trade in London for a while.'

They reached Essex Bridge.

'I'll leave you here,' Swallow said. 'You're nearly home and I'm going up this way to the Castle.'

'Thank you for your company,' she said cheerfully. 'You know, if you're interested in seascapes you should come into the shop sometime. There's an original by Van de Velde, and quite a few English and French works too.'

For a moment she frowned slightly.

'My father would always be glad to see you. In fact, at this time there is a matter that I think he would be happy to speak with a policeman about... a policeman he trusted.'

Then she brightened again.

'I would be glad to see you too. And since you're not being fed by your landlady any more, I could make you a very good *kosher* dinner, you know.'

FIVE

Exchange Court was at action stations when Swallow walked in off Dame Street. A grim-faced Detective Pat Mossop came bustling out the main door, followed by two constables. Three police side-cars jostled for space in the narrow confines of the Court.

Swallow winced to see the pencil-thin Mossop moving at speed. He was still under medical care, recovering from the gunshot wound he had sustained during the arrest of the presumed double-murderer, Simon Sweeney, just a few months previously.

'You're going like there's a fire lit under your breeches, Pat,' he called.

Mossop turned, but hardly slowed his stride.

'You'd better come with us. They've spotted Phoebe Pollock at the Northern Hotel. She must be making for the Liverpool packet.'

Swallow laughed, uncomprehending. He knew Phoebe Pollock. Crime investigations had brought him many times into the pawn shop on Lamb Alley.

'Why in God's name are you chasing Phoebe Pollock?'

'Come on,' Mossop took him by the arm. 'You mustn't have heard. Ambrose Pollock was found murdered this morning above at Lamb Alley.'

'Jesus Christ. What happened?'

Mossop climbed aboard the first of the police cars and beckoned Swallow to the seat beside him. He snapped at the driver.

'Northern Hotel, North Wall Quay. As fast as you can.'

He leaned across the car as the driver flicked the reins over his horse.

'It looks as if she's robbed the place.' He wheezed, drawing breath. 'And she's done for Ambrose. Stephen Doolan and a couple of bobbies from Kevin Street had to break in this morning. He's been dead a week or more. Phoebe's gone, and so is all the cash from the shop.'

'Jesus,' Swallow said again. 'Who's on the scene? Did they get Harry Lafeyre up there?'

'Boyle's in charge. Dr Lafeyre says the skull was crushed with an iron weight. They sent out an urgent ABC. A beat man down by the North Wall says he saw Phoebe going into the hotel there a couple of hours ago.'

The police driver was skilful. The horse's hooves sparked off the tram tracks as he weaved through Dame Street's traffic. They flanked the Bank of Ireland on College Green, turning into Westmoreland Street and clattered over Carlisle Bridge to swing eastward along Eden Quay.

Swallow gripped the handrail. His sense of excitement stirred as they picked up speed along the quay, the wind from the river whipping their faces. He liked this part of the job, the urgent challenge of the unknown, the almost childish delight at the prospect of adventure, danger perhaps. It compensated for the long days and nights of tedium and routine. Who could tell what might lie at the end of a dash like this?

They passed past Butt Bridge and Gandon's Custom House, the driver negotiating his way past the drays and delivery wagons that crowded the busy quayside. Swallow noticed that the first of the autumn leaves were dropping from the plane trees in the Custom House garden.

They slewed to a halt on the cobbled quayside. The Northern Hotel was a drab, functional building, put up in dark red brick between the Dublin Port and Docks Board's granite depot and the water's edge.

Its business was almost wholly based on feeding, watering and accommodating the passengers who travelled between Dublin and Liverpool. The cross-channel packet, *Maid of Cumberland*, was berthed at the quay directly across from the hotel, a wisp of grey steam hissing from the funnel.

The waiting constable who had spotted Phoebe Pollock stepped forward to meet them. Swallow knew him by sight. A senior man. Reliable.

'You're sure it's her?'

'Ah sure, I know her well from me days in th' A-Division. I checked that shop more times than I care to remember.'

'How long since she went in?'

'Comin' up on two hours.'

'On her own?'

'Yes. Carryin' two small cases.'

'You didn't think to arrest her?'

'No grounds,' he said sharply. 'And how was I to know at that stage that you fellas wanted to see her?'

'True enough,' Swallow conceded. 'Come on so.'

They took the front steps together while Mossop went to the back of the hotel.

A porter in a greatcoat that had seen better days hauled the front door open, bidding them good afternoon.

The lobby smelled of old cooking. Swallow's nose told him there was fish and vegetables and bacon fat in it. Two or three men sat reading newspapers or working on account books. An elderly couple were drinking tea at an alcove table.

A middle-aged man in morning dress behind the reception desk came to alert as they strode across the lobby. A small brass plaque on the desk said: 'JOHN L. BARRY, GENERAL MANAGER.'

'Police,' Swallow told him unnecessarily. 'We're looking for a lady on her own, seen coming in here maybe two hours ago. She was carrying two cases. Perhaps forty years of age. Respectable, but maybe a bit under the weather.'

The man gave a little snort. 'Lots of ladies come and go. It's a hotel. I imagine you can see that.'

'Less lip and more co-operation might be better if you want to keep your licence,' Swallow snapped. He turned to a grey-haired clerk seated behind the general manager.

'You there, you must have seen her,' he gestured across the lobby. 'Where did she go?'

The clerk jumped. 'She asked for a room. Said she was tired. So I told her she could sign the register later. She went upstairs. I gave her number nineteen.'

Swallow glared at Barry. The general manager raised his hands in a gesture of helplessness.

'I can't see everything.'

'Go and get a female member of your staff. We need her to go up there with us,' Swallow told the clerk.

The man scurried out through a door behind the desk. He reappeared after a few moments accompanied by a stout, unsmiling woman with black hair in a greasy bun. She scrutinised Swallow.

'Youse want me to fetch down a guest?'

Swallow nodded. 'I'd be thankful. We need to speak to her on police business.'

'I'm the housekeeper, not a bailiff.'

'Jesus, we seem to be dealing with a full cast of smart arses here.'

He affected an exaggerated politeness.

'Your assistance would be greatly appreciated, Madam, if you can spare us a few moments.'

'Am I riskin' me life in goin' up there? Is this individual violent?'

It was not an unreasonable question in the circumstances.

'Oh, not in the slightest,' he lied. 'And we'll be right behind you. We just need a female for the sake of decency.'

She led them along the first floor corridor and knocked at room nineteen.

'Housekeeper... this is the housekeeper.'

There was no response. She called twice more.

She put a key in the door, turned the handle and stepped inside.

'Youse must be practical jokers,' she called. 'There's no wan here.'

Swallow and the constable were through the door in an instant. The room was empty. Swallow got the smell of bitter almonds.

'Prussic acid,' he told the constable. 'A tincture of that and nobody lasts more than a minute or two.'

He scanned the room.

A pool of water had formed on the floor beside the bed with a shattered earthen pitcher and a wash bowl in the middle. Swallow surmised that they had probably been swept off the small dressing-table beside the window. The bed itself was at an angle to the wall, as if it had been pulled away. The coverlet was drawn half way up, creased and rumpled.

'Somebody musta tossed the place. Or there was a struggle,' the constable muttered.

'That's her bag anyway.' He pointed to a small travelling case on the floor at the end of the bed.

'She had it when I spotted her outside. But she had another one as well.'

Swallow saw a small brown bottle on the mantle shelf over the fireplace.

'Don't go near that. It's very likely the prussic acid.'

The desk clerk and the housekeeper hovered at the door.

'I'm closing off this room,' Swallow called. 'The medical examiner will be coming. Nothing's to be touched.'

By now, Pat Mossop had arrived, accompanied by Barry, the manager.

'Get across to Store Street,' Swallow told the constable. 'Message Exchange Court. Tell the duty officer we have a suspicious situation here. We need the medical examiner and the photographic technician.'

He lifted the small case to the dressing-table. Mossop snapped open the locks. There was a blue dress and a white blouse, a brush and comb set and a pair of shoes. Mossop reached into the case. He made a little whistle. When he withdrew his hand, he was clutching a bundle of money.

SIX

Dublin was a city where news usually travelled more quickly than the press could report it.

By early afternoon, before the evening newspapers were able to publish any details, most of the population knew about the murder of Ambrose Pollock and the disappearance of his sister, Phoebe.

It passed along the city streets from business house to business house. Passengers relayed it to cab men and tram drivers. It spread into the public houses and shops. It travelled through the courts and alleyways and into the tenement houses of the once-prosperous Georgian streets on both sides of the river. The prostitutes in the brothels around Gloucester Street and Mecklenburgh Street learned about it as they prepared to receive their early clients of the evening.

Reports of outrages might briefly engage the minds of all classes. But the pawnbrokers, the jewellers, the silver and goldsmiths and the watchmakers across the city were particularly alarmed.

Violent crime was not a frequent occurrence in Dublin. But if there were murderers and robbers abroad, any business that dealt in precious goods would be vulnerable. Their stock in trade, being portable, valuable and saleable, was highly prized by criminals.

The business community would draw little comfort from the newspapers' clichéd accounts of how the police were leaving no stone unturned. They knew the forces of law and order were preoccupied with the activities of extremists like the Fenian Brotherhood and its various splinter groups. Ordinary crime was very much a secondary concern.

In contrast to the shopkeepers and traders, the murder of a pawnbroker and furniture dealer in a poor part of the city did not impinge greatly on the consciousness of the professional classes. These things happened.

And indeed, they probably happened with less frequency in Dublin than in other cities.

Although the scene of the murder was less than a quarter of a mile away from the offices of the legal firm Keogh, Sheridan and James, the news scarcely registered with the partners, or indeed with the apprentices or the legal clerks. They were absorbed in their own business.

And business was brisk. The greatest transfer in property owner-ship since the clearances of the Scottish Highlands was under way across Ireland. Any half competent solicitor willing to do a little work could benefit from it.

Government money was flowing into the country from Her Majesty's Treasury to enable the smallholders to buy out their landlords.

The property owners got their cash, while the farmers got to own the land they had worked for generations. And a whole class of middlemen was set to make their fortunes, drawing off their fees and percentages as the torrent of Treasury money lapped around their doors.

Most of all, the lawyers did well. And the firm of Keogh, Sheridan and James did better than most.

Every transfer of property from landlord to tenant involved legal work. Apart from simple conveyance of ownership, there were boundary issues, challenges over rights of way and queries about title. Solicitors' offices in market towns across the country were crowded each morning with clients and supplicants, anxious to tie down the security of their new holdings.

Firms like Keogh, Sheridan and James were the 'town agents' for the country solicitors. Every transaction, every stamping, every registration executed in the capital carried a fee, usually calculated on a percentage basis of the property value.

As word of Ambrose Pollock's murder spread across the city, it was business as usual at Keogh, Sheridan and James. A sordid police case across the river, however unfortunate, would not distract the firm's part-ners and employees from their lucrative trade in deeds and affidavits.

Arthur Clinton was an exception.

Arthur recognised that he had some blessings. He was the senior clerk to the half dozen solicitors who made up the firm. It had been a long, hard road to get to this point. He had started fifteen years earlier as a junior clerk, working his way upward. But there was a world of difference between even a senior clerk and a qualified solicitor who held the parchment of the Law Society. In Arthur's view, he worked harder than any of them for a fraction of the reward.

He firmly believed he would make a suitable solicitor or even a partner, but the call never came. He had raised it with the firm, of course, but the partners were not inclined to the idea. Arthur remained a clerk.

He was reliable and conscientious. In recent months, he had been assigned to work on the conveyancing of a dozen large estates in areas west of the river Shannon. In all, more than 30,000 acres were to be transferred from the ownership of their landlords to almost 1,000 of their former tenants.

The discovery of the murder was reported initially in the afternoon editions of the *Evening Telegraph.*

Arthur Clinton saw it when the mid-afternoon edition was dropped on the desk in the general office by one of the office boys. He always had a quick look through it. He liked to check the afternoon figures from the Stock Exchange in London, even though he had no investments of his own.

He was interested in money. In truth, he was more interested in money than in the law, although he recognised that it was a vehicle through which the lucky ones could accumulate some wealth.

When he went home in the evenings to his house on the North Circular Road near Phibsborough, he did not discuss such matters. He provided as well as he could for his wife Grace and their three young children, he reckoned. But what a man did with the money he made by his own exertions was first and foremost his own business.

His heart thumped as he absorbed the three-deck headline.

'MURDER AT LAMB ALLEY NEAR CORNMARKET'
'MR POLLOCK'S BODY IS DISCOVERED BY POLICE'
'Investigation started by Inspector Boyle'

Arthur glanced around him. Nobody in the office seemed to have noticed his reaction. That was good. He folded the newspaper, his stock prices now forgotten, and walked slowly away to the shelter of his small office.

He reread the report slowly and carefully. There was nothing more than the barest details, probably gleaned by some reporter just minutes before the newspaper went to press. There was not necessarily any reason to be alarmed, he reasoned.

He went back to his work. When the offices would close later in the evening, he was due to meet a man who had more than a passing interest in the affairs of the late Ambrose Pollock.

SEVEN

To Swallow's surprise, 'Duck' Boyle's investigation into the death of Ambrose Pollock seemed to be running according to the book.

There was still, though, no trace of Phoebe Pollock. It was as if she had vanished into thin air. The constable who spotted her on the quayside was unshakeable in his identification, and the clerk in the hotel confirmed that he had allocated the woman a room, although he was hazy in his description of her.

That there had been some sort of disorder or struggle in the room seemed clear, although nobody had heard anything. One of the two small cases she had with her was gone, but nobody had seen her leave. Logically, she had to be somewhere on the premises.

First, every room in the hotel had been searched. Then they went through the kitchens and the pantries and the storerooms. They searched the staff quarters and the outhouses. There was no trace of Phoebe Pollock.

Perhaps she had managed to make her way unnoticed to *The Maid of Cumberland,* on the quayside. The vessel was searched before it cast off, and all passengers carefully scrutinised. She was not among them.

Swallow could make no sense of it. Had she been abducted? She would surely have taken both of her cases, with her clothing and the money, if she departed voluntarily. And what was to be made of the bottle of what he guessed would be confirmed by Harry Lafeyre as potassium cyanide – prussic acid?

He was back with Mossop at Exchange Court as the first Angelus bells started to toll from the city churches. Boyle had organised a conference for 6 o'clock. Perhaps twenty uniformed constables with a scattering of G-men had assembled. Swallow and Mossop were in time to take chairs by the parade room windows. The air was heavy with tobacco smoke and sweat after the men's exertions of the day.

Boyle had nominated Tony Swann to be his book man. The book man's role in any investigation was crucial. He entered and recorded every detail reported by the men on the ground. He indexed each item of evidence. He timed and dated every statement.

Boyle took the rostrum at the end of the parade room.

'The essential facts o' these tragic evints seem clear enough,' he intoned.

'The deceased, Ambrose Pollock, was done to death some days ago, mebbe as long as a week. It seems that his sister, Miss Phoebe Pollock, assaulted him with a heavy, blunt instrument and then tried to give th' appearance that the poor man was alive be tyin' his remains to a chair.'

He paused for effect.

'The same Miss Pollock this afternoon was traced be officers workin' under me own instructions to the Northern Hotel. It would appear she intended takin' the steamer to Liverpool, thus makin' good her escape. Unhappily, she was nowhere to be found when Sergeant Swalla' and Officer Mossop kem on the scene.'

He glared at Swallow and Mossop.

'However,' he added, 'there is reason to believe she may have been in possession of poison, to wit, prussic acid. Sergeant Swallow got the smell of it in the room, recovered a bottle, and this has gone to Dr Lafeyre to be analysed.

'So the principal business now is to locate the woman, be she alive or dead. Also, we must consider if there are any outstandin' lines of inquiry or action required. Dr Lafeyre will work late and conduct post-mortem examinations on the remains.'

'What about informing next of kin?' Stephen Doolan asked. 'The family came from somewhere in the north of England, as I understand it.'

'We got it out on the telegraph for all the English police forces,' Mossop said. 'But so far we've had nothing back.'

'One way or another we'll need an inventory of everything in the pawn shop,' Swallow interjected. 'We're required to trace the owners of any unclaimed goods.'

Doolan nodded.

'You're right on that. If there's no beneficiaries the Crown will claim the value of what's there. I think the Chief Commissioner is obliged to furnish a statement to the Solicitor General.'

'I'd already adverted to that particular requirement meself,' Boyle lied.

The unwelcome prospect of many days of hard, painstaking work at Pollock's loomed up in Boyle's imagination.

'That'll be a matter for the local division to take care of,' he announced. 'Sergeant Doolan, can you take a couple of reliable men and start that job tomorrow mornin' if you please?'

Doolan nodded in resignation.

'If Dr Lafeyre confirms the analysis, we'll need to check the poisons registers as well,' Swallow said. 'She might have got the stuff elsewhere. But if she bought it in any of the local chemists, we'd need to know. I'll circulate all divisions to check any purchases.'

'I was comin' to that aspect of things, Sergeant,' Boyle lied again. 'So it'll please me if you'll have that done and return any information here to Officer Swann.'

He turned to Swallow.

'What can you tell us, Mister Swalla', about what happened at the Northern Hotel? I believe a substantial sum of money was recovered.'

'We counted just over £300 in that,' Pat Mossop said, holding up Phoebe Pollock's case.

There were whistles and gasps as he lifted the lid to reveal the bundle of banknotes.

'Ill-gotten gains,' Boyle declared dramatically. 'Well, she won't have much use for thim now.'

Swallow caught Stephen Doolan's fractionally raised eyebrow.

'She's still a missing woman at this stage,' Doolan said. 'She could have been taken against her will. So finding her quickly could make the difference between life and death. I think we need to be a bit cautious before ruling anything in or out.'

'I didn't get to me present rank through bein' an incautious man, Sergeant,' Doyle answered testily.

Doolan shrugged with suppressed anger. Experience had taught him that 'Duck' Boyle could not open his mind to the possibility that his first conclusions on any matter might be ill-founded.

Swallow broke the tension.

'A lot of us know Phoebe Pollock from going in and out of the shop. We know she's a harmless poor creature, whatever trouble she's got herself into now. If she's alive and in the wrong hands she won't do well.'

'We're all sensitive to that, Swalla', and we're doin' what we can to locate her,' Boyle said impatiently. 'But there's other things to done as well, startin' with the post-mortem.'

'I'll attend there if you like,' Swallow offered. 'I'd take Mossop and Feore with me.'

It would be a relief from following Parnell around the city, he told himself. Or standing in the bloody rain outside his house watching the lights go off.

Boyle had the grace to acknowledge the gesture.

'That'd be a considherable help. Thank you, Misther Swalla'.'

He stepped down from the rostrum.

'As for meself, I've had an exhaustin' day. I'm goin' across the road to a certain licensed premises to take some refreshments up on a high stool. I'm that hungry, I could ate th' arse off a low flyin goose.'

EIGHT

The three G-men stopped at the Scotch Inn on Temple Bar.

'A lot of people think this place is named after Scotch whisky,' Mossop said amiably as they took three seats in the snug. 'But it's not. A fella from Aberdeen used to be head barman so the boys from the Scottish regiments used to drink here. That's why they called it… the Scotch Inn.'

'That's very useful information,' Swallow retorted. 'A great help when we're trying to conduct a murder investigation and find a missing woman.'

He ordered a Tullamore for himself, and a pint of Guinness's stout each for Mossop and Feore. Technically, the G-men were off-duty for their meal break. As they finished the first drink, Feore ordered the same again. When that was put away, Mossop bought a third round.

This time, Mossop drank Guinness plain, a halfpenny cheaper than the stout. Swallow had noted the small economy before. It irritated him slightly, but then he reminded himself that Mossop had a wife and four kids to maintain on a G-man's pay.

Once or twice he had been obliged to visit him where the family lived over a draper's shop in Aungier Street. The children always seemed well fed and noisily happy. Mossop's cheerful wife had occasional work as a seamstress, which supplemented the family income. As much as he understood the undoubted fulfilment in Mossop's life, though, he recognised that it had to be a struggle.

Sometimes he wondered how married life, perhaps with kids, might have been for him. There had been a girl he fell for when he was at medical school. A nurse from Tipperary, a doctor's daughter, bright and lively, training at St Vincent's Hospital on St Stephen's Green. Eventually, she gave him an ultimatum: choose her or choose alcohol. He made his decision. Later, he knew, she moved to Edinburgh. He often wondered what had become of her, and hoped that she was happy.

They crossed the Ha'penny Bridge, turned down Bachelors' Walk and crossed Sackville Street, making for Marlborough Street and the morgue.

Harry Lafeyre's assistant-cum-coachman, Scollan, was at work in the examination room. The evening light was weakening, and he had switched on the powerful, new electric lamps that Lafeyre had persuaded the authorities to install, replacing the old, hissing gas mantles.

'The stiff's over there,' Scollan jerked a thumb towards the examination tables.

He had strung a white linen mask across his mouth, looping the cords behind prominent ears. It was a fruitless attempt to alleviate the stench. The G-men blanched. Mossop put a thumb and forefinger up to pinch his nose. Feore removed his cap and stuffed it around his mouth and nostrils. Swallow clamped a cotton handkerchief across his face. Harry Lafeyre, in a heavy surgical gown, had come in the door behind them.

'Here, these will help.' He handed each of them a fat, brown cigar.

'The cheapest and foulest you'll ever taste. They smell like boiled horse shit. It's a trick I learned from an old pathologist in the Cape Colony.'

With the first puff, Swallow acknowledged silently that Lafeyre was not exaggerating. But the acrid, poisonous smoke in his nostrils and throat did partially counter the odours of putrefaction.

'I've tested the fluid in the bottle you gave me at the hotel with sulphide of ammonium,' Lafeyre said. 'The result for prussic acid was positive. It's deadly, of course, in its pure form, but diluted and properly applied it can be beneficial for some conditions. There was exactly an eighth of an ounce in solution in the bottle. That's the standard dispensing dose, so it suggests that none of it was used.'

'Yet I got the smell of bitter almonds in the room,' Swallow said.

'So the bottle had been opened. It would emit an odour on contact with the air. But you found it corked?'

'Yes.'

Lafeyre shrugged. 'So the bottle was opened but none of the solution was taken. Make what you will of that.'

He glanced at the wall clock.

'We haven't all night. Let's see how we get on with the brother.'

Ambrose Pollock's wrists and ankles were still bound. Scollan moved forward with a knife to sever the thin ropes so that Layfeyre could begin his examination.

'Make your cut well away from the knots on those ropes,' Swallow wheezed through the choking cigar smoke. 'I want to have a look at how they're made.'

Scollan ran the knife through the two cords, and laid them side by side at the end of the table. Then, with the tailor's scissors, he started to cut through the dead pawnbroker's clothing, putting each sectioned garment aside until the green-black corpse was bare. Mossop poised his pencil as Lafeyre started his narrative.

First, Lafeyre probed the broken skull. Fragments of white bone fell away from the rotted flesh. Then he used a steel spatula to take a dark mess of hardened blood and brain matter from the cavity.

'I won't require the sectioning saw,' he told Scollan. 'The visible damage to the skull is very severe. The trauma to the brain would have been enormous, causing an immediate loss of consciousness and death.'

Mossop worked his pencil swiftly, following Lafeyre's commentary. The medical examiner thrust a rubber-gloved hand under the corpse's head to turn it. With expert fingers he delineated the facial bones and probed around the eye sockets and the jaw. Globs of blackened skin and grey hair came away at the touch, showing further areas of dark red muscle and white bone.

'There's a fracture of the jawbone on the right side that tells us there was at least one further heavy blow. That's the only fracture I can detect. But the lateral cartilage just below the nasal bone appears to be compacted. That was probably a third blow. On its own it wouldn't have caused death, but it could have stunned him.'

Swallow interrupted. 'If he was struck on the back of the skull, and if there's evidence of a blow to the side and on the nose, doesn't that suggest attack from more than one direction? Maybe by two people?'

Lafeyre shrugged, puffing on his cigar.

'Not necessarily. The force of one blow could cause him to turn, maybe even as an attempt at self-defence. It could have been one person. It could have been two... or more.'

'You saw the two-pound weight that Stephen Doolan found at the scene,' Swallow changed tack. 'He thinks it's the likely murder weapon. Would that fit in with what you've seen here?'

'It would crack any bone. I took it with me from Lamb Alley. It's got blood spatters.'

He gestured to the storage cupboards that ran the length of the room.

'I have it safely if it's needed as an exhibit. I want to look at the blood spatters because there are finger-marks.'

Lafeyre made a 'Y' incision from the shoulders to the abdomen. Swallow had expected a wave of putrid gases, but Ambrose Pollock's body had advanced in decomposition beyond that point. One by one, Lafeyre removed the organs, stomach, intestines, liver and kidneys, placing them in variously sized steel trays. He probed around the organs.

'Nothing of significance,' he said finally. 'But any signs of injury would be masked by putrefaction in the soft tissues.'

Swallow had been fingering the severed sections of rope with which the pawnbroker's wrists and ankles had been bound. He offered the stump of his stinking cigar to Scollan.

'Is there some place that you could dispose of this… object… for me please? I need both hands to demonstrate something.'

Lafeyre drew heavily again on his cigar. 'If you don't mind, I'll persevere with this for the present. What's in your mind?'

Swallow took the length of rope that had bound Pollock's wrists and extended it, holding the severed ends at arm's length between thumb and forefinger.

'Look at the knot. It's a double hitch, right over left and then right over left again. It's the easiest knot in the book, the sort a child would make. But it could loosen with tensing and flexing.'

He placed it on the table and took up the section of rope that had secured the dead man's ankles. As before, he extended it at arm's length, displaying the knot in the middle.

'But this knot, as you'll see, is different. It's a double hitch, but it's right over left and then left under right, making it far more secure. The more tensing and flexing, the tighter the tie is going to be. It's a more professional knot.'

'Professional,' Lafeyre said. 'Do you mean like a sailor's knot?'

'It wouldn't have to be a sailor. A shop assistant would be trained to use it to tie a string around a parcel.'

Lafeyre ran an index finger over the section on the table, and then did the same with the length that Swallow still held.

'I can see they're different. Is this leading up to something?'

'Nothing that's absolutely conclusive. But it could indicate that the knots were tied by two different people. Most people use one kind of knot all the time. They don't vary it, particularly when they're repeating an exercise.'

'You're a mine of information.'

'I learned a few things at medical school when I wasn't drinking. Like how to knot bandages.'

Lafeyre started to remove his apron and gloves.

'I'll do some further testing on his organs since there's poison here somewhere in the story. And I'll see if there's anything to be learned from the marks on the iron weight.'

'Are you hopeful, Doctor?' Mossop asked.

'Who knows?' Lafeyre answered. 'Bodies can tell you a lot. There can be an eloquence about the dead. But you have to be able to interpret what they're telling you.'

Mossop sighed. 'If Sergeant Swallow is right about the knots, it seems that there might have been two people involved. Phoebe Pollock didn't act alone.'

'That's at least a possibility,' Lafeyre agreed.

Mossop put down his pencil and placed his hands over his face.

'But it could mean that we've got two murderers still loose.'

Swallow grimaced.

'The crowd in the Upper Yard will make a big meal out of it. But these things aren't supposed to happen where the Queen's loyal subjects live in safety, protected by the Dublin Metropolitan Police… and all that sort of shite.'

Mossop grinned mirthlessly.

'Hah. Loyal subjects, me arse. I'd find it hard to name any o' that kind up around Lamb Alley.'

NINE

There was a time when Arthur Clinton was content to drink in public houses like the Bleeding Horse on Camden Street. He enjoyed the warmth of its mahogany fittings and the brilliance of the polished mirrors in which he could admire himself.

He was rather handsome if a bit short. Intelligent looking, he thought. He dressed well. That was important if one did not want to stay forever as a poorly paid law clerk. But a man on the way up should be seen to patronise the better hotels rather than run-of-the-mill public houses.

Nonetheless, the Bleeding Horse suited the purpose of the meeting to which he had been summoned. The man he had to meet had to be discreet. His coming and going would not be remarked upon here. Their muted conversation would be lost in the hubbub of the bar.

The other man was there first. He sat with a whiskey and water in one of the booths by the small windows that gave on to Charlotte Way. A copy of the *Evening Mail* was spread out on the table, opened at the main news page.

Clinton ordered himself a brandy at the counter, and installed himself opposite. He nodded to the open newspaper.

'You've read the news.'

'Of course. What happened?'

'How would I know?' Arthur replied defensively. 'I only know what I've read in the newspaper.'

His companion could pass for a Londoner or even a Parisian with his pencil moustache, pale complexion and well-cut suit. Clinton reckoned him to be about the same age as himself, in his mid-thirties with cold, grey eyes. Arthur always found himself a little frightened in his presence.

He seemed to consider Arthur's answer for a moment.

'The current consignment of... merchandise... is still there? At his place?'

'As far as I know, yes.'

The eyes shone like ice.

'It's your business to know, Clinton. I've set up everything across the water. All you have to do is make sure the stuff is kept safe and then shipped. It's not very difficult.'

'You can say that. But there's a lot of organising. And there's paperwork at the office. I have to be very careful.'

'The reason I wanted to meet you is because I'm hearing reports... rumours... that some items are beginning to turn up in shops around the city. Can you throw any light on that?'

Arthur became defensive again.

'I told you, everything is taken care of. I don't know what you're talking about.'

The man nodded.

'I'll do my own checking. I just hope for your sake it's as tight as it should be.'

Arthur felt he had to defend himself.

'If you know so much, you tell me what happened to Pollock.'

'Don't be ridiculous. I'm as far removed from that sort of thing as could be. But I'll have to inform London. It won't be well received.'

He shrugged. 'It may just be that someone did for him, that's all. It happens sometimes, in that part of the city.'

'You've no reason to believe it's connected with our... business?'

'How can I tell?'

'It says there's an investigation. Do you think they'll... discover things?'

'That's usually what they do in an investigation.' The tone was sarcastic. 'It might be a simple robbery. In which case, nothing should emerge that would concern us.'

'But supposing it does. I've got to think of myself and my family. My livelihood.'

'We've all got to think of ourselves. You've been doing very well out of our efforts. Well enough to be able to make sizeable wagers on some doubtful racehorses, if my information is correct.'

Clinton felt himself flush.

'Sometimes I get a good tip… I know people in the bloodstock business. There's no harm in the odd wager among friends and gentlemen.'

The man snorted. 'What you do with your money is your own business. For my part, I'd count my fingers after shaking hands with some of those "friends and gentlemen".'

Clinton pointed to the newspaper. 'It says there's an Inspector Boyle been put on the case.'

'I know about him. I doubt if he could count two bottles on a table-top, so I wouldn't worry too much about his investigation. It says the police are seeking his sister to help in their inquiries. That's their way of saying she did it.'

He paused.

'Are you sure there's nothing for them to discover? No records, no papers, nothing traceable at the pawn shop?'

'I don't believe so,' Clinton said. 'I've been very careful.'

'In that case, we probably have nothing to be concerned about. It's an inconvenience, but no more than that. We'll find someone else for the job.'

Clinton's brandy was warming his gut. His companion's confidence made him feel a bit more comfortable. He downed the remains of his drink in a gulp, and signalled to the barman to replenish the glasses.

'I got a hell of a shock earlier,' he said, raising the refill to his lips.

The other man furrowed his brow and sipped again at his whiskey.

'I don't like the sound of that. You wouldn't be having some sort of doubts, or losing your confidence, I hope.'

It was not an expression of concern. It was a threat.

'No, I wouldn't be worried about that,' Arthur said after a moment. He attempted an unconvincing laugh, and put his empty glass on the table.

'That's good,' the man said. 'I'm travelling to London tomorrow anyway and I'll be seeing our friends there. I'll fill them in.'

'Now,' he drained his glass too. 'We'll drink to the late Mr Pollock'

TEN

In one respect, at least, Swallow had to acknowledge, he was blest in his sister. She believed that he had to be fed. And, contrary to her own modern, egalitarian principles, she had decided that she should play out an almost maternal role in her care for him.

Convinced that he would never look after his own nourishment, she insisted on providing for it herself. There had never been any evidence to justify her fears in the matter, but there was always food waiting for him no matter what time he arrived home. And so it was tonight.

Harriet was twenty-two to his forty-three. The gap between them, though, encompassed much more than a chronological span of years. His view of the world and hers were literally generations apart. They could agree on hardly anything: politics, music, religion, literature, the place of women – but above they quarrelled about politics.

Swallow cared nothing for it, and less for its practitioners.

'If the King of the bloody Zulus came to rule Ireland, I couldn't be bothered to see him ride down Sackville Street,' he had told her in an argument.

'The Zulus aren't the problem,' she retorted. 'It's a much more savage crowd – the English. And mind your language. It reminds me of your drinking days.'

She could still be angry about the grief he had caused at home when he threw away his medical studies for alcohol. Their parents had worked hard in the public house in rural Kildare to provide for their children's education. Swallow's father had died shortly after learning that his son had been expelled from the Cecilia Street College.

'Those days are long gone,' he had said. 'And I'd rather you didn't bring them up.'

'I don't want to,' she answered. 'But I can't pretend they didn't happen. I love you. You're my brother. But you hurt us. All of us.'

Harriet had been swept up by the new Irish nationalism over her time in the Blackrock teacher training college. Established to provide teachers for the newly formed national schools system, it had acquired a reputation as a seedbed of separatist thinking. Some members of the staff figured in G-Division's files, noted for their hostility to everything British.

Harriet's political views were potentially a problem for a detective sergeant in G-Division. On one occasion already, when she had become involved with a group calling themselves the Hibernian Brotherhood, he had to engage in some quiet skullduggery to get her out of trouble.

'Your own grandfather carried a pike to take a stand against England,' she had told him angrily afterwards. 'I appreciate that you're trying to look after me, and I love you as a brother, but don't ask me to respect what you do for a living, you and the rest of… of… England's hirelings in there in the Castle.'

He had learned to ignore the clichéd rhetoric, borrowed from badly printed pamphlets and political speeches reported in the press. Occasionally, though, he wished that she might acknowledge that it was his modest G-man's salary that would pay the rent until she moved up the teaching pay scale.

After Harry Lafeyre had completed the post-mortem on Ambrose Pollock, Swallow and Mossop had found 'Duck' Boyle drinking with a couple of clerks from the Army Office in Morton's bar in Dame Court.

'Bad news,' Swallow told him. 'It looks like there were two people involved in the attack on Pollock.'

Even with his brain fuddled with alcohol, Boyle realised that this was serious.

'Oh Jaysus. There must be some mistake. Is there any chance d'ye think that Lafeyre's slippin' up?'

'I doubt it.'

He knew there was no point in rehearsing the details of the knotted ropes to the half-soused inspector.

Boyle was anguished. Mallon insisted that information on all major crime developments be brought to him immediately, if necessary outside office hours at his house in the Lower Castle Yard. But he had enough sense not to turn up to his boss with signs of alcohol on board.

'Fuck it… fuck it anyway. We had it all grand and neat, hadn't we? You'll have to take this on, Swalla', seein' as I'm off duty now.'

He wiped froth from his beard with the back of his hand.

'Put it all in the report for tomorrow mornin' and drop a copy over to Chief Mallon's house.'

Swallow felt his fury rising. It was Boyle's case and Boyle's responsibility. He had agreed to attend the post-mortem in order to assist the investigation. But now he was being pushed into the lead role because his line superior was drunk.

Mossop saw his anger. He put a restraining hand on Swallow's arm.

'Ah sure, we'll get that done in half an hour, Skipper. C'mon, we'll go across to the office.'

For a moment, Swallow was going to brush off Mossop's gesture and knock the glass out of Boyle's pudgy fist. But an altercation between two G-men in Morton's would not be good for anyone.

'Fair enough, Pat.'

They stepped out into Dame Court.

'And at least the fucking thing will be done right,' Mossop said. 'Christ knows what he'd put in the report, the state he's in.'

Exchange Court was quiet. Mossop lit the gas mantles in the crime sergeants' office, and Swallow rolled foolscap and carbon paper into one of the G-Division's ageing Remington typewriters.

Swallow was the more proficient typist. He battered out the words as Mossop read from his notes taken at the morgue. They were finished by 11 o'clock. Swallow sent Mossop home, and he crossed the Lower Yard to deliver the report to Mallon's house.

Dublin Castle was no longer a castle in any architectural sense. Over the centuries, a jigsaw of yards and courts had grown up around the original site of the stronghold that had been put up in the reign of King John. Apart from the medieval Record Tower, all that was left of the early fortress was some underground foundations, now superimposed with faux crenellated curtain walls.

The courts and yards housed the many agencies and commissions that made up the British administration in Ireland. The most important of these, including the Office of the Chief Secretary, the Office of the Under-Secretary, the Gentlemen Ushers and others, were located in the Upper Yard around the State Apartments. This was where the Queen's deputy – the Viceroy – held his court, hosting receptions, balls and audiences in the Dublin 'season' from February to the end of March each year.

The Lower Yard, divided from the Upper by a three-storey block, accommodated the less prestigious agencies, including the separate head-quarters of Ireland's two police forces: the Royal Irish Constabulary and the Dublin Metropolitan Police.

The house allocated to the chief superintendent of the G-Division was a substantial one, more than sufficient to the needs of John Mallon and his family. Constructed in yellow-brown brick, it stood facing across the cobbled Lower Yard towards the apse of the Chapel Royal and the Record Tower beyond.

A light burning on the ground floor told Swallow that Mallon was still in his sitting-room. When the chief superintendent opened the front door in response to his tap on the window pane, Swallow found him clad in a woollen dressing-gown. The embers of a dying turf fire glowed faintly in the room behind.

'I'm sorry for disturbing the house at a late hour, Chief. There's been some developments in the Lamb Alley case from this morning. I've brought an updated file for you.'

'I thought Boyle was in charge of the case.'

'He is, Sir. He's gone off duty and he asked me to brief you.'

Mallon's grunt was ambiguous.

'Other than the delay in discovery, it seemed fairly straightforward from what I heard earlier.'

He gestured Swallow to an armchair.

'As I heard it, he was dead for several days and the sister had gone on the run. The last report from Boyle said that she'd disappeared at a hotel on the North Wall. Weren't you on the scene?'

'I was, Sir, but it's turning out to be more complicated. I was at the post-mortem with Mossop and Feore. There's a possibility that more than one person might have been involved in the murder.'

Mallon's shoulders slumped.

'Two murderers?' he said after a moment. 'Have you any idea where the sister is?'

'No, Sir. She can't be found anywhere. We're sure she was in the Northern Hotel, and there were signs of a struggle in her room. There was a bottle of prussic acid there too. Unused, apparently. And she had two cases. We recovered one of them with £300 in it. I'd be concerned for her safety at this stage.'

Mallon stretched out his hand.

'Let me see the report.'

He leafed through the file, his sharp eyes travelling across Swallow's typed pages. After a couple of minutes, he raised his head.

'It still looks as if Phoebe had a hand in it, doesn't it? The question is, who else was involved?'

'Yes, Sir, that's one of the questions.'

Mallon nodded.

'She might have met someone at the hotel. Maybe the person who was with her when the brother was killed? An accomplice?'

'It's possible.'

Mallon tapped the file. 'Find him – or her – and you've got either a prime witness or a suspect.'

'We're doing what we can on that, Chief. I put Mick Feore down there. I told him to get whatever help he needed from Store Street and to do all the usual things – seize the guest registers, employee lists and so on.'

'Feore's a good man. He'll get whatever there is to be got.'

'The Liverpool packet went out about an hour after we found her,' Swallow said. 'She wasn't on it. But it's possible someone who assaulted her or abducted her could be. It's due to dock around midnight. We've asked City of Liverpool Police to have someone at the gangway to run another check on the passengers.'

Mallon grunted approval.

Dublin and Liverpool were virtually one city as far as the criminal classes of both were concerned. The short sea crossing connected rather than divided them. Scores of Irishmen served in the Liverpool Police, many in the Criminal Investigation Department. In all probability, the officers sent to watch the arrivals would be Irish themselves, well able to identify any habitual criminals.

'There'll be a bloody great racket from the civil servants about Pollock being dead for a week,' Mallon said. He looked exasperated.

'The pawn shops are supposed to be checked regularly by the beat men. They musn't have been doing that up at Pollock's.'

'G-Division can't be blamed for that, Sir.'

'No. But we're the people who're expected to clean up the mess.'

Swallow left the Castle by the Ship Street Gate, nodding to the sentry. He passed the barracks, making for Heytesbury Street. He felt a pang of regret that he was not turning right, as he had done so many times in the past, to travel along Werburgh Street and Thomas Street towards Maria and the warmth of M & M Grant's.

At Bishop Street, the night smells of fresh bread came out on the air. Yeast, wheat, milk, all carried on a wave of passing warmth from the bakery.

It would be after closing time at Grant's now. The barmen would be clearing the counter and the tables in the snug, washing off the glasses and preparing to lock up for the night.

Maria would probably be gone upstairs. He would join her in the parlour, sipping a whiskey or sharing a late night pot of tea. If he was hungry there would be a hot plate of something prepared earlier by Carrie, Maria's cook, in the kitchen. They would tell each other about the business of their day, the good and the bad of it, its triumphs and its tribulations.

By contrast, Heytesbury Street seemed cold and empty. The terraced houses were silent and shadowed, their inhabitants safely in bed, lamps doused, sightless windows facing the street, doors barred.

In the kitchen, he lit the gas mantle for a few moments to locate the cold supper of ham sandwiches that Harriet had left on the work table before she retired. He took the plate with him, biting into the first of the sandwiches even as he climbed the dark stairs to his room.

FRIDAY SEPTEMBER 30TH, 1887

ELEVEN

The resources of the G-Division were stretched from early morning. At Lamb Alley, Stephen Doolan with three constables from Kevin Street had started to inventory the contents of Pollock's pawn shop and furniture store.

Knots of sightseers and idlers, drawn by morbid curiosity, continued to gather, peering through the grimy windows on Cornmarket. Mallon partially subscribed to the adage that the criminal sometimes returned to the scene of the crime. So he ordered that the G-men should watch the crowd and note their names.

The Exchange Court conference was brisk and brief. 'Duck' Boyle was hung over and liverish.

Swallow had half expected that Phoebe Pollock might have been located during the night. Every patrolling constable and G-man had been searching for her. But there was nothing.

'Orders of the day, Inspector?' he asked hopefully.

Boyle managed to wave a hand.

'Whatever ye think best, Swalla'. You're close to it all. Use yer rank and decide yerself.'

'The best chance of turning something up on Phoebe Pollock is probably at the Northern Hotel. I'll go down there again with Mossop.'

They checked every inch of the hotel room again. The water had dried around the shattered pitcher and bowl on the floor, but there were no clues to tell them why the missing woman had come here, much less where she might be now.

G-men and constables from Store Street questioned staff members and any guests who had been present the previous day. Did they see

Phoebe Pollock? Did she meet anyone or speak to anyone? Did anyone perhaps follow her to her room?

Other G-men went through the names and addresses of guests who had been present but who had since checked out. Details of delivery men and tradesmen who had called during the previous twenty-four hours were noted.

Beat men across the city divisions were detailed to check the poisons registers that every chemist and apothecary's shop was obliged to maintain.

Liverpool CID had met the steam packet from Dublin at the Pier Head Dock, and surveyed the passengers as they disembarked. They had no sighting of Phoebe Pollock and nothing unusual to report.

At mid-morning, Swallow knew the investigation was stalled. The questioning of the staff and the guests yielded nothing solid. A score of people had gone up and down the stairs in the half hour before the police had arrived at the hotel. Any one of them, for whatever reason, might have entered Phoebe Pollock's room.

'It's not looking great, Boss, is it?' Mossop asked, spooning sugar into his cup.

The G-men had wheedled a pot of tea out of the grim-faced housekeeper and were seated in a corner of the lobby.

Swallow took Mossop's question as rhetorical.

Mossop grimaced. 'What was she doing with the prussic acid in the first place?'

'I don't know. Maybe she intended to take her own life. Or maybe she was planning to poison someone else.'

Mossop ladled more sugar into his tea. Swallow often wondered why he didn't simply pour the tea into the sugar bowl and drink it straight.

'I wonder if she'd planned to meet anybody.' Mossop gulped at the hot, saturated mixture.

'Mind you,' he slurped again from his teacup, 'she must have been a fairly cool character. She probably did for the brother above in Lamb Alley and then stayed on for a week with his corpse in the office. That takes some nerve.'

'You're using the past tense about her, Pat. Do you think she's dead?'

Mossop looked sheepish.

'Slip of the tongue, Boss. She might be. Or maybe she's being held someplace against her will.'

Swallow nodded. It was at least possible that Phoebe had been murdered. But by whom? And if so, where was her body?

'We're not coming up with any answers here.' He sipped at his own tea. 'We'll need to start at the other end of the story. Her personal life.'

Mossop looked glum.

'By all accounts there hasn't been much to that. Herself and the brother lived like hermits.'

Mossop was pouring a second cup of tea when Barry, the hotel manager, crossed the lobby.

He was agitated.

'Surely to God you've finished your inquiries by now, Sergeant. You've talked to everybody, some people more than once. It's not helpful for business to have policemen questioning the guests. I have to run the place, you know.'

'A woman has disappeared in your hotel. There may have been a murder here, Mr Barry,' Swallow said testily. 'That doesn't help business either. Maybe you should have picked a different class of hotel to run, or maybe you should be running this one better.'

Barry's face reddened with anger.

'I'll have you know, Sergeant, I was a senior assistant manager at the Imperial Hotel in Cork. At the pinnacle of my profession. I understand perfectly well how to do my business. If the police could do theirs this sort of thing wouldn't be happening.'

He turned on his heel and strode away across the lobby.

Mossop sipped at his tea.

'You won't have a great friend there, Boss.'

'Bloody Corkmen. Jesus, they get up my nose. They think they're superior to the rest of the human race.'

He stood. 'You finish your tea, Pat. Keep the lads working on the lists. Have another shot at questioning the staff on duty yesterday. I'll start digging at the other end.'

The hall porter saluted and swung the front door outward for him. He took the first cab from the rank on the quayside and ordered the driver to take him back to the Castle.

TWELVE

The G-man on day shift in the public office at Exchange Court tapped the tabletop as Swallow came through.

'Letter here for you, Sergeant. Left in an hour ago by a lady... said she knew you.'

He grinned. 'It'd be a terrible waste if she was here on police business. Very easy on the eye, she was.'

He handed Swallow the cream laid envelope. His name and rank, in black ink, were written in a strong, looping script.

Jos. Swallow Esq.
Detective Sergeant.

And on the top right-hand corner:

Strictly Private to Addressee.

He tore the flap to read the single sheet of notepaper as he climbed the stairs to the crime sergeants' office.

Capel Street
Dublin   *September 29th 1887*

Dear Mr Swallow,

It was very pleasant to talk yesterday. I hope I may look forward to meeting you again at Miss Grant's painting class.

Perhaps you will recall my mentioning to you that my father is concerned about a matter that he feels may be of interest to the police. When I told him of our meeting, he immediately said that he would be glad of an early opportunity to talk to you. If your other duties permit, perhaps you might call to see him in early course?

Yours faithfully,
Katherine Greenberg (Miss)

A G-man lived by his contacts, and Ephram Greenberg had been a good one in the past, but Swallow could do without having to trek across the river to Capel Street at a time when there was a murder to solve and a woman gone missing.

On the other hand, if the old Jewish dealer wanted to talk to Swallow there was almost certainly a good reason for it.

He thought about putting Katherine's letter into the 'jobs pending' file on his desk. He would get to it in time. But something prompted him to fold it into in his jacket pocket. It would remind him to follow up her message sooner rather than later.

He filled two information requisition forms for Ambrose and Phoebe Pollock. They would be taken by a clerk to the criminal intelligence office beside the Commissioner's office in the Lower Castle Yard.

Every scrap of information about the Pollocks, their business, their background, their acquaintances and connections would be winnowed from the files. Then the trawl would widen to include the vast Dublin Criminal Registry at Great Ship Street where the three 'h's of every Dublin criminal were recorded: their haunts, habits and hoors.

Police clerks attached to the General Post Office would search the Post Office Savings accounts to find out if the Pollocks had cash squirreled away. If necessary, well-disposed agents or officials could check the accounts in the private banks.

Officially, of course, it did not happen. But every G-man knew that it did. The capacity to track funds was an essential weapon in G-Division's efforts to contain the Fenian threat. Subversion required money. G-Division had to know where it came from and where it went.

He handed the completed forms to the duty man in the public office.

'Get these moving for me like a good man. I'm going over to Lamb Alley to see how the search is going for Stephen Doolan and his fellows.'

He exited Exchange Court, and turned past the City Hall into Lord Edward Street. At the junction with Fishamble Street, he diverted to Currivan's public house, standing on the corner in the shadow of the cathedral.

Currivan's was not an establishment that he frequented very often, being off his usual track from Exchange Court into the Liberties. It was also a house frequented by individuals with little love of the police. Some were Fenians. Others were ordinary criminals. Inevitably, there were those also who straddled the worlds of politics and crime.

He was hungry. Apart from the tea he had drunk with Mossop at the Northern Hotel he had nothing to eat since morning. Currivan's had the reputation of serving good, fresh fish from Howth. He ordered a glass of ale along with some cold herring and Colman's Norwich mustard.

The patrons of the house referred to the proprietor, Matt Currivan, as 'Five Times' Currivan.

There were various schools of thought about the origin of the soubriquet. One held that he had fallen in the river on a Friday night, very drunk, and that he had been submerged five times before someone pulled him out.

The preferred story among G-men was that he had managed to perjure himself five times in one day in a trial involving the late Ces Downes, the woman who ran the Dublin criminal underground. Currivan's alibi testimony was credited with having Ces acquitted on all charges.

'Five Times' Currivan had the ability to play in several directions at once. Verbally at least, he subscribed to his clients' subversive sentiments. He also shared their dislike of authority in general and of the police in particular. But he also liked to keep on reasonable terms with the detectives of Exchange Court. Life was easier that way.

Currivan drew the frothy ale from the tap while the barmaid prepared the food. As the beer settled, the publican spread the *Evening Telegraph* on the counter-top.

'Shockin' to think o' that man killed up the street. Lyin' there all that time. And the sister disappearin' then. Have ye any idea why she killed him?'

He jabbed a finger at the double-deck news headline.

DUBLIN PAWN SHOP OWNER MURDERED A WEEK AGO

Sister disappears from city hotel

'Did you know him?' Swallow asked, ignoring the invitation to feed Currivan's curiosity. 'He'd have lived close enough to drink in here.'

Currivan snorted. 'I did, but he wasn't a customer here. I don't know that he took a drink at all. He wasn't a man for spendin' money if he could avoid it. But there was many a time as a young apprentice I pawned me watch or even me coat up there.'

He put the dripping glass on the counter, and reached across to where the barmaid had left the food. He clanked it down beside the beer along with a knife and fork. Swallow noted a trail of grease globs along the knife.

'A meaner bollocks never put an arm through a shirt, I'm tellin' you. I'd get five shillin' for hockin' me watch down in Mary Street. But Pollock would give you a bare half a crown. I'd take it though for the convenience of location, if you know what I mean.'

Swallow wiped the greasy knife with his handkerchief. If 'Five Times' Currivan noticed the reproof to the house's hygiene, it evoked no comment.

The cutlery might have been dirty, but the herrings were perfect; briny and firm. The barmaid had put two slices of fresh white bread, thickly buttered, alongside them. The Norwich mustard was smooth and strong.

Swallow forked fish and bread into his mouth. He nodded at the gold chain stretching across Currivan's waist and grinned. 'I'd say that whatever you've got fixed on at the end of that now is worth more than five bob.'

The publican grinned. 'Ah well, I was young then. I'm the licensee now. A man of business, you know. I can afford a bit better than an ould tin turnip.'

He assumed a solemn air.

'Still, we won't speak ill of the dead, will we? And whatever about Ambrose, I can tell you that Miss Pollock is a lady. Strange, distant... but a lady. And we don't get too many o' them in here, as you know. Perfect manners anytime she came in.'

Swallow had not expected that.

'Is she a regular?' he asked cautiously.

'Over the last few months, I'd say. I hardly knew the woman, 'twas so long since I'd seen her over there in the shop. But then she started comin' in once or twice a week maybe – with her gentleman friend.'

He had not expected that either. His next question had to be framed so that he might appear to know more than he did.

'She likes company all right. So which of the gentleman friends would that be? When she came in here, I mean.'

'There was only the one she ever came in here with anyway,' Currivan laughed. 'Well dressed, good suit, heavy set sort of fellow. Large Jameson twelve-year old, he'd take. She'd be on the port wine sometimes. Then maybe a gin or two. They'd be here comin' up on closin' time.'

Swallow decided to be direct.

'I'm working on the case. I'm on my way up to Lamb Alley now.'

He finished the last of the herring and placed his warrant card on the counter.

'What you're telling me might be important. Can you give me a better description of this fellow?'

The publican pushed the warrant card back to him. 'You can put that yoke back in your pocket. I didn't think you were sellin' insurance.'

He cleared Swallow's empty plate.

'He'd be maybe your own age, heavy set but shorter. Nicely spoken, but not a Dublin accent. Definitely an office man of some sort with the suit – always navy blue – cuffs, collar and tie.'

Swallow scribbled rapidly.

'Any unusual behaviour or characteristics?'

Currivan laughed. 'Unusual? Well, I suppose it's a bit unusual to find a couple of… well… their years, carryin' on, spoonin' at each other… and the like.'

'What about this fellow's height? Colour of hair? Clean-shaven or bearded? Any distinguishing marks?'

'Five foot seven or eight, but well built. Neat moustache but no beard. Dark complexion, hair brownish, going to grey. Good teeth too, with a bit o' gold in there somewhere, as I recall it.'

'You'd have made a great peeler,' Swallow told him. 'You've no idea how many folk seem to be blind and deaf when a *polisman* asks a few questions.'

'Five Times' Currivan was unsure if he should be flattered or disquieted at being well thought of by a G-man. But he was happier that there was nobody else in earshot.

Swallow grinned.

'Life would be easier if the Almighty had put more witnesses like yourself into the world.'

He set off past Christ Church for Lamb Alley. Was there something that sounded vaguely familiar about Phoebe Pollock's mysterious companion of the evenings? Something that reminded him of someone that he knew or that he had seen somewhere? The idea nagged at him as he walked, digesting his herrings and ale.

THIRTEEN

Margaret Gessel decided that in her first month in London she would stay at the Langham Hotel. Facing up Portland Place towards Regent's Park, her third-floor suite was comfortable and spacious. From her sitting-room she had a fine view in one direction along Regent Street and towards Marble Arch in the other.

There was a sense of liberation in leaving Mount Gessel. She was a healthy woman, energetic for her age. She could perhaps begin to enjoy life a little again. There were no more tenants, no more agents, no more armed policemen patrolling the driveway, no more shooting in the night.

But the Langham was expensive. And it seemed to be full of Americans. That was hardly surprising, she told herself, when she learned that the general manager was a former officer of the Union Army who promoted the hotel to his visiting fellow-countrymen as a desirable London address.

Although she had registered as 'Lady Gessel,' she found that official correspondence, including her weekly account, was addressed to 'Mrs Gessel.' She complained to an assistant manager, insisting that she should have her title.

'I am not 'Mrs Gessel.' I do not know anybody with that name. I am Lady Gessel.' She had demanded that someone in authority should come to her suite.

The assistant manager was young, but he was sufficiently experienced to understand that his only recourse was humility.

'I do most sincerely apologise, Lady Gessel. The error is unforgivable. A new clerk in the accounts office, you understand.'

'I do not understand. Do you not train these people?'

'Of course we do, Milady, but he is quite inexperienced. If I may say so, the title may not be very well known in London. It would not be one with which the accounts staff would be familiar.'

'Does the name Sir Richard Gessel mean anything to you?' she demanded crossly.

'Why yes, Milady... of course, I should have realised. We have had the honour of Sir Richard's presence here on occasion at the Langham.'

'Indeed you have. He called on me last week.'

'I can only apologise again, Lady Gessel,' the assistant manager pleaded. 'I assure you, there will be no repeat.'

In reality, she was both angry and disappointed at Richard's failure to make her welcome in London. He was a busy man at Westminster, she knew. He had a young wife and three children and lived in a smart house in Ebury Street. She knew from *The Times* that they entertained. But he had little interest in extending hospitality to an elderly Gessel relative lately arrived from Ireland.

He called on her shortly after she had established herself at the Langham. She thought he looked tired and strained compared to when he had visited Mount Gessel earlier in the year. He seemed nervous too.

'It must be very demanding to work in such a powerful position,' she said. 'Even for a young man it has to be stressful. Now that I am in London, perhaps I could be of some help? It's a long time since I had anything to do with small children, but I'm sure I could play the occasional role of an aunt very well.'

He had been polite.

'Thank you, Cousin Margaret. Perhaps when you have established yourself, become a little more accustomed to London, we could think about that. You must call upon us some day.'

He seemed more interested to know about the sale of Mount Gessel. How had her departure been viewed by other landed families in the district? Was the tenant purchase scheme considered to be successful? Would other landowners follow her example?

'It's essential to the government that the land transfer programme is taken up. The landlords are being offered good money,' he told her.

'I think some will do as I did,' she replied. 'But others are reluctant, understandably. They don't want to appear to be driven out. And some believe that they may get a better price in the future.'

'They're idiots,' he had told her. 'Don't they realise how difficult it has been to get agreement even among the Cabinet on putting up the money to buy them out? They won't get a better deal, I promise you. And if there were to be a change of government, the whole scheme could be withdrawn. Gladstone's party is divided on its Irish policies.'

A week later, she called at the Ebury Street house. None of the family was at home. Margaret had left her card with the maid who answered the door, but no response came.

She had not expected a bustling social life in London. London society was not especially warm in its welcome for middle-aged landholders from Ireland, even if their bank accounts were now a good deal healthier than before.

At the end of the first month, she found herself questioning the wisdom of her decision to leave Ireland. To her own astonishment, she even started to feel a hint of nostalgia for Galway and Mount Gessel.

FOURTEEN

The voyeurs and gawkers who had gathered at the pawn shop were gone now. Only the occasional layabout lingered on the pavement to try to peer in the windows of the notorious murder site. But a detective and a uniformed man remained on duty.

Swallow found Stephen Doolan shirt-sleeved in the basement. A young constable, similarly *déshabillé*, worked with a pad and pencil as Doolan told off the contents of the stacked shelves that ran from floor to ceiling. The place smelled of clay and damp. There was no natural light or gas and two Bull's-eye police lanterns smoked on the floor.

One wall was stacked with fiddles, violins and other musical instruments. Another section seemed to comprise items of medical and scientific equipment, their brass casings making dull gleams in the poor light. A collection of oil lamps was piled one on top of another in a corner.

Each pawned item had a numbered tag. The policemen's task would be to check each one against the shop's ledgers to ascertain their owner-ship. In theory, every customer would have to be given the option of redeeming their property and paying off the loan that had been advanced against it. Then, each item that had not been redeemed would have to be checked against the lists. The process carried no guarantee of success, but it offered a possible way of ascertaining what, if anything, had gone miss-ing. If Ambrose Pollock's killers had robbed the shop, they just might be traced along the stolen goods trail.

It was going to be a mammoth task.

'Jesus, we'll be here till Christmas,' Doolan mopped his brow with a handkerchief. 'This is like bloody Ali Baba's market. We haven't even started on the rooms with the watches and clocks, not to mention the jewellery.'

He jerked a thumb to the constable. 'Take a break for yourself. Go and make a drop o' tea upstairs.'

He leaned back against the shelving.

'Any progress elsewhere?' he asked.

'To be honest, not a lot. I've been down at the Northern Hotel with Mossop all morning. They've questioned the staff, the guests, any delivery men and so on. But there's nothing solid coming out of it.'

'Do you think she's gone? You know, deceased, dead?'

'Could be. Or she might be on the run. Or she could have been abducted. Held somewhere.'

'That wouldn't be a nice thing to contemplate,' Doolan said softly. 'She's not the strongest in her mind, I'd say.'

Doolan had worked often enough with Swallow to know the signs of an investigation that was stuck. There were gaps and silences between sentences. When he was frustrated, the G-man had a habit of staring at his feet and scuffing his shoes against each other. He was doing it now.

Then he grinned.

'But I did come across one interesting item of information. I was in Currivan's of Fishamble Street earlier. Matt Currivan tells me that Phoebe Pollock has been in and out of the place with a gentleman friend. And she's been well able to lower a few ports and gins.'

Doolan whistled. 'That explains why she was coming home as drunk as a fish the other night. Who'd have thought that she'd have found romance at that stage of her life?'

'There seems to have been another side to Phoebe, at least in recent times,' Swallow said. 'We're going to have to start a search of the living quarters to see if we can learn more.'

'It's a bloody big house,' Doolan said doubtfully. 'There's three storeys above this one. What are we looking for?'

He gestured around him. 'You can see for yourself. This could take weeks.'

'I'd start with her bedroom. If a woman has secrets, that's where you're likely to find evidence of them. We want information on her personal life, love letters, tokens, maybe a photographic likeness of this romantic gentleman. She probably had places for any letters and things.'

He saw apprehension in Doolan's eyes.

'I'll do a search of the bedroom myself,' he said. 'I might be lucky. But if we need a full search, I'll get you all the help I can. We'll need experienced men.'

By now, the shirt-sleeved constable had returned with three mugs of tea. Doolan took his and propped his backside against the window ledge. Sipping at his brew, he shook his head in disbelief.

'Phoebe Pollock. Who'd have thought it? As me old mother used to say, if you keep a thing long enough you'll likely find a use for it.'

FIFTEEN

Christ Church's bells announced 7 o'clock as Swallow left Lamb Alley. He had spent three hours searching Phoebe Pollock's bedroom and the living quarters over the pawn shop without any success.

He was not especially surprised that he found nothing in drawers, desks, or under mattresses. The search that would be necessary would involve nail bars, metal probes and lamps. Floorboards would be lifted. Hollow spaces in walls would be tapped and opened. Cupboards and panels would be prised out.

When he went to put on his jacket, he felt Katherine Greenberg's letter in the pocket. The air had been heavy and fetid as he worked through the upper rooms in Pollock's. It was at most ten minutes to Capel Street. The walk would be refreshing.

He crossed Cornmarket, and turned down High Street. Then he passed under the Christ Church arch to Winetavern Street, making for the river. The city was slow and quiet with the offices and shops now empty. A solitary tram, drawn by two tired horses, creaked slowly along Essex Quay, its proclaimed destination the Phoenix Park. Swallow reckoned that the willing animals were due their rest and a good feed at the end of the day.

A man walking upriver on Essex Quay called him by name through the dusk and stopped him. Swallow recognised him as Friar Lawrence from the Franciscan Monastery on Merchants' Quay.

'That's a shocking thing to happen up at Lamb Alley... absolutely shocking to think of a man done to death in his own business, may the Lord have mercy on him. Do you think you'll be long getting whoever did it?'

'Ah, we'll get them all right,' Swallow attempted to sound confident.

Friar Lawrence wagged a finger.

'It better not take too long. The people are frightened... terrified.'

He went on his way up the Quay, still muttering.

Greenberg's was one of the oldest houses on Capel Street. In its heyday, before Dublin society moved south to the fine squares around the Duke of Leinster's house, this had been the most fashionable street in the city, home to wealthy merchants and professionals. Greenberg's was a spacious Georgian building with the double-fronted shop on the ground floor and with living quarters above.

The Jewish community around Capel Street was not as numerous as it had been when Swallow was a young constable. There had even been a *shul* – a synagogue – close by, incongruously located in the site of the medieval Cistercian Abbey of Saint Mary.

Many families had migrated to 'Little Jerusalem,' the area around Clanbrassil Street across the river. But Capel Street still had a dozen Jewish businesses; tailors and hatters, a bakery, a kosher butcher. And there was Greenberg's, dealing in statuary and paintings, valuable coins and *objets d'art*.

Swallow knew the shop's cycle of business from his days on the beat. At 6 o'clock in the evening, Ephram Greenberg would draw down the blinds and fix a metal grille across the porch. Then he would lock the shop door from inside and climb the back stairs to the living quarters for his supper.

Swallow's haul on the bell cord at the side door was answered by a young female servant. When he stated his business, she led him up the narrow staircase and showed him in to the parlour at the back of the house.

He knew this room. Velvet drapes framed high windows that faced westward across the city to the Four Courts and the Phoenix Park. A heavy Persian carpet warmed the pine floor. Two matching Highland scenes in layered oils faced across from the walls. A Carrara mantle filled the space between the windows.

He remembered sitting here as a young beat man, talking with Ephram Greenberg, his Roman-style police helmet on the tabletop. There would be strong Arabica coffee and sometimes small iced cakes from the kosher bakery down the street. The household smells surged back, bridging the years; wax, camphor and something hinting of cinnamon.

'If you'll take a seat, Sir, I will tell Mr Greenberg that you are here.'

The girl's English was perfect, but deliberate and accented. Swallow guessed it was from somewhere in Eastern Europe.

He sat facing the windows, and realised he was looking at the scene that Katherine Greenberg had painted for Lily Grant's class. The silver fruit bowl and the fluted decanter sat on the same damask tablecloth. The backdrop of the tall mantle with its dark marble was true to life.

He heard voices in the corridor. When the door opened, it was Katherine.

'Mr Swallow. It was good of you to come. You got my letter?'

'I'm sorry I couldn't get to see your father at the shop while it was open,' he said. 'I've been engaged in a serious crime investigation all day.'

She smiled. She was wearing her hair full length to her shoulders. Swallow liked the way its dark gloss caught the evening light.

'I know about that. The whole city is terrified. Everybody is locking up early and putting up bolts and bars.'

'That's not difficult to understand. People are right to be careful. But there's nothing to suggest that there may be another attack.'

She nodded.

'I hope you're right. My father has gone to his room to fetch something he needs to show you. Can I have something brought in? Some coffee or tea, perhaps a glass of wine? There's a very fortifying Lebanese. My father likes a little of it in the evening.'

'That sounds very tempting, thank you.'

She moved to the door. 'I'll have the maid bring it. I hear my father coming down the stairs. He'll only be a moment.'

When he came in, Swallow could see that Ephram Greenberg had aged. He was stooped, and now he walked with a stick. His once silver beard and hair were snow white. Swallow knew that he should not be surprised. Ephram had to be well past eighty, but the brightness that he had always seen in his eyes was still there.

He placed a small wooden box on the table and shook Swallow's hand.

'Joseph, it's good to see you… very good to see you, after such a long time.'

'It's good to see you too, Ephram. I should have called long before now.'

Greenberg raised a hand dismissively. He laughed.

'No, Joseph, you have become a busy man, a famous detective. I always read about your exploits in the newspaper. I say to Katherine when I see your name that we must be proud to know such a famous and important person.'

Swallow smiled. 'When I get my name in the papers it's not classified under good news.'

'I understand,' the old dealer nodded. 'But it is important work. I see that you are working on that terrible business at Lamb Alley. Poor Pollock killed and then his unfortunate sister disappears. Do you think she has come to a bad end, Joseph?'

'We don't know. It may be that she was somehow involved in his death. Or she may be in danger herself. Or she may be dead too.'

'May his soul find peace. His time in this world was not very happy.'

'Did you know him?'

'I met him from time to time. Jewish people have a name sometimes for driving a hard bargain, but Ambrose Pollock was known as the hardest man in the business.'

The young maid came through the door with glasses and a decanter of red wine on a silver tray. She placed it on the table and withdrew silently. Greenberg poured.

'*Zayt gezunt...* good health, Joseph.' He clinked his glass against Swallow's.

It was strong, aromatic, heady.

'From the Beqaa Valley in Lebanon,' Greenberg nodded to the decanter. 'Better than any Burgundy, I tell you.' He smiled. 'It helps to keep me alive. So, tell me about yourself, Joseph. You have never married, never settled down? I would have thought you would be a fine catch for many a girl.'

Swallow smiled. 'No, Ephram. I came near to it once or twice but I'm still a free man.'

The old Jew wagged a finger. 'A man needs to have a wife, Joseph. I have a good business here. I have my daughter as a support in my old age. But I miss my Ruth every day... every single day.'

'She was a good woman,' Swallow said quietly. 'I remember her very well.'

Greenberg drank deeply from his glass.

'Now, Joseph.' He cleared his throat. 'Enough of this talking. I asked you to come here for a reason that has to do with your work.'

He reached across the table to the wooden box. He lifted out a section of green baize, perhaps a foot square. Then he gently tipped the box so that its contents came out onto the cloth.

Swallow was looking at six small, silver coins.

'Have a look at these, Joseph,' Greenberg said. 'Go ahead, get their weight. Feel them.'

The coins were smoothed with age, but Swallow could feel their detail under his fingers. The obverse depicted a human head with stylised hair, a strong nose and well-defined eyes. The reverse showed a bearded and seated figure with a bird perched on one hand and a sceptre or trident in the other. It reminded Swallow vaguely of Britannia on the penny.

Greenberg replenished their wine glasses.

'They're beautiful items,' Swallow said. 'But I know nothing of coins. I assume they're special, rare?'

Greenberg placed one in his palm, the head upwards.

'That's the face of Alexander the Great you're looking at, Joseph. More than two thousand years ago these were part of the currency of ancient Greece. They're called the tetradrachms, each one worth four drachmae. The silver is very fine, very pure.'

'And valuable?' Swallow asked.

The old dealer shrugged. 'They are not by any means the most valuable of ancient coins. Although personally I think they must be among the most beautiful. They are rare enough. In London, I would expect to get not less than £20 for each one.'

Swallow drank from his wine glass. 'So tell me why a policeman should be interested in these.'

Greenberg replaced the coins into the box.

'Because these, and other good coins, have been appearing in dealers' shops all over Dublin during the past couple of weeks. I was offered six, as you see. A shop in Camden Street has another two. I know that Isaac White, my neighbour here in Capel Street, has taken in three rare denarii. There may be more elsewhere. Ordinarily, you might come across one or two tetradrachms in a year of business.'

'If you want the police to know about this you must believe that they're stolen or somehow improperly on the market,' Swallow said. 'So where are they coming from? Who's selling them?'

Greenberg raised his glass. 'Yes, I believe they may have been stolen. As to where they are coming from, I have no idea. Who is selling them? My daughter may be of some help on that. I think it's best that she speaks for herself.'

He rang a small silver bell. A few moments later, Katherine re-entered the room. She smiled when she sat with them.

'It's been a long time since I saw you two talking here together.'

She reached to the decanter, took a glass from the tray and poured for herself.

Ephram Greenberg mused. 'I suppose it's a few years all right. You were a young girl then, Katherine.' He turned to Swallow. 'Now she is my partner in the business, you know.'

'*Zayt gezunt*. Good health, Joseph.' She sipped the wine.

'Your father has been telling me about these Greek coins, Miss Greenberg. I gather you dealt with the person who brought them in for sale.'

'Yes, I bought them. But before we go on, perhaps it's time to do away with "Mr Swallow" and "Miss Greenberg," wouldn't you say? You'll recall my name is Katherine.'

Swallow was momentarily unsure if he was impressed or mildly shocked by her self-assuredness. She had confidence and poise. On balance, he had to admire it.

'Of course, Katherine,' he smiled. 'And you know I'm Joe.'

It felt odd. He preferred the articulation of his name, rank and title. It was a shield, a barrier. He opened his notebook on the table.

'When did you acquire the coins?'

'It was on Friday of the week before last. My father always leaves the shop early to prepare for Shabbat, and I stay on until 6 o'clock. I am not at all a religious person, you see. The woman with the coins came in at around 5.30.'

Swallow thought he saw Ephram wince slightly at his daughter's peremptory dismissal of her family faith.

'Can you describe her?'

'She was about my own age, respectably dressed. She wore a wedding ring and a small engagement diamond. And she was quite nervous. It was obvious that she was not a dealer and that she was inexperienced in transacting business. She put the three coins on the counter and asked me what I would offer her. She clearly had no idea of their value.'

'You say three coins. But you have six.'

'Yes, she came back again last Friday at about the same time with three more.'

'So she's been here twice.'

'Yes.'

'Did you give her an especially good price for the coins on the first visit?'

Katherine looked momentarily embarrassed.

'No, that's the thing. When she offered the first three, she asked me what I would pay, and I said I would give her five pounds for each coin. I knew they could be worth probably four or even five times that sum. I expected her to bargain upward. But to my surprise, she accepted my price.'

'Did you ask her where she had got the coins?'

Katherine shrugged.

'When one is looking at a fine profit like that, one doesn't ask too many questions.'

Swallow grimaced disapprovingly. 'You might have suspected that they were stolen?'

'Greenberg's has never knowingly dealt in stolen property, Joseph.' Ephram's tone was sharp. 'You know that. If that were the case here, why would I have asked to see you this evening?'

Swallow decided to let it pass.

'I'm sorry. Please go on, Katherine.'

'I simply thought this was a naïve person who didn't have any idea of the value of what she had. She was a respectable woman. I guessed that perhaps she was in need. She wanted money and I saw an opportunity to buy at a very good price.'

'So tell me about the second visit. You say she came back with three more coins.'

'Yes, she was quite upset again on the second visit. She said she knew the coins were worth more than I had paid on the first occasion. But she was willing to give me the additional ones at the same price, so naturally I accepted.'

Swallow was less than impressed.

'So you have six coins, worth… what? Perhaps £150? You've paid £30 for them. Why do you want the police to look into it? It seems to me that you've had a good couple of weeks' trading, albeit through this woman's foolishness.'

Ephram Greenberg refilled Swallow's glass, and drained the last of the wine into his own. He rang the silver bell again.

'Because it isn't right, Joseph. There is something seriously amiss. As I said, there are other coins appearing in other shops too. There are tetradrachms, Roman denarii, silver shekels from Jerusalem. It must be that somewhere a sizeable collection has been broken up and is being sold off for a fraction of its worth.'

He stayed silent when the young maid entered, carrying another decanter of wine. She set it on the tray and removed the empty one. Katherine refilled the glasses.

'Those of us who love beautiful things from antiquity – things like these – do not like to see them thrown around, bartered by people who have no understanding, no respect for what they are handling,' Ephram said. 'And when it happens, it also causes confusion in the trade. Nobody knows what anything is worth.'

Swallow understood. Ephram might be an aesthete, genuinely pained to see treasures from the old world changing hands like greasy sixpences at a fair. But he also wanted to ensure that the bottom did not fall out of the market in which he traded.

He nodded. 'It's something the police will have to look into. For a start, we'll have to find this woman who sold you the coins. Have you any idea who she might be or where we might find her?'

'I think I might know her name, or part of it,' Katherine said. 'On the second visit, she left her bag open on the counter. I happened to see that she had a Post Office savings book with a name on it.'

Swallow poised his pencil over his notebook.

'What was the name?'

'I believe it was Clinton. That is what I saw.'

Swallow wrote it in his notebook.

There was nothing that could be done to follow it up until the next day. For the moment, he decided he would enjoy Ephram Greenberg's Lebanese wine from the Beqaa Valley, with the September sun settling behind the city.

SATURDAY OCTOBER 1ST, 1887

SIXTEEN

J ohn Mallon went through G-Division the next morning like an aveng-
ing angel come to punish.

Swallow had breakfasted early with Harriet in Heytesbury Street. Her
teaching schedule required her to be at the school on the South Circular
Road by 8.30. The local girl they had hired as a day maid had their porridge, fresh brown bread, some dried figs and tea on the table in the little
dining-room an hour before that.

He hated the figs. But Harriet insisted on them.

'They're healthy. Good for your bowels.'

'They'd want to be,' he told her. 'They taste like camel dung.'

'You don't know what camel dung tastes like.'

His protests made no difference. She instructed the maid to put them
on the table each morning.

He had returned late from Greenberg's. He and Katherine finished
the second bottle of Lebanese red after Ephram had retired. The young
maid had gone to bed too.

Katherine had gone to the kitchen and come back with a platter of
thinly sliced beef – she called it *speck* – with bread and cheese. They talked
about her mother, Lily Grant's painting class, his misspent days at medical
school, her training in the business, missed opportunities.

'I think maybe you and I could have more in common that might appear,'
she said when the wine was gone. 'We each might have had very different
lives. But here we are, drinking wine in Capel Street, telling stories….'

Swallow noticed how fine her hands were. They were beautifully
formed, tapering. Jeweller's hands that might have been doctor's hands, as
his own might have been. The warming wine and the conversation were
good. He had enjoyed the evening with Katherine.

She led him down the stairs, and let him out the front door on to Capel Street.

Harriet had been later still coming home. He knew that she would be at a meeting of some society or a political gathering. But his supper was laid out on the kitchen table. This time, there was chicken in the sandwiches. He nibbled at one for the sake of appearances, but the food at Greenberg's had taken care of his appetite for the evening.

He heard the front door closing sometime after midnight, followed by Harriet's footfall on the stairs as she made her way to her bedroom.

She greeted him at the breakfast table.

'*Dia duit ar maidin*'

Of late she had started to drop Irish phrases into her conversation with him. It irritated him intensely.

'I don't speak Norwegian.'

'You know very well I'm wishing you a good morning. It's a pity you can't be civil. And it's a pity you can't speak your country's native language.'

'We spoke English in Newcroft. That's my country.'

She sighed in exasperation.

'You seem preoccupied,' she said after an interval, spooning her porridge. 'And you look tired.'

The wine had been stronger even than he realised.

'I suppose so. There's a problem in an investigation. In fact, there's a whole lot of problems.'

She had become accustomed to hearing unhappy tales from him.

'I heard about the pawnbroker being murdered,' she said. 'It was in the evening papers. But what's happened to his sister?'

'I wish I knew.'

'Have you been assigned the case?'

There was no humour in his laugh.

'By default. My direct superior was drunk.'

He poured himself more tea.

'Did you do anything interesting last night?'

'Oh yes, I had a fascinating evening,' she said, choosing a slice of brown bread from the basket.

'I went to a meeting of a group called the Hermetic Society. It concerns itself with science, spiritualism, theology. And there are such interesting people involved.'

'I can imagine.' His tone was dry.

'Yes, we had an address by a young man called Yeats. I've met him before with some of my friends. He's about my own age. He's from a Protestant family in County Sligo, although he's spent time in England. He has fascinating ideas about the world of mysticism. He talked about Eastern philosophy and the old gods of Celtic Ireland. I could've listened to him all night.'

That sounded harmless enough, Swallow thought. The old gods of Celtic Ireland were less likely to cause trouble than some of the mortals currently around the city. He had heard of the Hermetic Society, but not of the young Mr Yeats. He finished his tea, and stood from the breakfast table.

'You look a little tired yourself. Since it's Saturday, you'll be finishing school early. You should take advantage of the free afternoon and rest here.'

'You haven't forgotten we're going to Maria's tomorrow,' she reminded him. 'She's arranging a special dinner for Michaelmas. It's an old Scottish tradition she follows from her husband's people.'

He had forgotten, of course. With a murder and a missing woman on his mind, social engagements were not high priorities. And the more he thought about it, the more he feared that the evening would be a challenge.

God knows what schemes Harriet and Lily might have in mind. Maria herself would be frosty and unforgiving. He would prefer to get out of the arrangement. But he knew he could not.

'Of course,' he lied. 'It will be a very pleasant evening, I'm sure.'

'Good. And I'll thank you not to lecture me when we're at Maria's. I've invited Mr Yeats to come along, and he has accepted. He respects me for my views and opinions. So I don't want to be treated like a child by my policeman brother.'

Early autumn dew had freshened the small rectangles of grass that fronted the terraced houses on Heytesbury Street. On the mornings when he walked to the Castle, he invariably encountered the cleaning women, cooks and maids who trudged in the opposite direction to work in the new, affluent villas of Pembroke, Rathmines and Rathgar. This morning, he noticed, many of the women clutched their shawls or coats against the chill.

The first portent of the day's vicissitudes was the newsboy's bawling of the morning headlines across the junction of Bride Street and Bishop Street.

'Journal, Times and Sketch… Journal, Times and Sketch… read about the shockin' crimes in Dublin….'

Swallow read the headlines on the news-stand.

PAWNBROKER WAS DEAD FOR A WEEK

Now his sister may be murdered too

INORDINATE DELAY BY DUBLIN POLICE

Shit and damnation, he thought. Some reporter had been tipped off. A policeman somewhere had a ten shilling note in his pocket or a few pints under his belt from one of the newspapers. It hardly mattered which rag started it. Once the story was out, they would all have it. Headlines about crime and murder would have the Castle authorities in an uproar. The civil servants and the Under-Secretary's coterie would be frantic.

Orders and demands, more often than not self-contradictory, would be fired off to the Police Office in the Lower Yard. The Commissioner would be down on John Mallon like a ton of bricks, and Mallon would be down on the crime detectives, driving for results.

Swallow's heart sank. It was not as if the inquiries into the death of Ambrose and the disappearance of Phoebe Pollock had got off to a good start. As of now, there were no leads and no identifiable suspects. There were no witnesses. There was no clear motive for the killing. And nobody knew where Phoebe Pollock was.

He turned into Golden Lane and followed the curtilage of the Castle wall until he reached the Ship Street Gate. He climbed the Castle Steps, making for Exchange Court, his heart heavy with each step.

The crime conference was set for 9.30, almost an hour away. But the building was already buzzing with activity.

Three police side-cars were drawn up outside the main entrance. Two constables stepped down from the first, a handcuffed prisoner between them. There were two more prisoners, similarly manacled in the second car. Swallow recognised them as junior members of the crime gang led until her death a few months ago by 'Pisspot' Ces Downes, and now directed by her former lieutenant Charlie Vanucchi.

Inside, the parade room was filling. Pat Mossop looked up anxiously as his superior entered.

'Mornin', Skipper. It's pretty lively here this morning.'

'So I can see. I read the newspaper posters as I was coming in.'

Mossop nodded. 'Yeah, the news is out about Phoebe Pollock. Chief Mallon is taking the crime conference himself, and he's startin' early. The shit's flyin' from the Upper Yard as you'd expect.'

The mornings that John Mallon chaired the crime conference were rare. Mossop gestured to a sheet of paper on the desk. Swallow recognised the Commissioner's distinctive stamp on the top.

'You'd better read that.'

DUBLIN METROPOLITAN POLICE
Chief Commissioner's Office
Lower Yard
Dublin Castle

Murder of Ambrose Pollock:/Whereabouts of Phoebe Pollock:

To all Divisions, Stations and Members DMP

A serious neglect of duty has resulted in an inordinate delay in the investigations into the above outrages. Appropriate disciplinary action is in hand.
All members are hereby instructed to accord absolute priority to these cases. This applies equally to members on general duties as well as to members of G-Division and others engaged in crime matters.
I have assured the office of the Chief Secretary that the police will spare no effort and will not relent until the perpetrators of these violent crimes have been apprehended and brought to justice.

J.J. Harrel
Chief Commissioner

With that gone out to every station and beat shift, the reporters' jobs were done for them, Swallow thought cynically.

Ten minutes after transmission on the telegraph system, there would be a copy in every newspaper office in the city. The Commissioner himself knew that, of course. It was clear now why half a dozen convenient suspects had been rounded up for questioning. The police had to be seen to have sprung into action.

A G-man put his head around the door.

'Conference is starting now. Mr Mallon's just arrived.'

Every chair and bench in the parade room was taken. Uniformed constables sat with their helmets on their laps. The G-men clustered together like barnyard fowl, muttering to each other, trading speculation and scraps of knowledge.

Even though the early September morning was cool, the air was heavy and laden with tobacco smoke. Swallow and Mossop found spaces to stand between the windows looking down into the Lower Yard.

John Mallon looked grim, as he intended.

Swallow tried to recall when last the chief of the G-Division had chaired a morning crime conference.

It was probably five years ago, at the time of the assassinations in the Phoenix Park.

The murders of the country's two top administrators had been a shocking lapse of security. But the aftermath swept John Mallon to the heights of power within the police structure. He assembled a team of G-men that smashed the conspiracy within weeks.

After that, Mallon, the Catholic farmer's son from Armagh, could do no wrong in the eyes of the administration. The current Chief Secretary, Arthur Balfour, was reputed to have told the Cabinet in London, 'Without Mallon we are nothing in Ireland.'

The buzz of conversation faded to whispers. 'Duck' Boyle, who would normally chair the conference, rose to face the room.

'Whisht now… whisht. We'll have quiet for Chief Mallon.'

When the silence in the parade room was complete, Mallon tapped the two green crime files in front of him.

'Members of the Dublin Metropolitan Police should hang their heads in shame. We're so far behind on these cases it's an absolute, bloody disgrace.'

He paused for effect.

'Ambrose Pollock was dead for at least a week. It took Sergeant Doolan to add two and two together from the beat reports before anyone even missed him. Is everyone else in the A-Division blind, deaf or just plain thick?'

He ran angry eyes across the room.

'If the "mules" down at Kevin Street had been on the job as they should have been, the likelihood is that Phoebe Pollock would be in custody.'

Swallow saw a uniformed inspector from Kevin Street, seated directly in front of Mallon, go pale. Most of the constables were A-Division men too. They sat with their eyes cast down. Some shifted uneasily in their seats. Two or three handkerchiefs were produced to mop sweat from faces taut with embarrassment.

'I don't have to tell you that we're in bad odour with the authorities over this. Bloody bad odour. The Lord Mayor and God knows who else has letters in to the Chief Commissioner.'

Mallon dropped his tone.

'Happily, I'm not the one who has to sort out the mess in the A-Division. My job, and your job now, is to locate the missing woman, clear up this case, find who killed Pollock and bring them before the courts.'

He looked directly at Swallow.

'I'm putting Detective Sergeant Swallow in charge. I want him to have all the resources he needs: men, cars, technical support. He'll report directly to me, hourly if necessary.'

Swallow silently flushed with anger. Across the room, 'Duck' Boyle's eyes bulged with fury at the brutal slighting of his own rank and seniority.

'There's a compliment,' Pat Mossop whispered in Swallow's ear.

He had his fill of compliments. He had played his role in the breaking of the Invincibles without any acknowledgment by way of promotion. The entire G-Division knew he was entitled to it. In June, he had cleared up the murders of Louise Thomas and her son at the Chapelizod Gate as well as the murder of Sarah Hannin near Portobello. Still there was no tangible acknowledgment of his successes. Now he was being pushed into the firing line again.

Mallon waited for an acknowledgment.

Eyes across the room turn expectantly towards Swallow. He felt the hot blood flooding his face as he fought to contain his anger. Conditioned obedience to authority won out. Slowly, the burning in his cheeks subsided. The pounding of the blood in his temples eased. He heard himself respond.

'That's understood, Chief. I won't let the job down.'

SEVENTEEN

Mossop was sympathetic.

'You got the shitty end of the stick again, Boss. But we'll crack this one. If I was Chief Mallon, I'd be lookin' to you too, instead of Boyle.'

The little Belfast detective was unconvincing, and Swallow was not in a mood to be comforted.

'It's fucking great to have a full-time optimist around,' he replied.

He knew the trail was stone cold. In fact, there was no trail worth talking about at this stage. His only consolation was that he had as good a team as G-Division could field.

Mossop was doing book man on the Phoebe Pollock investigation while 'Duck' Boyle had appointed Detective Tony Swann to that role for the investigation into her brother's murder.

Swallow was content to keep Swann on the team. He had the qualities a good book man required: grasp of detail, a capacity to spot patterns and connections and the ability to write passable English.

He retreated to the crime sergeants' office to think. He needed to consider how best to deploy his resources and to establish priorities.

He would leave Mick Feore to work on the guest and staff lists at the Northern Hotel. The big Galway man had an easy way about him that often worked with witnesses who were nervous or reluctant to help in police matters.

Stephen Doolan and his team would carry on with their task of inventory at the pawnbrokers. Beat men across the divisions would continue checking with the chemists and apothecaries to see if the prussic acid found in Phoebe Pollock's room might be traced.

Then there was the matter of the Greek coins appearing at Greenberg's and other dealers' shops around the city. Someone would have to be assigned to follow it up.

There was a possibly useful line of inquiry in the disappearance of Phoebe Pollock. Her drinking companion had to be traced. Would anyone else in Currivan's public house have recognised him? It was worth canvassing the clientele there.

There was no better candidate for the job than 'Duck' Boyle. He was generally a non-starter in crime investigation. But his garrulous manner, especially when there were a few drinks to be had, could be turned to advantage in a situation like this.

Boyle was in his office, a murderous look on his face. That was understandable, Swallow reckoned, after being humiliated by Mallon. Swallow raised his hands in a gesture of helplessness.

'I'm sorry about what happened in there. It wasn't of my choosing.'

Boyle glared at him.

'I'm not lookin' for sympathy. Just a little respect for me rank.'

'I want a bit of advice,' Swallow said. 'I need someone with experience to check on some intelligence we got on Phoebe Pollock.'

Boyle shifted the papers on his desk in an attempt to look preoccupied.

'I'm loaded with work, Swalla'. What is it you want?'

Swallow recounted what he had learned from 'Five Times' Currivan.

'We need someone to get into the public house, put a few drinks about and see if anyone can identify this fellow. It'll take an experienced, senior man to do it.'

Boyle's eyes narrowed as he saw an opportunity to escape the drudgery of regular duty, perhaps gain some kudos and do some drinking on the G-Division expense sheet.

He looked meditatively out the window.

'Well, like I said, I'm at the pin o' me collar here. But I recognise that ye need a reliable man on this. I'll try to clear things so I could get down there over the night couple o' nights. Mind you, I'm makin' no promises as to results.'

'That'd be great,' Swallow responded. 'I haven't a doubt you'll get them.'

He walked down the corridor to the public office.

Johnny Vizzard, just recruited from uniform as a trainee for G-Division, had been rostered as morning duty officer.

He sat behind the high, wooden desk meticulously countersigning release forms for the members of the Downes gang who had been freed from custody. None of them had anything to do with the Pollock murder. Their alibis were perfect. In fact, two of them had just been released from Mountjoy Prison that morning.

'Can you run a check on a name at the Post Office Savings Bank for me sometime during the day?' he asked.

Vizzard was already showing himself as a fast worker.

'Sure, Sergeant. Give us the details.'

A party of G-men worked each day and night at the General Post Office in Sackville Street. Their principal task was to intercept letters connected with suspected persons. These would be steamed open, and their contents copied or noted.

But the G-men could also gain access to the records of the Post Office Savings Bank, which now administered well over 200,000 accounts in Ireland alone.

'All I have is a name – Clinton – a Mrs Clinton, I think. She'd be a woman in her thirties maybe. I'm sorry I can't be any more precise. I'd expect her to have a Dublin address.'

Vizzard copied the details into his notebook.

'Leave it with me, Sergeant.' Swallow knew that he was flattered with the assumption that he was being brought in on a murder investigation.

'I'll have that for you by dinner time.'

Swallow silently gave thanks for the enthusiasm of youth.

EIGHTEEN

The urgent message from Stephen Doolan at Lamb Alley came in the middle of the afternoon. Swallow had succeeded in requisitioning four more constables to assist at the pawn shop.

The duty officer at Exchange Court climbed the stairs, and handed Swallow the note he had taken from a constable despatched from the search team.

D/Sergeant Swallow, Exchange Court
Some unusual items come to light here. Can you attend please as soon as possible?
Stephen Doolan (Sgt) 22A

The constable on duty at Pollock's had been told off to watch for him.

'Sergeant Doolan's in one of the back rooms downstairs. He said to go on down once you got here.'

Swallow descended the granite steps to the basement. The air was heavy with oil from the Bull's-eye lamps. He found Doolan with his constable assistant, seated at a pine table in a brick-walled cellar with a dirt floor.

Doolan's beard was streaked with perspiration and dust. Two opened pint bottles of Guinness's stout stood on the table beside a pile of ledgers and account books. A wooden crate, perhaps three feet square, stood on the floor with a Bull's-eye flickering beside it.

'That,' Doolan said, pointing to the crate, 'does not match anything I can find in the books here.'

He tapped the uppermost ledger in front of him. 'And when you see what's in the bloody box you'll understand why I thought you'd want to have a look for yourself.'

He reached across the top of the crate, leaned in and drew out a long silver salver. Swallow estimated it was more than two feet from end to end. The bevelled edging was chased in what looked like oak leaves. The salver glinted like moonlight under the police lamp. In the centre, an engraved coat of arms showed a helmet and a motto.

'Get the heft of that.'

Doolan offered him the salver. It was heavy. Swallow saw that the handles were inlaid with mother-of-pearl. He laid it on the table in front of Doolan.

'I'm impressed,' he said. 'The Pollocks were dealing in quality merchandise then, weren't they?'

'Well, that's just the point,' Doolan said. 'There's no paperwork here to show where any of this stuff came from. And there's crates of it.'

He looked at his notebook. 'So far we've listed 150 platters, plates, tureens, goblets, candlesticks... and we haven't even started counting the knives and spoons and forks.'

He tapped the salver on the table. 'I'm not an expert. But I've done my share of duty around the pawn shops, and I know quality silver from dross. This is the best... or damned close it.'

Swallow made a little whistle.

'There's nothing in the books to indicate where it came from or how it got here? Are you absolutely sure?'

'We've checked every scrap of paper. There's no invoice, no statement, no record, no pawn tickets – not that you'd be likely to have this sort of thing coming in here for pawn anyway.'

As if doubting Doolan's narrative, Swallow reached into the crate himself. His fingers fastened on a three-branch candelabrum wrapped in muslin. The silver shone dully through the translucency of the cloth. Underneath, in the crate, he could see a stack of servers, each individually wrapped.

'There's four o' them boxes, Sergeant,' the constable said helpfully. 'You can take our word. It's all the same stuff. We've been through every feckin' dish of it.'

Doolan slugged his stout.

'Thing is, I wouldn't believe it's here all that long. There was a coating of dust on the crates, but you can see there's hardly any damp. The floors here are saturated from the Liffey. If the boxes were here for more than a few weeks, you'd see the start of rot on the timber.'

Swallow turned the salver to the oil light to see the crest and motto more clearly.

'It's a coat of arms. A helmet, an arrow, some kind of a dog and there's a motto. How's your Latin, Stephen?'

'Ah Jaysus, Joe. How's yer own?'

Swallow chuckled.

'You forget I was going on to be a doctor. I had to know a bit of it. This says, *Sub Hoc Signo Morior* – 'I die under this sign.' At least I think that's what it means.'

'Very impressive,' Doolan muttered. 'All I can tell you is that this stuff didn't come in through the normal channels anyway. There's not a sheet of paper here on any of it.'

Every Dublin policeman knew that pawnbrokers were required by law to register each item received, the name of the depositor and the value accorded. Checking the pawn books was part of every recruit's formation.

'It's a damned fine set,' Swallow said. 'I suppose we could make a start in tracing it by trying to identify the coat of arms. If we can establish where it came from, then we might be able to find out how it got here.'

'D'ye think maybe old Pollock was murdered over this?' Doolan drained the last of his bottle of stout.

'Maybe. But if that's what happened, the killer or killers left the loot behind.'

'It took us two days with half a dozen men to find it,' Doolan answered. 'Most criminals won't hang around, especially when they've got a corpse to account for. Maybe they just couldn't locate it.'

Swallow made a simple sketch of the motto and crest in his notebook. He stepped to the door.

'Damned good work, anyway. Will you copy me the full inventory of what's here as quick as you can? I'll try to get some sort of a fix on this coat of arms and where it might come from.'

One of the oil lamps flared. In the brief, brighter light, Swallow could see that Doolan was exhausted.

'Why don't you pack it in for the day, Stephen?' he said. 'Put someone here to mind this stuff. Go home. Get a few hours' rest.'

When he got back to the crime sergeants' office at Exchange Court, the young novice detective Johnny Vizzard stuck his head around the door.

'I went down to the GPO over my meal break,' he told Swallow. 'There's two possible matches on that query.'

He opened his notebook on the desk.

'We've got ten Post Office accounts in the name of Clinton: six men, four women. One of the women seems to be a widow, with a date of birth in 1828. So she's around sixty. Her account was transferred five years ago from her deceased husband. Another has a date of birth in 1835, making her fifty-two years of age. They're fairly well outside the range you mentioned.'

'So far, so good,' Swallow said.

'That leaves us just two possibilities. There's a Mrs Annie Clinton living out at Howth. Her details show a date of birth in 1860, so she's twenty-seven. She has just over £80 on deposit. And there's a Mrs Grace Clinton at an address on North Circular Road, near Phibsboro. Her date of birth is 1859, so she's twenty-eight. She has £48 and 10 shillings.'

'Can you find out the patterns of business, deposits, withdrawals, balance and so on?'

Johnny Vizzard smiled with satisfaction.

'I got those, Sir. No withdrawals over two years for the woman in Howth, and a lodgement every three months of between £9 and £10. The sum is converted from US dollars, so it must be coming in from America. The other one has quite a few withdrawals over the past two years, but there's two deposits of £10, each in the past two weeks.'

'That's our woman,' Swallow told him. 'Mrs Grace Clinton. Now, here's your chance to do yourself a bit of good for your police career.'

He told Vizzard what he had learned from Ephram and Katherine Greenberg. The young G-man took swift notes.

'I'll get out to the house first thing once my tour of duty finishes here this evening. What's the line of questioning?'

'You can't let on that you know anything about her Post Office account,' Swallow reminded him. 'You'll have to say that she's been identified as the seller of these coins and that you need to know where she got them from. If she asks why, just play dumb. You're not at liberty to say anything more until you report back to your superiors.'

'So what are we dealing with?' Vizzard asked. 'Did she steal them? Or is she fencing stolen property? Maybe it's something bigger,' he said hopefully.

'How the hell do we know?' Swallow grumbled. 'We don't make assumptions. We ask questions and we get answers. Then we think about the answers we've got.'

'Sorry, Sergeant,' Vizzard was instantly downcast. 'I was wondering if any of this is connected with the murders. It'd be very big stuff for me.'

Swallow felt a pang of guilt at putting down his enthusiasm.

'Ah, you're all right. To tell you the truth, I don't know what this might be connected to. On the face of it, it sounds like stolen property. But it's not the usual stuff. The coins are rare enough.'

'I'll do my best, Sir.'

'I know you will. That's the annoying thing about detective work. You never know if there's a pearl in all the shit until you've waded through it. And usually there isn't.'

NINETEEN

Swallow left Exchange Court, and made for the Upper Yard to the office of the Ulster King-at-Arms.

The Ulster office was the authority on Irish heraldry, issuing coats of arms and banners on royal appointment. Swallow had a passing acquaintance with some of the staff, and he knew the current 'Ulster,' Sir John Burke, by sight. With any luck, he might get an early identification for the arms on the silver hoard at Pollocks.

The Bedford Tower that housed the Ulster office, though, was firmly shut. Swallow's profanity was loud enough to draw a startled glance from the sentry at the Justice Gate.

'Bloody civil servants, gone on the stroke of 1 o'clock on Saturdays,' he muttered to himself. He had lost track of time at Lamb Alley.

He wanted to kick the door. Only the reproachful eye of the sentry dissuaded him. Instead, he strode across to the Lower Yard and John Mallon's house.

Mallon was dressed as if to go out, with hat and cane in hand. Swallow caught a glance of Mrs Mallon crossing the half landing on the stairs, hatted and gowned. He surmised that they were bound for a social visit or perhaps to some official function.

'I thought you'd want to be brought up to date on things, Chief.' Swallow said. 'Is it a bad time?'

'I can take 10 minutes.'

Mallon led him into the parlour.

Swallow summarised. The leads were few and unpromising. The trawl of guests and staff at the Northern Hotel had yielded no result so far that might throw any light on the whereabouts of Phoebe Pollock. There was nothing coming in from the many informants the G-Division operated within the city's criminal underworld.

If there was any faint gleam of hope, it might be the possibility that when 'Duck' Boyle would have completed his inquiries at Currivan's of Fishamble Street, they might identify Phoebe's gentleman friend.

'I can't say I'm very impressed,' Mallon said testily. 'Forty-eight hours on, with the Security Secretary's office breathing down our necks, we don't even have even a suspect, unless we include Phoebe Pollock. And we don't know if she's alive or dead.'

Swallow was unwilling to let the reprimand pass.

'There's no point in laying that on me, Chief. You handed the case to me twenth-four hours after the event. I'm doing my best.'

Mallon sighed.

'Don't take it personally. Carry on.'

'There's been one other unusual development. It might be significant.'

He described the cache of silver plate uncovered in Stephen Doolan's search in the basement at Lamb Alley.

'It's a full set of silver, more than 150 pieces, I gather. I haven't got any estimate on the value, but we're talking about big money. It could be a very powerful motive for a robbery, or even murder.'

He showed Mallon his sketch of the crest engraved on the silver, and recounted his fruitless attempt to find someone at the Ulster Office in the Upper Yard who might help him to identify it.

Mallon gave a wintry smile.

'You won't find those gentlemen up there on a Saturday afternoon. It's only a part-time thing for Burke anyway. He's busy making money on his books about the peerage, pandering to the lords and earls.'

'That means it'll be Monday before I can get any fix on where this stuff might have come from,' Swallow said. 'If it's connected with the murder, it could be a costly delay.'

'I know that. But I wouldn't advise disturbing any of the officials from the Ulster office over Sunday.'

'Christ, I'd take great pleasure in rousing a few of those cosseted bastards and dragging them in to work.'

'Forget it,' Mallon said sharply.

He scrutinised the sketch in Swallow's hand.

'If you're right about the quality and quantity of this stuff, then Ambrose Pollock was way out of his league. When I was a young constable he generally traded in cast-off coats and bits of old clocks, that sort of thing. This wouldn't be the normal sort of transaction over in Lamb Alley.'

The parlour door opened slightly. Swallow knew it was a signal.

Mallon moved to the door.

'We're in dangerous times, Swallow... problematic times. Policemen have to tread carefully. That's why I wanted you to take these cases on instead of that clown Boyle. You do the detective work and let me look after the politics with the fellows in the Upper Yard.'

Swallow bit his lip. If he was so damned good, why was it not recognised where it mattered? Why was 'Duck' Boyle at the rank of detective inspector while he was stuck at sergeant for more than a decade?

He nodded.

'I understand, Chief. I hope yourself and Mrs Mallon have a pleasant evening.'

He was half way across the Lower Yard before he realised that he had not mentioned the business of the Greek coins that had been brought into Greenberg's in Capel Street. In the ordinary course of events it would be a matter worth mentioning, but until young Vizzard came back from interviewing Mrs Clinton he knew nothing himself.

With a murder to be solved and the disappearance of the chief suspect into thin air, it was not an immediate priority.

SUNDAY OCTOBER 2ND, 1887

TWENTY

Sunday morning's murder conference was low key. In reality, Swallow knew, there was little point in holding it at all. But even if there was no progress in the investigations, appearances had to be kept up to satisfy the higher authorities.

The only man in uniform was Stephen Doolan. He had sensibly told his constables to take a rest day, leaving just one man to guard the pawn shop. Detective Mick Feore's glum expression confirmed that the trawl of guests and staff at the Northern Hotel had not yielded anything positive. The two book men, Mossop and Swann, were pretending to cross check witness statements in case there were any potential connections that had been missed. There were none.

Swallow attended Mass at 8 o'clock at the Franciscan church on Merchants' Quay. He liked the Franciscans and the Carmelites at Whitefriar Street, preferring their humility to the sense of high authority exuded by the parish clergy of the Dublin Archdiocese. That enabled him to be at Exchange Court to chair the conference at 9 o'clock.

The duty man handed him a note as he arrived. It was from Vizzard.

Sergeant Swallow, G-Division

Sir,
I wish to report that I visited the address of Mrs Grace Clinton at North Circular Road at 7.15 last evening. There was no response at the front door and there did not appear to be anyone present in the house.
I identified myself to a neighbour, who advised me that Mr Clinton, Mrs Clinton or their children hadn't been seen that day. Sometimes on a Saturday

they went to visit relatives, he said. He advised me that Mr Clinton works as a clerk in a solicitor's office in the city centre. He was unable to state the name of the firm.

I will revisit this address again tomorrow (Sunday).
I remain your obedient servant,

John Vizzard (Constable)

Nothing much of benefit there either.

He had felt increasingly tetchy since the previous afternoon. The closure of the Ulster office continued to rankle, and Mallon's insistence that the civil servants should not be disturbed annoyed him more.

With no leads and no new developments, the conference was going to be little more than a formality.

'Would you tell the team about the silver in Pollock's, Stephen?' he asked Doolan. 'It'll take the bare look off the morning's work.'

Doolan described the crates of silver plate in the basement at Lamb Alley. Eyebrows were raised. G-men scratched details in their notebooks.

'I'm trying to get an identification for the coat of arms,' Swallow said. 'But the Ulster office is shut until Monday.'

'But there's nothing to link it to the murder, beyond the fact that it's well out of the range of ordinary trade at Pollock's,' Pat Mossop interjected.

Doolan shook his head.

'Look, there has to be a connection. This silver isn't recorded anywhere in the books, so it's got some sort of a story to tell. Ambrose Pollock is dead. The sister is missing. It links up some way, I've no doubt.'

At that moment, 'Duck' Boyle arrived. He installed himself on a chair beside the door, looking somewhat the worse for wear.

Swallow allowed himself a smile. 'That must've a tough night, Inspector, drinking with the select clientele across at Currivan's.'

Boyle attempted a countering grin.

'Well now, Swalla', the pint in Currivan's isn't too bad. And when you're spendin' official money and not your own it's even better.'

He leered around the room with a satisfied look.

'I can reveal that Miss Phoebe Pollock has been in the habit recently of repairin' to Currivan's o' Fishamble Street in the company of a gentleman.'

There were expressions of surprise. One or two G-men giggled.

'In consequence, I took up duty in the said establishment last night. And, as the sayin' goes, I spread me bread upon the waters to see what would happen.

'In the evint, I think the Chief Commissioner's money wasn't entirely wasted.'

Boyle paused momentarily for effect. 'I might've got a name for Phoebe Pollock's gentleman friend.'

Heads jerked up in sudden interest.

'Tell us more,' Swallow said.

Boyle opened his notebook.

'There wasn't any point after a while in trying to present myself as anythin' other than a G-man. I just moved around from one client to the next and asked did anyone remember Phoebe Pollock drinkin' in the place in the past few weeks.'

He grinned.

'I offered a fair share of drinks, and they weren't refused, I can tell you. I pressed one or two fellows fairly hard because they told me they were regulars – every night in there. And sure enough, I got two witnesses who said they remembered her, always in the snug, comin' in wid yer man, maybe half an hour before closin' time.'

'So who is the bloody man?' Swallow interjected, impatient at the laboured narrative.

Boyle glanced at his notebook.

'I didn't get a full name. But I got a good description. Well dressed, comfortable lookin'. The two fellows said they heard her call him 'Len' at one stage and 'Lennie' at another.'

'Len,' Stephen Doolan said. 'That's all?'

'She didn't exactly introduce him around to the social circle in Currivan's,' Boyle said defensively.

'Len,' Swallow repeated bleakly. 'Or maybe Lennie.' He shrugged. 'I suppose we'll have to try to work on it.'

The ever-optimistic Pat Mossop fell into role again.

'Ye're right, Skipper. Work on it we will. Isn't it better to light one candle than sittin' here cursin' the feckin' darkness?'

TWENTY-ONE

The aroma of roast goose permeated the upper floors of Maria Walsh's house on Thomas Street.

Swallow had taken a corner chair in the parlour directly above Grant's public bar. A turf fire burned in the grate, sufficient to take the edge off the chill of the October evening. Harry Lafeyre had poured him a Tullamore, to which he had added a dash of soda water, giving it a nice lift. In other circumstances, he reckoned, he might be happy to relax and enjoy a sociable gathering. This, though, would be an evening fraught with peril. It would be his first extended encounter with Maria since he had taken up the rented house at Heytesbury Street with Harriet.

The interval of three months had done little to clarify his thinking, whatever about Maria's. She declared that she'd had enough of the uncertainty and unpredictability of his job. He had been hesitant about making a commitment that he felt he might not be able to sustain.

'We can't go on indefinitely like this,' she had told him reasonably, two years into the relationship. 'Your work makes terrible demands, and you say yourself that it's not acknowledged. You could make all the difference to this business if you were prepared to do so. And we could plan for some sort of a life together.'

If she found the situation this evening in any way stressful, it was not showing, arranging herself with her back to the windows that faced the street. Her fine, blonde hair was stylishly shaped in her customary French roll. It contrasted classically with a green silk dress, stitched with small pearls at cuffs and neckline. When she laughed, the evening light caught her strong, high cheekbones. Swallow had not forgotten how strikingly attractive she was.

Lily and Lafeyre, along with another guest, were already seated in the parlour when Swallow arrived. Lafeyre introduced the stranger.

'I'd like you meet a friend of mine from my Cape Colony days, George Weldon.'

Swallow had heard Lafeyre mention him, and that he was connected to a landed family in the South of Ireland. He knew that Weldon was now a civil servant, acting in some sort of a liaison role between Whitehall and one of the Chief Secretary's departments in Dublin.

Weldon dressed well, and there was a faint scent of an expensive cologne. Swallow estimated he was in his mid-thirties. He smiled broadly and his handshake was firm

'Mr Swallow. I know you do a lot of work with Harry.'

Swallow was about to sit with his whiskey when Harriet arrived, accompanied by a delicate looking young man with longish hair and gold-rimmed spectacles.

She introduced him to Maria and then to each of the others.

'This is my elder brother, Joseph,' she said when it was Swallow's turn. 'And this is Mr William Yeats.'

Swallow extended his hand.

'Mr Yeats. Very nice to meet you. My sister has told me about you.'

'Now,' Harriet said, taking her guest by the arm, 'we'll have Harry get you something to drink.'

Weldon took a chair beside Swallow.

'I read in the newspapers that you're a busy man,' he said. 'I'm sure you're glad to get away for a few hours from that murder case.'

Swallow realised now that had seen Weldon on occasion at the Castle. The body of officials controlling the country from within the walls of the Castle, and in the various government offices around the city, numbered no more than a few hundred. But each cohort guarded its privacy. A policeman and a civil servant might recognise each other. A bureaucrat might identify an army officer out of uniform. They might even know each other's names. But they would rarely socialise.

Swallow wondered if Weldon had been invited to dinner because of his association with Lafeyre, or as a not-so-subtle attempt to remind him that other men might come into Maria's line of sight.

'Detective work doesn't follow the clock, Mr Weldon,' he smiled. 'You have to fit your social life around it.'

He shot a sidelong look at Maria, but she had turned to talk to another of the guests, the Franciscan, Friar Lawrence from Merchants' Quay. The elderly friar was seated across the room from Swallow.

'Will you say Grace for us, Father, when we go across to the dining-room?' Maria asked.

Lawrence smiled and raised his glass of whiskey, well-filled earlier by Harry Lafeyre.

'Of course, Mrs Walsh. That lovely smell of cooking coming up from below is almost sinful, you know. We'll need a prayer.'

'Oh, you must think of this dinner as a religious occasion, Father,' Maria laughed. 'We're celebrating Michaelmas, the feast of St Michael. It's a tradition to eat a goose. At least, I'm making it a tradition now.'

'I understand in Scotland it's called a "stubble goose" because at this time the fowl are feeding in the harvested fields,' Yeats said knowledge-ably. 'Although why it should have any relationship to St Michael, I don't know.'

Maria smiled. 'I don't know either. It was a custom in my late husband's family.'

Swallow saw the slight sadness in her face, and he picked up the catch in her voice. Jack Walsh had gone down with all his fellow crew members when their ship foundered off the Welsh coast five years previously, leaving Maria widowed at twenty-five.

He was still a presence in her conversation when Swallow first came as a lodger to Thomas Street. Once their relationship developed into inti-macy, though, she rarely spoke of Jack afterwards.

'I believe it's time to go to table,' she said. 'I think I hear Tess on the stairs.'

The party of eight arranged themselves around the mahogany din-ing-table. Maria sat at the end nearer the door. Some swift choreography by the other guests obliged Swallow to take the seat to her right. He had no doubt that it was contrived. Weldon sat opposite. Friar Lawrence sat at the other end of the table, between Harriet and Yeats.

He tucked back the sleeves of his habit, and made a benediction with his hand.

'May the Lord bless us all, bless this food we are about to eat and bless those who have prepared it.'

They had a chicken broth, and then a warming vegetable soup, followed by steamed cod in white sauce. Then Carrie, Maria's cook, brought in the goose on a blue platter. Lafeyre carved, while Tess the maid ferried platters of the meat along the table. There was Hock and Claret. Swallow stayed with the claret, a velvety Château de Pez from Saint-Estèphe.

'You're a poet, Mr Yeats, I understand,' Maria said. 'Is that something that one can be trained to? Or is it a natural gift?'

'It is a gift given to some, Mrs Walsh,' the young man answered. 'Often it is part of a larger gift, the gift of vision, of being able to connect with worlds that exist elsewhere.'

'Like the Moon, or Mars?' Swallow knew he was being provocative.

'You know very well that Mr Yeats is not talking about the Moon or Mars,' Harriet said icily. 'He is referring to the spiritual dimension. It is a matter of vision.'

'Quite right too,' Friar Lawrence said, raising his glass approvingly. 'We must not allow our horizons to be bounded by the material world.'

'Would you have any vision of where a missing person might be, Mr Yeats?' Swallow asked. 'I'm trying to find a woman who might have been murdered. Or maybe she just ran away with a lot of money.'

'Oh for Heaven's sake, Joe,' Harriet said.

'Don't be upset,' Yeats told her. 'No, Mr Swallow, I don't think I could help you there. But I might know somebody who could.'

'And who might that be?'

'Have you heard of Madame Blavatsky?'

Swallow knew of the Russian mystic, who had followers in many countries across Europe. G-Division knew that such a group had formed in Dublin. In police circles, it was considered harmless if eccentric.

'No, who's she?'

One never knew what might come up with a bit of fishing.

'Those of us who are interested in the mystic believe that she has powers of sight, vision if you like. And she can draw out those powers in certain others who may have them too. There are several people, followers of Madame Blavatsky, in Dublin who could probably tell you where to look for your missing woman.'

Swallow resisted the urge to be sarcastic again.

'I think I'll rely on more conventional methods just for the present, Mr Yeats. If they don't work, maybe I can make contact with your Madame Blavatsky.'

By the time Lafeyre offered second helpings of the goose, and notwithstanding the wine, the atmosphere at Swallow's end of the table had grown frigid. Maria had not addressed a single word to him. Weldon too seemed to have picked up the sense of unease.

'Tell me, Mr Swallow,' Weldon asked, 'what message might I bring to my superiors in London about the state of Ireland? Do you think the government's land policy can bring peace around the country? The police must have a good sense of whether it's working.'

'Outrages are down. But how much of that's due to the land policy, I wouldn't be able to guess. So I wouldn't want you to base your report back in London on anything I say.'

Weldon laughed.

'Don't worry. I won't have you held accountable. But I can speak with some personal experience. My family has – or had – land in County Limerick.'

He laughed again.

'Unfortunately, I'm on the poor branch of the tree. The inheritance laws worked against us. Otherwise, I wouldn't be labouring as a civil servant. But the Weldons have been there since Cromwell. Never a night's peace with shootings, arson, cattle being driven off, until my cousin decided to accept the government money and sell out to the tenants. It's a peaceful as an English meadow down there since.'

'You were probably wise to choose a civil service career, Mr Weldon,' Maria said, casting a reproving eye at Swallow. 'I'm sure it's much more pleasant than being shot at by Land Leaguers and Fenians.'

Weldon smiled.

'To tell the truth, I'd never have had any interest in the land even if I had the opportunity. That's why I went to Africa for a spell. But my background gave me an understanding of issues in the ownership and the management of property. So the government in the Cape Colony put me in charge of the office that dealt with land transfers. Now I'm doing something similar for Ireland.'

'Quite a few of the Dutch in the Cape wanted to sell out to English farmers,' Lafeyre explained. 'Each wanted the business done according to their own legal code. And Dutch law and English law are very different. Then the Xhosa people had their own claims on the land too. George acquired a reputation as a skilful negotiator.'

'So what exactly do you do now, Mr Weldon?' Maria asked.

'Like any other Irishman, I want to see the land issue settled once and for all. If the people secure ownership of the farms, their grievances are taken away. My task is to advance that process as completely and as rapidly as possible.'

'Rightly so,' Friar Lawrence said. 'Down in my own county of Cork, the tenants are taking up the scheme in their thousands. Mind you, there's a few of the big landlords who won't budge for love or money. They'll hold on for spite, I think. '

Harriet clanged her knife and fork noisily on her plate.

'We'd be very foolish to think that Ireland can be pacified simply by giving the land back to the people from whom it was taken in the first place. We need to break the connection with England, to rule ourselves and to make our own destinies.'

'Miss Swallow is a Home Ruler,' Lily Grant said to nobody in particular.

'I agree with her,' Yeats interjected. 'Ireland must find its own soul. Home Rule may be part of that. But we have to reach back into our history, into the spirit of the nation and reclaim the days when a race of giants, heroes ruled our country.'

'I'd hate to think of us being ruled by a race of giants,' Lafeyre laughed. 'They'd probably eat us.'

'You don't think I mean giants in the biological sense, Doctor?' Yeats said irritatedly. 'I mean in the intellectual sense, in their capacity for imagination, thought.'

Lafeyre shrugged. He disliked abstractions.

'So you're a follower of Mr Parnell, Miss Swallow?' Weldon said amiably.

'Yes, she is,' Lily said.

Harriet's eyes lit with anger.

'I can answer for myself, thank you, Miss Grant. I consider Mr Parnell to be a compromiser. He negotiates with England as if she had rights in this country, which she does not. Mr Parnell's objective of

Home Rule, secured on England's terms, is a selling of Irish nation-hood, nothing less.'

Swallow groaned inwardly. He heard Lily's sharp intake of breath at the far end of the table. Lafeyre sought to dispel the chill. He leaped to his feet.

'Maria, would you like me to serve more wine?'

She nodded and smiled nervously. 'Please, Harry.'

But if Weldon was offended, he cloaked it well, even elegantly, Swallow thought.

'Well put, Miss Swallow. In a way I agree with you about the man,' he said pleasantly. 'For my part, I see him as a traitor to his own, the Protestant landowning people, the backbone of this country.'

He looked up the table at Yeats.

'I think they're your people too, Mr Yeats.'

'Protestant, yes,' Yeats replied. 'But landowning, no, except in a very small way. My father is an artist and my mother's people have a business in Sligo'

Weldon nodded.

'From my background, I could say Mr Parnell is a compromiser too. So are the politicians in power at Westminster. They'll not defend my family's right to their land, and they'll sell us out to some Dublin parliament where we'll have to bow and scrape to Parnell's cronies. That much being said, I have my job to do, and I shall do it to the best of my abilities.'

This was a point, Swallow recognised, at which a sensible police-man should say nothing. He gratefully extended his glass as Lafeyre went around the table with the claret.

Now Friar Lawrence's face glowed with agitation.

'The backbone of this country, Mr Weldon, are the loyal Catholics on their farms and in their villages. They're the true Irish, descended from the noble Celts. Many of the people you speak of are no doubt upright and God-fearing. But they're planters and usurpers. They have no busi-ness here at all.'

Weldon snorted derisively.

'The Celts? Are you telling us the Celts were Catholics, Father?'

He turned again to Yeats.

'You'd better come to my aid here, Mr Yeats. You know about such things. Do you think the Celts were Catholics?'

Yeats frowned.

'I think they were far too wise to have anything to do with our kind of religion, in any of its branches.'

Swallow thought Weldon's riposte to the old friar was unnecessarily brusque.

He caught a glance of alarm pass between Lily and Lafeyre. If the Michaelmas dinner had been a ploy to bring Maria and himself back into harmony, it was not going to plan. It was turning into a heated evening of political argument.

Maria decided to exercise her prerogative as hostess.

'We'll have an end to this. The dinner-table isn't the place for a political debate. We're here for a pleasant evening. It's time for pudding. Carrie has prepared one of her specialties. It's a special compote. So I propose that we move on to the next course and talk about more pleasant subjects.'

As if on cue, Carrie bustled through the door supporting two big dishes of her fruit compote, one on each hand. Lafeyre began to say something about the current programme in the city theatres, falling in with Maria's injunction against further talk of politics.

'I apologise,' Harriet said. 'I shouldn't have been so outspoken. Please forgive me everybody.'

Swallow plunged his spoon into Carrie's pudding.

His sister was right, he knew. But if Parnell could be kept in place for a while longer, the chances of transition to a peaceful, new order on the land would be greater. There would be fewer shootings, fewer arson attacks, fewer deaths.

The compote was good. Lafeyre refilled the wine glasses. Outside, the October evening had turned to night.

TWENTY-TWO

Trainee Detective Johnny Vizzard travelled out to Grace Clinton's house on the North Circular Road for the second time on Sunday evening, at about the hour that Maria Walsh was showing her dinner guests to the table.

The possibility that his assignment might touch upon the investigation of the Lamb Alley murder had given an added edge to his zeal. He would show enthusiasm and thoroughness, two qualities that were highly prized in the Detective Office.

He left Exchange Court at the end of his duty shift, and took a tram from Sackville Street to Phibsborough. On a Sunday evening, Vizzard reckoned, most families would be gathered at a meal or around the fireside. Even if they were religious to the extent of attending evening service, they would be home by now.

If the husband were present, he knew, he would have to be explicit about the reason for his visit. And Arthur Clinton, working in the law, would know the limitations of a police officer's powers in a private house. He would be more likely to get honest answers from a woman on her own. But the likelihood was that the husband would be at home on a Sunday evening.

Ideally, he would put off the visit until Monday, but Sergeant Swallow wanted answers as quickly as possible.

The lamplighters had been along the North Circular Road before he stepped down from the tram, but not long before. The gas lamps were showing a thin, lemon-white. It would take a while before they strengthened to their full luminescence.

The lights were coming on in the houses too. Here and there, through laced windows, he could see families reading or in conversation. In one front sitting-room he saw a tall, full-bearded man, a woman and several young children around him. It was a cameo of comfortable suburban life.

This was respectable, God-fearing Dublin; streets and avenues in which a policeman could not only feel safe but actually be welcome.

These were the homes of a striving middle class, with the occasional professional or middling business family. Vizzard felt a pleasant reassurance from these illuminated glimpses of domestic order as he made his way towards his destination.

But when the novice G-man reached the Clinton house, there were no lights burning. His hauling on the bell and his hammering on the door knocker echoed through silent rooms. He bent down and pushed his fingers through the letter-box, forcing the flap back on its spring so that he could peer into the hallway. He could see only darkness.

He heard the scrape of an opening door from the adjoining porch. The neighbour, of whom he had made inquiries on his previous visit, poked his head out and then stepped out into the evening gloom.

'You won't find them here now. You've missed them again.' The man wagged a finger reprovingly.

'They were all away out of here in a big cab first thing this morning. They took an amount of stuff with them too, cases, bags, boxes. Even the poor children were carrying their luggage.'

'Did they say where they were going?'

'Mr Clinton said he had to go away on business. But it didn't look that way to me. The wife was in a bad way. You could see the tears. And the children were upset too, what with being taken out of their beds at that hour.'

A slow, queasy realisation of what had happened began to form in Vizzard's head.

'You didn't tell them I was looking to talk to them, did you?'

'Of course I did, as soon as they came back last night.'

'What did you say?'

'I said there was a G-man here, wanting to see them. Sure what else would I tell them?'

Vizzard understood with a sinking heart that his quarry was gone. And he knew that the situation in which he now found himself was of his own making.

It was a lesson that would stay with him for the rest of his career. In later years, when he had risen high in the G-Division, he would caution novice officers when they were going about inquiries. 'Pretend you're looking for a stray dog. Pass yourself off as a salesman. Say you're giving out bibles in order to save souls. But, never, ever say you're a *polisman* and that you'll be calling back tomorrow.'

TWENTY-THREE

The house had settled into quiet after the guests had gone. Maria heard Tom, the senior barman, lock the front door downstairs. She followed the sound of his departing footsteps along Thomas Street. Then she heard Tess climb the stairs to her room at the back of the house.

Carrie's dinner had been a great success. St Michael's stubble goose had been reduced to a clean carcass. The last of the fruit compote had been cleared off by Friar Lawrence. The wines had been well appreciated. Port, whiskies and brandies had followed when the party repaired to the parlour. But the evening had left her drained.

Maria did not believe in the custom of ladies withdrawing after dinner to allow the gentlemen to smoke and talk among themselves. Lily thought it a mark of gentility. It was common in the professional classes in which she moved as Harry Lafeyre's fiancée.

'It's my house,' Maria told her firmly when they rehearsed her programme for the guests, 'I'm not going to be shooed off to where I can't engage in the conversation of the evening.'

She found herself sitting beside Swallow in the parlour after the meal. She thought he looked strained.

'I suppose you're working very hard,' she said.

She surprised herself with the sympathetic tone that she had resolved to keep in check for the evening.

'It's fairly brisk, as you might imagine,' he smiled. 'Mallon has landed the latest murder on my lap.'

'You mean the case down at Lamb Alley? Ambrose Pollock?'

'Yes, and the disappearance of Phoebe Pollock as well.'

'I saw about it in the newspapers. I presume that's what you were referring to when you had that exchange with Mr Yeats at dinner?'

'Unfortunately, yes.'

'Did she kill him? Or am I allowed to ask?'

'You can ask. But I don't know the answer. I don't even know if she's alive herself.'

He forced a lighter tone and added a polite lie.

'But I've good fellows with me on the job. And I wouldn't have missed this evening.'

She tried not to think of the countless ruined meals and cancelled arrangements over the time that they had shared their living arrangements.

'I'm glad you were able to come,' she said simply.

She wanted to tell him that she missed his presence, irregular and unpredictable though it always was. She wanted to say that she missed their conversations and their outings – when they could get them – to the Park, or to the Zoological Gardens or along the strand at Sandymount. And she wanted to say that she missed his practical help in the business of running M & M Grant's.

'How do you find your house in Heytesbury Street?' she asked instead.

'It's fine. There's plenty of room for Harriet and myself. We've taken on a day maid. Harriet is gone to teaching early, so she keeps the place for us and she has breakfast ready every morning. '

'That's very satisfactory. I'm delighted to hear it.' She hesitated for a moment. 'Of course, if you would ever like to come here for supper or for dinner, you'll always be welcome. I mean, if you find yourself caught on duty... or whatever.'

'Thanks.'

She blushed with embarrassment, then with anger.

Thanks. What a flat, empty word. He could hardly be more graceless, she thought. She forced herself to change the subject.

'Lily tells me how much you're enjoying her painting class.'

'Yes, but I'm also discovering how much I don't know,' he grimaced. 'There are some very talented pupils there.'

'She tells me you met an old friend in the class,' she said. 'That must be nice.'

He picked up the undertone of hostility.

'I don't know what your sister may have told you. But I've known Katherine Greenberg since she was a child,' he said tersely. 'She runs the family business now in Capel Street with her father.'

'Yes, I know the shop. A bit unusual for a Jewish girl to go into business and not to marry, isn't it? '

He shrugged. 'It's not something I've given a lot of thought to.'

She could see that he was becoming tetchy. No matter where she tried to bring the conversation, it seemed to go wrong. She got to her feet.

'I think we'll have a little music to round off the evening,' she said in what she hoped was a tone of levity.

'Harry, to the piano, if you please.'

Lafeyre played while Lily sang *The Minstrel Boy*. Friar Lawrence recited from Goldsmith's *Deserted Village*. Weldon sang poorly from *The Gypsy Prince*. Maria briefly took the piano seat from Lafeyre and played a Mozart sonata. Harriet recited some lines of poetry in Irish. William Yeats recited one of his own poems.

Maria said she liked the metre of the poem, which, Swallow deduced, was about dogs and hunting. Beyond that, he acknowledged silently to himself, he could make neither head nor tail of it.

Swallow pleaded a lack of talent when his turn came to perform, but Maria persuaded him to try a few verses from Thomas Gray's *Elegy Written in a Country Churchyard*.

But there was no more talk of politics, or crime, or land as the night drew to an end. Lafeyre's driver and assistant, Scollan, arrived with the brougham. They took Lily to Alexandra College, dropping Yeats at St Stephen's Green, then they brought Swallow and Harriet to Heytesbury Street before returning to Lafeyre's house.

George Weldon and Friar Lawrence decided to walk together towards their respective abodes. The Franciscan monastery was at nearby Merchants' Quay. Weldon offered to accompany him, since his own lodgings were just across the river on Ormond Quay.

Swallow reckoned that Weldon was trying to compensate for his earlier brusqueness to the elderly friar.

Maria was unsure what she had hoped for from the night.

Did she want Swallow to ask her if he could come back? Hardly. She could not contemplate resuming their relationship as before in all its ambiguities and uncertainties. Was she expecting to hear him say that he would leave the police, marry her and share in the business? She knew he would see that as an undignified surrender. Was she simply hoping that being together for the evening would reignite the spark between them that had never fully gone out?

Whatever she had wanted, it had not worked out. The idea of meeting in company with the others had seemed a clever device when suggested by Lily, but it had been all wrong. She had embarrassed herself by mentioning the Jewish girl that Lily had told her about. And she had shown herself as over-eager by telling Swallow that he would be welcome to supper whenever he felt like it.

The night had been a disaster. Maria was always moderate in her consumption of alcohol, but now she felt completely enervated. Before she doused the oil lamps, she poured herself a very large glass of port and drank it down neat.

MONDAY OCTOBER 3RD, 1887

TWENTY-FOUR

Next morning, trainee Detective Johnny Vizzard discovered, more or less, where the Clinton family had gone after they departed their house early on Sunday.

Smarting from the embarrassment of losing his quarry through his own fault, he was resolved to affirm his detective skills to the degree that might be possible by trying to establish their destination.

He reasoned that Arthur Clinton was likely to have hired the cab from the nearby stand at the village of Phibsboro, or at Hanlon's Corner where the cattle dealers and the drovers congregated. But the cattle markets were closed on Sundays, and there would have been few fares for the cabmen.

His deduction proved to be correct. Clinton's neighbour had described the vehicle as a closed carriage, dark in colour, drawn by a grey horse with the driver a short fellow, bearded and stout. Vizzard found him with his horse and cab, all matching the neighbour's description, queuing for early morning business alongside St Peter's Church at Phibsborough.

He was surly until Vizzard showed his warrant card. Then he became co-operative, and demonstrated a surprisingly good memory for detail.

'Yer man kem up to hire me around eight in the mornin', all urgent and in a hurry. So we go down to the house and collected the wife and the young wans. I think there was three o' them. But I thought to meself 'twas a hardship to have them out in the chill o' the mornin' like that.'

'Where did you take them?'

'I brung them down to the railway terminus at the Broadstone. I heerd one o' the little girls askin' the father would it be warm on the train. So they were goin' travellin.' And sure they were loaded down with bags and boxes. I must 'iv loaded a dozen 'iv 'em into the luggage racks there.'

'Any idea what train they took, or where they went?'

'Nah. I asked yer man, just to be conversational, like. But he gev ne'er an answer to me. I'd have said the man was nervous, very upset. And the wife was cryin' an' she leavin' the house.'

Morning trains ran each day from Broadstone, Sundays included, to the west and northwest, stopping at scores of stations in between, and with connections to regional lines.

The Clinton family could be in Galway, Sligo, Cavan, Donegal, Mayo or anywhere along the lines. But a family of five, burdened with bags and boxes, might not go unnoticed at the railway terminus, especially in the relative quiet of a Sunday morning.

Within the hour, after he had jogged the recollection of the foreman porter for the price of a couple of pints of stout, Vizzard had what he considered to be relatively good news. The Clintons were not gone to the far-flung reaches of Connaught or Ulster. He was satisfied that they had bought tickets for Trim, in County Meath, just thirty miles from Dublin.

He had at least narrowed the field to the extent that he could claim some progress when he would report to Joe Swallow later in the day.

TWENTY-FIVE

In the morning, Swallow revisited the Ulster Office at the Bedford Tower.

His ill-temper of Saturday afternoon had not abated after he had found the civil servants gone for their half-day. If anything, it had been exacerbated by the tensions of the previous evening at Maria's.

Carrie's stubble goose and her compote of autumn fruits, both delicious in the eating, had lain heavily in his stomach during the night. And he was angry, although he was not sure who to be angry with, about what he knew had been a set-up to get Maria and himself back on track together.

There was little to report at the morning crime conference. Not that he had been expecting much. Nonetheless, it dragged on as the book men checked and re-checked statements and cross-references. It was repetitive and painstaking work.

He exited Exchange Court and made his way to the Upper Yard, noting that the sentries at the Justice Gate had been issued with their greatcoats. Autumn was tightening its grip.

The clerk at the Ulster office knew him by sight, but not by name. He bade Swallow a good morning and invited him to take a seat.

Swallow showed him the sketch of the crest that he had drawn in the basement at Lamb Alley. The clerk considered it for a moment.

'You've an eye for detail, Constable... I'm sorry, I didn't catch your name.'

'Swallow, Detective Sergeant. And you are?'

'Harrington, Deputy Chief Clerk to the King-at-Arms.'

Swallow tried not to look impressed. But the man's demeanour was helpful.

'The sketch is a bit rough, Mr Harrington. But it's accurate. I assume it's the arms of a family, or maybe an institution. Do you think you can help me to identify it?'

Harrington peered again at the notebook. 'Ordinarily, we ask people to submit any request in writing. And it can take weeks, months maybe, to search the records. They go back a very long way, you know.'

'This isn't "ordinarily", Mr Harrington. I'm investigating a murder, and the disappearance of a woman.'

'I understand,' Harrington said quickly. 'And of course we'll do what we can to help. I was simply saying that with the best will in the world it can take time. Tell me, from where did you copy this image?'

'It's stamped or chased into a set of household silver. Our problem is that we don't know whose it might be, or how they came to be parted from it.'

'I see. Do you know is it Irish silver? Or English? Or something else? That could save us a lot of time and effort. You could take it to the Assay Office in Great Ship Street and they'd tell you in an instant. But they only operate on certain days of the month when they stamp new manufactures. They're closed today and tomorrow, I believe.'

'I don't have that much time to wait for an answer,' Swallow replied, 'but I think I know somebody who could tell me.'

He rose to leave. Harrington raised a hand to stay him.

'Find out what you can. But before you go, show me that drawing again.'

Harrington took a sheet of tracing paper, and with swift, short pencil strokes started to make a copy of Swallow's sketch.

'I'll put someone to work on the records straight away. The arms are very likely English or Irish, possibly Scottish. But you couldn't rule out something from the Continent.'

'Can you make a guess?' Swallow asked.

'I could. But I might be wrong. There are thousands of family arms for Ireland, and many tens of thousands for England. To the untrained eye, many of them seem very alike. I could send you on a complete wild goose chase. If we can narrow the search, it'll certainly make it faster.'

He finished his tracing.

'There's a coronet on the shield there. That coronet indicates enno-blement, some sort of titled line. The hallmarks will tell you the maker. They should have records, and that would be easiest way of getting the information you need. On the other hand, if you try to trace it through our records here, and if you can narrow our search, I daresay we might have a result for you in a day or two.'

Nobody knew more about silver than Ephram Greenberg, Swallow reckoned.

'I think I know where to go next,' he told Harrington. 'With luck, I'll be back in an hour or two with the information you need.'

TWENTY-SIX

Fifteen minutes later he was at Pollock's.

'If we can identify the country of origin, they might be able to give us a name to match the crest within the day,' he told Stephen Doolan.

Doolan took a small dish from one of the crates. He checked that the engraved coat of arms was clear, and wrapped it in some brown paper from Ambrose Pollock's office.

'That's a good sample,' he grinned, nodding to the package. 'Very clear detail. I'm becoming something of an expert myself.'

He hailed a cab on Cornmarket. The driver clattered down Winetavern Street to the river, and turned across Essex Bridge towards Capel Street. It was coming to dinner hour, when most Dubliners would take their main meal of the day. Many of the premises on Capel Street were already rolling in their awnings or drawing down their blinds to herald the shop staffs' hour of freedom.

Some of the tailors had already closed. Swallow smiled at the sight of three or four young apprentices making their way from one of the tailoring shops to the welcoming doors of Jack Feehan's pub. He speculated mentally on the numbers of pints they would put down before resuming their places at the cutting tables at 2 o'clock.

The street was busy, and the traffic slowed the cab. Swallow nudged the driver when they were within stopping distance of Greenberg's. He paid him his fare and stepped to the footpath.

A constable patrolling towards the river passed the shop's double windows and nodded discreetly in recognition. As a security precaution, G-men were never saluted in public.

A moment earlier Swallow had noticed two men on the pavement outside Greenberg's. Now they were nowhere to be seen, and the shop door was shut. That was not quite right. It was still a couple of minutes to the hour, and Swallow knew that Ephram Greenberg would close at 1 p.m. on the dot, not a second before or later.

He shielded his eyes with his hand to look through the glass. Inside, he could see one of the men, a squat, moustachioed fellow, turn to draw down the blind.

He peered through the slit between the blind and the door jamb.

He could see a glint of blue steel from a revolver in the first man's hand. Ephram Greenberg was coming from behind the counter towards the gunman, his right fist raised. Behind him, he saw Katherine, her features fixed in alarm as the second man came towards her.

He yanked the Bulldog from his shoulder-holster and banged hard on the door with the other hand. The patrolling constable on the street swung around at the noise and started to sprint back.

'Gun!' Swallow snapped. 'Two fellas in there. They have the old man and the daughter.'

The constable took a step back, raised a nailed boot and kicked hard at the lock with his heel. The frame splintered and the door swung inward.

Swallow saw the barrel of the gun impact against Ephram Greenberg's face. The old man dropped to his knees, hands clawing at his attacker's coat. Blood spurted from where the skin had been split along the cheekbone.

Now the second man had his arm around Katherine's neck, dragging her towards the counter. There was a double-bladed knife in his right hand.

Swallow knew that the man with the gun posed the greater threat. But for the split second that he used it to club Ephram, that threat was in abeyance. He swung the Bulldog towards the knifeman and fired twice.

The first of the big .44-calibre slugs took the man in the upper chest under the right shoulder, the impact hurling him against the counter as the knife dropped from his hand. The second shot grazed his face as he went down. Freed from the knifeman's grip, Katherine threw herself forward through the gunsmoke to her father on the floor.

Swallow swung the Bulldog back to the gunman to find that the constable had closed with him, grasping the Colt revolver with one hand while he sought to force the man's head backwards with the other. They reeled across the shop floor, cursing and scrabbling at each other's faces.

The policeman's helmet came off. He appeared to be getting the better of his opponent, but the gunman succeeded in getting his feet against the policeman's stomach. He kicked, sending him staggering backwards against Swallow.

The attacker was on his feet before either of them could recover. Then he was out the door, gun in hand. Swallow saw him turn towards the end of the street in the direction of the river.

'Let him go,' Swallow shouted. 'We have this bastard....'

But the constable was already gone.

Swallow turned to the knifeman on the floor. There was blood seeping through his jacket, darkening his front.

He checked that the man was not carrying another weapon, then he clicked a handcuff around the man's left wrist and attached the other part of it to the brass kick-rail on the shop counter.

The double boom of Swallow's shots had echoed out into the narrow confines of the street. People had started crowding through the shop door, heads strained in curiosity and shock, noses wrinkling at the pungent smell of cordite.

'Get a doctor... whoever's nearest!' he called. 'There's a man shot and another injured. If there isn't a doctor nearby, get over to Jervis Street to the infirmary and bring one here.'

A man wearing a shopkeeper's apron was tending to Ephram. He raised him into a kneeling position, and then got him to his feet. The old dealer swayed, examining the bloodstained sleeve of his coat in puzzlement.

Swallow saw shock in his eyes. There was blood running down to his collar and shirt. He knew from his own medical training that it was a wound that would stitch. The greater danger, he reckoned, was that Ephram would suffer a seizure and collapse.

'Go across to Feehan's. Get some brandy for him and bring it over here,' he told another man. 'And get him sitting down. There's a chair behind the counter there.'

Katherine helped her father to the seat, dabbing at his wound with a linen towel that someone had handed to her.

The young constable came through the door, gasping for breath, his baton dangling from its leather thong.

'Bastard got away…' he wheezed. 'He was ahead o' me at the bridge. Turned and put the bloody gun straight on to me. I couldn't get in close to tackle the fucker. I had… had to let him go.'

'You did right,' Swallow said. 'You'd be a corpse for sure. We'll find out who he is when we get this other character patched up and back in the Castle.'

He squatted to look into the wounded man's face.

'What's your name, fella?'

The prisoner grimaced in pain and clanked the handcuffs against the brass bar.

'You fuckin' shot me… you fuckin' shot me. I'm dyin'.'

The accent was English. Cockney.

'You bloody will die if you don't lie still until the doctor gets here,' Swallow told him. 'I'm asking you again, what's your name? And who's your pal that's legged it away off down the street?'

'Fuck off.'

Swallow reached down and grasped him roughly by the ears, twisting his face upward to the circle of onlookers.

'Anyone know who this hero is? Anyone get a name for him?'

Nobody did. Heads shook.

The constable had retrieved his helmet. Swallow made a mental note of his number for mention in his report. He saw that he was trembling.

'Take a couple of deep breaths,' he told him. 'I want you to go across to Exchange Court. Tell them what's happened here, and say that Detective Sergeant Swallow wants armed support to hold a dangerous prisoner. Then give them as good a description as you can of the fellow with the gun that you chased down to the bridge.'

A young doctor and a nurse came hurrying across Capel Street from the direction of the infirmary. The wounded man's eyes had half closed, and small, frothy bubbles were forming at the corners of his mouth.

'He needs to get to hospital,' the doctor said after a quick examination. 'He's losing blood and he's in shock. He'll be in serious trouble if we don't stop the bleeding.'

He pointed to the handcuffs holding the man's wrist to the bar. 'Get those things off him. There's a stretcher on the way.'

Swallow handed his Bulldog to one of the constables.

'Do you know how to use it?'

'I do, Sir.'

'Take it. Go with them to the hospital. Shoot him if he tries to escape and shoot anybody else who tries to help him.'

He started to open the wounded man's handcuffs. The young doctor got to his feet.

'You can't come into the hospital with a gun.'

'Suit yourself. In that case, the handcuffs stay on and he stays here. This fellow has at least one armed accomplice out there on the street. So the constable here is going to have my weapon to protect himself, the prisoner and you, Doctor and your nurse.'

The young doctor blinked, unsure how to respond to the challenge to his authority. It was the more experienced nurse who broke the impasse.

'I'm sure it's all right, Doctor. We've had the police in the infirmary before in situations like this. They're very civil and discreet.'

Swallow leaned down to open the handcuffs.

'What the nurse says is true, Doctor.' He tried to keep the sarcasm from his tone. 'That's what we're noted for in G-Division when we come across bastards like this: civility and discretion.'

TWENTY-SEVEN

Ephram Greenberg insisted that he would not go to his bed.

The doctor had examined the gash on his head. He said that it would need stitching that would be better done at the infirmary. Swallow and Katherine had walked the old man slowly the short distance to Jervis Street, where his wound was washed, disinfected and stitched.

When they got back to the shop on Capel Street, though, he insisted that it was time to open for the afternoon's business.

'Look… look at the hour,' he gestured impatiently to the clock over Feehan's. 'It is almost 3 o'clock. Greenberg's should be open by now.'

Swallow wondered at his resilience. And his daughter seemed to be cut from the same cloth. She had been manhandled, threatened at knife point and seen her father pistol-whipped. Swallow's two shots, taking down the knifeman, had come within inches of her head. Strong men would be quaking after less.

Her concern was for the old man.

'You've had a bad shock. If you won't go to your bed, then at least go to the parlour and lie on the sofa.'

'Do as Katherine says,' Swallow told him. 'I need to ask both of you some questions.'

With Ephram settled reluctantly on the parlour sofa, the young maid with the Eastern-European accent brought them coffee.

'Something stronger would better,' Swallow said.

Ephram raised a hand. 'No, not at this time. I want a clear head.'

'I'm sorry I had to do what I did,' Swallow said. 'They could have killed both of you.'

'I don't doubt that they would have,' Katherine said angrily. Swallow saw her shudder.

'I've never seen such hard eyes as the man with the gun. He didn't have to do that to my father. He's not young or strong. He could have just pushed him away.'

'Do you know who they are, Joseph, these fellas?' Ephram asked.

'From the accents I'd say they're English. The fellow I shot certainly is.'

'English?' Katherine said. 'Have you any idea of who they are?'

'We'll find out about the character with the knife when the doctors are finished with him. The other managed to get away. But we'll locate him in time.'

'The man you shot… will he survive?' she asked sharply.

Swallow guessed that the question was pragmatic rather than humanitarian.

'He'll have lost blood, but the bullet didn't hit anything vital. Will you tell me what happened?'

She poured the coffee.

'It was all very sudden. I was arranging some trays in the display cabinet and my father was behind the counter on the other side of the shop. The first I heard was the door opening and closing. One of them pulled the blind down, and the one with the gun pointed it at my father.'

'I saw him,' Ephram interjected. 'I saw the lousy *harah* take the gun from his pocket and I knew it was trouble. So I didn't wait. I started out at him. I nearly had him by the throat when he hit me.'

'That was brave,' Swallow said, 'but it was also foolish. An unarmed man is no match for somebody with a gun.'

Katherine sighed with exasperation.

'So many times… so many times we spoke of this and we agreed, if there was a robbery, we had a plan.'

She waved her hand for emphasis.

'We have a box of trinkets behind the counter. They look expensive, but they're just baubles. We agreed that we'd just hand these over and hope that they'd take them and run.'

She looked back at her father. 'But this foolish man forgets the plan. He just rushes out and nearly gets us both killed.'

Ephram pushed himself up on his elbow.

'That plan would not have worked. These fellows weren't going to be fobbed off with a few paste brooches.'

He reached for his coffee.

'They said they wanted the Greek silver.' He cackled. 'I don't suppose they didn't know how to pronounce tetradrachms. They said, "Give us the Greek coins and tell us who sold them." Lousy *harahs*.'

'Are you sure of this?' Swallow looked to Katherine for corroboration.

'That's true. What my father says is correct. I... I hadn't had time to think about it until now.'

She raised a hand to her forehead, recalling what had happened.

'Yes, I heard the man with the gun say "We want the silver coins." He said to me, "Where did you get the coins... give us the name or we'll cut you." It was something like that.'

'I need to get this clear,' Swallow said. 'They didn't just want to take the coins. They wanted to know where they had come from.'

Ephram nodded from the sofa.

'Yes... yes they did.'

'That raises the question: how did they know that you had them here?'

The old dealer shrugged.

'There is talk around the city dealers. We all keep in touch, you understand. They tell me what they have taken in... I tell them what we have bought. It has been known that certain shops had been approached and had bought the coins. As you know, Katherine got them from a young woman who did not identify herself. You remember, we gave you a name but it was not a full name and we have no address.'

He paused.

'This was why we had thought it best to tell the police. Did you discover who the young woman is?'

Swallow shook his head. 'No. We're working on that. We think we know her full name now, but so far we haven't been able to find out where she is.'

'Ah, I thought you might have been coming to tell us you had located her.'

'No, I was coming to ask you about something completely unrelated to the tetradrachms.'

'What was that?'

'It's in connection with the murder of Ambrose Pollock. We found a lot of silver in the basement of the pawn shop, and I'm trying to trace who it might have belonged to.'

He took the small silver dish from inside his pocket, unwrapped it and passed it to Ephram.

'I need to know what you can tell me about that. Who might have made it, and who might have owned it?'

Ephram turned the dish in his hand.

'It's a nice little piece, no doubt. It's got the Britannia mark, which means it's not absolutely the purest silver. But it's still very good of course.'

He reached to a side-table, and took a small glass that he screwed into his eye.

'There's a crowned harp. So it's Irish – Dublin – no doubt about it. The capitals are a bit worn, so it's difficult to be precise about the date, but I'd say it was made around thirty to forty years ago. And the maker's initials are there too: *J.M.* That was a silversmith called Joseph Mahony. Quite well known. He had his shop at Crampton Court, just off Dame Street. But he's dead now, and the shop is gone.'

'What do you know of the coat of arms?'

Ephram shook his head. 'I've no knowledge of heraldry, Joseph. I imagine it's some titled family. But the silver is Irish – Dublin – so it must be likely that it was commissioned by an Irish family.'

Swallow rewrapped the silver dish.

'I have to bring it to the Ulster King at Arms at the Castle. I want to get an identification on it as quickly as possible.'

He stood.

'As soon as I can, I'll be back. I want to question the fellow in the infirmary. There'll be an armed policeman on duty outside here.'

'We still have the coins,' Katherine said. 'What are we to do about them?'

'Put them in a safe, or in the most secure part of the shop. They'll be evidence in court when we catch these fellows.'

He moved to the door.

'Some of my colleagues will need to interview you about what happened. They'll want details of what the men said, what they were wearing, their accents, anything that will help to trace them. They'll want to take statements and they'll ask you to sign them.'

'Of course,' Ephram said. 'We will do what we can to assist the police.'

Swallow hesitated. 'There's one other thing they'll ask. They'll want to know what happened when I shot the man with the knife. It's important they understand that your lives were under threat.'

He paused again.

'They need to know I shouted a warning before I shot him... that he could have put down the knife as I ordered him to.'

Ephram blinked slowly. 'I'm not sure that I heard....'

Katherine raised a hand, stopping her father in mid-sentence.

'We heard you warn him. He had the knife to my throat and I was in fear of my life. There will be no misunderstanding about that. No misunderstanding.'

TWENTY-EIGHT

After a month at the Langham, Margaret Gessel knew it had been a mistake. She could afford the hotel's charges. That was not the problem. But she resented paying so much to live in a place where her days were long and uneventful.

London might be the capital of the Empire, but there was little that a respectable lady could do on her own. There was a limit to the hours that could be spent reading in her suite or in the residents' private drawing-room.

She knew that some other landed families from Galway had decided to live out of town. Of those she knew, one had gone to Hastings, the other to farm somewhere in Sussex. She found their addresses and wrote to them.

The replies were cautious. In one case, a widowed lady of similar circumstances whom she had known through the East Galway Hunt indicated that she was thinking about returning to Dublin. Another suggested that she might consider moving to the fashionable little town of Dymchurch on the East Sussex coast. It was little more than an hour by train from Victoria.

A week later, on a bright spring day, Margaret travelled down to see it.

The town was pretty, with some surprisingly good shops and fine houses. The houses were far better maintained than in Ireland. Its prosperity contrasted sharply with what she had known in the grey market towns of Galway. At the end of the month, she decided to vacate the Langham and moved to the George Hotel on Dymchurch's High Street.

She wrote to Richard at his Ebury Street address, telling him of her plans. Her letter was calculatedly polite, but couched in terms that could leave him in no doubt about her sentiments. She was hurt and angry. There had not been a single gesture of civility from the Gessel household.

'I regret to say that I have found London quite uncongenial,' she wrote. *'So I believe I will be happier where I can breathe country air and re-engage with persons of my own class.'*

She was not entirely surprised when, on the following morning, a maid came to her suite with Sir Richard Gessel's visiting card.

'This gentleman is in the morning-room, Milady. He would be pleased if you would agree to see him.'

She kept him waiting for fifteen minutes to make the point. When the maid led him to her private sitting-room, she made no attempt to offer him any refreshment.

'I'm sorry that you're leaving town, Cousin Margaret,' he said. 'It's unfortunate that we haven't seen more of you.'

'Yes, I can imagine your disappointment.'

She allowed a hint of irony in her tone.

'A pity when families can't keep better contact with each other.'

'Perhaps when you came back to London on occasion you might call on us.'

'I'll not be back with any frequency. And when I do, it will be to visit my bankers. There's rather a lot of money to be managed, as you know.'

'Well… I'm glad that you decided to take my advice about selling Mount Gessel. I was… able to help there.'

For a moment, she wondered if he was about to ask for a commission for his services. If he was, he thought better of it. She stood to indicate that the interview was over.

'Goodbye, Cousin Margaret.'

She was relieved when he had left the room.

While it was comfortable and inexpensive by London standards, the George at Dymchurch was in reality little more than an improved coaching inn, patronised by local big-wigs, commercial groups and political parties. But she liked its bustling air. The staff were not nearly as polished as at the Langham, but they were obliging and cheerful, not unlike some of the servants in better times at Mount Gessel.

In the absence of a social life, she determined to fill the days in learning about the area, visiting its places of interest and exploring its antiquities. She hired a pony and trap from the hotel's livery. Initially, there were some misgivings about allowing a lady out alone on the roads and byways of East Sussex, but she quickly showed her skills in managing the pony and so, on fine days, she could set off along the coastline or through the farmland and the villages.

First, she explored the coastal road to Lydd. On the first fine afternoon, she strained and peered out across the channel thinking that she might see France. It was impossible, of course, they told her later at the hotel, although some people claimed to be able to see the lighthouse beacon at Calais in the night time.

She drove east as far as Dover, then west along the coast towards Hastings, pausing to explore the Martello towers put up to defend England against Napoleon. She travelled inland to the edge of the Weald. She had not realised how beautiful the English countryside would be.

The country people that she met were courteous and friendly. There was none of the caution and suspicion that she almost invariably sensed among the peasantry around Mount Gessel. But equally, she felt, there was not always the same quick-wittedness or nimble-mindedness. On occasion, she would be invited into a wayside cottage and offered tea or milk or cider. The people's houses were very different from those in Ireland. They were more spacious, brighter and very much better furnished. This was countryside, she realised, where prosperity and peace had been the norm for generations.

In time, she made connections. She discovered that the vicar at St Peter and St Paul's Church in the town was from County Armagh, and a graduate of Trinity College Dublin. His wife called on her at the George and invited her to visit. She met a retired Major General who had served in Dublin and his wife. They both knew the Galway countryside for shooting and fishing. Gradually, a small circle of pleasant acquaintances formed in her life.

After six months at the George, she determined her establish her own independent household. She took a lease on a new house that had been built on the Folkestone Road by a banking agent who had moved to Eastbourne. He had named it 'The Orchard' because the land behind it was planted with fruit trees. It was perhaps a little isolated, but it would be easily maintained. It was suitable for modest entertaining. It had accommodation for staff, and it was comfortably within her financial capacities.

She advertised in the local newspapers for a maid, a cook and a coachman. Within a week, she had hired all three. They came with excellent references. She vacated her rooms at the George, and moved to her new home, The Orchard. She told herself that although she had failed to secure some of the things that might be considered necessary to make a happy life, she could be at ease with the world for whatever years might be left to her.

TWENTY-NINE

Once Swallow had confirmed to Harrington that the silver from Pollock's was of Irish provenance, it took his staff at the Ulster office less than an hour to identify the shield and motto.

Harrington was pleased with himself.

'Your silver's engraved with the coat of arms of the Gessel family. They've been around East Galway since about the end of the eighteenth century.'

He rummaged through a buff-coloured file. 'This particular arms was issued for the First Baronet Gessel in 1801. They were throwing titles around like currant buns at the time of the Act of Union. According to our records he died in 1818, so your silver is probably about sixty years old.'

Swallow jotted the details in his notebook.

'So where do I find these… Gessels? Presumably somebody inherited the title, land, a house and all that?'

Harrington shook his head. 'The title's extinct. The Second Baronet, John Gessel, died in 1848. His only son, also John Gessel, never married, and died in 1867 in India, with the army, I gather.'

He looked at his notes.

'Do you know anything about Sir Richard Gessel?'

'No. Who's he?'

'He's the only other Gessel I can find in Mr Burke's *Landed Gentry*. He's an Under-Secretary at the Cabinet Office in London. Bigwig, obviously, even though he's a young man, born in 1857, I see. He seems to be a distant relative.'

'There must be somebody around,' Swallow felt himself becoming exasperated. 'Wouldn't it be likely that someone would have taken over the property?'

Harrington shrugged. 'Perhaps. One can't be certain. A lot of these estates have been so burdened with debt, and so badly managed, that the families have just wanted to get out. You could try locally around the family seat. It's a place called Mount Gessel, predictably enough. But your colleagues in the RIC would be the ones best able to answer your questions, I'd guess. The nearest town is Loughrea.'

Swallow thanked him. He made his way to the Lower Yard and the Police Telegraph Office, and instructed the constable-operator to despatch information requests to the office of the District Inspector of the RIC at Loughrea. He planned to retreat to the Crime Sergeants' Office to start work on a statement about the shooting at Greenberg's.

Johnny Vizzard was waiting for him in the corridor. He leaped to his feet when Swallow came up the stairs.

'I heard what happened over at Greenberg's, Sergeant. Is it connected with these coins?'

Swallow decided this time to be gentler in his response to the young recruit's zeal.

'Hard to tell. We don't know yet who these fellas are and who they're working for. But they didn't cross over from England and decide to rob Greenberg's on a whim. They wanted to know who had sold the coins.'

He led Vizzard into the office.

'Did you make any progress in finding this Mrs Clinton?'

'I did. The family left the house yesterday morning with a fair amount of luggage. They hired a cab to the Broadstone. I established that they caught the 9.30 train to Athboy in County Meath. There's stops at Ashbourne, Dunboyne and Trim.'

'You've notified the constabulary?'

'Telegrams gone this past hour.'

'Good man. How are you rostered now? You should try to see what you can pick up from the train crew, conductors and ticket men.'

Vizzard was a 'live-in' man. Newly recruited members of G-Division were required to reside in Exchange Court for a year. This ensured a ready supply of manpower for unexpected circumstances. And it caused little resentment among young detectives who saved money in accommodation and messing.

'I'm on protection duty at the Viceregal Lodge tonight, ten to six. Give me a couple of hours' sleep after that and I can be back on the inquiry tomorrow morning.'

'I'll have you rostered so you can talk to the train crew.'

He returned to the office to get a start on the paperwork.

No sooner had he rolled the first sheets of foolscap and carbon paper into the Remington typewriter than Inspector 'Duck' Boyle put his head around the door.

'I kem to tell ye, Swallow, I'm th'investigatin' officer in this shootin' yer after bein' involved in. Ye'll have to do me a statement.'

Swallow was not unduly concerned. Regulations required that when a policeman opened fire it had to be investigated by an officer of more senior rank. And 'Duck' Boyle, for all his faults, had a reputation for making things as easy as possible for any man involved in a spot of bother while on duty.

'Don't worry, Inspector, I have it in hand. Give me an hour.'

'I will.'

Boyle hesitated awkwardly.

'You done good work there, Swalla'... from what they tell me.'

'Thanks. I got a chance at a good shot. The bastard could have killed the woman.'

'Aye, that's what they're sayin'. Anyway, there's two of the lads sittin' at the fucker's bedside across in th' infirmary, waitin' until the doctors are done with him. I imagine you'll be goin' back to have a talk wid him.'

'I'm looking forward to it.'

'Right so. I'll let ye get on with it here.'

'No progress in finding the second fellow with the gun?'

'Nah, he got away. But whin we – whin you – get this first fella' talkin' we won't be long findin' him.'

Swallow was anxious to get started on the Remington.

'Let's hope so.'

'We put out a request to the English forces askin' if any of their clients were known to be in Ireland,' Boyle said. 'But so far we've got nothin' back on that.'

Before closing the door behind him, he added 'And ye'll remember to put in the bit about shoutin' a warnin' before ye fired?'

An hour later, as he finished his statement for 'Duck' Boyle, a constable from the Telegraph Office brought a telegrammed message from the District Inspector's clerk at Loughrea.

From: District Inspector's Office, Loughrea; Division of County Galway.
To: Det Sgt Jos Swallow, G-Division, DMP, Dublin Castle.

Re Information Request in respect of Gessel family, Mount Gessel House.

Sir,
I beg to inform you as follows.

The above family are no longer resident in this District, having disposed of their estate, with houses and outbuildings, in accordance with the terms of the Land Acts recently applied.

Approximately 1,250 acres of land were purchased by the Land Board and have been distributed among 45 local farming families. Full details are available if required. A large house, numbering more than 30 rooms in all, has been vacated and remains unoccupied since May of 1886.

The vendor to the Land Board was Lady Margaret Gessel, widow of the Second Baronet Gessel, who deceased in 1855. Her last known address, as advised today by her solicitors here, is at The Orchard, Folkestone Road, Dymchurch, Sussex.

The family have been established in the area for many generations, and would have been held in high regard by persons of quality. However, a number of agrarian outrages have been committed in this District and some of these have been directed at the family and its property.

For further information, please be aware that Sir Richard Gessel, an Under-Secretary at the Prime Minister's office in London, is a relative (second cousin) of the late Second Baronet Gessel.

I remain Sir, your obedient servant,

John Kelly (Clerk)
(On behalf of DI)

Swallow felt himself wearying.

Establishing the provenance of the silver was proving to be a long and tortuous challenge. Now it seemed that the person most likely to throw any light on how it had ended up in Ambrose Pollock's cellar was a widow living somewhere in the depths of rural Sussex. Was the game worth the candle? Even if he succeeded in establishing the story behind the silver, would it bring him any closer to solving the murder or locating the whereabouts of Phoebe Pollock?

One side of his brain told him it was a side-issue. He would be better to focus on the technical clues that had been yielded from the murder scene, from Harry Lafeyre's post-mortem and from what they could learn about Phoebe Pollock's love life. But something more instinctive than deductive told him that the story of the Gessels' family silver was also at least partly the story of Ambrose Pollock's murder and the disappearance of his sister.

If the trail had led to the widow in rural Sussex, then so be it.

He reached for *The Police Directory for England and Wales.*

It listed the town of Dymchurch within the jurisdiction of the East Sussex Constabulary. Not surprisingly, it did not have a detective office or any equivalent of the G-Division. His inquiry would have to be routed through the Special Irish Branch at Scotland Yard.

He would brief Mallon in the morning. But he needed to eat and to get across to the infirmary at Jervis Street. When the doctors would have finished their work on the captive knifeman he had questions for him.

Evening was closing in as he left Exchange Court. It would be quicker and more convenient to go to the police canteen in the Lower Yard, but he did not relish the barrage of comments and questions he would face from colleagues, however well-meaning they might be. He decided to treat himself instead at the Dolphin Hotel on Temple Bar.

He took a mixed grill along with a pint of Guinness's stout. He savoured the Dolphin's sausage, bacon, a lamb chop and pudding. After a large Tullamore to clear his palate, he set out across the river for Jervis Street.

THIRTY

The doctors at the Dublin Charitable Infirmary on Jervis Street had done well for the knifeman.

He had been brought from the operating theatre to a room on the first floor of the hospital with two G-men posted outside. Swallow's .44-calibre slug had lodged in the muscle of the right shoulder, and the doctors removed it without difficulty. There had been considerable blood loss, but the man was strong and healthy.

When Swallow arrived, the man was conscious although his eyes were glazed. Swallow guessed that he had been given a heavy dose of laudanum to dull the pain. He seemed childlike and thin in the grey, hospital-issue nightshirt. His left wrist was handcuffed to the iron mattress-frame. Swallow estimated he might be twenty or younger.

He gestured to the G-men to move to the corridor and drew a chair to the bedside. The young man had the pinched, hollow face that spoke to Swallow of childhood malnutrition and hardship.

He leaned forward.

'Detective Sergeant Swallow. I want to talk to you.'

The prisoner turned his head away.

'Fuck off.' The voice was a whisper, dulled with the laudanum.

Swallow tapped him smartly on the cheek.

'Mind your language, young fella, and pay attention. I want your name for a start.'

'I told… you… to fuck off.'

'And I told you, I want your name. I want the name of your pal with the revolver. And I want to know what you were after in that shop.'

The man burrowed his face into the pillow.

'I said I wanted your name,' Swallow said sharply.

The response was something between a snort and a laugh.

'Take a… guess. Maybe I'm… the Duke of fuckin' York.'

Without rising from the chair, Swallow kicked hard at the metal bolt that secured the mattress-frame to the iron bed end.

Frame, bed ends, mattress and prisoner collapsed in a sequence of bangs and crashes. The young man screamed as the heavy frame fell across him. Swallow planted his foot on it and pressed hard. The scream rose louder as the steel springs bit through the flimsy nightshirt into the flesh.

'Jesus… Jesus Christ… you're fuckin' killin' me! Mad Irish bastard!'

Swallow added more weight and, for good measure, kicked again with his heel at the mattress-frame.

'By the time I'm finished you'll see how mad I am… and how much of a bastard I am. Now, what's your name?'

The door opened and one of the G-men peered in, looking alarmed. Swallow waved him away.

'Bit of a mishap here. Keep everyone out for a bit.'

The prisoner raised his free hand. He tried to bring his eyes into focus, fighting the effects of the tranquiliser.

'I'm Darby… Jack Darby.'

'Address?'

'Forbes Street. You wouldn't know it.'

'London?'

'Where else?'

'And your friend? The hero with the gun?'

'Calls 'imself Teddy. I… don't know 'is full name.'

Swallow did not believe the last bit, but he eased the pressure on the mattress-frame.

'That's a bit more like it.'

He pulled him to his feet, and sat him lopsidedly on the chair, his wrist still manacled to the mattress-frame.

'It's best to be truthful with me, Jack, because I'm going to check everything you tell me through criminal records. The quicker I can do that, the sooner you'll get back into your comfortable bed here.'

He lifted the mattress-frame and propped it against the wall so that the pressure was taken off the prisoner's manacled wrist. Then he caught him by the hair and turned his face upward.

'If you feed me any false information you'll be taken out of here to Dublin Castle where I'll beat the living shit out of you for as long as it takes. Do you understand that?'

The young man nodded. The eyes were a little clearer, but the expression was still dull and slack-jawed. Swallow wondered if what he had taken for the effects of laudanum might not, in part at least, be symptomatic of some mental deficiency. He reopened with a soft question.

'How long are you in Dublin, Jack?'

Darby's face was vacant. 'A few days, I think.'

'No idea beyond that? Can you read the calendar?'

'Nah, never 'ad any need to.'

'All right, how did you get here?'

'I come up from London, didn' I? I met Teddy in a pub. I knew 'im from doin' a stretch… Wandsworth. There wos this geezer with 'im. A toff. And 'e says there's a job for us to do in Dublin. Says 'e's got a few quid for us. Showed us the money too. Said there'd be more when we'd come back wiv the job done. So we gets on a ship and 'ere we are.'

He looked quizzically at Swallow.

'This is it, then, ain't it? This is Dublin…?'

Swallow was sure now that Jack Darby was not the full deck of cards.

'Who was this toff type you met? Have you a name?'

'Nah, it wos Teddy wot knew 'im. But I'd figger 'im again if I seen 'im.'

'What was the job? What were you told to do?'

Darby attempted a grin.

'Just go to this bloody shop, get some fucking old coins that the Jew girl 'ad bought. Find out who 'ad sold 'em to 'er, come back to London. That was it.'

'That was it? So why the gun and the knife? You could have just gone in and done your business like you were told.'

'It wos Teddy's idea. 'E said we could 'it two birds wiv one stone, like. We'd get the information and then 'elp ourselves to whatever was lyin' around in the shop. You know, rings, watches, wha'ever. But it was all Teddy's idea, you understand. I let 'im do the plannin' and thinkin'.'

Swallow saw his opening.

'If that's true, if it was his idea and you just followed along, I might be able to do something for you, Jack. But I need to find Teddy.'

He saw a flicker of caution in the dull eyes. Darby might be borderline intelligent, but he knew he might have something to trade. He glanced around him as if he feared someone was listening.

'I'll give evidence, Guv. I'll swear against 'im... if you and I can come to some sort of deal.'

Swallow reckoned that lies and evasions were Jack Darby's natural defences against the cruelties of the world. Indeed, they might be the young man's only defences. But he was probably telling the truth, at least insofar as he was willing to rat on Teddy if he could save his own skin.

'Where's Teddy then, Jack? How do I find him?'

Darby shrugged. 'We moved around a bit. But last night we wuz stoppin' in a place called the Windsor Hotel.' He grinned. 'But 'e's not goin' to be back there, is he?'

Swallow didn't think so. The Windsor was a dive on Mecklenburg Street, a haunt of prostitutes and vagrants. It was well accustomed to the attentions of the police. But it would have to be checked and searched, just in case.

He moved to the door.

'You made a bad mistake coming to Dublin, Jack. We've enough of our own troubles here. So we're not going to have much of a welcome for fuckers like you and Teddy. And you made a worse mistake in taking a knife to that lady. She's a friend of mine. If it had even grazed her, my third shot would've been through your bloody head.'

Jack Darby's pinched features wrinkled in puzzlement.

'I didn't know abaht that, did I? Abaht you and 'er... like. 'Ow could I? She was just a woman in the bleedin' shop.'

Swallow was unsure if he should feel more pity than anger towards young Jack Darby. He pushed his way out through the door of the hospital room.

THIRTY-ONE

Teddy Shaftoe did not scare easily. The fact that he had survived to see this thirtieth year on the streets of London's East End testified to his nerve, his cunning and a willingness to use force that he could deliver swiftly and brutally with gun, knife or cosh.

But he was scared now. What had seemed like a simple job in Dublin had turned into a nightmare thanks to his own greed. He had been promised good money to get some simple information and to retrieve some old coins. But to Teddy, the jeweller's shop with its elderly Jewish owner seemed too easy a target to pass up.

He knew that the woman in the shop had bought the coins. That was what he had been told when he was given the job. The man he had met at The Mitre public house in London had been clear in his directions about what he and Darby were to do. Their task was to find out who had brought the coins into the shop. The sight of Darby's knife should be enough to do it. If not, a quick slash along the arm or the side of the face would get results. The old man would not be a problem either. The gun would make him cower and plead with Teddy to take what he wanted. Not for a moment had he imagined that he would come at him from behind the counter with his bare fists.

He had no idea how the coppers had got there so quickly either. The plainclothes one had a bloody big gun. The coppers at home had no guns. How was he to know that the Dublin coppers had them? It made no sense. Dublin should be the same as England, shouldn't it? But the plainclothes fellow had shot Darby. Teddy had no idea if he was alive or dead.

Now all he wanted to do was to get home. To lay low in London. Darby would tell the coppers everything to try to save his own skin. They wouldn't have to try very hard to get him talking. They would know his accomplice's name by now.

Teddy was always fast on his feet. He had learned as a boy how to duck and weave through the streets of the East End. He could scale walls like a cat. He knew the trick of rolling under a moving carriage, gaining vital seconds from pursuers in a chase.

He had outpaced the Dublin policeman, fleeing across the river and then making his way through streets he did not know, trying not to draw attention to himself by moving too quickly. He clutched the Colt in the right pocket of his coat, partly to conceal its shape but also to be able to draw it quickly if challenged by anyone.

He found a church in a side street and slipped inside. Its interior was dark, comforting and silent. He chose a back pew in a side chapel. There were candles burning in a brass tray. He liked the warm smell of the wax.

Churches were good hides, he had always found. A few worshippers came and went, but they paid no attention to him. When he thought it might be safe to leave, he noticed that someone had left a man's cap on a window-ledge in the nave. He had lost his Derby hat in his flight, so he put the cap on. A change of headgear was always a good disguise. When he emerged from the church, the light was fading.

He had only the vaguest idea where he was. He wandered for perhaps another hour through dirty streets, populated by ragged children and weary-looking women. London's East End was no paradise. But these streets were even more miserable, the children more wretched-looking and the houses more dilapidated than at home.

At a street corner a news vendor was putting up a new billboard.

'SEARCH FOR GUNMAN'
'SHOTS IN CITY RAID'

It was bloody unreasonable, he told himself. He had fired no shots. It was the copper with the big gun who fired. He had an overwhelming sense of the unfairness of it all.

He came to what seemed a busy commercial area. A cast-iron street sign overhead told him it was called The Coombe. Odd bloody name to call a street, he thought. On the pavement ahead he saw two constables, booted feet moving in unison as they came towards where he stood. He realised he was directly outside a public house. He turned, pushed the swing door and stepped inside.

Teddy had no clear idea of how much time had passed since then. Now, as far as he could judge, he was in the cellar of that public house. He knew he had been carried and dragged and then bundled down a flight of stairs. They had flung him on the freezing floor, his hands bound behind his back, a foul-tasting cloth gagging his mouth.

He had lost track of time. Was it dark because it was night or because no light penetrated down here?

He remembered that when he went inside the pub had been noisy, and that the air was heavy with dirt and sweat. There were perhaps a dozen clients at the bar with a card school going in one corner. Heads turned in curiosity. The faces were hard, unsmiling.

He had gone to the bar and ordered a pint of bitter. That was another mistake, it seemed. The barman had laughed. But it was not a friendly laugh.

'Only an Englishman would ask for his pint o'bitter. D'ye know the name of what ye want? There's Perry's or MacArdle's and that's about it.'

'I'll have the first one, the Perry's.'

The barman started to draw the brown-red ale into a glass. At the same moment, Teddy realised that two men had moved in on either side of him, pint glasses in their fists. He kept his hand on the butt of the Colt in his pocket.

'Bit of a shortenin' in th'evenin's now, isn't there?' The man on his right was about his own age. Teddy might have taken him for a cab-driver or a porter. He had several days of stubble on his face.

'Oh, it won't be long now before the winter's down on us,' the other chimed in.

He looked into Teddy's eyes inquiringly. 'I suppose you'd have better weather now in your own part of the world... wherever that might be.'

Teddy tried to appear jovial. He laughed. 'It's the fog... the bleedin' fog's the big problem in London.'

'Oh, London, begod. Ye've come all the way from London?'

'That's right.' He knew his accent was a giveaway. It was best to give an appearance of frankness.

The first man put out his right hand. 'The name's Murphy.'

Teddy had to relinquish his grip on the Colt in his pocket. He shook the man's hand.

'A pleasure, I'm sure.'

Then the other man extended his hand. Teddy turned to shake it.

That was when the one who had called himself Murphy hit him with his closed fist on the side of the head. At the same moment, his companion drove his knee hard into Teddy's groin.

He saw red and yellow flashes as the pain shot through him, doubling him over. His hand scrabbled to his pocket for the Colt. One of them grabbed his wrist, pulling him off balance and bringing him to the floor. A boot came down, clamping his neck and cutting off his breathing.

He felt a hand going to his coat as the Colt was pulled out. At the same moment, a cord or rope was being circled around one wrist and then another, forcing his arms behind his back. The boot came off his neck, and he gulped for air. Rough hands turned him over on his back so that he was looking at the ceiling.

'That's a neat little item,' Murphy said, hefting the Colt in his hand. He snapped the magazine open. 'Fully loaded too. Very useful. Go through his pockets there.'

Searching hands reached the wallet in his coat.

'Jesus fucking Christ, there's more than fifty quid here.'

'Get him in the back,' he heard someone say. 'You'd never know who'd come in that door.'

A hinged flap was lifted in the bar. He saw the barman looking detached and unconcerned as he was bundled through, down a corridor and into a storeroom. It was dark. One of his captors struck a match to an oil lamp on the wall.

They sat him on a porter keg.

The man who called himself Murphy had a knife in his hand now. He ran the flat of the blade slowly along Teddy's cheek from his eye to his jaw, turning the razor edge against the skin through the last inch or so. Teddy felt sick in his stomach and his legs started to tremble. He made a desperate effort of will to control them and not to piss himself with terror.

Murphy laid the knife on a keg.

'First, yer name.'

'Jones... the name's Jones,' Teddy stammered. He could see no imme-diate advantage in the alias. But his instinct was to be untruthful.

'So, you'd be best tellin' me yer business in Dublin, Mr Jones, and why yer in a public house frequented by Mr Vanucchi while yer carryin' this firin' piece.' He waved the Colt with his other hand.

'I... have the gun for self-protection,' Teddy stammered. 'And I don't know anythin' about the gent you just mentioned. I never 'eard of him and that's the truth.'

'Yer not a bobby,' the other man snarled. 'We know all the G-men. So what are ye, and where'd you get all this fuckin' cash?'

For a mad moment, Teddy wondered if he should simply tell them the truth. That he was a robber come to Dublin whose luck had gone wrong. He was unsure if it would help his odds of survival or simply seal his fate. He decided not to take the chance.

'I'm a... salesman... sent 'ere from London to do some business. Look, why don't you just take the money and let me go? I'll not say a word about what's 'appened and I'll be on the first boat back to England.'

The man called Murphy punched him hard in the face so that he fell to the floor. A boot crashed down and he felt cartilage crack in his nose. Then there was a warm gush of blood down his lower face and neck.

Now Teddy finally lost control of his bladder. He felt the hot urine run down his legs and soaking his trousers.

'Speak when yer fuckin' spoken to,' the man who called himself Murphy said. 'Answer my fuckin' questions. Salesman, my arse, yer up to no good, crawlin' around the Liberties of Dublin all fuckin' day. Did ye think ye weren't noticed?'

The door opened, and a man stepped into the room. Teddy tried to focus through eyes blinded with pain and tears. He had the impression that the newcomer was tall and well-dressed. A smell of cologne con-tested with the foul air of the storeroom.

Teddy's tormentors came to attention after a fashion. They stepped back from their victim on the floor.

'Mr Vanucchi,' the man called Murphy said respectfully. 'You... you heard we have this fella here.'

The visitor peered down at Teddy's huddled and bloody form as if examining something suspect on a market stall.

'Who is he?'

'An English fucker. Says the name is Jones. Says he's a salesman. He had a bundle o'cash, more than fifty quid. An' a gun.' Murphy took the Colt from his pocket.

'What were you plannin' to do with him?' Vanucchi asked.

'Knock him on the head, wait till dark and drop him down the drain behind the brewery,' Murphy said in a tone that anticipated approval.

Vanucchi thought silently for a moment.

'Ah no, I don't think so,' he chuckled.

He drew an *Evening Mail* from his pocket and held it out.

'I think this fella' is too valuable to be let off down the sewer.' He tapped the newspaper. 'This fella is in the news. If he's who I think he is, every bobby in Dublin is lookin' for him. I can do us a couple of favours with the lads in the G-Division over this.'

He gestured to the porter keg.

'Sit him over there and clean him up.'

They dragged Teddy to a sitting position. One man produced a flannel handkerchief and rubbed it across his features. Vanucchi leaned forward.

He caught the odour of Teddy's urine and stepped back a pace.

'Jesus, you're a stinky fucker. Pissed yerself.'

Teddy sat in terrified silence.

'Let me to introduce meself. My name is Charlie Vanucchi. You can call me 'Mister Vanucchi.' I'm a fella of, let's say, a lotta' influence around these parts. Me associates here would be happy to drop ye in the Liffey and, for meself, I couldn't care if they did. But I think it might be in yer own interests and mine if we were a bit more imaginative. Do ye get me drift?'

Teddy nodded stiffly.

'Good. Now we're gettin' somewhere. So I suggest ye start by tellin' me who ye really are, why ye came to Dublin to do yer robbin' when ye've plenty of places to rob in England and who yer boss is.'

Teddy knew that if he was ever again going to see his beloved East End, this Charlie Vanucchi was his best hope. He realised that he had to tell all.

TUESDAY OCTOBER 4TH, 1887

THIRTY-TWO

Swallow presented himself at Mallon's office in the Lower Yard shortly after 9 o'clock. The chief's clerk was coaxing a turf fire into life in the grate so that he could boil a kettle for tea.

'You'll not see him until th'afternoon,' the clerk announced on his knees in front of the feeble combustion. 'Gone to the military across at Parkgate. There's a meeting with the brass, and then there's the usual luncheon. I'll put you down for 3 o'clock.'

'Three o'clock. Sure, there's no hurry on anyone. Good luck with the fire. You'll have a fair thirst by the time you get the tea made.'

The clerk did not miss his sarcasm.

The morning conference held no great promise. For most of those present there was more interest in getting first-hand details of the attempted robbery and shooting at Greenberg's than in the murder investigations.

'Great shootin' I heard,' Stephen Doolan grinned. 'A bloody marksman.'

Various G-men went through their reports, detailing their inquiries over the previous twenty-four hours.

The Windsor Hotel on Mecklenburg Street had been raided, searched thoroughly and then put under observation for the night. Not surprisingly, though, the gunman called Teddy had not returned.

Nor had there been any sighting by the beat men. That was surprising. Unless a fugitive had a particularly good hideout, the Dublin Metropolitan Police machine could usually locate its quarry fairly quickly.

'Duck' Boyle was engaged in the unusual business of exercising his imagination.

'Mebbe these two done th' Ambrose Pollock killin' too. If they were plannin' on knockin' off Greenberg's mebbe they had a sort of a practice run at Pollock's?'

'It's an angle that could be considered all right,' Swallow said. 'But we don't know if they were even in Dublin when Ambrose Pollock was murdered. The Darby fellow is of borderline intelligence. He can't read the calendar and he doesn't know if he's been here for days or weeks.'

'Well, Dr Lafeyere says Pollock was dead for a week whin he was found,' Boyle agreed. 'And that's five days since. So they'd have had to have been here twelve days ago. Fellas like thim woulda' made their presence felt before now. They'd a been in some kind o' trouble.'

Swallow reckoned that Boyle was probably right. The police network was well tuned to pick up the presence of any new arrivals into the city's underworld. An observant constable, a curious G-man or an informant would have spotted them and notified Exchange Court.

'We can question the second fellow about Pollock's when we get him,' Doolan said.

'First he has to be found,' Boyle retorted. 'I can't figger why he hasn't been spotted around the city.'

Stephen Doolan raised a hand.

'Did you manage to trace where the silver at Pollock's came from?'

'It was made for a family called Gessel. Big landowners in Galway, somewhere close to Loughrea,' Swallow answered. 'They just sold out recently and the place was broken up. It seems there's a Lady Margaret Gessel now living in Sussex who was the last of the family there.'

'Are we going to try to talk to her?'

'I think we have to. It's worth trying to bring it a bit further. I'm going to see Chief Mallon later. I'll ask him to have one of his London contacts to interview her down in Sussex.'

The conference was about to break up when Mick Feore arrived.

'Sorry I'm late, Skipper,' he told Swallow. 'There was something I needed to look in to.'

'What's on your mind, Mick?' Swallow asked.

Feore had his notebook open.

'There's a hall porter at the hotel with a record for assaults on women and for larceny. He's a fella called Jimmy Rowan, from Limerick, aged around forty. He's done time in Limerick and Mountjoy. We didn't get on to him until now because he's been working under an assumed name. He calls himself Regan now – his mother's name.'

Swallow sensed a frisson of interest around the room. In his mind's eye he recalled an image of a porter in a not-too-clean coat operating the front door of the hotel.

'How did you cop the false name, Mick?' Doolan asked.

'He's not too popular with some of his fellow workers. Aggressive. Throws his weight about, they say. A chambermaid passed the word to one of the Store Street constables. How she knew about his past, I haven't an idea.' He smiled with satisfaction. 'Anyway, when I questioned this fella he admitted who he is and told me about his form. I've just been down at DCR asking them to pull out his file. They'll have it in an hour.'

'You'd better stay with that inquiry,' Swallow said. 'And let us know what they have on him. Any idea of his movements around the time Phoebe disappeared?'

'The Store Street lads are working on that now. He admits that he was in the hotel, but he claims he was nowhere near the first floor any time around then.'

'I'll cross check the statements we already have,' Mossop offered. 'It's possible that someone could've mentioned his whereabouts.'

'Do that, Pat, it might come right.' Swallow said. 'God knows, there aren't too many other possibilities.'

THIRTY-THREE

John Mallon had mixed feelings about luncheons with the army brass. Government policy was to keep the army away from the dirty business of politics and the Land War, and to have the police in the front line. But the civil power might ultimately have to rely on the strength of the military, and so regular briefings with exchanges of intelligence were essential. And, after all, there had to be lunch.

Mallon liked the military for their directness and practicality. They made a refreshing change from the civil servants in the Upper Yard with their careful ambiguities and their cultivated subtleties.

The food and the wines at the officers' mess were always first class. But the soldiers all seemed to be married to each other's sisters or cousins. And they came overwhelmingly from a background that Mallon had nothing in common with. He enjoyed the hospitality, but he was always glad to get back to the comfortable familiarity of the Lower Yard at the Castle.

He sensed when Swallow came into his office that he seemed more eager, more energised. He took the chair that Mallon indicated in front of the big oak desk.

'Good work at Capel Street yesterday, Swallow. The newspapers are full of praise for a change. Do we know anything more?'

'Not a lot, Chief. The young fellow I shot, Darby, is simple-minded. He's a known petty criminal in London. A string of convictions for everything from larceny to assault. It's fairly clear he was the number two man on this job. The other one with the gun hasn't been picked up yet, which is strange because he doesn't know his way around Dublin.'

Mallon stroked his short beard. It was a characteristic mannerism when he concentrated.

'What were they doing here in the first place? They hardly came over specially to rob old Ephram Greenberg. Were they on the run?'

'Well, that's the strange thing about it, Chief. It seems they did come to rob Greenberg and his daughter. They wanted some Greek coins she'd bought in recently. And in particular, they wanted to know who she had bought them from.'

'Greek coins? They're valuable I assume.'

'According to old Ephram they're worth decent money, maybe £20 each in London. But you wouldn't cross the Irish Sea for them. They're not the most valuable items known to collectors.'

'Numismatists,' Mallon said.

'Sir?'

'People who make coin collections, Swallow. The opposite of what you did in medical school, according to yourself.'

Swallow surmised that the wines at the army lunch had been good.

'So,' Mallon continued, 'what does this young Darby fellow say?'

'He's told me what he knows, I think. He says the gunman's name is Teddy. They did time together in Wandsworth. He says that he hasn't got a second name for him. Ordinarily I wouldn't believe that two lags who were in together wouldn't know each other's full names, but he's slow-witted. They met some man in London and he set them up for the job. Darby doesn't know his name either. He says he's a toff type. I think that's genuinely about all he knows.'

'Toff type, eh? Someone with enough money to have their dirty work done by somebody else.'

'Sounds like it.'

'What's so special about the coins? What do the Greenbergs say about it?'

'It was the daughter, Katherine, who bought them in the shop. The seller was a woman called Grace Clinton with an address on North Circular Road near Phibsboro. She's married to a law clerk called Arthur Clinton. We've checked the register at the Law Society, and it shows him employed with Keogh, Sheridan and James. They're on the Quays there just up from the Four Courts.'

'A law clerk? Unusual to have a law clerk's wife going around selling trinkets.'

'That's true. Mrs Clinton doesn't seem to have understood the value of the coins. Greenberg says they'd fetch maybe £20 apiece in London, but Grace Clinton sold them to Katherine for a fiver each.'

'Have we questioned this Mrs Clinton?'

'That's part of the problem. I sent young Vizzard out to the house. But she and her husband and their children seem to have left. They took off to the Broadstone station on Sunday morning in a cab, taking a lot of bags and luggage. They boarded a train that goes down into County Meath as far as the town of Athboy, with the usual stops in between. We've got inquiries out with the railway staff to see if we can pinpoint where they got off, but so far we've nothing back.'

Mallon's forehead creased in puzzlement.

'It's bloody hard to make a lot of sense out of all that.'

He looked up as if he had suddenly remembered the murder investigation and the search for Phoebe Pollock.

'Leave that for a bit. Any progress on the Pollocks?'

'There's a couple of things.' Swallow drew his notebook.

'Mick Feore discovered that the hall porter at the Northern Hotel is a fellow called Jimmy Rowan, with a lot of form, it seems, including violent assault. He's from down south, Limerick. A Store Street constable got a whisper from one of the staff.'

Mallon pursed his lips.

'Hmm… we'd need to be careful in case he tries to make a bolt for it.'

'We're checking with other witnesses now, and we're pulling down his file from DCR.'

'Good work by Feore… you said there were a couple of things.'

'We traced the silver in Pollock's basement.'

'How did you do that?'

'The Ulster Office got moving on it. In fairness, they were very helpful once they came back to work.'

Mallon grinned.

'You'll have learned a bit more about diplomacy so?'

Swallow ignored the jibe.

'The silver is connected to this Gessel family. The last of them at the place down in Galway was a Lady Margaret Gessel, now living in England. She might know where the stuff went after the house and its contents were disposed of. We have an address for her in a town called Dymchurch, in Sussex.'

Mallon scratched his beard again

'There's a fellow called Gessel in Downing Street. One of the Under-Secretaries at the Prime Minister's office. Any connection?'

'He's a distant relation. I don't think he comes into this picture. The property came down to the widow.'

Mallon reached for his notebook.

'I'll jot down those details about this Lady Margaret. I'll be on the telephone later to Jenkinson at Scotland Yard. I'll have him send someone out to interview her.'

'We still don't know for definite that there's any connection between this and the murder,' Swallow emphasised. 'So it's a bit of a shot in the dark, Sir.'

Mallon shrugged. 'Of course, but like I said, this sort of merchandise would be very unusual in Ambrose Pollock's line of business. It's worth a try.'

Swallow retraced his route across the Lower Yard to Exchange Court. As he passed the apse of the Chapel Royal, Harry Lafeyre and another man emerged from the Medical Examiner's office. He recognised Lafeyre's companion as George Weldon, lately their fellow dinner guest at Maria's.

Lafeyre waved a greeting. Weldon gave a polite nod.

'You look pleased with yourself, Swallow,' Lafeyre bantered. 'It's nice to see a man who's happy with the way he finds the world.'

'Happy would be too strong a word, but I'm making some progress.'

'With the Pollock case?'

'What else? The boss has the job nailed between my shoulder blades.'

Lafeyre nodded. 'I thought maybe it was to do with that shooting in Capel Street yesterday. You're all over the newspapers, as I'm sure you know.'

'Indeed. Any progress on your end with the blood spatters on the weight that Pollock was skulled with?'

Lafeyre shook his head.

'Not yet, I'm afraid. I've been dealing with a bad outbreak of food poisoning at a house in Rathmines. There's a couple of young children and their mother who're very ill. I'll need a bit more time.'

It was part of the price paid by the authorities for not employing a City Medical Examiner full time. In order to make a decent living, Lafeyre took private patients. He had built a reasonably good practice among the middle-class families of the new affluent suburbs to the south of the city.

Lafeyre jerked his thumb toward the Castle Street Gate.

'George is staying for a few days. We're going over to the Burlington for a drink and maybe a bite of food later. Do you want to join us?'

Swallow was hungry. He had not eaten since breakfast and he could tackle a pint or a large Tullamore. But he had work to do first.

'I've to complete a report for Chief Mallon on the Pollock business. It'll take an hour. I'll follow you there.'

Weldon raised an eyebrow inquisitively. 'Are you likely to make an arrest?'

Civil servants, other than in the security offices at the Castle, did not habitually ask G-men about their work. Swallow took refuge in a policeman's favourite generalisation.

'Ah, it's just a routine matter, Mr Weldon.'

THIRTY-FOUR

The Burlington Hotel was a five-minute walk away on St Andrew's Street. Its *habitués* were the bankers, stockbrokers and insurance managers who populated the grand offices on Dame Street in sight of Trinity College. Castle officials and G-men would not generally figure in the usual run of clients in the bars and lounges on the ground floor or in the restaurant on the level above.

That was fine with Swallow. There were times when he was happy to step out of the world of policemen and criminals. Not that he was under any illusions about the fellows with the stiff collars and the striped pants on Dame Street. Like any other sector of the population, there were good and bad among them. The bad ones in the banking offices did not carry knives or guns as a rule. Their crimes were effected with dodgy account books, fake signatures, bogus deeds and the like.

Lafeyre and Weldon were in the Burlington's Empire Lounge. Weldon beckoned to a waiter as Swallow sat.

'My round, Mr Swallow. What are you having?'

'A Tullamore please.'

'Make it a large Tullamore,' Weldon said amiably.

The whiskey was welcome. Swallow relaxed into the club-like atmosphere of the bar. He raised his glass.

'Your health, gentlemen.'

'Do you remember that old Xhosa chief out beyond Stellenbosch, Harry?' Weldon laughed. 'He loved his Irish whiskey, when I could get it for him. We got many a boundary settled and many a problem solved over a couple of bottles of John Power.'

Lafeyre smiled. 'I always thought it a paradox that Irish whiskey could be helpful in settling land disputes in Africa. It tends to have quite the opposite effect here at home.'

The exchange prompted a linkage in Swallow's head.

'Did your department ever have any business with an estate in Galway at a place called Mount Gessel?' he asked Weldon. 'A family by the name of Gessel. They sold up under the land acts in the past year or so.'

Weldon appeared thoughtful for a moment.

'If they've moved out as recently as that, the transfer would have come through one of the offices here in Dublin. I've heard the name all right. There's a Gessel at the Prime Minister's office. But it can't have been a very big estate, or I'd recall it. Why are you interested?'

'Something came up in relation to missing property,'

Swallow was instinctively vague again. But that was silly, he told himself. It was he, after all, who had raised the query with Weldon.

'We're hoping to talk to a family member through our colleagues in London.'

'Gone off to England, have they?' Weldon asked. 'A lot of the landed families have done that. Once they get a bit of money in their hands, it usually seems an attractive option.'

'The widow of the last Baronet sold up,' Swallow said. 'She's gone to live on her money at a place called Dymchurch on the Sussex Coast.'

Weldon nodded.

'She'll have fewer problems there with the neighbours than she had in Galway.'

'Indeed,' Swallow gestured to the waiter, but Weldon raised a restraining hand.

'Nothing more for me, thank you. I'm away. I have an engagement to keep.'

He checked his pocket watch.

'I'm taking a lady to the theatre,' he smiled. 'The charming Mrs Walsh. I musn't keep her waiting.'

THIRTY-FIVE

Swallow knew from his medical student days that he did not make a pleasant drunk. Not that he was so very intoxicated, he reckoned, when he left the hotel on St Andrew's Street some time before midnight to make his way home.

His walk was steady, but he had felt the anger building inside as he drank through the evening with Lafeyre.

Weldon was off to the theatre with Maria. Well, good luck to them. Why should it bother him? She was a free woman. If a well-placed senior civil servant wanted to keep her company, let her get on and make the most of it. Was she not doing better with George Weldon than with an embittered G-man more than a decade her elder?

Lafeyre was embarrassed. 'I had absolutely no idea about this. Neither did Lily, I'm sure. He never mentioned it to me. He must have called on Maria or sent a message. If I had known, I'd have said it to you, of course.'

Swallow called to the waiter for more drinks.

'You needn't worry. It's got nothing to do with me. I've more important things on my mind.'

He knew he sounded unconvincing, even to himself.

'Don't take me for a fool,' Lafeyre snorted. 'You've got fury written all over your face. In one way, man to man, I can understand. But you're not in a position to have any grievance. You walked away from her. She doesn't owe you a thing.'

'I'm not claiming that I'm owed anything, am I?' Swallow snapped. 'And I'd prefer if people stopped trying to manage my personal affairs for me. I came along here for a drink because you invited me, remember? So that's what I'm doing.'

They had three more drinks in the bar, Swallow throwing back large Tullamores while Lafeyre cautiously nursed his claret.

They went upstairs to the dining-room. Swallow ordered a bottle of Burgundy before they chose their food, and then another before they had completed the main course. They finished with brandies. He mellowed eventually with the accumulation of alcohol and insisted that he would take care of the bill. It would wipe out a week's pay, but he did not care.

'Look, forget about George Weldon,' Lafeyre said. 'Is there any progress in the murder investigation or in locating Phoebe Pollock?'

Swallow seemed glad of the change of subject.

'Mick Feore has fingered the doorman at the Northern Hotel as a fella with a violent record. Name of Rowan. Working under an alibi. A bad character. So we're going to bring him in.'

Lafeyre nodded thoughtfully.

'It's a possibility. You're then looking at perhaps a different story. It'll be interesting to hear what this Rowan has to say. When I get through a few house calls I've got a couple of tests I want to do on the weight that was used to kill Ambrose. I have an idea that might tell us a bit more.'

But by now Swallow's mind was starting to be fuddled with the Tullamores, the Burgundy and the brandy. He had a busy day ahead tomorrow and he needed to get his sleep. Lafeyre checked the hour.

'It's getting late. A walk homeward will do us good.'

The night was cool and dry, and the air was refreshing after the heat of the dining-room, the heavy food and the alcohol.

They walked through Wicklow Street and Grafton Street and along the western side of St Stephen's Green. Two constables in night capes and blackened badges nodded a goodnight as they passed the Royal College of Surgeons. They parted at the bottom of Harcourt Street, where Lafeyre turned for his house. Swallow continued through Cuffe Street, making for Heytesbury Street.

His head was clearing now. The walk had loosened his limbs and stirred his digestion, heavy from the long drinking session and the rich food at the restaurant table. At the corner of Pleasants Street, just twenty paces from his house, a man started towards him out of the darkness. Swallow's right hand moved to the butt of his Bulldog in its shoulder holster, now aware that the man might have been watching for him.

He got the scent of eau-de-Cologne on the night air. It was Charlie Vanucchi.

The chief of Dublin's criminal underworld was a notoriously violent man, but he was also one of Swallow's informants, arguably his most important one. He was no threat. The Bulldog stayed where it was.

'Jesus, Charlie, don't come up on me so suddenly in the bloody dark. You could get yourself shot.'

'Do ye never come home at a decent hour, Misther Swalla'? I've been waitin' in the feckin' dark all night. Will ye for the love o'Jaysus let me inta the house before I ketch me death a' pneumonia.'

Swallow led him down the steps to the side door and into the back kitchen. He lit the gas mantle and pushed a chair to Vanucchi. The house was silent. Harriet was in bed and probably asleep.

Swallow told himself that he could not manage any more alcohol. But the relationship demanded that he offer something to his informant. The only choice in the house was rough Tipperary Colleen that he had confiscated in the street one night from a drunken boy. He poured a stiff dose of the cheap whiskey for his visitor.

Vanucchi grimaced and wiped his lips with the back of his hand.

'Yer taste is deterioratin', Misther Swalla'. The liquor isn't what it used to be when ye were stoppin' above in Thomas Street with the Widda Walsh.'

'You didn't come by to lecture me about my choice of whiskey, Charlie. What has you around at this hour of the night?'

'True enough.' Vanucchi swallowed half of the Tipperary Colleen in a gulp. 'I have a... well... I suppose you could say, I have a present for ye.'

'Go on.'

'Youse are lookin' for an Englishman, after yer shootin' his pal over in Capel Street.'

'The dogs in the street know that, Charlie.'

'Yeh, well the dogs in the street don't know where he is. And the geniuses of the Dublin Metropolitan Police don't fuckin' know either. But I do, if yer interested.'

Against his better judgment, Swallow decided to take a shot of the Tipperary Colleen. He laughed as if he had heard something amusing.

'Ah, I don't know. I'd be mildly interested, but no more than that. There's not a lot of money around after all the cash we had to put out during the Queen's jubilee.'

Vanucchi nodded solemnly. 'And that money was very well spent, Misther Swalla'. The *polis* o' Dublin city done a fine job o' keepin' the place safe in them dangerous days. But this'd be worth a tenner.'

'A tenner? Jesus, Charlie, if you brought me Napoleon Bonaparte and the evidence to hang him, I couldn't get you a tenner. This is some Johnny English on the run from the London Metropolitan. He may be important to someone over there, but not to me. Two quid.'

Vanucchi sipped his whiskey. 'I think when you hear the tale this Johnny English has to tell, Misther Swalla', ye might have a different view.'

'If the story is that big I might rise to three quid, Charlie. That's being generous. Take it or leave it.'

'Here's a deal, Misther Swalla'. Three quid down, and when ye hear this fella's story we'll talk again. If ye're impressed ye can raise another two quid.'

Swallow threw back the last of his whiskey. He took an informant payment slip from his wallet, pencilled in the agreed sum and handed it to Vanucchi. Over the coming days, he knew, someone acting on the informant's behalf, perhaps a child or a woman, would present it at Exchange Court and depart with the cash.

He reckoned that his night's sleep, already foreshortened, was forfeit. 'So where is he?'

'I'll come to that in just a minute, Misther Swalla'.' He leaned forward across the kitchen table. 'But first, let me tell ye what I heard from this Johnny English and why I think ye'll want to talk to him yerself.'

THIRTY-SIX

The bells started to ring for 2 o'clock across the sleeping city.
Shift workers, insomniacs and other *habitués* of the night sometimes remarked that every one of Dublin's churches seemed to have a
different version of the hour. This meant that the pealing actually lasted
for several minutes. One sequence of chimes would end as another would
start in the next steeple.

As the last peals faded, Swallow led the party of G-men with a uniformed constable to the boundary railings of St Patrick's Cathedral. The
moon had dipped to the west of the city rendering the tower and the
ancient Norman walls a dark bulk against the night sky.

Earlier, the constable had roused the sleepy verger from his bed in
nearby Cathedral Lane to unlock the high gates fronting onto Cathedral
Close. To the verger's discomfiture, he found that the locks were undone,
even though he swore that he had secured them earlier at 10 o'clock as he
was obliged to do each night.

Swallow was working hard to get his head around what Charlie
Vanucchi had told him about the gunman from the East End of London
who had walked into the wrong public house in The Coombe.

'This fucker is called Shaftoe,' Vanucchi had told him. 'First he said
his name was Jones. How fuckin' imaginative could that be?'

'But you managed to persuade him to be more open with you, I suppose.'

Vanucchi grinned.

'He became very... what's the word... eloquent all right. He kem
here to find some fucking coins that shouldn't be on the market. He's
been sent over from London just to do that. He tells me he's workin' for
some rich bastard over there. It sounds like big-time stuff.'

He put his glass on the table.

'I'll tell you where to find him, Mr Swallow. He won't give ye a bit o' trouble, I promise. But he's not in the best o' shape.'

The G-men slipped silently through the open gates and made for the sheltering darkness of the cathedral wall. Then they moved forward, pressing in against the granite until they came to a stone staircase leading below ground level.

Swallow signalled two of the detectives to take positions on either side of the heavy wooden door below.

They merged into the shadows, revolvers drawn. He had taken them from sleep in the dormitory above Exchange Court and briefed them on their task. There could be no noise. Pockets were emptied of keys and coins. Every man's boots were muffled inside heavy woollen stockings.

A third G-man with a shotgun gave cover from the top of the steps while Swallow and the constable went down. When he reached the bottom step, gun in hand, Swallow heard the sound from beyond the door.

It might have been a child's moan or the noise a small animal might make in distress, an injured dog perhaps. The constable heard it too. Even in the darkness, Swallow could see it register on his face.

'Light the bull's-eye,' he said softly.

The constable struck a match to the police lantern, and yellow light flooded across the stone floor to the wooden door. Swallow tugged the iron handle with one hand, his revolver poised in the other. The door swung out. He saw that the lock had been smashed, its innards of springs and screws littering the floor beneath.

The lantern light extended only a few feet into the room. It caught workmen's tools, spades, a pick, buckets. They took a step forward, then another. The sound came again, this time more a whimper. Swallow's eye caught movement at the periphery of the bull's-eye beam.

A shape formed where he had seen the movement. When the constable held up the lantern, Swallow saw the man's face, eyes wide with fear above streaks of blood and dirt. His mouth was gagged with a fabric strip, knotted tightly at the side of his face. The torso seemed to be covered by a canvas or tarpaulin. When Swallow leaned forward to take it away, he saw that the man's arms were pinioned behind his back with the wrists roped to an iron embrasure set in the wall. He stank of stale urine and blood.

Thus, sometime after 2 o'clock in the morning, in a workman's store-room, under the south transept of St Patrick's Cathedral, Edward 'Teddy' Shaftoe, of Mile End, London, an ambitious but ultimately inept, small-time criminal, was taken into the custody of the Dublin Metropolitan Police.

The constable used his penknife to cut through the rope that bound him to the wall. Then he cut through another set of ropes that ran around his ankles, biting deep into the skin. Strong hands got him to his feet, and stood him upright. When he saw the helmet and uniform in the lantern light, Teddy started to weep with joy.

THIRTY-SEVEN

An hour later, in a cell at Exchange Court, Teddy Shaftoe was still shaking.

They had searched him swiftly on the off chance that he still had the Colt revolver. Then they had taken him from the fetid storeroom to the freshness of the night air and on a police side-car to this place.

Swallow reckoned that Charlie Vanucchi's assessment had been on the mark. Teddy Shaftoe had broken. He was gone beyond hysteria to a whimpering, almost hopeless state where he was certain he would die. He had reached the point where he might have welcomed that if it meant no more beatings.

Every part of his body ached. His groin and testicles were swollen from kicking. His scalp was criss-crossed with cuts and bruises. His tongue rasped across what remained of the broken teeth in his mouth.

But he would live. The trick, Swallow knew, was to have him talk before he started to recover to the point where he would begin to feel safe. He knew from experience that it could happen quickly. He had seen suspects, at first just grateful to be alive, who re-attained their instinctive defiance half an hour after getting a hot meal and a dry bed.

A doctor arrived. He cleaned Teddy Shaftoe's cuts and dressed his wounds. There was bruising up and down, and rope burns to his wrists and ankles, but the doctor could find no broken bones.

A plainclothes man gave Teddy a shot of strong liquor in a tin mug. It stung the inside of his mouth where the flesh had been cut by punches and blows, but it felt good coursing down his throat and warming his stomach.

A constable brought him a bowl of water, a bar of rough soap and a small towel. Thankfully, he also brought a surplus pair of police uniform trousers and an old shirt. Slowly, painfully, Teddy cleaned himself and gratefully changed his stinking clothes.

When they left him alone in the cell, he lay down on the bunk-bed. It hurt to move, but he could not stay upright. He closed his eyes and tried to think straight. He was in the shit, he knew. He had no idea how the Dublin coppers had found him, or what they planned to do with him. But he was alive. And the beating had stopped. Teddy had dealt with hard men. He had taken his share of fist and boot, cosh and knife. But the bastards who had got him this time were animals. He shuddered and drew the grey cell blanket around him. He wished he had some more of the liquor the copper had given him upstairs.

Swallow reckoned on allowing him a quarter of an hour, no more, no less. That would be sufficient to have him rest just a little, to allow a little relaxation of his guard, to lull him into a false sense of security.

So far, Vanucchi's information had been good. He had said that Shaftoe would be in the gardener's workshop under the cathedral. It was a safe, secure location, implicating nobody once the Englishman had been brought in there and left under cover of darkness. He would not be a pretty sight, but he would pose no threat.

He flung the cell door open and then banged it behind him. Teddy Shaftoe lifted his head an inch or two from the mattress to see his visitor. Swallow placed himself on the three-legged stool beside the bunk.

'Swallow. Detective sergeant.'

'Who?'

'We met when you tried to rob Greenberg's. I shot your idiot friend, Darby, the hero with the knife.'

Teddy blinked. He seemed puzzled.

'Darby's been singing like a thrush, Teddy. So you'd better give me your version of things now while you can.'

'I'm an innocent man,' Teddy croaked. 'And I'm injured.'

Swallow raised his voice.

'You'll know what it is to be injured if I hand you back to Vanucchi's crowd. Don't piss me off. Any man who puts a gun in my face is fair fucking game as far as I'm concerned.'

'You can't do that,' Teddy made an effort to sound confident. 'I know me rights. You've got to let me go or bring me to a magistrate. An' he's got to get me a brief, a lawyer.'

'Well, Jesus pity you,' Swallow laughed. 'You're in Ireland now, my friend. We've different rules here thanks to a certain Mr Balfour, a countryman of your own. You wouldn't know much about the Coercion Act, but it means I can keep you here for as long as I want or put you back on the street if I want.'

Teddy was still able to muster some defiance.

'You can't prove nothin' against me. I'm bein' bleedin' victimised, so I am.'

Swallow laughed again.

'You're talking shite, Teddy. I can give evidence of identification at Greenberg's. You'll be done for attempted armed robbery, assault with a deadly weapon and possession of a firearm with intent to endanger life. You're looking at twenty years in Maryborough Convict Prison.'

'Where?'

'It's in the bog. It's colder and wetter than any place you've ever been. Wandsworth or Brixton are like hotels compared to Maryborough.'

Teddy was silent for a moment.

'Look, I got into fackin' deep waters. All I want is to go 'ome and forget about this bloody place. If you can do that for me, I can tell you where to catch some really big fish, if you're interested....'

Swallow smiled.

'You're not in a position to make deals. If you're lucky you'll spend the next twenty years buried in Maryborough. That is definitely not something you would enjoy. It might be more merciful to put you back in that cellar where Vanucchi's gang can finish you off.'

Teddy struggled to a half-sitting position.

'I know 'ow it works for coppers. You gets a conviction, it adds to yer good record. It might even add to yer pay. You can put Darby away. I'll swear against him, no bother. And, if you just put me on the boat back to Liverpool, I'll give you a score that any copper in London would give 'is right eye for.'

Swallow cocked his head.

'I doubt it very much, Teddy. Some poor bugger that's been dumped in the Thames or some inkie printing banknotes in his kitchen isn't of any interest here. But I'm listening.'

'It's much bigger than any o' that. Wot I'm talkin' about is big money gettin' took away from 'er Majesty's Treasury. An' it's 'appenin' 'ere in bloody Dublin, innit.'

Swallow tried not to look impressed. But he was. So far, what Teddy Shaftoe had told him tallied with what Charlie Vanucchi said his men had beaten out of him in the cellar under the public house in The Coombe.

'Go on.'

Teddy hesitated. He calculated that he had to give a bit more.

'It's like this. I meets this bloke back 'ome. He works for the government down at Whitehall. From time to time 'e calls me in when 'e 'as jobs that need to be done, for the government, like.'

Teddy was upright now.

'So,' he said, seeming to draw energy from his own narrative, 'this bloke sends for me a couple o' weeks back and asks would I like to do a bit o'work in Ireland? So I says, Teddy's not proud, I'll work for anyone wot pays me up front.'

'What's his name, this fellow who works for the government?'

'Aha, that's fer me to know at this stage and fer you to wonder at,' Teddy attempted a grin. 'That's the kind of information you jest might get... if we can... come to an understanding.'

'Go on,' Swallow said again.

'So I says to 'im, I says, I always wanted some recognition for me talents. Wot is it exactly 'er Majesty wants me to do? And 'e says, "It ain't exactly 'er Majesty you'd be workin' for. You'd be workin' for my boss and 'e works for the gov'ment, so, indirectly sort of, you'd be workin' for the gov'ment too."'

'So you're telling me now that you're working for the government?'

'I s'pose so. Bit like yerself, in a way,' Teddy laughed. 'Yeh, I've got maybe a dozen jobs over the year that required my skills. They pay me well. But I know, don' I, I'm doin' their dirty work for 'em because they can't afford to get caught doin' it themselves, can they?'

Swallow had no idea what Teddy was talking about, but it seemed best to agree.

'What sort of jobs?'

'Went for some posh Irish geezer in the street outside Claridges' hotel wiv' a knife. I 'ad to cut him but not too badly. I 'ad to stick a letter in 'is pocket as he went down. I seen it. It said "GET OUT OF IRELAND OR DIE." It was wrote in big, red letters.'

'You can tell me who he was. I can check that easily in the crime records.'

'True enough. Okay, 'e was a big bloody landowner somewhere. I done a right good job. Got 'im just in the ribs, not too deep though. Just enough to bring a squirt o' blood and a good squeal.'

Swallow recalled the incident. The Earl of Dunmanway was a leading landlord. The attack on him as he came out of his London hotel had been attributed by Scotland Yard to Irish land agitators. A few weeks after the incident, the Earl had sold out his estates.

'It doesn't sound like the sort of work government usually undertakes. What else did you do?'

'There was a couple more jobs wiv me knife. I 'ad to threaten a woman once. He told me she wasn't to be 'armed, and she wasn't. I just frightened 'er.'

'You're not making any sense, Teddy. Why would somebody in Whitehall want to threaten or injure these people?'

Shaftoe cocked his head.

'I've a pretty good idea it's connected with sellin' or buyin' land 'ere in Ireland.'

'What makes you think that?'

'Once I was meetin' this geezer at The Mitre – that's a public 'ouse – he had papers wiv 'im and 'e left 'em on the bar when 'e went to answer a call o' nature. So I 'ad a look. It was all about acres and deeds and who owned these fackin' farms. There was big money bein' mentioned too. I seen figures of £2,000 and £5,000 in there. 'E come back from outside and sees me lookin' at the stuff and 'e was fackin' furious wiv me. I reckon he thought I couldn't read.'

'What did he say? Exactly.'

'When 'e calmed down, 'e said I didn't need to know abaht all the stuff 'e was dealin' wiv. 'E said there was a lot of business to be done over land across in Ireland an' if I was smart there'd be work in it fer me.'

'So who is this geezer, as you call him?'

Teddy's eyes narrowed. 'There you go again. Like I said, that's the kind of detail that'll cost you.'

'All right,' Swallow conceded. 'If this story stands up, I reckon I can do something for you. But it'll take time, and I'm making no promises until I get a solid case out of it all.'

Teddy grinned. 'That's good. You're a man wot knows a good chance when 'e sees one.' He leaned forward. 'Wot this is all about is makin' a lot o' money for a few clever people, if you ask me. Me, I'm jest gettin' crumbs while I'm takin' all the risks.'

'What was the job here in Dublin?'

'It's been a fuckin' disaster, ain't it? 'E gave me a 'undred quid and said "Go to Dublin." I was told that someone in Dublin was sellin' these facking coins. Said they knew there was some of 'em bought by in this Jewish shop called Greenberg's. I was to buy 'em up, find out who was sellin' em and get back 'ome.'

'But you didn't stick to the job, Teddy. You got greedy.'

'That's the truth. I cased out the bleedin' shop with that fackin' idiot Darby. It looked easy…. They got some good stuff in that shop, believe you me.'

He winced in pain.

'From the moment we went in that bleedin' place, it's all gone wrong. First, you turn up with the bobby and your fackin' gun. I didn' know the coppers 'ere had guns. It ain't right, you know. Then when I gets away, I falls into the 'ands of a bunch of fackin' cannibals.'

He lay back, exhausted.

'Now, you've got a lot from Teddy. So what abaht Teddy gettin' somethin' from you?'

Swallow got to his feet. 'You have me interested, Teddy. But things take time and it's been a long night. You just relax here now and enjoy the hospitality. I'll go away and do a bit of thinking.'

He turned as he reached the door.

'One other thing. When did you get here to Dublin?'

'Three days ago, it was Sunday, I think. Why?'

'Just curious.'

If Shaftoe was telling the truth, then he and Darby were still in London when Ambrose Pollock was killed. Swallow was not surprised. But it helped to seal off at least one line of inquiry.

WEDNESDAY OCTOBER 5TH, 1887

THIRTY-EIGHT

Morning was breaking east of the city when Swallow emerged from the police canteen in the Lower Yard. A thin sun was spreading in from the bay, and there was a hint of ground frost on the cobbles.

There had been no point in making for Heytesbury Street or his bed.

He had no sleep, and he had drunk far too much the night before. But the initial sense of exhaustion when he had made it home after dinner with Lafeyre had given way to exhilaration at the arrest of Teddy Shaftoe at the cathedral.

As the new day formed out of the dawn, he began to feel a little better. The alcohol was beginning to pass out of his system. He thought briefly of Maria's evening at the theatre with George Weldon, and then pushed the subject to the back of his mind before his anger would take over again.

He focused on what Shaftoe had told him about the job he had been sent on from London. If his story was true, it was serious news for the authorities both at Westminster and in Dublin. If it emerged that the land transfer process was corrupt, it could collapse the entire programme. He would have to brief Mallon as early as possible.

But how did any of it connect to the coins that the Clinton woman had brought in to Katherine Greenberg? Johnny Vizzard had still not located her. Wherever she was, she and her family were almost certainly now in danger.

So too was Katherine. But with an armed G-man around the clock at Greenberg's she could be protected. Vizzard's efforts to find the Clintons would have to yield results sooner rather than later.

In the meantime, he had to hear what Mick Feore's inquiries might have turned up in relation to the front hall porter at the Northern Hotel.

He needed the soakage of the police canteen breakfast. He had sausages, bacon, black pudding and two fried eggs. There was bread in from the bakery, butter and strawberry jam in a big glass pot. It was a blessed change from Harriet's porridge and figs. He filled his mug three times with strong tea.

The canteen was abuzz with the dramatic events of the night. Uniformed constables plied the G-men for details. Two of them sat on the bench seat facing Swallow across the trestle table.

'Busy night, Skipper,' the younger one grinned, forking half a sausage away under his moustache. 'You grabbed this English character above in the cathedral, I hear. Did he give any trouble?'

Swallow cursed silently. If the morning uniformed shift knew about Shaftoe, it would in the newspapers by noon. He could have done with a bit of slow time before it became public knowledge.

'Nah,' he answered. 'Just a small-time gurrier that got out of his depth. Should have stayed in London.'

He finished his breakfast and checked the roster to see if Johnny Vizzard was back on duty after his night protection duty at the Viceregal Lodge. He had returned to the Exchange Court dormitory just an hour ago. Swallow reckoned he would let him sleep for a while before rousing him.

He went down to Mallon's office in the Lower Yard.

'What time will the boss be in?' he asked the clerk. 'I want to brief him on a few developments.'

'Come back at half nine. He's got an appointment with the Security Secretary in the Upper Yard an hour after that.'

Pat Mossop and Mick Feore were waiting for him at the crime sergeants' office. Swallow told them the story behind Teddy Shaftoe's arrest at the Cathedral.

'He's a lucky man that the Vanucchi crowd didn't do for him straight away,' Feore said.

'There's got to be some connection with the murders, Boss.' Mossop shook his head. 'I'm damned if I can see it, but all my instincts tell me yes.'

Swallow shrugged.

'Maybe so.'

He turned to Mick Feore. 'What new on your friend Rowan?'

'I got the file from DCR. He's ex-army. Did two years in the glass-house at the Curragh for robbery with violence of a camp shopkeeper. Then he's got convictions for assault in Limerick and Kilkenny. In all cases the victims were women.'

He turned a page on his notebook.

'He says he was never near the first floor of the hotel at the time Phoebe Pollock went up there. But we have a chambermaid saying she passed him up there on the corridor. The reception clerk says that around the same time there was no porter on the front door. He had to keep an eye to it himself in case anyone needed assistance.'

'What do think we should do, Boss?' Mossop asked.

'I think it's clear enough,' Swallow said. 'Bring him in.'

THIRTY-NINE

John Mallon felt good about the day.

The divisional crime reports for the previous night on his desk offered nothing other than the usual. The city's six divisions, from the crowded, poor 'A' to the affluent, coastal 'F' had an almost crime-free night. A street fight here and there. The usual drunk-and-disorderly incidents. A housebreaking at Drumcondra.

The most important report was always that compiled by the duty sergeant at G-Division, and this morning's was positively good news. It narrated the arrest, in the precincts of St Patrick's Cathedral, of the second man believed to have been involved in the attempted robbery at Greenberg's jewellers shop on Capel Street two days previously.

He riffled through the morning newspapers, the *Freeman's Journal, The Irish Times,* the *Daily Sketch.* He could find nothing critical of the police. There was a matter-of-fact paragraph in *The Irish Times* about the Lamb Alley murder and the presumably connected disappearance of Ambrose Pollock's sister, now almost a week ago.

He was due to meet the Security Secretary at his office in the Upper Yard, and he would be the bearer of at least some good tidings. The Pollock murder was still unsolved. Phoebe Pollock was still missing. But the arrest of the Capel Street gunman was evidence of the police force's exertions. He relaxed a little behind his desk, satisfied that he could put a fair gloss on things for the day.

When Swallow arrived shortly after 9.30, the conversation helped his mood initially. Swallow related what Mick Feore had learned about Rowan, the hall porter at the Northern Hotel.

'We'll bring him in, and if he's our man we'll get it out of him fairly quickly,' he told Mallon.

'Good work,' Mallon enthused. 'You'll keep me informed, of course.'

But ten minutes later into the conversation, when Swallow had relayed what he had been told by Teddy Shaftoe, Mallon's happiness was ebbing.

'Jesus, do you believe what this character is saying?'

The chief of detectives appeared to have deflated in his chair.

'I'd say he's telling us the truth as he understands it. Or enough of the truth to get himself out of Dublin and out of trouble if he can manage it.'

Mallon put a knuckled fist to his temple.

'Let me get this straight. He says he's working for some toff in the government in London. He's going around stabbing and threatening people and pretending he's from the Land League or some other crowd of assassins. He's been sent here to find out who's putting these bloody Greek coins about. And somewhere, there's a gang aiming to make money out of land deals here in Ireland. Is that it?'

'That seems to be it.'

'Jesus, at least it's original, I'll give him that. God be with the days when all we had to deal with was old-fashioned murder and robbery.'

'What do you want me to do, Sir?' Swallow said after an interval.

Mallon rose to pace the room.

'If this is true, Swallow… and mind you, I'm saying, "if," it could destabilise things more effectively than any of the extremists ever thought possible. It's been the devil's job to get either the landlords or the tenants to believe in the land transfer scheme. If it turns out that some crowd are on the make it could bring the whole bloody thing to a halt.'

'I realise that, Sir.'

Mallon scratched his beard.

'What's the significance of these Greek coins… these tetra… whatevers?'

'Tetradrachms. We don't know. But they must be important to someone if Shaftoe was sent here to find out who's been putting them into circulation.'

'I assume we've still got protection on the Greenbergs.'

'There's a G-man over there on special post since the attack.'

'Is there any progress on locating this Clinton woman who sold the damned things to the Greenberg girl? Didn't we send out an information request to the constabulary?'

'Johnny Vizzard is following that one. But there's nothing back from the RIC, which seems strange. They got on a train at the Broadstone, and went off to County Meath. They must have got off someplace.'

Mallon snorted. 'The RIC will always claim that they can find anybody, anywhere in Ireland in twenty-four hours.'

Swallow hesitated. 'There's one other thing. It may be just coincidence, but I'm wondering if there might be more to it than that.'

'Yes?' Mallon cocked his head impatiently.

'I was wondering about that silver turning up in Pollock's basement. It comes from one of the big estates in Galway that's just been broken up. There might be a connection to the land story that Shaftoe is telling.'

'I see where you're going. But there's nothing we know of to connect the two.'

'No, Sir. I acknowledge that. Could I ask, when do you expect to have some word back from London about interviewing this Lady Gessel?'

'Lady Gessel?' For a moment, Mallon seemed to have forgotten her. 'I'll probably hear something over the next day or two. I didn't ask them to treat it with any particular urgency. Do you think I should have?'

Swallow diplomatically avoided the question.

'If there's nothing to it, we're better off knowing that. We can close down one line of inquiry to follow others.'

'I'll telephone London again,' Mallon said. 'In the meanwhile, what do we do about Shaftoe and Darby?'

'Darby's only a hang-on. He's feeble-minded, and he hardly knows if Dublin is in Ireland or India. But Shaftoe is a smarter type. Let's assume his story is more or less true. He knows the one thing we'd want is the identity of this fellow in London who sent him over here. But he knows that the moment he gives me that he'll have nothing left to trade.'

'Does he know he could be looking at a lot of years breaking stones in Maryborough?'

'I've used that line. But he's clever enough to realise that putting him away for a stretch is of no great profit to us. On the other hand, he knows that anything involving high-level corruption could be important in political terms as far as we're concerned.'

Mallon mused silently.

'You could threaten to give him back to Vanucchi's gang. They'd get the name out of him fairly quickly.'

Swallow gave a hollow laugh.

'In principle I'd not have much against it. But we can't just throw him out the Ship Street Gate.'

Mallon resumed his chair. 'What do you propose?'

'I think we'll have to play his game,' Swallow said. 'Let's hold off from charging him over Greenbergs, at least for a while. We can charge Darby, but there might be a case for doing a deal with Shaftoe.'

'What would that entail?'

'A ticket to London.'

'You mean let him go?'

'I mean we send him back where he came from… with conditions.'

'What conditions?' Mallon sounded doubtful.

'That we'd get the identity of who set him up for the job,' Swallow said. 'And if we get that, we might learn what this land business is about, along with the names of anyone else involved.'

'He could give you the names of Robin Hood and his merry men. Once he's out of here we'll not see him on these shores again.'

'I agree, Sir. We need some way to verify what he tells us while we still have a grip of him. But he won't tell us anything useful until he feels he's safely away.'

Mallon sighed.

'I'm due up with the Security Secretary. I think I'll say nothing about this land business just for the present. I'll confirm that we have two men in custody for Greenberg's and that we're taking a suspect in for questioning on the Phoebe Pollock case.'

He swept a sheaf of papers from the desk into a file cover.

'So you go and do a bit more thinking, Sergeant.'

'Yes, Chief.'

Swallow moved to the door. 'By the way, Sir, there's a request I'd like to make.'

'What's that, Swallow?'

'You know I've been going to a class at the Metropolitan Art School on Thursdays and I'm due another class tomorrow. I'd be glad if I might have the afternoon free.'

Mallon paused.

'Art class? I thought you were going to tell me about something else.'

'Chief?'

'I'd heard you'd gone to new accommodation. I thought you'd have stayed on at Thomas Street. You seemed to be well looked after there by Mrs Walsh.'

'It wasn't an altogether satisfactory arrangement.'

'Well, that would be a matter for your own judgment. I gave you certain advice in the past, told you to make a decent woman of her. But I won't repeat myself.'

'Thank you, Sir. Was that a yes or a no to my request for leave?'

'If that's what makes you content, go ahead. Good luck to you.'

THURSDAY OCTOBER 6TH, 1887

FORTY

The numbers in Lily Grant's painting class were down. That always happened, she knew, after the first few lessons. Some pupils lost their courage or their confidence. Lily was indifferent. She believed a good art teacher should ruthlessly identify talent and let the no-hopers go their own way.

She was mildly surprised to see Swallow among the early arrivals this afternoon. The newspaper had been full of crime stories all week, and he seemed to have figured in most of them.

Although she was reluctant to admit it to herself, she was also embarrassed by the disaster of Maria's Sunday evening dinner party. Having largely engineered the event in an effort to get Swallow and her sister back into some sort of civil dialogue, she knew that she carried much of the responsibility for the debacle.

'I wasn't sure we'd see you this week,' she said cautiously. 'You've been a busy man.'

'That can't be denied,' he laughed. 'But I'm committed to this. A murder or two wouldn't keep me away.'

Katherine Greenberg had taken the chair next to him.

'There might have been more than one murder if Mr Swallow hadn't been so promptly on the scene on Monday,' she said.

'Of course, Miss Greenberg. What an ordeal you've had. And your father. I read about it in the papers.'

She stared hard at Swallow.

'Was it just a coincidence that you were on the scene? It was very fortuitous, wasn't it?'

'I was in Capel Street on police business,' he said icily.

Katherine cast him a look of admiration that was almost possessive. He knew it was intended to be.

'Sergeant Swallow didn't hesitate,' she said. 'If he had, I might be dead by now, and my father. The newspaper accounts couldn't do justice to the courage he showed.'

'I wouldn't doubt it,' Lily said tersely. She turned to Swallow, her back to Katherine.

'It was very pleasant to see you at Mrs Walsh's – Maria's – for dinner on Sunday evening. I hope you enjoyed it.'

He was calculatedly sharp.

'She went to a lot of trouble. It was nice to know that Mr Weldon returned her kindness by taking her to the theatre during the week.'

Lily's expression betrayed nothing.

The room was filling with the hum of conversation. Easels and paintboxes clattered onto tables. Chairs scraped across floorboards as the would-be artists took up their favoured positions. She walked to the front of the classroom and clapped her hands.

'Good afternoon. I hope everybody has done their homework.'

She slipped quickly into professional teaching mode.

'I shall be going around shortly in order to see what each of you has accomplished. But first, I want you have a look at something very unusual. When you see it – or him, more accurately – I want you to think about how you would paint him, what colouring you might use, what pigments you might mix.'

She looked to the back of the room and gestured to a man of about Swallow's own age, standing in the doorway, clad only in a woollen blanket. It took Swallow a moment to recognise the Neapolitan features of Charlie Vanucchi.

'Please come in, Charles,' Lily called.

Vanucchi made his way to the front of the class and sat on a low dais beside her. He drew his blanket around him and gave a wide, beaming grin to the class.

'I'd like to introduce you to Charles,' Lily said. 'He has very kindly agreed to act as our model this afternoon. Now, this is not a drawing class so I'm not asking you to consider too closely any of the rules of anatomical drawing. What we're concerned with here this afternoon is how to bring the right colours together to paint Charles as he is.'

On cue, Vanucchi dropped the blanket to the side of his chair, leaving only a small, white loincloth to protect his modesty. Charlie Vanucchi was practiced in this routine, Swallow reckoned.

At the same moment, he realised the immensity of Lily's challenge to her pupils' amateur talents.

Italian, Irish and God knows what other bloodlines had merged to give Charlie Vanucchi's body a combination of flesh tones that ranged from waxen white to pale brown. The face and hands were dark, but the torso was light as a church candle.

'Charles has unusual colouring,' Lily said. 'This is why we're so grateful to him for his willingness to help here at the Art School. The task for you all this afternoon is to see if you can devise colours using your basic pigments that can accurately reflect the complexity of the tones you see in front of you.'

At that moment, the naked Vanucchi recognised Swallow. The grin widened and he gave a thumbs up sign. He called cheerfully across the class.

'Ah, howya, Misther Swalla'? I didn' know ye was involved in this caper. Talk to ye later, wha'?'

Mixing colours to paint Charlie Vanucchi was indeed a challenge. When Lily Grant called the usual break, an hour into the afternoon, Swallow's effort was a hotch-potch of greys and creams with streaks of brown that prompted various unsanitary comparisons in his imagination.

Katherine Greenberg seemed to be doing marginally better. She had achieved a translucent white that to some degree picked up the tones of the model's torso. But the nether regions, which she had attempted to depict in a mix of grey and pink, had clearly defeated her.

Swallow put down his brush and palette and strolled to the front of the class.

'You're doing a bit of modelling on the side then, Charlie?'

Vanucchi had drawn his blanket around himself again. Someone had supplied him with a mug of hot tea.

'I started doin' it as a kid,' Charlie grinned. 'A shillin' for two hours. Sure it was money for jam. But I like it too. Mebbe it's the eye-talian in me. Very artistic people, ye know. That fella' who done 'The Last Supper,' he was a cousin on me grandmother's side, I think. She was a Vinci, ye know, the Vincis are big around Napoli.'

'I wouldn't doubt a word of it,' Swallow said. He lowered his voice. 'Your fellows must have given our Mr Shaftoe a fair going-over. We're still trying to sort out how much of his story is true.'

'Oh, I think you'll find its true enough, Misther Swalla'. He wasn't keepin' much back by the time the lads was done with him. I wouldda said he was uncooperative at first. An', of course, you'll remember ye owe me the balance of a fiver at th' end of it all.'

Katherine tapped him on the shoulder.

'I'm going to the cafeteria downstairs for a cup of tea, Joe. Would you like to come?'

'I think I could do with stretching the legs,' Swallow was glad of the excuse. 'And the tea would be welcome.'

The cafeteria in the basement of the Art School was crowded and noisy, but they squeezed into a table in a corner. The two teas Swallow ordered from the waitress were served immediately.

'This man that you arrested in the cathedral,' she asked, 'is he the one… the English man who… had the gun at the shop?'

She sipped her tea.

'I believe so. He's under lock and key, so he won't be a threat to you.'

'What did he tell you?'

'We're questioning him still. He says he was hired by somebody in London to find out who sold you the tetradrachms.'

She shrugged.

'It makes no sense. They're worth a few pounds, yes. But why come all the way from London for them?'

Swallow had decided that Katherine did not need to know anything further about Teddy Shaftoe's story.

'That remains to be seen,' he said, finishing his tea. 'In the meantime, until we get to the bottom of it all, we'll be keeping a detective at the shop night and day.'

Katherine smiled.

'You're very vigilant for us. And it's greatly appreciated.'

They worked through the second half of the class. Lily circuited the room, offering a word of advice here, an admonition there.

By the end of the lesson, Katherine had made progress, even in the challenge of colouring Charlie Vanucchi's nether regions. Swallow's board was by contrast a mess. No human form ever carried the hues and shades in which he sought to represent the leading figure of the city's criminal underworld.

Lily shook her head silently and passed on.

As the class ended and the first pupils exited to the corridor, a moustachioed constable, helmet in hand, put his head around the door. He gestured urgently.

Swallow folded his portfolio and crossed the room. The policeman backed into the corridor.

'Sorry to be waylayin' you, Sergeant,' he apologised. 'I was ordered to wait 'till ye were finished inside but not to let ye away. This is from Chief Mallon.'

Swallow opened the official envelope and read the message from the office of the Chief Superintendent, G-Division.

Swallow,

I regret that notwithstanding it being your rest day, I require you to attend here as soon as possible. Significant information has come to hand.

Yours faithfully,

John Mallon (Detective Chief Superintendent.)

As he finished reading, Charlie Vanucchi, swathed in his woollen blanket, emerged from the classroom. He beamed at Swallow and the constable.

'An' a very good afternoon to yiz, gentlemen. I was lookin' at yer efforts there Misther Swalla'. What yer lackin', if ye don't mind me advisin' ye, is a touch a' this new shade they've invented. They're callin' it beige.'

The constable's eyes popped. Like every other beat man across the city he knew Charlie Vanucchi and every one of his runners by sight.

Vanucchi pushed through the doors, back into the classroom.

'Is that who I'm thinkin' it is,' the policeman asked, 'or are me eyes mistakin' me?'

'No mistake,' Swallow replied. 'Very artistic people, these Italians, or so I'm told.'

FORTY-ONE

When Swallow got to Mallon's office, the chief was hunched over a file of papers on his desk. He scarcely glanced up when Swallow entered the room.

'Ever in London, Swallow?' he grunted.

'No, Sir. I went to Coventry once to bury an uncle.'

'Well, you're going to London in the morning.'

He waved Swallow to a chair.

'I think this story of Shaftoe's is standing up. Sir Edward Jenkinson at Scotland Yard telephoned me. He sent a man from the Special Irish Branch down to Sussex yesterday to see this Lady Gessel. In fairness to them, they move fairly quickly over there when you ask them to.'

He gestured to the notes on his desk.

'She says the silver disappeared when she sold out the place down in Galway.' He glanced at the notes. 'Mount Gessel.'

'So it's stolen property then?' Swallow said.

'It's not as simple as that. According to what she told the man from the Yard, it was her solicitors in Galway who told her it was gone. They said it must have been lifted out of the house by some of the tenants before the contents were auctioned. But if that's the case, nobody seems to have notified the constabulary down there.'

'That's odd,' Swallow said. 'A load of good silver goes missing and nobody reports it to the peelers? Wouldn't her solicitors have done that?'

'You'd have thought so. But it doesn't stop at that. There's other things missing from the house. Some fine china and glassware. Paintings too. And ... something else very significant.'

Swallow waited expectantly.

'According to Lady Gessel's information, the missing property also includes a collection of rare coins, Greek and Roman, put together by her late husband's grandfather, as far as she knows.'

Swallow felt a frisson of comprehension.

'And are you going to tell me that the coins included Greek tetradrachms?'

Mallon shrugged. 'I don't have those details. But I'd lay a penny to a pound they did.'

Suddenly he seemed animated.

'You might say it's straws in the wind. But by God, there's a stack of them. Here's this Gessel woman telling us her property has gone missing. It's turning up here in Greenberg's and in Ambrose Pollock's pawn shop. We have your friend Shaftoe in the cells, telling us he was sent here to find out where it came from. And he claims he's working on behalf of some unknown characters pulling money out of the land transfer process.'

'It seems to fit together.'

Mallon grunted again.

'If this is real, the authorities will have to be told. The government will need to take the landowners' and the tenants' representatives into their confidence. They'll have to hold the process together while they sort out whatever is afoot.'

'So when are you going to alert them?'

'I'm not sure. If I do that now there are two problems. First, we could be wrong, in which case we'll undermine our own credibility and become a laughing stock. Second, if the word gets out that we suspect something, it could get back, giving these characters the opportunity to cover their tracks.'

Swallow understood Mallon's anxiety not to be seen to get it wrong. The Assistant Under-Secretary for Security, Howard Smith Berry, had his own cabal of detectives, mainly English and Scottish, working directly under him in the Upper Yard. Their leader, an obnoxious former Army officer, Major Nigel Kelly, was a constant critic of the G-Division and of Mallon's methods.

'Just like you said, we need to know who's running this fellow Shaftoe,' Mallon said. 'Who's his boss, and who sent him here? You'll have to cut a deal with him, as you suggested. I've been thinking how we'll do it.'

Swallow felt he could indulge his own sense of vindication.

'So I was on the right track.'

Mallon ignored it.

'You'll bring him back to London, like you said. You'll lodge him in a cell at one of the prisons. We'll try to avoid places like Wandsworth or Brixton or Pentonville. I'll arrange it with Jenkinson.'

'How will we hold him? Or rather, how will they hold him?'

'He'll be sentenced to fourteen days on some minor charge, maybe public disorder or drunkenness. Then he'll have to identify who he's working for. If the information is good, he'll be released at the end of his two weeks. Otherwise, you produce this.'

Mallon handed him a document topped with the Royal Arms of the Lion and Unicorn.

'It's an warrant entitling you to bring him back to Dublin to face charges of attempted murder, attempted armed robbery, possession of a firearm with intent to endanger life and conspiracy. All you have to do is countersign it.'

Swallow understood.

It was more than clever.

Shaftoe would not like it. It still left his fate in Swallow's hands. But as an alternative to Maryborough prison, a short spell behind bars in London before regaining his freedom would have to be an irresistible offer.

He pocketed the warrant.

'What about the Pollock murder investigation here? Mossop and Feore are bringing this fellow Rowan in this morning for questioning.'

'I'll make sure that they stay on top of the case. But I need someone with a bit of wit and diplomacy to do the London end of things.'

Swallow thought for a moment.

'I'll need help in London. I can find my way about. I might even enjoy the sights. But this sort of trick will only work if the authorities there are on board.'

'I'll arrange that through Jenkinson. And you won't have much time for seeing the sights. I want you to go down to this place, Dymchurch, in Sussex, and take a formal statement from Lady Gessel. If we end up charging people we'll need to prove that she was the lawful owner of the silver and the coins.'

Swallow could still be impressed after more than twenty years working for the man by John Mallon's ability to see around corners he had not even reached yet.

'Now,' Mallon said, 'today was supposed to be a rest day for you, Swallow. I suggest that you make the most of what's left of it, go home, pack a suitcase and be back here at nine in the morning. My clerk will have your tickets and a cash advance ready for you to take care of accommodation, subsistence, that kind of thing.'

He sat, indicating that the conversation at an end.

'Collect Shaftoe from the cells after that. Explain the deal to him and be on the noon sailing from Kingstown. When you're settled in London, telegraph me.'

The shadows of the October evening were darkening the Lower Yard as he left. A chill wind, hinting of the coming winter, cut across the cobbles from the direction of the river.

He met Pat Mossop and Tony Swann going out the Palace Street Gate. They were in good spirits.

'"Duck' Boyle is standin' for everyone in the Dolphin,' Mossop said. 'He's got notification that he's on the list for superintendent. Are ye comin' with us, Joe?'

He thought about declining the offer, but it would be interpreted as begrudgery. He went to the Dolphin.

Mostly he listened to the gossip, keeping his counsel, standing his round to the other G-men and accepting theirs. When the wall clock in the bar showed close to eleven, he decided to go. Packing for London would not take long, but he needed to explain to Harriet that he would be away for a few days.

He felt the cool air in his lungs when he left the Dolphin. He turned along Parliament Street and, at the top, turned right out of habit towards Lord Edward Street. Without willing it, his steps took him across High Street, past the two churches of St Audoen and into Thomas Street.

His progress should have been towards the rented house on Heytesbury Street but some instinct was bringing him back along Thomas Street to Grant's and Maria Walsh.

When he came abreast of Grant's he crossed the street and sought the shadows get a better view. The upstairs rooms were in darkness, but the lights in the bar were warm and inviting. He recognised the rituals of closing time, the barmen clearing the counters, customers draining their glasses. And there was Maria moving across the illuminated rectangles of the windows, elegant in her dark, formal dress, her blonde hair catching the light.

He sensed a convergence of emotions. He felt angry, but he was not sure at whom. At himself, perhaps more than anyone else, he guessed. There was sadness too. Or was he just feeling sorry for himself? By right, he should be in there, in the warmth and comfort of Grant's, with Maria. But instead he was standing, half drunk, on Thomas Street with wind and rain whipping around him. Well, whose fault was that but his own?

He shut his eyes, closing off the picture, and turned for Heytesbury Street.

FRIDAY OCTOBER 7TH, 1887

FORTY-TWO

At about the time that Swallow was wakening Detective Johnny Vizzard in his bunk at the Exchange Court dormitory, the station sergeant of the Royal Irish Constabulary in the small market town of Trim, County Meath was preparing to resume his duties.

Sergeant Timothy Devenney had been granted a five-day furlough on compassionate grounds. The purpose was to enable him to attend the obsequies of his wife's mother in County Roscommon.

His leave had started at noon on the previous Sunday. At the same hour on this Friday he would again take charge of the Trim barracks, relieving the replacement sergeant who had been transferred temporarily from Navan to take his place.

Devenney was never content merely to be on time. It was his lifetime habit to be early. He believed it was a good maxim for a policeman, offering a margin of protection against surprise inspections and sometimes yielding other advantages. Thus, while he was officially free of duties until noon, 11 o'clock found him descending the back stairs from the married quarters to the offices below.

Once he entered his office, he saw the tell-tale signs of laxity over the period of his absence. Ash spilled from the remains of the turf fire onto the hearthstone. The station registers were scattered untidily across the table. A copy of Thursday's *Daily Sketch,* opened at the sports pages, was spread out beside the official books.

Of infinitely greater seriousness, potentially at least, was the bundle of unopened post in the wire tray on the sergeant's desk.

He cursed under his breath. The replacement sergeant from Navan was a notorious idler, heavy on the alcohol and addicted to the racing of any species of animal upon which bets could be placed.

Five days away from the oversight of his superiors at Navan would have been a boon for the shirker, an ideal opportunity to indulge his favourite pastimes without having to undertake the inconvenience of duty. And it was very likely, Devenney reflected, that he would have found a keen apprentice in the young recruit constable lately posted to the Trim barracks as well.

Devenney had tried to do his best for him since his arrival, but he knew that the new recruit had no natural inclinations to police work. Only hours before he had started his period of compassionate leave, the sergeant had marched with him to the railway station, there to observe the comings and goings of passengers on the Great Southern and Western Railway, as required at regular intervals by routine orders.

He had sought to instruct him regarding the ways in which a policeman should observe a train.

His position in daylight hours should be in the waiting-room, or in a railway office from which he had a good view of the platform. He should use a window receiving direct daylight so that its reflection on the glass would render him invisible to passengers or others on the platform.

At night, the opposite procedure should be applied. A man in a lighted room is clearly visible to anyone outside in the darkness, while at the same time his capacity to see them is greatly reduced. The watching policeman in hours of darkness should choose the exterior shadows of a building, taking care not to allow reflected light to catch his buttons or badges.

He knew that his apprentice was not listening, being more interested in the progress of some young ladies as they made their way aboard the Galway train. If Jesus Christ and the Twelve Apostles landed on the platform at Trim, he reckoned, the recruit constable would hardly notice them.

Sergeant Devenney swept the dated newspaper aside, sat at the table and started into the unopened post, reordering it so that he could start with the oldest. He saw Post Office Telegram in its distinctive red and blue envelope dated from Monday. He cursed again. His replacement's laziness was such that even a telegram, by definition an urgent communication, had remained unread.

He slit the envelope and read the telegram.

FROM DI/RIC NAVAN

INFORMATION REQUESTED G-DIVISION DMP WHEREABOUTS OF MR MRS ARTHUR AND GRACE CLINTON THREE YOUNG CHILDREN TRAVELLED BROADSTONE TRAIN SUNDAY MORNING STOP URGENT CRIME INQUIRY

Oh Dear God. Although it was the greater part of week ago, Sergeant Devenney recalled clearly the young couple with their three children, laden with bags, as they stepped down from the Dublin train on Sunday morning.

Devenney had seen the man cross the station platform to approach a jarvey on his side-car in the forecourt. He watched as the jarvey helped the woman and children to board the car and then loaded the baggage.

Devenney calculated quickly. Wherever they went, they could not have travelled far. Two hours later, when the sergeant and Mrs Devenney had gone to the station themselves to take the train to Athlone on the first stage of their sorrowful journey, the jarvey was back on the forecourt. Were the sergeant not preoccupied with comforting his wife in the circumstances of her bereavement, he believed he would have inquired of the driver, out of professional curiosity, who his passengers had been and the destination to which he had brought them.

Four days on and the damned telegram had not even been read. He would report his replacement's slothfulness and deal with the recruit constable's neglect of duty in due course, but an urgent situation had now arisen.

Fifteen minutes later, Devenney was questioning the jarvey at his cottage in a laneway off the main street of Trim. Where had he brought the young couple, their children and their baggage?

The driver was co-operative. He told Devenney how the husband had resisted his friendly efforts to have him identify himself or to state their business in the area. But the young wife had cried with joy when they came in sight of the solid, two-storey house in the townland of Clonlar that she told the driver was the home of her widowed mother, a Mrs Armstrong.

Devenney knew Elizabeth Armstrong as he had known her late husband, James. They had almost 100 acres of good land at Clonlar. There were no Armstrong sons, and after James's death the land went to local farmers. The sergeant knew there were two daughters, Helen and Grace. The coincidence of names, he surmised, probably meant that Grace was the elusive Mrs Clinton.

He hurried to the Post Office on the main street. Once inside, he composed an urgent telegraph:

FROM DEVENNEY SERGT IN CHARGE TRIM STOP REPORTING LIKELY LOCATION OF CLINTON FAMILY PER DMP INFORMATION REQUEST SUNDAY STOP INSTRUCTIONS PLEASE

He handed it to the postmaster and told him to wire it personally and immediately to the District Inspector's office at Navan.

FORTY-THREE

Jimmy Rowan, alias Regan, had a lot of experience of police stations. He knew the procedures. First, they would take everything you had off you. If that included anything valuable, like money or a watch, you were likely not to see it again. Then they would throw you in the cell. Depending on the mood of the peeler who took you down, there you might get a few belts of a baton on the way. Then there would usually be a long wait in the dark among the odours of bodily excretions and coarse disinfectant.

Eventually, a couple of them would fetch you from the cell and take you to an office. One would tell you what you were to be charged with. Sometimes the charge was right, sometimes not. Sometimes, where drink might have been involved, you might not even be sure yourself. It hardly mattered. In the end, perhaps after some show of defiance followed by a hammering, you would sign the statement of admission. It never varied.

It was a surprise to find that it seemed to be a bit different in Dublin, at least with the plainclothes fellows at the Castle. They had been polite as they went in and out of the hotel over the days, and he had come to recognise them by sight.

When Barry, the general manager, told him that two of the G-men wanted to talk to him, he had briefly entertained the notion of fleeing. He guessed that they had found his record. One way or another it would mean the end of the job at the hotel. When he saw that two constables had been strategically positioned on the street outside, though, he reckoned it was best to go willingly to the manager's office.

Feore, the big fellow with the west-of-Ireland accent, led the questioning.

'We won't waste each other's time,' Feore said. 'I know who you are and what you are. Your name is Rowan. You've six convictions for violence and a few more for theft, drunkenness and obstruction.'

Rowan shrugged.

'So ye know who I am,' he said, throwing a sidelong look at Barry, who stood to one side. 'I'm usin' a false name here. If I didn't, there'd be no work for the likes of me.'

'You're right on that,' Barry interjected.

'I've done me time,' Rowan ignored him. 'I'm not on yer books for anythin', so go ahead. Ask me any questions ye want.'

'For a start, you're on the books again on suspicion of theft,' Feore said. He tossed three leather wallets on the desk. 'We found these in the cupboard beside your bed. There's no money in them now, of course. But it's a fair bet that when you lifted them, maybe from fellows with a few drinks on them, there'd have been cash in there.'

'You can't prove that.'

'We'll trace the owners easily enough, or some of them. They'll have reported them as lost or missing. They'll recognise their own property.'

Rowan shuffled his feet.

'There might have been a case where a gent let his wallet fall out of his pocket and I picked it up.'

Feore laughed. 'Indeed there might have been. When you're a front door porter you probably see a fair few opportunities like that.'

Rowan was silent.

'You weren't truthful about where you were at the time the woman was last seen,' Feore said tersely. 'You told us you were never on the first floor that afternoon. But we have a witness who says differently, and we have another witness who says you were absent from the hall door where you should have been.'

'I'm sure ye have.' Rowan's tone was bitter. 'There's always plenty a' witnesses when youse are tryin' to put some fella away. I wasn't near the first floor. I never touched the woman. I never even saw her. I admit I wasn't on the door when I should've been. The reason was I went down the road to Hayden's public house for a couple of shorts.'

He turned to look at Barry.

'Ye might as well know I done it often enough. You'll have me out of the place anyway. You had me standin' at that fuckin' door ten, maybe twelve hours a day with the bloody wind comin' in offa the river, cuttin' through me. A couple o' drinks was the only thing to keep me warm.'

Mossop looked up from his notebook.

'There'll be witnesses down at Hayden's who'll back up your story?'

'Yeah, g'wan down and ask the head barman there. He knows me well.'

They kept him in the manager's office while a constable was despatched to Hayden's, a couple of hundred yards along the quay. When he returned, he put his head around the office door and beckoned to Feore. The G-man returned to the room a few minutes later. He sat in front of Rowan.

'I'm afraid you're in trouble now, Jimmy. The head man down in Hayden's says he hasn't seen you there in a month. How do you explain that?'

Jimmy shrugged.

'I don't know.'

'Well, you'd better do a bit of thinking about it because you're going to Mountjoy on remand for theft. In the meantime, you've become a suspect for the disappearance of Phoebe Pollock.'

FORTY-FOUR

'The Tower of London? You're lockin' me in the facking Tower o' London?' Teddy Shaftoe was unsure whether to be flattered or frightened.

The two detectives from Special Irish Branch who met the mail-boat train at Euston had a set of papers from Bow Street Magistrates' Court. The documents detailed Teddy's fictitious sentence of fourteen days' imprisonment for drunkenness at Charing Cross Road.

Swallow had plenty of experience of cooked-up charge sheets, but a ready-made order for imprisonment was impressive, even by the standards of Dublin perjury.

'If we put him in Wandsworth or Brixton he'll be back among his pals,' one of the Yard men told Swallow. 'Our guv'nor pulled a few strings and got him a nice little place where you can talk to him without anyone ear-wigging.'

Teddy quickly started to feel better on home ground. He had stopped complaining about the injuries he had suffered at the hands of Vanucchi's gang. Now he peered through the windows of the police hansom, calling out familiar landmarks, mainly licensed premises, as they made their way through the darkened streets of Clerkenwell and Houndsditch.

'Oi, there's the White Feathers. Great fackin' public 'ouse, that. An' there's the Crown. Solid lads and lively ladies in there, I promise.' He giggled with happiness.

The senior Scotland Yard man was a detective sergeant called Montgomery. He introduced his colleague as Detective Constable Bright. Bright had a soft, regional English accent that Swallow could not place.

Teddy had gone for Mallon's deal, but with conditions. He wanted a pound in cash so he could drink at the bar on the packet from Kingstown to Holyhead. And while he accepted that he would be handcuffed to Swallow for the train journey to London, he wanted the handcuffs off at sea.

'I mean, Mr Swallow, wha' would be the point of me tryin' to escape out on the fackin 'igh seas? What am I goin' to do? Jump in the fackin' briney? An' I'm not goin' to be a threat, what with you 'avin' that bloody big shooter. An' if the facking ship 'its a rock an' sinks, a man's got to 'ave a chance to swim for it, ain't 'e?'

Teddy drank steadily across the Irish Sea. Pints of brown ale, alternating with whiskies. Swallow handcuffed Teddy's wrist to his own as the mail packet started to dock at the Admiralty Pier at Holyhead. It was hardly necessary since his prisoner was semi-comatose with alcohol. He stayed that way for nearly all of the seven hour train journey to London.

The arrangements for Teddy's accommodation at the Tower of London were far from intolerable. A senior warder with two fox terriers at his heels showed them to a spacious room in St Thomas's Tower. It was fitted with a bed, a table and two chairs. A small coal fire burned in a grate.

'Gets a bit damp if we don't keep up the fire. But there's a nice view of Father Thames in the mornin' there,' the warder quipped. The salty, sulphurous smell of the river was strong, seeping through the thick stone walls.

With Teddy installed in St Thomas's Tower, the Yard men took Swallow to the lodgings they had chosen for him off Farringdon Road. A sign proclaimed it as Frost's Hotel, but it was a boarding house. While the detectives waited in the hallway, the eponymous proprietor-cum-manageress, Mrs Frost, showed him to his room. It was a good deal smaller than Teddy Shaftoe's in the Tower, but it was comfortable, warm and clean.

'And we 'ave a bathroom, Mr Swallow,' Mrs Frost told him proudly. 'Just put in this year. Very modern, I am. If you want to use it, let me know and the maids will fill the 'ot water for you from downstairs. Lots of p'lice lads stay 'ere when they 'ave official business in London,' Mrs Frost said. 'But you're the first we've seen from Dublin. My mother was from Belfast, as a matter o' fact.'

Swallow surmised that Mrs Frost was probably a police widow. A photograph on the landing, showing a platoon of helmeted constables in front of a station somewhere, reinforced his assumption.

The Yard men took him to a nearby public house. It reminded him a little of Grant's, only noisier. They found an empty booth.

Montgomery ordered whiskies. Irish for himself and Swallow and a House of Commons Scotch for Bright.

'God speed the plough, as we say in Donegal.' Montgomery raised his glass.

'Donegal?' Swallow said. 'You don't sound like a man from Donegal.'

'Two generations out of it. My grandfather came to London, took up policing and never went back.' He grinned. 'But it sounds more interesting than saying I'm from Hackney.' He sipped at his whiskey. 'Then my old man became a copper too. Lots of Irish in the job.'

Swallow understood. Men who would shun the police in the land of their birth were often happy to wear the Queen's blue serge on the streets of England or Scotland. Bright shook his head. He looked confused.

'But that's a bloody English sayin', Sarge – this "God speed the plough." We 'ad it in Devon when I were a lad growin' up.'

Montgomery sighed. 'It means the same thing wherever it's from. It means good luck for the job in hand.'

Swallow felt that Bright did not seem to get the point.

'Now, here's the ground rules, as I've been briefed by Sir Edward Jenkinson, our guv'nor,' Montgomery said. 'You've got access to Shaftoe at the Tower any time you like, night or day. You can question him all you want. If he's cheeky and needs a clip on the ear, that's a matter for yourself. But he's not to be marked. Am I clear?'

Swallow nodded.

'As I understand it,' Montgomery resumed, 'you've a deal with Shaftoe. He's got the name of someone engaged in some sort of fiddle over the land transfers in Ireland. Once you're satisfied that you've got what you need from him, we turn him loose. Is that right?'

'Yes. And if he feeds me bullshit, I've a warrant to bring him back to Dublin to face half a dozen charges that'll put him out of circulation for a long time.'

'That could easily tempt me,' Montgomery said. 'Shaftoe's one of the worst. He'd as soon knife you as buy you a drink. The lads in the H-Division down at the East End will tell you that.'

He raised a hand.

'Don't worry. I know you're playing for higher stakes here. If the price of that is to see Teddy Shaftoe on the streets again, then so be it. It won't be too long before CID will have him in again anyway. When will you start with him?'

'Tomorrow morning. I'd plan to be at the Tower by 9 o'clock.'

'Fine. I'll be at Frost's at 8.30. We can take the underground railway to Mark Lane. It's close to the Tower. I gather you're going down to Dymchurch to take a statement from Lady Gessel as well?'

'I think that'll be after I've made some progress with Shaftoe. We'll need a statement from her if we bring charges.'

'I know she's connected to Sir Richard Gessel. He's one of the big men at Downing Street. Very close to the PM, I understand.'

'They're distantly related. But I don't think he's got anything to tell us about this business. They share a name going back a few generations. That's all.'

Montgomery grimaced. 'That's a relief. The less a copper has to do with the political types the better. Anyway, if you're going to Dymchurch one of us will travel down with you. It's about an hour by train out of Victoria.'

Bright signalled to the barman for a fresh round of whiskies.

When the drinks had been served, Montgomery raised an index finger.

'The one thing Sir Edward insists upon is that we know everything you hear from Shaftoe. So Jack here, or myself, will be there when you question him. He won't see us or hear us. There's a listening hole up in the wall in his cell.'

He laughed. 'It's probably there since old King Henry was locking up his wives. But it works so that a man in the room above can hear every word.'

'That's fine with me,' Swallow said. 'We'd do the same if you were in Dublin.'

'And,' Montgomery added, 'any police action as a result of information you get will be taken by us. It's our patch.'

'I can't see that anything else would be practical,' Swallow said. 'But I'll need to be on the inside track. It's no good to me if you simply run off with the investigation, leaving me no wiser.'

'I'd be sympathetic to that,' Montgomery said. 'But I can't give a promise on it. At the end of the day, our guv'nor is the Home Secretary; yours is the Chief Secretary for Ireland. If they disagree on something, we've got to do what our man tells us.'

The argument was unwinnable, Swallow knew. And it was probably unnecessary.

It was his round.

FORTY-FIVE

The effectiveness of Robert Peel's Irish policing system derived from three organisational imperatives: strong central control, a rigid chain of command and uniformity in procedures and processes.

These very strengths, however, also sponsored the system's significant weaknesses. While information and instructions could move efficiently, if slowly, up and down the chain, they did not travel laterally. Thus, information gleaned by a policeman in one sub-district might take several days before it reached his colleagues in adjoining sub-districts, even though their barracks might be within marching distance of each other.

Important intelligence went up and down the full length of the command chain, through the offices at district and county level and thence to headquarters in the Lower Yard at Dublin Castle. Then it would be notified downward along a similar chain until it reached the men in the small barracks and posts around the country.

If the intelligence was destined for transmission between the Constabulary and the Metropolitan Police, the process was even more tortuous.

Once received at Constabulary Headquarters in the Lower Castle Yard, and considered at the appropriate level of authority, it would be conveyed manually to the headquarters of the DMP across the Yard.

In normal office hours, it might go directly to the office of the Commissioner. Outside of office hours or, in the case of 'special' intelligence relating to subversive crime, it might go to the office of the Chief Superintendent of G-Division.

Sergeant Devenney's information on the possible location of the Clinton family was transmitted from the Trim Post Office late on Friday morning. Then, after dinner hour, it moved through the offices of both the District Inspector and the County Inspector at Navan.

In the County Inspector's office, a clerk decided to leave the telegram for transmission to Dublin until the late afternoon. Then he would take it to the Post Office along with the rest of the official mail. Thus, when the telegram reached Constabulary Headquarters in Dublin, the clerical staff in the DMP Commissioner's offices across the Yard had finished their day's work and were gone.

The duty officer at the Constabulary Office knew that, in these circumstances, intelligence should go the office of the Chief Superintendent of G-Division or, indeed, to his house in the Lower Yard. But because of a temporary shortage of the special blue file covers that carried correspondence relating to intelligence, the duty officer had placed the telegram in a buff-coloured file of the type used to carry routine administrative information.

The messenger deposited it in the letter-box on the door of Commissioner's clerk.

There it remained overnight, setting at naught the urgency with which the diligent Sergeant Devenney had pursued his investigations and transmitted his valuable information.

SATURDAY OCTOBER 8TH, 1887

FORTY-SIX

Teddy Shaftoe was anxious to be co-operative after just one night in the Tower.

'He was as big as a fackin' rabbit, Mr Swallow. Wiv a tail about a foot long. An' that was just the first of the fackers. Got 'im wiv my boot, didn' I? But then all of 'is facking brothers an' sisters comes in after 'im.'

A pile of four or five dead rats in the corner of the cell corroborated Teddy's tale of voracious rodents who were masters of the night in St Thomas's Tower. Swallow understood why the warder the previous evening had insisted on being accompanied by his two terrier dogs.

Montgomery and Bright had been at Frost's, as promised, at 8.30. But the hotel's breakfast of thin porridge, toast and watery marmalade was an unsatisfactory start to the day.

The Yard men led the way to the underground railway station on Clerkenwell Road. Swallow was looking forward to the experience of the travelling under the earth.

In the five-minute walk from Frost's Hotel to the station, he saw why London's engineers and builders had embarked upon this radical transportation plan.

He had never walked in streets so noisily congested, or with such foul air. Dublin had the gentle pace of a market town by comparison. Carriages and cars contested for space between delivery wagons, huge drays and lines of steam-driven omnibuses. Drivers and porters manoeuvred for advantage, shouting for room and cursing their rivals.

The sheer number of people was overwhelming. In Dublin, a walk on a city street was a pleasure. Here, phalanxes of pedestrians crushed and jostled against each other, grim-faced and without salutation.

The underground railway was a novelty, but not a pleasant one.

Swallow had read descriptions of the miniature carriages, plunging through the dark, earthen channels under the city. What he was not prepared for was the belching steam and smoke from the engine, funnelling backward towards the passengers, driven by the vehicle's own subterranean velocity. He was grateful to gulp fresh air, briny from the river, when they emerged at Mark Lane.

At St Thomas's Tower, the warder secreted Montgomery and Bright in the listening hole above Teddy Shaftoe's cell. When Swallow entered, he found Shaftoe sitting on his bunk, feet tucked under him. A heavy boot in his right hand was in readiness as a missile in the event of a daylight appearance by the rodents.

'The quicker you tell me what I need to know, and the quicker I can verify it, the quicker you'll be out of here, Shaftoe.' Swallow had no desire to spend any longer than necessary himself in the dampness of the Tower.

He drew a chair and sat at the table, notebook ready.

'So, what's the name of the fellow who contracted you and where do I find him?'

Shaftoe cautiously left his bed, crossed the cell and took the chair opposite.

'I didn't ever exactly say I knew 'is name, Mr Swallow. I know wot 'e looks like and I know where 'e works, or where 'e says 'e works. An' I know where 'e drinks. Or at least I know where 'e drinks when 'e wants to meet me.'

Swallow's temper rose.

'This is bullshit. I set up this deal on the basis that you'd lead me to the fellow who sent you to do the job in Dublin. You'd better do that, no fucking about and you'd better do it now.' He brought his fist down on the table. 'Or I'm off to Bow Street with my warrant and you'll be back on the boat to Dublin with me tonight. And you won't be drinking the Queen's money in the bar either.'

Shaftoe raised a hand defensively.

'I said I'd do that, Mr Swallow. An' so I shall. So I shall. It's just not as straightforward as that. I'll 'ave to send this geezer a message that I wants to see 'im, won't I? Then, when 'e shows, you can 'ave 'im.'

Swallow bottled his anger.

'Right,' he said reasonably, 'how do you send him the message?'

'I drops the word into the public 'ouse. Someone passes it on. I goes back and I gets a time from the guv'nor when to come back. Then my man shows up. Sometimes I 'ave to wait around for a couple hours. But that's no 'ardship in a decent 'ouse, is it?'

'What's the public house? You know that much, I'll warrant.'

'Yeh, it's The Mitre, innit? Right there in Ely Court, off 'Atton Garden.'

Swallow knew of Hatton Garden, as did every police detective in the Kingdom.

Lying between Gray's Inn Road and Farringdon Road, it was emerging as the centre of London's burgeoning trade in jewellery and precious metals. The vast majority of its business was legitimate and above board, but inevitably, among its scores of workshops and trade houses there were some that offered opportunities to those with stolen gold, silver or diamonds to dispose of.

'Right, we're going for a visit, Teddy. You'll bring me down to the Mitre and you'll leave a message to meet this fellow. I'll be watching you at every moment. Try to bolt and I'll plug you.' Swallow tapped the Bulldog Webley in its shoulder-holster. 'And you know from what happened at Greenberg's that I don't miss.'

When Swallow met the Scotland Yard men an hour later, Montgomery was unhappy with what he had overheard from his listening post above Teddy Shaftoe's cell.

'I don't have authority to let him out at this stage, even into your custody,' he told Swallow. 'And if he's to deliver a message in The Mitre without arousing suspicion, he'll have to be uncuffed and unaccompanied.'

'We can manage that, I think,' Swallow said.

Montgomery looked doubtful.

'I don't like this any more than you do,' Swallow conceded. 'But I've got to follow this trail down to the end. I'll take responsibility if anything goes wrong.'

'We can cover the place,' Bright said. 'It's in an alley called Ely Court. Just two exits. One onto Hatton Garden; the other into Ely Place.'

In spite of Montgomery's reservations, an hour later saw Teddy Shaftoe step through the door of The Mitre close to the Holborn Circus end of Hatton Garden. Swallow placed himself against the railings of the shop next to the entrance to Ely Court, pretending to read a newspaper. Directly opposite, Montgomery peered in a shop window, apparently examining trays of rings, but with a perfect mirror view across the street. Jack Bright had taken up position at the other end of the laneway at Ely Place.

'You've got to give me some time in there, Mr Swallow,' Shaftoe pleaded. 'I've to deal with the guv'nor. It could be when I goes in that 'e's dealin' wiv a customer. I may 'ave to wait until 'e can talk to me.'

Shaftoe went into Ely Court, and Swallow watched him go through the front door of the public house. A moment later, Swallow heard his own name being called. It was a woman's voice.

'Mr Swallow… Joe. What are you doing here?'

Katherine Greenberg was standing on the pavement not a yard away. Swallow fumbled with the newspaper. The last thing he needed or expected was to be recognised.

'What a coincidence,' Katherine laughed. 'Are you gone into the jewellery trade?'

'I'm on duty,' he pitched his voice low. 'Pretend you don't know me. Just go about your business.'

She understood. Her expression became serious.

'Of course,' she too dropped her voice.

'It's just so… amazing. I come here regularly.' She looked past him to the shop front. 'I have business in here. I hope you'll excuse me.'

She stepped to the shop door and then turned back to him.

'I don't know how long you will be in London, but I'm here until Monday. I'm at the Grosvenor, beside Victoria, if you are free to call.'

He had no time to answer. Teddy Shaftoe stepped out into the street from the alley. He did not as much as glance at Katherine, but the alarm in her face told Swallow that she recognised him. She looked away quickly.

Shaftoe turned left towards Holborn Circus. Swallow followed. He saw Montgomery flanking them on the pavement opposite. They crossed Holborn Circus into Fetter Lane and made for a public house called The White Swan, as they had planned.

Swallow bought Teddy Shaftoe a pint of ale and whiskies for the Yard men. He ordered a pint bottle of Guinness's light porter for himself and a Cornish pasty to fill the hole left by Mrs Frost's poor breakfast.

'Well,' Swallow asked when they had settled over their refreshments, 'what's the plan?'

Shaftoe drained off his ale in two great gulps.

'Another o' those would do very nicely, Mr Swallow, so it would.'

Swallow signalled the barman.

'At The Mitre,' Shaftoe said. 'That's where 'e'll be. Tomorrer' around noon.'

FORTY-SEVEN

Swallow spent the afternoon at the National Gallery on Trafalgar Square. They had returned Teddy Shaftoe to the Tower after they left the White Swan on Fetter Lane.

'Would we have time to make it to Dymchurch to interview Lady Gessel this evening?' Swallow inquired once Shaftoe was locked up.

'I don't think so,' Montgomery shook his head. 'We'd need to give notice to the East Sussex Police. They'd have to notify her. And we've no way of knowing if she'd be available for interview without arrangement.'

'A pity.'

'There's nothing to be done until the morning. We'll collect Shaftoe then and bring him down to The Mitre.'

The Special Branch men returned to Scotland Yard. Swallow caught a steam omnibus to Trafalgar Square.

He was struck by the similarity between the Nelson Column in the centre of the square and its Dublin counterpart. But London's monument was somewhat taller. The four bronze lions at the base were impressive.

He thought to climb it for the view. But then he discovered that the column's slender Corinthian proportions did not allow of an internal staircase as in Dublin. Swallow felt a small surge of pride that his own city had probably done a better job.

He felt affirmed, too, when he compared the Gallery itself to the National Gallery in Dublin.

Francis Fowke's building on Merrion Square was not nearly as magnificent at Wilkins' temple facing Trafalgar Square, but he fancied that the Italian collection in Dublin could hold its own with what he saw here. While the English and French collections were on a grander scale, he reckoned that the quality of Dublin's acquisitions compared favourably.

He was absorbed in the Barry Rooms when the staff started to call the end of viewing. Men in blue uniforms moved from gallery to gallery, ringing small handbells and calling out.

'Clowsin' time… clowsin' time please.'

He asked a porter how he might find the Grosvenor Hotel.

'Bucking'am Palace Road, across from Victoria Station, Sir. Can't miss it. Bloomin' great buildin,' must be six storeys 'igh. Lovely walk along the Mall, if you're not in a 'urry.'

Swallow was not in a hurry. He crossed Trafalgar Square and set off along The Mall. The trees in St James's Park still held just a little of their summer greenery. The footpaths were busy with strolling ladies and gentlemen. Fine carriages with uniformed footmen and drivers went up and down.

Halfway along The Mall, he saw the gates of Buckingham Palace open and a column of Life Guards ride out. A minute later they trotted past him, magnificent in silver breastplates and helmets, every man fixed perfectly in the saddle as if he and his horse were one. He felt that he was starting to understand the difference between an imperial capital and a national one.

Many times in his head during the afternoon he had turned over Katherine Greenberg's invitation to call. Was it just social nicety? Two people who know each other cross paths in a strange city. What could be more appropriate than that they should agree to meet, perhaps for a drink or to dine?

Or was it a sense of obligation? Here were two people recently thrown in each other's way by dramatic and dangerous events. Her life and her father's life had been threatened.

Or was there something more? Was it ridiculous to think that there might be some glimmering of a romantic interest on her part? He had seen a look in Katherine's eyes when they talked in Lily Grant's painting class that seemed to go beyond friendliness. The air between them had seemed, somehow, alive. But he was old enough to be her father. No, that was not true. An older brother, perhaps. And yet, she had seemed to grow warmer towards him with each successive encounter. And since he had started in the painting class he realised that he had begun to look forward to Katherine's company each Thursday afternoon.

He hoped that she would be at the Grosvenor when he got there, and he found himself worrying that perhaps he might not be looking as well as he should for an engagement with a lady.

FORTY-EIGHT

Katherine chose a supper house on Drury Lane called The Albion. 'London hotels are stuffy with dining-rooms like a morgue,' she said. 'And the fancy restaurants would break anyone's bank account. We can eat well at The Albion and we won't be thrown out at 9 o'clock.'

When Swallow had inquired for her at the Grosvenor Hotel, the reception clerk nodded. Yes, the hotel had a guest of that name staying, and yes, she had advised that she was expecting a visitor. A bell boy would be sent to Miss Greenberg's room with a message. Would the gentleman care to take a seat in the lobby?

The Grosvenor was almost on the same vast scale as the great railway terminus nearby, whose passengers comprised the bulk of its clientele. Swallow found a vacant chair under a colonnade of arches that reached to an elaborately decorated ceiling. Glittering chandeliers reflected on walls panelled with high, burnished mirrors.

Ladies and gentlemen with porters and servants bustled in and out of the lobby. Liveried hotel staff greeted guests, directing them to the various dining areas and lounges or towards the lifts that would carry them by electric power to their accommodation on the upper floors.

A few minutes later he saw Katherine emerge from one of the lifts. She spotted him as he rose from the chair, made her way across the busy lobby and kissed him lightly on the cheek. Swallow was unsure whether he should be embarrassed or pleased at the unaccustomed intimacy. He felt himself blush.

'It's good that you came,' she said. 'I didn't know if you could, being on duty this morning when we met. There's a private lounge here for residents. We can at least hear ourselves talk in there.'

The residents' lounge was surprisingly uncrowded. She led the way to a place by the windows, looking out onto Buckingham Palace Road.

'Wasn't that an extraordinary coincidence that we should meet this morning?' she said smiling. 'When did you come over from Dublin? And what are you doing here, or can you tell me?'

'Business,' he said. 'Police business.'

Her face darkened momentarily. 'I assume it has something to do with that wretched man who beat my father with the gun. I only saw him for a few seconds when they attacked us, but I recognised him going into Moser's.'

He grimaced.

'I can't tell you everything. But yes, it's to do with him. I'm working with some detectives from Scotland Yard on it. You wouldn't have seen them at Hatton Garden, but they were with me this morning.'

A waiter appeared. They ordered tea.

'And what about you?' he asked. 'What are you doing here?'

She waved a hand at her surroundings.

'Oh, this is a regular visit. I come to London from time to time in connection with the business. My father isn't strong enough to make the journey any longer. He used to love it, meeting his old friends in the trade, making bargains, all of that.'

'So what do you do when you come here?'

'I usually bring stones, rings, watches, rare items that we know we can make a good profit on. Coins too, of course. The Dublin market is small, and there's a much greater demand in London. You'll always get a good price.'

'Are you telling me that you travel on your own from Dublin carrying these things? Don't you realise that you're a dream opportunity for robbers? Some of them would murder a woman for a sixpence.'

She shrugged. 'The only time anything ever happened was last week in our own shop in Dublin, as you know. And I'm not foolish. I take suitable precautions.'

Swallow believed her. He wondered what they might involve.

The waiter brought the tea. She poured for them both.

'Now, we've had enough discussion of police work and the jewellery trade for a while,' she laughed. 'What are your proposals to entertain me for the evening? Or do I act as your guide?'

They agreed that the programme should be a compromise. He would entertain her to dinner. She would choose the venue. There was still an hour of light in the October evening. She would use it to introduce him to some of the London sights that he not seen.

They walked to Westminster. She showed him the Abbey and the Houses of Parliament. They waited to hear Big Ben strike the hour before crossing Bridge Street to the Victoria Embankment.

Katherine slipped her arm through his as they made their way along the river front. To anyone watching, they might be any courting couple taking the Embankment air, he reckoned.

The gas lights had been lit, forming a pearly chain that followed the river's curve to Waterloo Bridge. The Embankment's wide pavement was dotted with strolling couples. Here and there a brazier glowed where men roasted chestnuts for sale.

She pointed towards the arches of Waterloo Bridge.

'Did you know that Constable painted this scene? And Monet too.'

Swallow did not know that, but he could understand how the perfect proportions of the bridge, the reflection off the water and the backdrop of the city would appeal to an artist. For a moment, he allowed himself to think that what he was looking at was actually a painting. He was aware that increasingly he tended to frame the world in terms of art. It disturbed him. He came back to reality.

'I thought Constable always liked to paint rural scenes,' he said. 'Trees, lakes, river crossings, that sort of thing.'

'I imagine it was a commercial decision. For many years the poor fellow didn't sell very well in England. Nobody was particularly interested in images of the countryside.'

'You know your London well.'

She laughed.

'I should. I lived here for three years, you know. My father put me to an apprenticeship with a friend of his who had a fine business. He had a workshop near Hatton Garden and a really good outlet at Bond Street. Very fashionable. I learned a lot about the jewellery trade. It wasn't usual for a girl, of course, but my gender has never been a problem in the business. It might even have been an advantage.'

'You obviously liked it here. You weren't tempted to stay?'

They came to Cleopatra's Needle. She stopped, looking out across the river.

'I fell in love,' she said. 'But the man didn't love me. Oh, he said he did, of course. There was a year of courtship. In the end, he didn't think the daughter of a Dublin Jewish shopkeeper was a good enough match.'

'Was it a question of religion? Was he of your faith?'

'Oh yes, he was Jewish. As Jewish as you can get.' There was an edge of anger to her voice. 'His family were high up in the community here. Big people in the synagogue. They finally drove me away from any religious practice.'

'But your family was well established in Dublin. And well off too. Your parents built up a good business.'

'By their standards they saw us as struggling.' For a moment she looked sad. 'I went back to Dublin as soon as my three years were up. My mother was gone. My father needed support. It was time to put what I had learned back into the business.'

They left the river front at Lancaster Place, and walked through Aldwych to Drury Lane. By now the light was fading, and the streets were filling with theatre-goers. Elegantly dressed men and women stepped down from carriages or emerged from the restaurants and chop houses. The pavements were alive with the buzz of laughter and conversation.

The Albion was warm and welcoming. They were offered a glass of cider punch, and shown to a table with a cheerful view of the fire. They were early diners, the waiter told them. The place would really only get busy when the theatres began to close.

The menu of the evening was chalked up on a blackboard that stood beside the fireplace. Swallow had never seen such a thing. The supper house had an air of informality that he liked.

They chose from the menu, starting with fried eel, on Katherine's advice.

'They're a London specialty,' she told him. 'They catch them in the Thames estuary and they cook them in a flour batter. They're very tasty.'

When he had finished, Swallow was sure he would not seek them out again.

They had a glass of Hock with the eel. Then they both decided to take the waiter's guidance in favour of the house beefsteak. Swallow ordered a bottle of Medoc when they had finished the Hock.

'So how much are you going to tell me about your business in London?' she asked. 'I imagine that Mr Shaftoe must have turned out to be a serious criminal to bring you all the way to Scotland Yard. It makes me nervous to think of him on the loose again.'

'You needn't worry for the moment. He's safely locked up in the Tower of London now.'

'In the Tower? I thought they only used that for kings' wives before they cut their heads off.'

Swallow smiled. 'Well, they do. But it has other uses too.'

He sipped the Medoc.

'We know he was sent to Dublin by someone to find who had sold the tetradrachms. We're not sure who sent him or why he wanted the information. And we're still searching for Grace Clinton, who sold them to you. '

'That poor woman. I didn't know who she was or where to find her.'

'We'll locate her eventually, I hope.'

'I don't understand. The coins are not worth sending someone from London with a gun.'

'Shaftoe tells us that there's a plan here in London and in Dublin to defraud the Treasury in the transfer of land in Ireland.'

She looked puzzled. 'But what has that do with the coins?'

'I don't know. I think it might have something to do also with the murder of the pawnbroker Ambrose Pollock a couple of weeks ago.'

'My father knew him, but I don't think I ever met him.'

'It seemed at first that he'd been killed by his sister. It might have been some sort of family dispute. But it became clear once we started into the investigation that there were two people involved in his death. She might have been one, but she's gone missing. We don't know if she's alive or dead.'

Katherine looked puzzled. 'Then it wasn't his sister?'

'I can't say that. I can't say much with any certainty. This may not be the glittering peak of my police career.'

'I don't know much about how the police authorities view these things, but it seems to me that you've had lots of successes,' she said firmly. 'I've been forever reading about you in the newspapers. It would be unfair if you were to feel down because of one case.'

'You're only as good as your last job in the police. Credit for past successes dries up pretty quickly.'

By now the supper house had become busy. The theatres were emptying, and tables began to fill with couples and larger groups, animatedly discussing the shows they had just seen.

The waiters redoubled their speed of service and the air became thick with cigar smoke. When an attractive young woman entered on a gentleman's arm and was shown to a reserved table by the window, the restaurant broke into a round of applause and cheering. Swallow surmised that she was a leading lady or at least a prominent role in some nearby stage production.

The Medoc was finished. He ordered a second bottle.

When the wine was poured, the waiter asked if they would like to choose a dessert. They both opted for raspberry sorbet.

'They're good,' he said approvingly, savouring the raspberries. 'But they're not as good as the ones my mother grows in Newcroft.'

She smiled. 'Where's Newcroft? Is that where you grew up?'

'It's a little place in Kildare, hardly on the map. It's not even a village, more a crossroads really. My people have a business there. The usual combination, a public house and a grocery. My father died a few years back, but my mother still runs it.'

'Were they disappointed when you left your medical studies?'

'It wasn't so much that I left them,' his tone was serious. 'I told you before. I threw them away like a fool because I was too fond of drink.'

'Wouldn't you be interested in going home to take it over? Or is there someone else in the family to do that?'

'No, I'm an only son. My sister is a teacher, and she doesn't want to go back to it.'

'Maybe it's not my place to ask,' she said cautiously, 'but would it not be… well… suitable for yourself and Mrs Walsh?'

'Mrs Walsh was my landlady.' He knew his tone was sharp. 'And we… found each other's company congenial. In other circumstances, there might have been more to our relationship in the long run, I won't deny that. But there's no commitment and no expectations on either side now.'

She seemed to recoil a little at his vehemence.

'Oh, I'm sorry. It's just that you seem, well, unhappy.' Katherine finished her drink. 'I've had my own experiences of unhappiness,' she said, 'and I can recognise it when I see it.'

They had reached the end of the Medoc. A troupe of three men in evening dress with violins was making its way across the restaurant, playing for each table party. Katherine smiled and reached across and touched his hand.

'I'm not one for music, really. I think you should see me back to The Grosvenor.'

FORTY-NINE

No shot had not been fired in anger in Dymchurch for as long as anyone could remember. Some older residents claimed to have heard of an incident many years ago, when a gang of smugglers had been intercepted by Revenue men one winter's night on the Folkestone Road.

There was virtually no crime there, apart from poaching and, occasionally, some petty thieving from outhouses, usually the work of vagabonds or gypsies.

It had taken Margaret some time to adapt, to move away from the routine of constant vigilance that she had been required to follow at Mount Gessel. At the height of the Land War she had slept with a loaded shotgun by her bedside. She never went out in the open car or on horseback without her small .32 Smith and Wesson revolver.

Each night every door and window at the house had to be locked and barred. Her bedroom door had been reinforced with steel stanchions from the smithy at Loughrea. When the attacks on landlords' homes were at their height, she slept lightly, subconsciously registering the tread of the sentries on their rounds under her window.

The dimensions of her new house were exhilarating after the confines of living at the hotel in London. She delighted in the spacious proportions of the hall and the gallery, and she determined that she would make full use of the drawing-room and the dining-room when she had established herself socially in the town.

The well-tended orchards from which the house had been named were a delight. When she moved in, the apple blossom was full, scenting the air around the house. Now the fruit had been taken by the pickers with their ladders and wicker baskets, but the trees still held their leaves. She wondered how they would look after the first winds would have stripped them for winter.

For the first few weeks, she had been thorough about the house's security. She instructed the servants to ensure that the doors to front and rear were locked and bolted every night and that the shutters on the ground floor windows were folded out and barred.

That particular precaution fell away after some weeks when the maid asked for permission to go home at night because her mother was ill.

Margaret agreed to the request. The girl started to come to work late in the mornings. When Margaret came downstairs, the rooms were in darkness because the maid did not have the time to open the shutters before serving breakfast.

She reprimanded the girl, whose punctuality improved. Through some misunderstanding or neglect, though, the nightly routine of shuttering the windows ended. Margaret was conscious of the change, but she did not make an issue of it. She liked the way the morning sun came through the windows, pouring the day's light into the house. This was Dymchurch, East Sussex and not Mount Gessel, Galway.

The man who crouched, hidden in the darkness of the orchard in the October night, quickly identified the vulnerability of the un-shuttered windows. One of his skills was to locate the weak spots in a house or building. It might be a flimsy door, an easy drainpipe or a rusted grille. Domestic windows were easy. He would simply wait until the last of the lights went out.

When he made his move from the shadows, the glow of the lamp from the upstairs room had been extinguished for more than hour. He had surmised that was where the woman slept.

The man used a diamond cutter to make an almost perfect circle in the drawing-room window, just under the sash. Then he smeared the circle with gum and overlaid it with a small square of coarse flannel. In a minute or two the night air would harden the gum, melding the cloth with the glass. Then a sharp blow to the weakened area of glass would allow him to take it out silently, glued to the flannel.

He undid the clasp on the sash. The window went up noiselessly. Once inside, he lit a small candle in a reflecting holder. It gave him all the light he needed.

He moved quickly across the room to the hall and up the stairs. He halted outside the bedroom door and took the knife from its sheath. He turned the door handle.

Margaret heard it turn, just as she had heard the faint creak of the stairs a few moments earlier.

Even before that, when he had raised the window in the drawing-room, she had sensed the slight stirring, a change of pressure, in the air. Her translation from Mount Gessel to Dymchurch had not changed her pattern of shallow, fitful sleep, or diminished her alertness to the sounds of the night.

When the door opened she saw the man's form outlined behind the candle in its holder. She levelled the Smith and Wesson .32 revolver that she had taken from its place under her pillow and fired twice.

SUNDAY OCTOBER 9TH, 1887

FIFTY

Swallow was to rendezvous with Montgomery and Bright at Great Scotland Yard at 10 o'clock. They would travel to the Tower, collect Teddy Shaftoe from his cell and take up positions near The Mitre Tavern at Ely Court.

He was disappointed by the ordinariness of the famous police headquarters. It might have been any office building in the usage of some commercial company or some department of the civil service. The only indication of its status was the presence of a solitary constable in uniform at the gate facing towards Whitehall.

Jack Bright was waiting.

'Morning, Sir. My guv'nor, Sir Edward, wants a word.'

He led Swallow through the main building and up a broad staircase to the first floor. He knocked on a door and opened it on a call of 'enter.'

Swallow was struck by how much Edward Jenkinson reminded him of John Mallon. They were approximately the same age. They had the same lithe build and the same sharp, agile features.

'Swallow,' he extended a hand. 'I've heard about you.' He waved him to a seat. 'You'll be interested in this.'

He handed him a single carbon sheet.

'This came in just half an hour ago. I have the top copy.'

Swallow read the telegram.

East Sussex Constabulary Headquarters; West Street, Lewes.
From: Captain George Bentinck Luxford, Chief Constable.
To: Sir Edward Jenkinson, Special Irish Branch, Great Scotland Yard.

ADVISING RE INCIDENT AT DYMCHURCH HOME OF LADY GESSEL STOP YOU INQUIRED ON BEHALF SWALLOW DMP STOP INTRUDER WITH KNIFE SHOT BY HER EARLY HOURS THIS MORNING STOP SHE UNHARMED STOP BODY PRESUMED INTRUDER FOUND LATER WITH GSW STOP USUAL PROCEDURES BEING FOLLOWED AWAIT ANY INSTRUCTIONS STOP

The implication was as clear as it was disquieting. Unless Lady Margaret Gessel had been the victim of a random criminal attack, which was unlikely, she must have been targeted because someone wanted her silenced or out of the way. Only a handful of people, though, could have known that he was going to interview her. Fewer again would have known where she lived in rural East Sussex.

Someone, whoever it was, had to have a line into government and security intelligence.

'I need to copy this to my boss in Dublin,' he told Jenkinson.

'It's done already. Mallon and I always share information of this kind.'

Swallow was impressed if not particularly surprised.

'I spoke with him earlier this morning by telephone,' Jenkinson said. 'He's asked that we provide armed protection for Lady Gessel, which we've arranged.' Jenkinson added quickly, 'We'd have done it anyway, given her connections… Mr Mallon and I agree that the attack on the lady must indicate a security breach at senior level. In the circumstances, he wants you to return to Dublin for a review as soon as you've completed your task with Shaftoe. We can arrange for somebody to take a statement from Lady Gessel, maybe Montgomery or Bright.'

'Yes, Sir. I can see the implications.'

Jenkinson walked to the window.

'Is your visit going to pay dividends, Sergeant? Will you identify whoever is behind this business?'

'I hope so, Sir.'

'My fellows giving you all the co-operation you need?'

'Very much so.'

'Good. I'm glad to hear it.'

He went to the door, but paused as he reached for the handle.

'You've a strong reputation, Swallow. It travels before you, in case you don't know. If you ever felt like a transfer to Scotland Yard, I'd be interested in seeing if we could arrange something. I could set it up with Assistant Commissioner Monro here make it worth your while in pay and rank.'

For a moment, Swallow thought he had misheard.

'Are you… offering me a transfer? Here?'

'Mallon wouldn't thank me if you left Dublin, I know. But you could carry your pension with you. There's a standard CID allowance and a special allowance when you're attached to the Irish office as well.'

'Thank you, Sir. I'll certainly give that some thought.'

'You should. Irish fellows do very well in this job. You can write to me in confidence here.'

He felt elated. The compliment was a big one, and the offer was more exciting because it was unexpected. Christ, it would be one in the eye for Mallon and Harrel and Boyle back in Dublin to see him lined up for a fine job at Scotland Yard.

Suddenly, the day seemed a lot more attractive.

Bright was waiting in the corridor.

'Now,' Swallow said lightly. 'Let's go and collect Mr Shaftoe so we can get to meet his mysterious employer.'

FIFTY-ONE

Swallow took up position in a cafe whose windows looked out across Hatton Garden towards Ely Court and The Mitre. The Sunday streets were quiet, and for a time he was the only customer. He ordered a pot of tea.

The morning was clear and dry, giving him a clear view of the approach to the alleyway. Shortly before noon he saw Montgomery cross the street with Teddy Shaftoe to turn into Ely Court. He knew that Jack Bright was already in the public house. Between them, the two Scotland Yard men would ensure that Teddy could not make a bolt for freedom.

Teddy was to detach himself from Montgomery and go to the bar once they entered The Mitre. Montgomery had given him a sixpence, enabling him to buy two pints of ale.

'When your mark arrives, you're to go to him and tap him on the arm,' Montgomery had instructed. 'When I see that, I'll give Jack the nod. He'll exit the pub and get to the corner of the alley. His signal to Mr Swallow will be to put his hat on.'

As they crossed Holborn Circus, two men were setting up a chestnut stall on the pavement.

'CID,' Montgomery said under his breath. 'I arranged to have them on hand. They'll be useful if Shaftoe has friends here. Don't worry about the security end of it. They know nothing they don't need to know.'

Swallow had to admit silently that he was impressed. Scotland Yard's Special Irish Branch seemed to know their business. Jenkinson's job offer got more attractive the more he thought about it.

Once noon had passed the streets became busier. Londoners who had attended morning religious services were on the move, some returning home, others making their way to visit to family or friends. The

Sunday morning markets had closed by now, and traders and customers were repairing to their favourite public houses.

Swallow watched perhaps a dozen men and one or two women proceed along Hatton Garden and turn in for The Mitre. From their dress and demeanour he reckoned they were locals. He saw no one who matched Teddy Shaftoe's description of the well-dressed gentleman from whom he claimed to take his orders.

He heard 1 o'clock strike from the nearby tower of St Etheldreda's Church. Then he heard the half hour. There was still no sign of Shaftoe's contact or Jack Brights' signal when the clock struck 2.

Swallow saw one of the CID men sauntering up Hatton Garden from his chestnut stand. It was likely, Swallow reckoned, that he too sensed that something had gone wrong.

He was on his third pot of tea, shortly after the clocks struck 3, when he saw a young boy of perhaps twelve or thirteen years scamper into Ely Court. A minute later he came out again and took off along the street, heading in the direction of Clerkenwell Road. He had scarcely passed from Swallow's sight when Montgomery emerged from the alleyway.

The Scotland Yard man made no attempt at secrecy. He waved to Swallow to step out into the street. He looked dejected and frustrated.

'I think we must have been rumbled. There's no sign of any contact in there.'

'Where's Shaftoe?' Swallow asked.

'I left Bright minding him inside.'

He jerked his thumb towards the public house. As he pointed, there was a crack that Swallow knew was a gunshot. Then another. And another.

Montgomery swung around. There was commotion at the doorway of The Mitre. Customers were spilling out, scrambling past each other. A man half-stepped, half-fell into the alley and shouted.

'Murder... murder! Someone get the coppers!'

They sprinted up the alley and into the bar. Swallow heard a woman scream as he went through the door. Two other women with frightened faces pushed past him, making their way out to the street.

Inside, the air was acrid with gunsmoke. A ring of customers was pressing around two human outlines on the floor. A dark, spreading pool was forming under them. One of them stirred, then rolled over and attempted to rise, clutching at the wound in its side. It was Jack Bright.

The other did not move. Swallow saw a neat, round hole in the middle of Teddy Shaftoe's forehead. He was quite dead.

MONDAY OCTOBER 10TH, 1887

FIFTY-TWO

Summer attempted a brief comeback in Dublin on Monday morning. For half a day, the October chill gave way to bright sunshine with sufficient warmth to induce a sense of well-being among a citizenry that had become reconciled to the inevitability of shortening days and dark skies. Gentlemen temporarily shed their overcoats and ladies substituted parasols for rain umbrellas.

Nursemaids took children into the gardens on the great Georgian Squares in the morning. Labourers and porters threw off their jackets and worked in their shirtsleeves. There were reports that bathers had appeared at Sandymount and other beaches around the bay.

The city's shopping streets were busy. The pleasant weather always encouraged ladies to travel into town from the affluent suburbs of Rathmines and Pembroke. They crowded the fashionable shops on Grafton Street and South Great George's Street, or met to gossip in the coffee shops.

The surge in social and commercial activity also meant a surge in crime. Before Inspector 'Duck' Boyle briefed the morning shift at Exchange Court, constables had reported the movement of pick-pockets around the shopping streets. Known thieves were reported to be in the vicinity both of Pim's and Switzer's department stores on Grafton Street.

'Duck' Boyle had gone through the morning post diligently, including the bundle of letters and circulars that had been delivered earlier from the Commissioner's office. Correspondence addressed to the 'Member-in-Charge' or to 'the Detective Office,' he opened himself. Where items were addressed to particular officers, he conscientiously placed them in a rack of pigeon-holes, each one named for an individual G-man.

Trainee Detective Johnny Vizzard came into the parade room a moment after the news came in of a felonious threat to Switzer's. Boyle jerked a thumb towards the door.

'Don't even take yer hat off, Vizzard. Get up to Grafton Street. There's robbers been spotted in Switzer's and the doors barely opened fer business.'

It was said among G-men that the General Manager at Switzer's was a senior figure in the Freemasons, and that he mixed socially with senior officials from the Upper Yard. For whatever reason, the security of commerce at his store was an unchallenged priority.

Vizzard knew the score.

'Yes, Inspector.' He turned on his heel and made for the door.

It was three hours later, after a fruitless game of hide and seek around the counters and floors of the department store, when Vizzard got back to Exchange Court. He picked Sergeant Devenney's telegram out of the pigeon-hole with his name over it.

'Christ,' he said out loud. 'We have her.'

'Duck' Boyle was not challenged by a great imagination. Once the connections between things were set out to him, though, he could quickly sense the importance of a situation. He read and reread Devenney's telegram, then he went down the Yard to John Mallon's office and reported its content to the chief.

'Swallow is supposed to be crossing from London today,' Mallon said. 'We'd be best to delay things for a few more hours until he gets here. After this length of time it's not going to make a big difference. He'll have to be briefed, and we'll need to have the Constabulary move on this,' he told Boyle. 'The old RIC fellows have a nose for anything out of the ordinary. Have Swallow met off the mail boat at Kingstown.'

FIFTY-THREE

The Holyhead packet landed Swallow at Kingstown's Carlisle Pier in the early afternoon.

There had been little he could do at The Mitre once the initial investigation by the CID had got under way. Teddy Shaftoe was dead, it was reckoned, before he hit the floor, a revolver bullet through his brain and another in his heart. Detective Constable Jack Bright was going to survive the knife slash to his side that he sustained as he tried to grapple with the gunman who had emerged from somewhere at the rear of the public house.

The eyewitness accounts were poor. The assailant was tall and short, dark and fair, bearded and clean shaven. The only point on which they concurred was that he was fit and fast, but nobody at The Mitre had seen him before.

Shaftoe had been downing the last of his ale, one man said, when the first shot was fired. Bright had lunged at the gunman, possibly not seeing the heavy-bladed knife in his other hand. The gunman fired twice more, and lashed out at Bright with the knife. Then, his work done, he had run back through the rear of the house, scaling a low wall to make his escape along the alleyways and yards leading to Farringdon Street.

Montgomery was distraught.

'If I hadn't left Jack with him on his own it wouldn't have happened,' he insisted to Swallow. 'The bastard saw his chance when I stepped out to talk to you.'

Privately, Swallow did not disagree. But there was nothing to be gained from saying so.

'The important thing is that Bright's going to recover,' he said. 'He's lucky the gun wasn't turned on him.'

The CID men who had been masquerading as chestnut vendors had commandeered a cab and taken Jack Bright to Charing Cross Hospital. Other CID men had arrived swiftly at The Mitre along with a photographer.

A sceptical detective sergeant took Swallow's witness statement. He had difficulty understanding what an armed G-man from Dublin was doing on his patch. Montgomery had to invoke the authority of the Special Irish Branch and Sir Edward Jenkinson to persuade him that his presence had been sanctioned at the highest levels.

Later, Montgomery took him to Euston Station for the Holyhead train.

'I know my guv'nor was going to talk to you about maybe coming to work at the Yard,' he said as the cab drew up at Euston. 'I'd like that if you did. Will you think about it?'

'I will,' Swallow told him.

He meant it. He turned Jenkinson's offer over in his head as the train sped through the night, across the midlands, over the Welsh Marches and on to Holyhead. The idea of a completely fresh start excited him. At forty-three, not many got that sort of chance. A whole new life.

Then he thought of Harriet. God knows what scrapes his young sister was going to get into with her politics and her romantic notions. He felt he needed to be around to steer her through the next few years until she got sense. But he couldn't be on hand for ever. Sooner or later, she would have to learn to fend for herself.

There was the home place in Kildare too. His mother was getting on. While she accepted that he had no interest in the business, she still looked forward to his visits when he took leave. Maybe the business would have to be sold, passing from their family hands.

A new life in London would be attractive, but it would come at a price, and that was before his relationship with Maria came into the calculation. He realised with a start that she had been crowded from his mind since he left Dublin.

Johnny Vizzard was waiting for him at Kingstown.

Summer's brief resurgence was already on the wane, and the sky across the city was filling with dark clouds from the west. They took the train into Westland Row. Vizzard recounted the intelligence they had received from County Meath as they travelled.

'I knew they were gone somewhere on the Great Western, but I'd thought they'd be farther away. The damnable thing is it took so long for the constabulary to find them.'

'Mr Mallon wanted us to wait until you got back,' he explained. 'We're ready to move as soon as you are. He's telegraphed the County Inspector at Navan. There's an arrest and search party of RIC being assembled at Trim police barracks at 6 o'clock.'

Swallow made a quick diversion to Heytesbury Street for a wash, a shave and a change of clothes. He thought again about Jenkinson's offer as he shaved, examining himself in the mirror. He looked well, he knew. He was fit and healthy. Not a bad catch for Scotland Yard. Not a bad catch for a younger woman either. He felt energised as he made his way back to the Castle.

An hour later, along with Johnny Vizzard, he was on a train out of the Broadstone station.

FIFTY-FOUR

It was a quarter of an hour by trap from Trim Barracks to the townland of Clonlar.

There was no reason to anticipate any trouble, but the County Inspector was taking no chances on a matter that had been referred directly to him by the head of G-Division. The police party, in two traps, consisted of six armed constables, Devenney and a Head Constable from Navan who knew the area well. Swallow and Vizzard travelled with Devenney in the lead trap.

Sergeant Devenney had garnered some additional intelligence. Mrs Armstrong had sent a servant girl into the town twice during the week to buy groceries and supplies. From discreet inquiries among the shopkeepers he learned that the purchases were out of pattern, including extra bacon, flour, sugar and cured fish.

Later, the sergeant had sent a constable in plain clothes to walk the road past the Armstrong house. From a distance along the avenue he could hear the sounds of children laughing at play somewhere around the house.

Elizabeth Armstrong opened the door, allowing candlelight to faintly illuminate the steps of the house. From her strained features, Swallow surmised that the arrival of the police was not entirely unexpected.

'Sergeant Devenney, good evening to you.' Her voice was even but controlled.

'Good evening to you, Mrs Armstrong. This is Detective Sergeant Swallow and Detective Vizzard of the Dublin Metropolitan Police. We'd be glad of a word.'

'Please, come in.'

She led them into a well-furnished parlour, already lit with oil-burning brass lamps as if they had been expected. It was the house of a comfortable farming family, Swallow reckoned, owning their own land over generations, and very probably unconcerned and untouched by the struggle between landlord and tenant that raged across much of the country.

She did not invite them to sit. Somewhere in the back of the house, they heard a child's voice calling.

'The Dublin Metropolitan Police?' she unsuccessfully attempted a smile. 'This is a surprise out here in County Meath.'

'Sergeant Swallow and Detective Vizzard would like to speak to your daughter, Mrs Armstrong,' Devenney said. 'That would be your daughter Grace, Mrs Clinton, I believe.'

'In what connection would that be?' Now there was a tremor in the voice.

'I'm afraid I can't disclose that to you Ma'am,' Swallow said. 'It's in connection with a police inquiry. We'd need to speak to Mrs Clinton herself.'

'Have you authority to do that? Outside of Dublin?'

'Strictly speaking, no, Mrs Armstrong,' Devenney said, clearing his throat. 'This matter is now under the jurisdiction of the Royal Irish Constabulary. But these men will be operating under my authority. I promise you it'll all be in order.'

The door opened, and a dark haired woman walked in. Swallow reckoned she might be thirty, perhaps thirty-five. There was no doubting that she was Elizabeth Armstrong's daughter. The same strong build, sallow skin, rounded features.

'I'm Grace Clinton. I know why you're here. There isn't any need to speak to my mother about your business. She's got nothing to do with it.'

For a moment Swallow thought the older woman was about to step between her daughter and the policemen.

'Thank you Ma'am, ah… Mrs Clinton. My name is Swallow. I'm a detective sergeant of the DMP. We've been trying to find you for some time. We need to talk privately. May I ask, is your husband here?'

'Yes, he's resting upstairs. He's been under a lot of strain.'

'Then I think you should tell him that you need to discuss something with us pertaining to a police matter. And I may need to see him later.'

'I believe you will, Mr Swallow,' she said flatly.

She turned to her mother.

'Will you tell Arthur the police are here, Mother? And tell him I've agreed to speak to them. It's for the best now.'

FIFTY-FIVE

'Will you sit down, Sergeant… Mr Swallow, Mr Vizzard?'

They settled themselves, drawing notebooks and pencils.

'I think it'd be best if you tell us what you think we should know, Mrs Clinton,' Devenney said. 'But you understand this is a serious matter. You're under suspicion for a crime. And I must tell you that anything you say after this may be written down and used in evidence at a trial.'

She drew a small, embroidered handkerchief from her dress. Swallow suspected that she was close to tears, but whether they might indicate relief, distress or self-pity he could not guess.

'I've been foolish,' she said after a moment. 'Very foolish.'

'Our concern here is with the coins that you brought into Greenberg's jewellers shop on Capel Street, Mrs Clinton,' Vizzard said softly. 'We need to know how you came into possession of them.'

Swallow was surprised by Vizzard's manner. He had a gentleness in his approach that belied his zeal.

'I… I found them.'

'Where?'

'In the street. Yes, I found them in the street, near St Peter's Church. They were in a purse.'

'When was this, Mrs Clinton?' Devenney asked.

'A few weeks back, I can't remember exactly when.'

Devenney's response was diplomatic, but there was a harder edge to his voice.

'If someone found something valuable like that, they'd have a duty to bring it to the police, Ma'am.'

'I… I suppose I should have.'

'Indeed, Mrs Clinton,' Swallow said. 'There's an offence known as stealing by finding. I'm sure your husband, being a legal man, would have known that. It can carry a heavy sentence, depending on the value of the goods involved.'

She twisted the handkerchief between her fingers.

'I don't know what to say... what will happen?'

Swallow could not sustain Devenney's qualities of patience.

'What happens will largely depend on yourself. Are you sure about finding the coins on the street? Because we've reason to believe they were taken elsewhere in a criminal action. We're also investigating a murder case and the disappearance of a woman who may be in danger or even dead. These coins may be important as evidence. If you tell the truth, and if it helps us, it'll work to your benefit. Now,' his tone was sharp, 'wouldn't you like to reconsider your version of this? We know there's a reason why you and your family left your home and why your husband left his place of employment.'

There was a silence. Then Grace Clinton began to sob into her handkerchief.

'I... I discovered the coins in my husband's wardrobe at our house. I know I shouldn't have taken them. But... I found it very difficult... impossible to keep the house on the allowance that he provided. One of the children has been ill and... there were doctors' bills. Arthur has debts... big debts to pay.'

Sergeant Devenney scribbled hurriedly in his notebook. He exchanged a look with Swallow.

'You're telling us you stole... took... the coins from your husband,' Vizzard said. 'Why would you need to steal with a good salary coming into the house?'

She dabbed at her eyes with the handkerchief.

'It's... not as simple as that. Arthur has been a gambler all his life. It isn't easy for me to speak of this but I must, I know. He wagered money that he didn't have. He'll wager money at cards or on horse races. He owes money that I don't think he'll ever be able to pay. I had to look after our children, don't you see?'

Devenney put down his pencil.

'I can understand that. A man given to gambling... that's a cross to bear for any family. Do you know where your husband might have got these coins from?'

She shivered, although the room was not cold.

'I do now… unfortunately. And that's why we had to get away from Dublin to where we thought we would be safe… with my mother. Arthur's life was in danger and so was mine… and maybe the children's.'

'Would you explain that to us, Ma'am?' Vizzard said.

Before she could answer, there was a scream in the hallway. The door of the room was flung open. Elizabeth Armstrong rushed in, followed by one of Devenney's constables.

The older woman seized her daughter by the arms.

'Oh Grace… Dear God… Dear God.'

The constable's face was white. He looked helplessly at Devenney and the two G-men.

'It's the husband, Clinton. He's out in the barn. He's after hangin' himself.'

FIFTY-SIX

Arthur Clinton probably reckoned he had done a good job of it. He had climbed to the top of the winter hay, stored high in the barn behind the house. Then he worked his way out along a roof beam. From there, he looped the rope around one of the rafters and launched himself, as he hoped, into eternity.

Now he was dangling eight feet above the ground, where the yellow light from the police lanterns caught the kicking and thrashing of his legs. A constable had tried to manipulate a ladder to reach him but it had fallen short, bringing the man and the ladder crashing on to the floor.

Vizzard was first through the barn door.

'Here, give me that.'

He seized the nearest constable's sabre from its scabbard before the man could react, then he was scaling the piled hay and scrambling his way out along the beam.

If Clinton's intention had been to make a quick end of himself by breaking his neck with a hangman's knot, he had miscalculated. Instead, he was being slowly strangled. Even as Swallow and Devenney gazed up in horror the thrashing of his legs started to slow.

Vizzard swung himself forward on the rafter, one hand grasping the rough timber, the other reaching out with the sabre to where Clinton had looped the rope. The steel cut through the fibres with the force of Vizzard's downward slash, sending Arthur Clinton plunging to the floor below.

Swallow and Devenney heard the crack of bone. His face had turned purple around bulging eyes, the rope scarcely visible in the deep groove it had cut into the neck. Devenney dashed forward and started to dig his fingers between ligature and flesh. At first, he could get no purchase, but then he got one finger under the cord and pulled hard, drawing it away half an inch. He cut the noose with a swift upward stroke of his pen-knife. For several moments, Clinton was immobile, apparently unable to breathe, then he started drawing air.

Grace Clinton had followed Swallow and the other G-men from the house into the barn. When she saw her husband immobile on the floor, she screamed.

'Oh Jesus, no… no.'

For a moment she failed to comprehend the scene of Johnny Vizzard climbing down from the hay, sabre in hand, to the congratulations of the constables.

Then she saw the severed rope and understood.

'Get that off its hinges and take him into the house,' Devenney ordered, indicating the side door of the barn. 'Put him lying down and get blankets to keep him warm.'

They put the would-be suicide on it and carried him to the house, laying him on a sofa in the parlour. Both of his feet were at a crooked angle, and a splinter of white bone protruded from one leg above the ankle.

As he came to consciousness, the pain flared in his broken bones and the contusions around his neck.

'The big danger is shock,' Swallow said. 'Is there anything to stimulate the blood? Whiskey? Brandy?'

Elizabeth Armstrong found brandy in the sideboard cupboard. Devenney uncorked it and held it to Clinton's lips. He took a little, swallowed and then drank some more.

There was a sudden commotion as two little girls burst into the parlour, eyes wide with fright and confusion. Elizabeth Armstrong intercepted them as they ran to their father on the sofa.

'Hush now, girls… hush… out of here.'

She ushered them back to the door and into the arms of a woman that Swallow reckoned to be a maid or a cook. He heard their wailing as they were taken away to some more tranquil part of the house.

'Your husband is badly injured,' Devenney told Grace Clinton. 'We'll need to get him to hospital. It looks to me as if he's got two broken ankles and maybe more fractures. The open car is the fastest and the safest way of getting him there. I'll send two men with him.'

'You'd better go too,' Swallow told Johnny Vizzard. 'And get a message to Mr Mallon. Tell him what's happened.'

When they had gone, Devenney and Swallow went back to the parlour with Grace Clinton and her mother.

Elizabeth Armstrong had regained much of her composure. Her daughter, by contrast, had collapsed, sobbing into a chair, her face buried in her hands.

'I'm sorry to have to press you,' Swallow's tone was firm, 'but if there's to be any salvation out of this for yourself... for your children... you'd be best to tell us what's been going on. What drove your husband to that desperate course?'

She emitted a long, deep sigh.

'I know... I know. I've already told you about the gambling... and the lack of money. To be reduced to coming home here to my mother... in these circumstances.'

She started to sob bitterly again.

'I took the coins from Arthur's wardrobe, but when he found out, he flew into a terrible rage. When he heard that there had been an attack on the shop in Capel Street where I sold them, he got into a panic. Then we learned that the police had been at the house. He said we were all in mortal danger and that was why we came here... for safety.'

'Safety?' Swallow asked. 'What was the danger?'

'I don't know... I don't know... I tried to get him to explain, to tell me. He told me he shouldn't have had the coins at all, but he would never tell me what he meant by that. He was like a man being hunted.'

'I think, Mrs Clinton,' Swallow said slowly, 'that the coins, and maybe some other valuables, had to do with his work on some land transfers.'

'I think that's so. And I think he had got caught up in something that was wrong and that he couldn't get out of. He's not a bad man; he's just not very strong in certain ways.'

'Did it occur to you at the time that the coins might not be his? Or that he had come by them improperly?' Vizzard asked.

'Arthur is not a thief,' she said indignantly.

Devenney shifted uncomfortably in his seat.

'Of course Ma'am. Nobody was suggesting that.'

Swallow wished Devenney had stayed quiet.

'You say he told you he shouldn't have had the coins. What do you make of that now?'

'I don't... I don't know.'

She fell silent, staring at the floor.

'Is that all, Mrs Clinton?' Swallow asked after an interval. 'There's nothing more you want to tell us?'

When she looked back at him, he saw that her eyes had hardened. Swallow decided that this was a woman who could mobilise strength under a show of grief.

'No... I've told you everything.'

'We're going to have to go to the infirmary to interview your husband now. You'll be needed here with your children. Sergeant Devenney will leave some of his men here so you'll be safe. You don't need me to tell you that someone badly wants to know where the coins came from. And they're prepared to use any means to get that information.'

'Are there... legal consequences for my daughter from what she has told you?' Elizabeth Armstrong asked.

Swallow answered carefully.

'On the basis of what she's told us, I doubt it. She took property that belonged, as she thought, to her husband. Unless he wants her charged, I can't see that she has committed any crime.'

But he knew he was still only hearing parts of the story. What Grace Clinton had told him was not nearly the full version.

FIFTY-SEVEN

An hour later, Swallow and Devenney joined Johnny Vizzard at the Navan Infirmary.

The open police car had bucked and swayed along the rutted road from Clonlar, its lamps flaring against the trees. The October night was dark and a strong wind had picked up, whipping their words away across the bogland.

'I presume you know what's going on here?' Devenney called against the gale. 'Because I'm damned if I do. What's this land business and the thing about stolen coins?'

'I'm not a lot wiser than you,' Swallow shouted back, cupping his hands to his mouth to amplify his voice. 'I think it's basically about stripping the big houses that are being closed down in the land transfers.'

He was not going to have a local sergeant of the RIC, living among a rural community, aware of a possible corruption of the land transfer process.

'So you think Clinton was fingering this stuff? Making a bit of extra money on the side, lifting property out of the estate?'

Swallow shrugged. 'Maybe. Hopefully he'll tell us. The wife had been selling the coins for a fraction of their value. Our job was to find out where she got them from.'

His voice trailed off as the wind picked up. Now there was rain too, driving across the scrub, spinning leaves and bits of branches before it. By the time they reached Navan, they were soaked. They were thankful to dismount and find the shelter of the Infirmary's gloomy hallway.

But Arthur Clinton was not in a position to tell them any more than they knew. The expression on the doctor's face was grim. Clinton's legs were encased in plaster and he had been heavily dosed with laudanum to counter the pain of his two shattered ankles. Even so, shortly after arriving he had begun to vomit blood.

'We did our best,' the doctor told Swallow, 'but I had to pronounce him half an hour ago.'

'What happened?'

'We'll do a post-mortem shortly. At a guess, given what I'm told, I'd say there's a punctured lung or maybe the pericardial sac. There's four or five broken ribs. Any one of them could have thrown out a splinter. He drowned in his own blood, I'm afraid.'

Devenney groaned in frustration. He finally abandoned the disciplined restraint he had maintained since returning to duty.

'Ah, Fuck it. Fuck it, anyway, after all that. If he'd hanged himself properly at least we'd be warm and dry.'

FIFTY-EIGHT

Just after 4 o'clock in the afternoon, while Swallow and Vizzard were on their way to Clonlar, policemen with warrants signed by Dr Henry Lafeyre, the City Medical Examiner and *ex officio* Justice of the Peace, visited a number of premises around Dublin. They included a number of dwelling houses, as well as Greenberg's jewellers shop on Capel Street.

Three bangs on the door of the Clinton house on the North Circular Road failed to elicit any response, so a constable put a jemmy bar to the lock and levered it against the frame. There was a sharp snap as the bolt was sprung from the receiver. The door swung open. Lafeyre led the way in.

'Nobody here to be interested in this,' he muttered, waving the search warrant in the air before putting it back in his pocket.

'Where do you want to start, Doctor?' Stephen Doolan asked.

'The bedrooms first, then work down.'

A brass-framed double bed, two wardrobes and two matching dressing-tables identified the principal bedroom on the first floor. It was a bright, airy room, recently decorated. Lafeyre opened one of the wardrobes to reveal dresses on hangers.

He drew a grey metal box from his bag, along with a small, fine brush.

'You won't mind if I watch?' Doolan asked. 'I've heard of this but never seen it done.'

'Of course. This is fine graphite,' Lafeyre told him, dipping the brush into the open box.

He dusted the polished surface of the wardrobe with the black powder. Then he opened the wardrobe door so that it caught the light from the window.

'Have a look at this.'

Doolan angled himself to peer along the mahogany.

'Christ, I wouldn't have believed it. You can see the finger-marks like they were put on with pen and ink.'

'Over here please,' Lafeyre signalled to the photographer. 'Get your lens to take the same angle as the Sergeant and you'll see the marks.'

The photographer trundled his tripod and camera across the room. He adjusted it for height and range. Then, firing off phosphorescent flashes, he started taking pictures.

As the room filled with acrid smoke from the flashes, Lafeyre and Doolan went downstairs, making for the front garden and the fresh air.

'So how does it work from here?' Doolan asked.

Lafeyre grinned.

'I'll tell you that in a few days when I know the answer myself.'

When the photographer had finished, the police party mounted the open car and made for Capel Street and Greenberg's.

The G-man on protection duty recognised Lafeyre and Doolan. He accompanied them into the shop.

Doolan introduced himself to Ephram and Katherine.

'Beg your pardon, Sir... Ma'am... for the inconvenience. I have instructions to take photographs for evidence. It'll only take half an hour at most. Can I take it you have no objections?'

Ephram spread his hands in a gesture of helplessness.

'As you can see, there are no customers here. You are welcome to do what you must, but please be as quick as you can, and if any customers come in please understand that I will have to deal with them as a matter of priority.'

Lafeyre beckoned to the street. The photographer and his assistant climbed down from the car and came in, burdened with their equipment.

'Is all this necessary?' Ephram Greenberg asked Lafeyre. 'And who are you?'

'I'm Dr Henry Lafeyre, Justice of the Peace and also the City Medical Examiner. These men are photographers who work for the police. As the sergeant told you, we'll only be a short time here.'

'Are you investigating the attempted robbery here?' Katherine asked, puzzled.

'Yes, Miss. That, and a number of other crimes.'

'Is the case not being investigated by Detective Sergeant Swallow?'

'Yes, we work together. He's engaged in other duties today.'

'I don't understand,' she said sharply. 'We made full statements to the police. What are you looking for? Nobody told us to expect a visit from... photographers.'

'Put the camera there,' Lafeyre instructed the photographer, pointing to the glass counter top in front of where Katherine stood.

'That may be so,' he told her firmly, 'but there are matters on which I have to gather evidence. I would hope for your co-operation. If I need to, I am possessed of a warrant that I can invoke.'

'I'd like to see it, please.'

He drew the warrant from his pocket and handed it to her. She scrutinised it carefully before handing it back without a word.

While the photographer assembled his equipment, Lafeyre dusted the glass with graphite. Then he angled himself so that he was looking across the smooth surface of the glass towards the window giving on to Capel Street.

'This will do fine,' he told the photographer. 'You'll hardly need any flash at all, I'd guess.'

When he had finished, Lafeyre thanked the Greenbergs and made for the street with the photographer.

'What's the quickest you can get me prints?'

'It'll take maybe twenty-four hours, Doctor, because I'll have to use different lights to bring them up. That's slow with all the chemical changes as well.'

'You'll do your best for me, I know. There may be answers to a few nasty questions in what you bring up.'

TUESDAY OCTOBER 11TH, 1887

FIFTY-NINE

It was past midnight by the time Swallow and Vizzard reached the city on a slow goods train they had boarded at Trim. Notwithstanding the hour, Swallow knew that the chief would expect his briefing from London as well as an up-to-the-minute report on what had happened at Clonlar.

Mallon listened intently to his narrative, taking occasional notes. Swallow wondered if he knew that Jenkinson had offered him a job in London. If he did, he gave nothing away.

'There's very big stakes being played for,' Mallon said finally. 'Someone took a hell of a chance in killing Shaftoe under the eyes of the Scotland Yard men. And Margaret Gessel's lucky to be alive.'

He had opened a bottle of Bushmills, and poured one for each of them.

'Arthur Clinton must have been pushed beyond the brink of sanity to do what he did. A man with a young family, like that…'

'It's a pity we didn't get to him sooner,' Swallow said. 'The RIC slipped up badly.'

'You think Clinton's wife – widow – has more to tell?' Mallon asked.

'I don't doubt it.'

'You'd be as well to bed down in the dormitory. I'd like you to be available in the morning. I'm going to brief the Commissioner and the Security Secretary and I'll want you there.'

Swallow was glad to make it to the Spartan comfort of the Exchange Court dormitory. In spite of the hard bed, and the comings and goings of G-men on early shifts, he slept like a baby.

'Dr Lafeyre was in. Said he was hoping he'd see you, Skipper,' the duty G-man at the public office told him when he emerged on the following morning.

'When was that?'

'Ten minutes ago. I didn't know you were billeted above. I told him I'd give you the message when you got in. He said if you had a minute would you drop down to his office.'

Harry Lafeyre usually worked from the morgue on Abbey Street or from his house, but he was also provided with a small office in the Lower Yard, near the Army Pay Office. It gave him convenient access when working with the police, and it provided a secure place to store exhibits that might be used for evidence.

Swallow had not yet had any breakfast, but the thought that Lafeyre probably had some news for him spurred him on.

'Sure. I'll go down. If anyone wants me, tell them where I am.'

'You've been travelling, I hear,' Lafeyre quipped as Swallow came in. 'Off to London to see the lady?'

Swallow was shocked. How could Lafeyre have heard about his encounter with Katherine in London?

'What do you mean? How did you know?'

'I assumed you'd have an audience with Her Majesty. Didn't you do a lot to make her dim-witted grandson's visit a success here in the summer?' Lafeyre grinned.

'Sorry, I thought you meant something else,' Swallow mumbled. 'I was trying to identify who's running this fellow Shaftoe. But then somebody plugged him under my nose in a public house.'

Lafeyere grimaced. 'Dear God. That's dramatic.'

'That's not the half of it.'

He recounted what had happened at Clonlar during the night. Lafeyre shook his head as if disbelieving.

'You've had a run of bad luck it seems. And enough drama too. Dead men everywhere. But I may have a bit of news that might help a little.'

He drew a file from his bag.

'It's to do with Ambrose Pollock. You felt that two people were involved in his killing, or at least in tying the knots that fastened him to the chair. I think I can tell you something about them.'

He opened the file.

'I've been keeping up with new developments in the identification of fingerprints. Do you know anything about it?'

Swallow shrugged. 'Not a lot. I know there's been some research. In India, I think. Nobody seems to be sure how to make any use of it.'

'It's vague still, but the basic premise is valid: that every human's finger ridges are unique. That's accepted universally. The difficulty is how to match the finger-marks made at crime scenes to particular individuals.'

Swallow smiled. 'I suppose you'll tell me you've found a way to do it.'

'Afraid not,' Lafeyre shook his head. 'There's some work being done by a Scottish doctor called Faulds and also an Englishman called Galton. He's a relation of Charles Darwin, actually. But what I've been working on is a technique for bringing up finger-marks that aren't always visible to the naked eye.'

'So you found something at Lamb Alley?'

'Indeed I did. The researchers who've been at this up to now have used ink powder or even fine sand to bring up finger-marks. The fingers have sweat glands. They leave a patterned mark on a smooth surface. You may not see it, but it's there. Dusting it with ink powder or sand will bring the patterns up, and in certain light you can see them. You can even photograph them if you have the right equipment.

'Now,' he said, 'I was watching Lily one evening sharpening some pencils and I noticed the very fine graphite that she pared off the lead, as it's called. It's lighter and finer and it's more adhesive than ink powder. So I collected a quantity of it and I dusted the smooth surfaces around Ambrose Pollock's chair and desk.'

'Go on,' Swallow said, 'this better be leading somewhere. I'm supposed to be going to a meeting up the Yard with Chief Mallon any minute now.'

'Just be patient,' Lafeyre waved a hand. 'Have a look at these.'

He dropped half a dozen photographic prints on the table. Swallow could see that each showed the distinctive whorls and loops of a human fingerprint

'I brought these images up from Pollock's desk and chair,' Lafeyre said. 'Do you notice anything unusual about them?'

Swallow shook his head. 'Well, I can see that they're not all identical. Should I see something else?'

'You're right. These marks are made by two different individuals. And they're actually blood marks. Even better than sweat marks.'

'So they were made by the killer or killers?'

'It's not as simple as that. One set was quite freshly made. The blood was not coagulated, so that tells us the marks were made in or around the time of death. And they were on the iron weight that we think was used as the murder weapon. The others were much stickier, if I can use the term. You can see that if you put them under the microscope.'

'So they were made later?'

'Anything from a few hours to the next day.'

'Let me get this absolutely clear,' Swallow said. 'You have finger-marks from one person who was at the scene at the time of death. Then there are marks from someone else who was there later?'

'Yes. We know the likelihood is that Phoebe was involved in this somewhere. I think she used the rope to tie him in his chair so anybody looking in would see him there as usual. That's why the knots were different. The person who killed Ambrose tied one rope. Phoebe tied the second.'

'I was right, then,' Swallow said. 'There were two different knots tied by two different people.'

'That's a sustainable thesis now that we know there were two people on the scene.'

'It still doesn't bring us any closer to knowing who the killer is.'

Lafeyre wagged a finger.

'Don't be so negative. I think I can take this a bit further. You don't have anything to scale them against, but in my view both marks were made by women. They're smaller than the marks made by a man's fingers. The French scientist, Bertillon, gives estimates for the dimensions of women's finger-marks, and these fall within his measures. They could be children's of course, but I guess we can rule that out as a serious possibility.'

'Women? Are you saying that Ambrose Pollock was murdered by two women?'

Lafeyre grimaced.

'Look, you've got your meeting in the Upper Yard. Come and see me after that. I'll give you lunch at the United Services Club. I think I might have something very important to tell you then.'

SIXTY

'The Chief"'s gone up to the Commissioner and the Security Secretary this past hour. He wants you up there on the double.'

Mallon's clerk had left the sanctuary of his office to deliver the summons to Swallow in the crime sergeants' office.

'Christ knows what's up. He got a call from Mr Jenkinson in London there around 9 o'clock and took off like a scalded cat. He's been up there since.'

'All right, thanks. I was expecting he'd send for me,' Swallow said, making for the door.

He crossed the Upper Yard to the Georgian block that housed the Chief Secretary's department. A clerk led him through an outer office populated by a cohort of other functionaries to the Under-Secretary's room.

In spite of the chilly October weather and the early hour, the room was warm. It was also more crowded than Swallow had ever seen it on any previous visit.

The Under-Secretary, West Ridgeway, sat at his desk, flanked by the Assistant Under-Secretary for Security, Howard Smith Berry. Swallow thought that Smith Berry looked distraught.

John Mallon sat on a straight-backed chair in front of the desk. The Commissioner of the Dublin Metropolitan Police, Sir David Harrel, sat beside Mallon.

Major Nigel Kelly, the head of the secret service group established to report directly to the Assistant Under-Secretary, stood by the window, staring down into the Lower Yard. Swallow and Kelly had clashed in the past. Swallow detested Kelly, and he knew the feeling was mutual.

'Sergeant Swallow,' West Ridgeway greeted him solemnly, pointing to a vacant chair beside John Mallon.

'It appears that we have a situation on our hands that is potentially very serious for the government. Mr Mallon has briefed us. Is there any further news from London?'

'I'm afraid there's none that's either conclusive or very helpful, Sir.'

'I've briefed the meeting on the purpose of your London visit as well as what happened last night in County Meath,' Mallon said. 'Would you take us on from there?'

'I hoped to find the principal mischief maker, the top man, in London,' Swallow explained. 'Shaftoe had undertaken to identify him for me. But Shaftoe's dead, shot almost in my sight.'

West Ridgeway nodded. 'Do you suspect that there was a leak somewhere? Was this top man, as you call him, tipped off?'

'It's hard to say with certainty, Sir, but it looks like it.'

'Outrageous,' Kelly said, turning from the window.

West Ridgeway gestured him to silence.

'That would be a matter of the utmost seriousness, but as of now it is only speculation. Go through last evening's events in County Meath, Sergeant.'

'Cutting it short, Sir, the RIC found the Clintons on this farm at Clonlar. It's not far from the town of Trim. Mrs Clinton's home place, it turns out. She says she took the coins from the husband. So the next question is: where did he get them? And then, while we're interviewing her, he hangs himself out in the barn at the back of the house.'

Mallon raised a hand to pause the narrative. Swallow could hear shouted commands below in the Yard at the changing of the guard at the Justice Gate.

'Mrs Clinton told Sergeant Swallow enough to confirm his original suspicion,' Mallon said. 'Clinton was engaged in conveyancing the assets of the Mount Gessel estate, and he was stripping off valuables as he did so. That's how he got the coins. It seems likely that he also misappropriated the Gessel family silver and arranged for it to find its way into Pollock's basement.'

West Ridgeway nodded.

'It's a pity that Clinton isn't around to tell us more. I still can't see how this connects to the murder of Ambrose Pollock.'

Smith Berry waved a hand impatiently.

'With respect, Sir, the Pollocks don't matter. What's at issue here is a challenge to the government's policies. The Devil knows, it's been hard enough to get the Land Leaguers and the landlords to agree to anything.'

'Oh, I can understand Sergeant Swallow's concern about the Pollock murder.' Kelly's tone was mocking. 'He's a policeman first and last. A squalid murder in a squalid laneway by definition engages his interest. He's hardly worried about government policy.'

Mallon shot Kelly an icy look.

'You seem to forget that I too am a policeman, Major Kelly. The sergeant and I are well aware of the importance of the land transfer programme. But so far the only crime that we can say for certain has been committed is the murder of Ambrose Pollock. Are you suggesting that we should be indifferent to murder?'

'Gentlemen,' West Ridgeway raised his hands. 'This isn't very helpful. I need to determine our actions from this point and to do so swiftly.'

He swivelled to Mallon.

'Chief Superintendent, please summarise what you know and what you suspect. And make the distinction clear between the two.'

'Very well, Sir,' Mallon shifted a little in his chair. 'I'll start with the murder of Ambrose Pollock. It's a reasonable surmise that his death had something to do with the fact that he had several thousands of pounds worth of stolen silver in his premises. That silver came from the Gessel estate in Galway. The family and their solicitors locally have no idea how it ended up in Pollock's possession. They believed it had been sold as part of the estate and its effects. We're fairly sure it was misappropriated by Arthur Clinton. He somehow arranged for it to be diverted to Pollock's.'

'Gessel,' West Ridgeway said. 'I know Sir Richard Gessel at the Cabinet Office. Is that the same family?'

'Distantly related,' Mallon said. 'I know Sir Richard too. He's not a member of the immediate Mount Gessel family.'

He gestured towards Swallow.

'The detective sergeant has told us how Arthur Clinton died by his own hand. We know that he worked on the conveyancing of the Gessel estate. It seems that he also misappropriated a collection of rare coins, some of which were sold to Greenberg's of Capel Street by his wife.'

He paused.

'Then we have the information passed by the late Teddy Shaftoe to Sergeant Swallow. He says he was sent to Dublin from London with his accomplice Darby in order to find out who had sold the coins and to recover them, using force if necessary.'

He raised his hands in a gesture of finality.

'That's what we know as fact, no more, no less. Now, if I may, I'll speculate on what we suspect and try to draw it all together.'

'Please do so.'

'It's my belief that Shaftoe's information was essentially correct. Clinton's firm are the Dublin agents who handled the break up and transfer of the Gessel estate. I believe that he was engaged in some sort of plan with other persons to defraud the Crown and perhaps other parties. I suspect that somehow Ambrose Pollock was involved as well and that he was killed, perhaps in a dispute among thieves, perhaps for some other reason that we can't yet ascertain.'

'There's rather a lot that you people haven't ascertained,' Kelly shot in.

Mallon glared.

'Pollock's sister Phoebe remains missing. In spite of the best efforts of G-Division, and the police in general, no trace of her has been found. We don't know. We don't even know if she's alive or dead.'

'Finally,' he allowed his gaze to swivel across the room, 'I will be more forthright than Sergeant Swallow. I believe that there is a security breach somewhere at senior level, probably within the Castle here. Last night an attempt was made at her home in Sussex on the life of Lady Margaret Gessel. She'll be an important witness and a key source of information if we succeed in bringing charges in these matters.'

He raised a hand in reassurance.

'Thankfully, the attempt was unsuccessful and rather than becoming a victim, she shot and killed the intruder. It seems she's well accustomed to the use of firearms. My colleagues at Great Scotland Yard have identified him as a known criminal from the East End of London.'

'What do you propose we do now, Mr Mallon?' West Ridgeway asked quietly.

'As a first step, I believe we need to secure and examine all the documentation relating to the breaking up of the Gessel estate. Depending on what we find, I believe we'll have to question particular people who have been involved in the processes. I'd start with the files in the offices of Keogh, Sheridan and James.'

'That can be done in either of two ways,' Smith Berry offered. 'We can get an order of the court to search and seize, or we can ask for their co-operation.'

'I'd very strongly urge that we get a court order,' Mallon said. 'If we start a process of negotiation it will take time, and it would tip off people with things to hide.'

'I'm inclined to agree with John,' West Ridgeway said. 'What else should we be doing, Chief Superintendent?'

'A land transfer, as I understand it, requires three official documents for completion: a certified map, a title deed and a certificate of purchase. I'd want to examine these in relation to all of the property transfers at Mount Gessel. So I'll require warrants for Keogh, Sheridan and James, the Land Office and probably a couple of banks.'

Kelly snorted.

'Is that all? You want to invade most of the administrative and commercial institutions across the city? It would take every man under my command and every second solicitor and accountant on the Crown pay-roll to do it.'

'I wouldn't intend that it be done by your men or by Crown solicitors or accountants, Major Kelly. I would intend that it be done by officers of G-Division, directly under the supervision of Detective Sergeant Swallow.'

Kelly threw his hands in the air.

'You're saying you don't trust Crown officials, Mr Mallon. And I'm saying I doubt if G-men would have the competence to do the sort of job you're talking about.'

'I believe our men can do it,' Swallow interjected. 'In G-Division we've got some of the best analytical minds I've come across in my career.'

'Oh, I wouldn't doubt that for a moment,' Kelly sneered.

'I'm going to go along with Mr Mallon's argument,' West Ridgeway said. He turned to Mallon. 'How long will you need?'

Mallon shrugged. 'If I get my court order, I'll deploy my men today. I'd estimate there's a week's work in it.'

'Very well, Mr Mallon. Is there anything else you need?'

'Two things, Sir. I want to arrest Mrs Clinton for further questioning. It'll be a bit of a ruse, but Sergeant Swallow believes she has more to tell us. I'd like to get her out of her mother's house and into Exchange Court for a while.'

'Gentle pressure?'

'If you put it that way, yes.'

'Anything else?'

'With your agreement, I'd like to ask Lady Gessel to return to Dublin for a short time to assist us. If we find evidence of dirty work in the transfer of her property, she's the person most likely to recognise it.'

'I agree. There will be costs, I'm sure. She'll have to be offered decent accommodation and so on, given her position and her connections. We'll make sure that's taken care of if you let us have the details. I have to say I'd rather look forward to meeting this lady who's such a crack shot.'

SIXTY-ONE

Swallow disliked the United Services Club.

Its membership extended to military and naval personnel, both serving and retired. It could never fully make up its mind up about policemen, although it welcomed senior officers from the Colonies, like Lafeyre. As he had learned on previous visits there as Harry Lafeyre's guest, however, the food was good. He wasn't particular.

It was a ten-minute walk from the Castle to the club on St Stephen's Green. Although he was glad to get the freshness of the street air after the hotel, he felt the October chill was sharper than in recent days. Dublin certainly felt colder than London, Swallow reflected. Even in the short walk from the hotel, a blast of icy air blew in from the east. Swallow was happy to reach the warmth of the club.

The waiter offered them a table at the window overlooking the Green.

'Business is slow,' Lafeyre remarked ruefully, glancing around the dining-room.

'You said you might have something important to tell me,' Swallow got to the point without ceremony.

Lafeyre drew his watch. 'I'm expecting something from Scollan. He'll probably arrive while we're eating. So, tell me about London,' he said. 'What did you think of it?'

'Noisy, crowded, dirty – but quite a place if you had the time to enjoy it.' He wondered if he should say something to Lafeyre about Jenkinson's job offer.

'Will they make any progress on the shooting of this fellow Shaftoe?' Lafeyre asked. 'From what you say, the fellow who killed him must have been a professional.'

'It isn't looking good. The witnesses were poor. I think it all happened so quickly that even if they wanted to be helpful they mightn't have much to tell.'

'Sounds like a waste of time,' Lafeyre said, tapping the wine list to indicate that he wanted a bottle of the house claret. 'Did you get to do any sightseeing? Bit of a shame to get to London and not see the place.'

'By coincidence I met someone who knows it well. She might be described as an expert guide.'

'She?' Lafeyre raised an interrogative eyebrow.

'Katherine Greenberg. She's in Lily's painting class. And she's the woman who bought the tetradrachms from Grace Clinton.'

'I know who she is. Lily told me,' Lafeyre said cautiously. 'Was that just coincidence?'

'Of course. She goes to London on business. I literally almost bumped into her in Hatton Garden.'

'I see.'

The silence that followed might have been broken if Swallow wanted to expand on the encounter. He remained silent.

'And I got a job offer,' he said instead.

'A job? Well done. At Scotland Yard?' Lafeyre seemed impressed.

'Yes. They want men for the Special Irish Branch. It'd be attractive money-wise, and they'd honour my DMP service for pension purposes.'

'Will you take it?'

'I'm going to think about it. There isn't much prospect of advancement here, is there?'

'That's a matter you have to judge carefully,' Lafeyre said.

He seemed to want to change the subject.

'Have you decided what you want to eat?'

They ordered mutton broth, to be followed by loin of pork. The waiter poured the claret for them.

'What are you going to do about Maria?' Lafeyre asked as they finished their soup. 'You may tell me it's not my business, and if I were asking as her sister's fiancé you'd be right to do so. But I'm not, I'm asking as your friend.'

Swallow sipped the claret. 'I'm not sure it's appropriate that I "do" anything, Harry. She seems to be enjoying the company of Mr Weldon very much, and I don't see myself having any right to cut across that.'

Lafeyre clattered his soup spoon into his plate, exasperated.

'For God's sake, you've a few years on me in age, but your seniority hasn't imparted much sense. Does it have to be spelled out to you that she took up an invitation from Weldon just to send a message out to you?'

'I'm not so sure. I can't see it as clearly as that. What I see is that she showed me the door. So I've set up with my sister in Heytesbury Street and I'm doing fine there, thank you very much.'

Lafeyre shook his head as if in despair. He reached for the claret bottle as a familiar voice called.

'Lafeyre, Swallow, how's the battle against crime?'

As if on cue, George Weldon strode across the dining-room towards them. He had detached himself from a threesome who had occupied a table down the room.

There were handshakes all round. Weldon jerked a thumb in the direction of his companions.

'Some colleagues in from Whitehall. I've to keep them fed and watered,' he laughed.

Lafeyre smiled. 'They won't do badly here. The mutton broth will keep the chill out, I promise.'

Weldon's expression was serious. 'I hear there's been squads of your fellows all over the city for the past couple of days,' he said to Swallow. 'What on earth is going on?'

'Stolen property,' Swallow answered, not untruthfully. 'Quite a lot of it.'

Weldon nodded as he retreated to join his colleagues. 'I see. I hope you get to the bottom of the problem.'

'We'll do our best, Mr Weldon,' Swallow said with forced pleasantness. 'Isn't that all any of us can do, in any walk of life?'

The waiter came to their table.

'Dr Lafeyre, your driver is in the lobby. He says he has a message for you.'

Lafeyre threw down his napkin.

'I'll need a few minutes,' he told Swallow. 'Help yourself to the claret.'

When he returned, Swallow could see that he looked pleased.

'You'd best finish up your wine and come outside with me. You'll need to see something outside in the carriage.'

When they were seated in the brougham, Lafeyre reached into his bag. He drew out a file and laid in on the seat beside Swallow.

'Open that.'

The file contained four photographic images of finger-marks.

'What do you make of those?'

'I can see that they're not the same, just like yesterday. They're quite different in fact. And they're small, as you said. I assume they're women's marks.'

'Well done. The pictures on the left are the marks left by two different women at the scene of Ambrose Pollock's murder.

Now Lafeyre was grinning.

'So, my dear Sergeant, I have to tell you that the first photograph on the right shows the fingerprint of Phoebe Pollock. I lifted comparisons from the glass top of the dressing-table in her room. It matches the more sticky marks, if I can use the term again. Phoebe Pollock was at the murder scene some time after Ambrose was killed. But this other mark tells us that another woman left her finger-marks on the iron weight at the time he was killed.'

Swallow stared at the pattern of loops, whorls and points.

Lafeyere reached into the bag again and produced two more prints. He laid each one side by side with the first set.

'You can see that those match,' he said, indicating the prints on the right. 'Those are the mark left by Phoebe Pollock along with her fingerprint as I have recorded it from her belongings.'

He tapped the other print.

'And the second photograph on the right is the fingerprint of Katherine Greenberg. It does not at all resemble either of the marks left at the murder scene. Katherine Greenberg can be eliminated from the investigation.'

Swallow was speechless.

'Eliminated? Are you telling me...?' he finally spluttered, '... that you decided Katherine Greenberg was a suspect and that you took her fingerprints?'

'Yes and yes,' Lafeyre said. 'She had to be a suspect. She and Pollock were linked by stolen property from Mount Gessel. It turns out that she had come into possession of it inadvertently, but we only had her word and that of her father for that. So I managed to get her fingerprints surreptitiously. She never knew she was a suspect, and she need never know now. She's in the clear.'

'You bastard, Lafeyre. You've cut across my investigation. You could have told me.'

'Leave the recriminations for now, Swallow,' he tapped the third print on the right.

'This fingerprint matches the mark that was left in fresh blood on the weight when Ambrose Pollock was killed. Now,' he smiled enigmatically, 'let me tell you whose fingerprint this is.'

SIXTY-TWO

Mallon secured his court order from a judge in chambers at the Four Courts just after noon.

Shortly before 2 o'clock, as Dublin's clerks, book-keepers and officials made their way back to their offices from their dinner-time break, the G-men moved in on the targeted locations across the city.

Swallow and Pat Mossop, with the enthusiastic Johnny Vizzard, led the party that went to the offices of Keogh, Sheridan and James at Inns Quay.

'I'm expecting a prisoner to come in from the constabulary in County Meath,' Swallow told the G-man on duty in the public office. 'It's a woman, name of Grace Clinton. I want her to be made as comfortable as possible, and have me notified as soon as she's here.'

'Duck' Boyle and two G-men went to the Land Office, downriver at the Customs House.

Mick Feore and another detective presented themselves with their warrant to the manager of the National Bank on Dame Street.

Mallon's instructions were succinct. All papers, records, deeds, notes and any other things relevant to the sale of the Mount Gessel estate were to be seized.

The partner who greeted the G-men at Keogh, Sheridan and James was bemused but courteous. He scrutinised the warrant that Swallow proffered before handing it back.

'Naturally, this firm will co-operate. We are, after all, officers of the court.' He attempted a thin smile. 'Might I inquire, Detective Sergeant, why you are interested in this particular land transaction? We've handled a great many such here since the passing of the Land Acts.'

'We believe that some valuable property from the Gessel estate has gone missing, probably stolen,' Swallow told him, not inaccurately. 'It would be very helpful to us to have a word with whoever handled the papers for this transaction on behalf of the firm,' he added in what he hoped was an inquiring tone.

'That would be one of our senior law clerks, Mr Clinton, Mr Arthur Clinton,' the partner said stiffly. 'Unfortunately, he isn't here at present. He sent word some days ago that he is obliged to attend to family business somewhere down the country. I don't know when he will return.'

It was just as well he did not know, Swallow thought to himself. The longer that Clinton's death could be kept out of public knowledge, the better.

The G-men were shown into a small room at the back of the building. After a short interval, a clerk arrived carrying two black deed boxes, which he placed on a tabletop.

'Sale of Mount Gessel Estate,' he said sullenly. 'There's more to come.'

When there were six boxes piled on the table, he wiped his hands.

'That's it. Everything we have.'

Swallow took one box to himself. Pat Mossop, with Vizzard sitting beside him, took another.

The first mortgages were dated from the 1840s. From that point on, it became clear that Mount Gessel was borrowing to keep itself going. Tranches of land were sold off. An agent working on a nearby estate purchased 500 acres from the second Lord Gessel. Five years later, he purchased another 1,000 acres. There were three transfers of Gessel land to adjoining estates. According to the deeds, when the reduced Mount Gessel estate was finally bought with government money and divided among its tenants, the acreage was just over 1,200 acres.

Shortly before 6 o'clock, the clerk came back.

'We're closing now. You'll have to leave and come back in the morning if you need to.'

Swallow shook his head.

'You can go home if you want to. We're staying here. And we'll need access in and out of the building. We have to eat at some stage. If that's a problem, I can have a constable put at the door for safety.'

The clerk might have considered protesting for a moment. If he did, he thought better of it.

'That won't be necessary. I'll stay on until you're done.'

Mossop and Vizzard had gone through one box of new title deeds, recording the transfer of more than forty holdings to their new owners. On each deed, the certifying clerk was Arthur Clinton.

'It all seems fairly regular, Boss,' Mossop said, raising his head from behind a mound of files.

'There are forty families or so with their own farms now. The valuations look pretty much as you'd expect. I can't see anything here to suggest any skulduggery. Clinton certified them all, as you'd expect.'

Swallow pointed to the still-unopened deed boxes on the table.

'It's early days yet, Pat. I wouldn't expect to find anything much on the recent land transfers. It'll be a tale of lucky tenants getting to be landowners at the stroke of a pen. It's when we get into the disposal of the house and the contents that I'd expect to find dirty work.'

He took a meal break after 6 o'clock. He found himself a quiet stool at the bar in Traynor's public house on Chancery Street and ordered a cold pork pie with a pint of Guinness's stout. The food and the beer lay heavily in his gut, so he had a Tullamore to settle it before he went back to allow the others to get their break.

The papers relating to the sale of the house and its contents were in the third deed box he opened. By now, Mossop and Vizzard had returned from their own refreshments at Traynor's.

Swallow passed a file across the table to Mossop.

'Have a look at that. It's the sale catalogue for the contents of the house.'

Mossop laughed. 'I'd say we're getting warm now.'

Swallow took out another file, which was divided in two sections. The first was an inventory of contents put together by Lady Gessel's steward before the sale of the house. There were lists of farm equipment and tools that were to be sold off. It included everything from ploughshares to pig troughs, from harnesses to hammers, all listed alphabetically and numbered.

The second was the steward's inventory for the contents of the house itself. In the kitchens it listed pots, pans, skillets, kettles and so on. The laundry and wash-house listed tubs, buckets, wringers, mangles and ironing-boards. The linen lists showed that Mount Gessel had more than 200 sets of sheets, pillows, bolsters and blankets.

The great rooms where the Gessels spent family time, dined and entertained their visitors, listed furniture, carpets, chandeliers, paintings and books.

There were details of the Gessel coin collection and the family silver. More than 1,500 coins were listed. Swallow saw tetradrachms and denarii among them. The silver collection numbered more than 200 pieces, from plates to sauce-boats to candlesticks.

He called to Mossop.

'Let's check this list against the sales catalogue you have there.'

'Righto, Boss.'

Mossop started through the catalogue, calling out the furniture, paintings and valuable items one by one. Swallow followed, ticking them off in the steward's list. When Mossop went through the contents of the drawing-room and the dining-room, though, there was no mention of the silver or the coin collection.

'The silver and the coins were included when the steward compiled his list,' Swallow said, 'but they were gone when the sales catalogue was put together. Here,' he instructed Mossop, 'give me that catalogue.'

He flattened the book on the tabletop. When he pressed it out he saw a wafer-thin gap in the gutter between the open pages. He pressed down harder and gently drew the pages apart.

There were loose threads of gum in the narrow gap. A page, or maybe more than one, had been neatly removed from the catalogue.

'I think we have it,' he said. 'Clinton took the coins and the silver out of the sale and then removed any trace of them from the catalogue. He simply took the pages out.'

He handed the catalogue back to Mossop.

'Go ahead, look. You can see there's a page gone, maybe more than one.'

Mossop drew his magnifying glass, peered through the lens and whistled.

'You're right, Boss. There's a few pages gone. The coin collection and the silver never went on sale. My guess is that they went straight to Ambrose Pollock's.'

Swallow shut the catalogue and replaced the other documents in the deed box.

'It's ten o'clock. I think we're entitled to a celebratory drink back at Traynor's.'

A constable was coming up the steps as they exited the building.

'You lads look as if you were goin' somewhere pleasant.'

'I imagine you're here to tell us differently,' Swallow said.

'You're wanted back at Exchange Court. I'm to tell you that your prisoner has arrived.'

SIXTY-THREE

The October night was drawing a mist off the river when the two RIC men, along with Sergeant Devenney's wife, who had been assigned to accompany the female prisoner, reached Exchange Court with Grace Clinton.

Abandoning the promised pleasures of Traynor's, Swallow, Mossop and Vizzard crossed the river at Richmond Bridge and climbed Winetavern Street towards the Castle.

Swallow signed the exchange certificate proffered by the senior RIC man. Grace Clinton was now in the custody of G-Division.

'I'm sorry that we have to meet again under such circumstances, Mrs Clinton. You've had a lot to deal with.' Swallow said. 'This is Detective Mossop and you know Detective Vizzard.'

Johnny Vizzard, not yet appointed to detective grade, swelled a little.

Swallow thought Grace Clinton looked terrible. Her hair was dishevelled, her eyes sunken in two dark pools. Her hands were balled into tight fists. Even though the room was warm, and although she had a good woollen coat, she shivered, sitting on the public office bench. She said nothing, staring straight ahead, trance-like.

'Mrs Clinton, I'm investigating the murder of a man called Ambrose Pollock. I think you may know about this.'

There was no response. Swallow waited a moment.

'It's important that you understand me, Mrs Clinton. Do you know where you are?'

'I do.' It was a whisper.

'Good. Mrs Clinton, I believe that you murdered Ambrose Pollock at Lamb Alley at a date unknown last month.'

'I understand.' The voice was stronger now, but the shivering had not abated.

'Can I get you a cup of tea, Ma'am?' Vizzard asked. 'Or maybe something stronger? Would you like something to eat?'

'Some tea, if you don't mind,' she said after a moment.

'I'm going to take you to my office now,' Swallow said. 'Detective Vizzard will bring you the tea there. I have some important questions to ask you.'

The crime sergeants' office was deserted and quiet. Swallow drew three chairs around a desk, where light pooled from the gas mantle. Vizzard arrived a few minutes later from the canteen carrying a tray with four mugs of tea.

Swallow sat directly opposite Grace Clinton.

'Mrs Clinton, I have to warn you that you are now under caution. You're not obliged to say anything, but if you do, it will be written down by Detective Mossop and it may be used in evidence. Do you understand this?'

'I do.'

'What do you know about the death of Ambrose Pollock?'

She sipped cautiously at her tea.

'What will happen to me?'

'That's not for me to say, Mrs Clinton. I'm a policeman. I collect evidence and then it's up to the court, a judge and jury, to decide on the basis of the evidence, whether you're answerable for a crime.'

'I'm not concerned for myself,' she whispered. 'It's the children, the girls. My mother will be there, but she's no longer young.'

She raised her eyes, looking to each of them.

'Do any of you have children of your own?'

'No, Ma'am,' Swallow said. 'Detective Vizzard and I are both single men.'

'I do,' Pat Mossop said. 'There's four at home.'

She dropped her eyes, seeming to absorb this information for a moment.

'I told you before, my husband wasn't a bad man.' Her voice was stronger now. 'He was influenced by others.'

'With respect, Mrs Clinton, we're not asking questions about your husband. He's deceased, God rest him,' Vizzard said. 'The death of Ambrose Pollock has to be cleared up and it's in your own interests now to co-operate with us.'

'I know enough of the law to know that I can send for a solicitor,' she said.

'That's true,' Swallow's tone sharpened. 'But under the Coercion Act I'm not under any obligation to allow him to see you. And even if I did, you can't meet with him in private.'

She managed a thin smile.

'I won't press for it, Mr Swallow, in that case. I've probably seen enough of solicitors anyway. Don't forget that I was married to a man who worked for them. And I'm here because of the way he misused his position of trust.'

'That may be so,' Swallow said, 'but my concern now is with the death of Ambrose Pollock. So I'm asking you again, what do you know about that matter?'

She cupped her hands around the canteen mug, then she closed her eyes as if concentrating. For a moment, Swallow wondered if she had actually fallen asleep in the chair. She opened her eyes.

'I defended myself... he was a vile man.'

'Are you saying you acted in self-defence?' Vizzard shot in.

Swallow raised a hand to silence him.

'You're acknowledging that you were involved in his death? That you were at the pawn shop when he was killed?'

'Do you need me to admit that?'

Swallow wondered if Grace Clinton sensed some uncertainty behind their questioning.

'No, I don't in fact. I have evidence that you were there and that you used a measuring weight to strike Ambrose Pollock. It's scientific evidence.'

She looked puzzled.

'Scientific, you say? What do you mean by that?'

'It's a science called fingerprinting. By using certain chemicals and with the aid of photography it's possible to know when someone has touched a particular object.'

'What object?'

'In this case, we have evidence of your finger-marks on the weight that was used in the killing of Ambrose Pollock.'

'I just... seized it... picked it up. I hit him with it,' she said after a moment.

'What happened?'

'Mr Vizzard said it was self-defence. So it was. Won't a court believe that, Mr Swallow? Won't they allow me to go home to look after my children?'

'I can't speak for a court, Mrs Clinton. And you understand that I can't offer you any inducement. But if that is to be your evidence, and if the court accepts it, I think it possible that you might be spared the worst extremities of the law's punishment.'

'You have a very formal way with words, Mr Swallow. "The worst extremities of the law's punishment." You mean that they mightn't hang me.'

'Yes,' he said flatly.

'I told you at my mother's house about my husband's gambling. I was sometimes reduced to taking things, things that he had brought into the house, to sell them in order simply to pay for household necessities.'

'Yes, Ma'am,' Vizzard nodded. 'You told us that.'

'One day, while he was at work, I found a small cardboard box at the bottom of my husband's wardrobe. When I opened it, I found these coins. They seemed to be silver and gold. They had heads and writing on them that I couldn't understand. I presumed they had to be valuable.'

Mossop wrote steadily.

'I had no money to pay the house maid. I had barely enough to put supper on the table for the children. So I took them. Then I realised that there was a note, a scrap of paper really, underneath the box. There was writing on it, not in my husband's hand. It said, "Pollock, pawnbroker, jeweller," or something such and it gave an address at Lamb Alley, off Cornmarket.'

She drank the last of her tea.

'I told myself that this had to be where Arthur was going to bring the coins. They were obviously people who dealt in such things. So I decided that instead of Arthur selling the coins and putting the money into his gambling, I would sell them to meet the household costs.'

She seemed to hesitate.

'Go on,' Swallow said.

'I found the pawnbrokers shop – Pollock's – and went in there one afternoon just as they were closing. There was a woman at the counter who looked at the coins. She said she would give me £10 for each of them. I had twenty of them, I think. I was absolutely delighted. But then, this... man appeared from behind the counter. He was very angry. He told the woman to get back to her work and he called me into this back office.'

She halted. 'This is very difficult.'

'I'm sure it is, Mrs Clinton, but you have to tell us what happened.'

'I showed him the coins. He seemed very interested and he offered me £2 each for them. I said "But the woman outside offered me £10 each." He got more angry and told me I wasn't to pay any attention to her. Then his mood changed. He began to smile and came forward. He started to stroke my hand and tell me how attractive he found me. If I would be "nice" to him, he said, he'd consider raising the price a little.'

She hesitated.

'Then he said he knew who I was, that he did business with Arthur. And he said he was sure that Arthur wouldn't want to know that I had come to sell these coins to him. But he would tell him if I didn't do as he wanted.'

She shuddered. 'He... put his hands... on me. I pushed him away and then... he sprang on me, pushing me back on the table. I felt this iron weight in my hand – I didn't even know what it was – and I brought it down on him as hard as I could. I think I heard his head crack.'

She put her hands to her face and covered her eyes as if she were afraid to see.

'He... sort of... staggered. He was bleeding. But he came at me again. He was shouting and cursing... foul language. I hit him a second time... and I think maybe a third. He collapsed back into his chair and he... he was there. He wasn't dead though. He was bleeding a lot but he was breathing.'

'So what did you do then?' Swallow asked.

'I... I'm not sure what happened next. I was afraid that he would attack me again, that he would get up from the chair. There was a piece of rope on a shelf nearby. I took it and wrapped it around his arms and tied it behind the chair so that he couldn't move. You see, he had the coins. I needed to get them back.'

'Did you not think to get help, Mrs Clinton?' Johnny Vizzard asked.

'I was in a panic... I didn't know what to do. I was going to call for help. Then the door opened, and the woman came in. She saw what had happened.'

'The woman, you mean Pollock's sister, Phoebe?' Swallow asked.

'I didn't know she was his sister. I thought she just worked in the shop. She saw what had happened, and I thought she would attack me too… or run for the police. But she didn't. She just looked at him and then back at me and she asked what happened. So I told her. She said to me, "Go home and don't tell anyone." I don't really remember leaving or anything else. The next thing I knew, I was at home. I had blood on my coat and on my dress, so I burned them in the fire.'

'You took the coins with you?' Swallow said.

'I realised when I got home that, yes, I had taken them.'

'You had sufficient presence of mind to do that.'

'I didn't know what I had or didn't have. But yes, I took them home.'

'Did you not feel it necessary to inquire, perhaps the following day, what had happened to the man?' Vizzard asked.

'Well, there wasn't anything in the newspapers. And I went down to Cornmarket two days later to see what had happened. All I could see was that the pawnbrokers was open and doing business. I assumed that the man was all right, even though I knew he was injured. I thought he was afraid of saying or doing anything about what had happened because it had been his… attack… on me that caused him to be injured.'

'You went back to the scene?' Vizzard prompted her again.

'Yes. But I didn't go into the place. I couldn't. I knew there was a jeweller's on Capel Street. Greenberg's. And then I went to the shop on Capel Street and I sold the coins to the woman there.'

'When did you know that Ambrose Pollock was dead?'

'I only understood what was happening when I read that his body had been discovered a week later. Then my husband found that the coins were missing. He was so angry that I had to tell him what had happened.'

'Did he not suggest that you should go to the police at that stage?' Swallow asked.

'He became hysterical. He said that if the police got involved they'd find out about everything and that he would be a dead man. He said I would be in danger too, and the children.'

'What do mean when you say the police would find out about everything?' Swallow asked.

'Arthur… told me what had been going on. He said he and the others had been making false claims for land to be purchased for the government. But he had been greedy. He had been making his own profits on the side by taking valuables from the houses and the estates that were being redistributed. He was taking silver, coins, good paintings, furniture, and he was selling it to Ambrose Pollock. Mr Pollock had an exporting business to London, it seems.'

'False claims for land?' Swallow asked.

She shook her head.

'I didn't ask. I didn't want to know.'

'I can understand that your husband wouldn't want the police involved,' Johnny Vizzard said. 'But if you felt yourself and family to be in such danger, would it not have been better to tell them?'

'I thought about it. I said it to Arthur. He said the police couldn't protect us. That what he was involved in went higher than the police. He persuaded me that our only hope was to disappear. So we went to my mother's, down in Meath.'

'Who are the people who were involved with your husband in this… enterprise?' Swallow asked.

'I… really don't know… I think he said there were quite a few people involved in the paperwork. I suppose that's how things are done officially. Arthur said he wasn't the only one doing it.'

'Do you know any names?'

'No. He never told me,' she said wearily.

Mossop's notes by now ran to many pages. Swallow saw that Grace Clinton was exhausted. She had probably told them what she could.

He stood.

'Mrs Clinton, I'm going to charge you in connection with the death of Ambrose Pollock. I'll arrange for you to be transferred to Kilmainham Jail. The conditions for women there are safe and reasonably comfortable. Is there anything that you would like us to do for you?'

'You could have someone notify my mother of what's happened.'

'Of course. Would you like me to arrange for your children to visit you?'

'No, not at the present. They're safe with my mother for the moment.'

Swallow nodded to Vizzard to send for the car to transfer her to Kilmainham. At the same moment, Mick Feore put his head around the door.

'We've finished up at the bank, Skipper. And we have the information you need, whenever you're ready.'

Swallow's watch was showing past midnight. Ordinarily, with something as significant as a murder confession, he would go straight away to brief John Mallon at his house. But it was more urgent to know what had been learned at the bank.

He would prepare a report for Mallon and leave it for his clerk in the morning.

It was going to be a long night.

SIXTY-FOUR

Swallow sensed something different in Harriet's demeanour immediately they sat to breakfast in Heytesbury Street. She seemed hesitant and cautious, a contrast to the enthusiasm with which she usually met the new day.

'I have no school this morning,' she told him. 'There's an inspection of school stock, so classes are cancelled.'

'Any plans for the day?'

'Yes, in fact I have. Plans that may involve you.'

He was instantly suspicious.

'You're not in some sort of trouble again, I hope. Out to turn society upside down?'

She placed a hand on his arm.

'I'm very worried about you. You seem so tired and so worried about these cases.'

He knew he looked drawn. He had seen it in the mirror as he shaved himself earlier. It was hardly surprising. It had been close to 4 a.m. when he reached his bed.

'Fair enough. I won't deny it. Bear in mind that I've had to go over and back to London with a prisoner. I've seen two men dead, a woman widowed and a family orphaned.'

He thought about telling her of Jenkinson's job offer, but he thought better of it. The last thing he needed was a lecture about being lured into the heart of the Imperial machine.

'I think I can help,' she said. 'Or at least some of my friends can help.'

'What do you mean?'

'You remember at Maria's that Willie Yeats spoke about the gift of vision and you asked him if he could trace a missing woman?'

So now, Swallow noted, the young Mr Yeats had become 'Willie.'

'Of course.'

'Well, he asked me the other evening at a meeting of the society if you had located her yet. I said I didn't think so. But he said if we were to ask some of the members to try to vision her, they might have some information that could help you.'

'Vision her?'

'Yes, try to locate her using psychic powers.'

He tried not to sound impatient.

'Interesting. So what are you going to do?'

'I'm meeting two of them this morning, and we're going down to Lamb Alley to where the woman lived. We're going to try to vision where she is, whether she's still in this world or gone to the spirit world.'

He chuckled cynically in spite of himself.

'It's a total waste of time, Harriet, though I appreciate your concern.'

'You're completely ignorant,' she said hotly, 'but I've seen things happen that have surprised me. Now, it would be especially helpful if you could arrange it so that we can get access to the house. It would make it much easier to pick up some sense of the woman.'

'It's out of the question. It's private property... and it's a crime scene.'

'You could come with us. Make sure we don't interfere with anything. Or you could send someone else if you can't go yourself.'

Only brotherly tolerance prevented him from standing from the breakfast table and ending the conversation.

'I can't go. And all my men are busy.'

'Give us just one hour. Surely you can spare somebody. What harm can it do? You're not making any progress on this case.'

Extraordinarily, he heard himself agree.

'Right. Just one hour. I'll arrange for Pat Mossop to meet you there. What time?'

She smiled clapped her hands.

'That's wonderful. We planned to meet there at 11 o'clock. Oh, I know you think this is all poppycock. But you just might be glad of it.'

He finished his breakfast, carefully avoiding the dried figs, and set out for Exchange Court.

SIXTY-FIVE

The G-men had worked late into the night, piecing together the information they had gleaned from the files at Keogh, Sheridan and James and from the National Bank.

Swallow was in by 8 0'clock. To his surprise, Pat Mossop was hovering around the crime sergeants' office.

'The very man,' he told Mossop. 'I need you to go up to Pollock's at Lamb Alley at eleven and meet some people there. Show them around the shop and the living quarters. Don't let them touch a thing, and don't give them more than an hour.'

Mossop blinked, uncomprehending.

'I could take a long time to explain it,' Swallow said, 'will you just do it? They call themselves mystics. They think they might be able to help us to locate Phoebe.'

'Righto... Boss,' Mossop said slowly. 'If that's what you want. But it isn't like you... if you know what I mean.'

'It's to do with my sister... Harriet.'

Mossop nodded.

'Ah, fair enough, I understand.'

He hesitated.

'I think I might have something on Phoebe's disappearance, Boss. But sure, it'll wait until after the conference.'

The diminutive Belfast detective had a rare capacity to pick up connections between things that might at first seemed unrelated. He could see patterns in the masses of information that a major investigation would throw up. And he never disregarded a detail, however trivial it might appear.

Sometimes, Swallow wondered if Mossop was affected by some unusual ordering of the mind. He knew from his own foreshortened medical studies that doctors specialising in what was called 'psychiatry' were only starting to classify such conditions. The man's capacities for concentration and focus could be unnerving. Conversely, his limited ability to understand or anticipate people's emotional responses was a serious handicap.

'We've an hour before the conference. Out with it.'

'We have this fella Jimmy Rowan, the hotel porter, above in Mountjoy on remand,' he said, lowering his voice. 'He's got a record of violence against women, and his alibi didn't stand up.'

'Sure,' Swallow said. 'They found a few wallets he'd lifted.'

'Yes. So he's on remand for that. He gave us an alibi that fell apart when we checked it, but we haven't been able to connect him to Phoebe's disappearance at all. He's been interviewed time and again, and he's sticking to his story. He says he never even saw her.'

'So?'

'Well, you'd have wonder if we should believe him at this stage. And I think we might have something else on the case.'

He drew his notebook from his pocket.

'As a matter of fact,' he said, 'it's not that we've got anything new on Phoebe herself. But we might have a fix on her gentleman friend, this fellow called Len or Lennie.'

Swallow felt a stir of optimism. Mossop did not go out on a limb unless he was fairly sure that his information was solid.

'Tell me more.'

Mossop flicked through his notebook.

'You remember that when we went to the Northern Hotel on Thursday, the first fellow you met was the General Manager?'

'Yes. Barry.'

'Do you remember his name?'

'John.'

'No, his full name.'

'That's what he said his name was.'

'Yes, but the plaque on the desk in the lobby gave his name as JOHN L. BARRY. I wrote it down.'

Swallow guessed.

'You're telling me the L stands for Len or Lennie? Are you saying he's Phoebe's gentleman friend?'

Mossop grinned.

'You're quick enough off the mark, Boss. You've got the ear for accents and you said he was from Cork. So I got the RIC to check the parish registers in Cork city against the date of birth he gave us when we got him to sign his statement.'

He took two sheets of paper from his pocket and spread them on the table.

'This fella was born John Leonard Barry in 1842 in Cork. There were eight other John Barrys born that year in Cork, and probably every year. The bloody place down there is crawling with Jack Barrys. So he'd naturally use his middle name.'

Swallow smiled with the pleasure of comprehension. 'And we only ever heard the staff call him Mister Barry. He'd be the right age for Phoebe's drinking companion, and he'd fit the descriptions we have.'

Mossop's eyes were alight with enthusiasm.

'And he'd have had access all around the hotel without anybody taking notice of him. He could have been up around the corridor by Phoebe's room on any number of occasions and nobody would have remarked on it.'

'What do we know about him, our Mister John Leonard Barry?' Swallow asked. 'I'll be surprised if you haven't been through the records already.'

'I've got a good bit,' Mossop riffled through his notebook. 'Aged forty-five, born in Cork, as you know, no convictions. I pumped some of the staff down there. He's not known to have ever married, but there's been talk of some romantic encounters with women working at the hotel.'

He flicked another page on his notebook.

'He patronises one or two of the local public houses, which is a bit odd for a respectable man of commerce. The taverns are all as rough as a terrier's arse down there.'

He turned another page.

'He has two rooms at the top of the hotel, a bedroom and a sitting-room or parlour. He takes his meals in the dining-room downstairs.'

Swallow grimaced. 'Not exactly the profile of a brutal murderer. But he's the only Len or Lennie in the scene so far.'

'There's one other small thing, Boss,' Mossop added. 'According to the local public houses, when he does drink it's Jameson Twelve-Year-Old, same as Phoebe's man, as you heard it from 'Five Times' Currivan.'

Swallow smiled appreciatively. Mossop missed nothing.

'I think we should take this Barry fellow in and do a search on his rooms at the hotel. We'll go down at a decent hour and do it discreetly. The man is entitled to a bit of privacy until we know for sure that he's the fellow we want.'

WEDNESDAY OCTOBER 12TH, 1887

SIXTY-SIX

Swallow was at Mallon's office at nine. Boyle and Feore were there before him, waiting in the outer office.

'He'll have had a report from me last night,' he told the clerk. 'I think he'll very likely want to see us.'

'Right y'are. Yer to go in the minute you were all here, that's what he said.'

Mallon was at his desk, the crime sheets spread out in front of him. Swallow saw the file he had put together late the previous night. The three G-men drew chairs to the front of the desk.

'Jenkinson just messaged me,' Mallon said. 'He's got Lady Gessel on the evening sailing out of Holyhead, accompanied by one of your friends from Scotland Yard. We'll meet them at Kingstown and take over the escort.'

'That's fast work, Sir.'

'She's a very angry woman. That's good from our point of view. She wants to do everything she can to pin down whoever's behind the attack at her home.'

'She sounds a formidable individual.'

'You'll get your chance to make a judgment for yourself on that,' Mallon said. 'We're putting her up at the Shelbourne. Under-Secretary's instructions. I'm aiming to interview her tomorrow morning, and I want you there.'

'Now,' he reached for the file. 'You had a productive night. Grace Clinton confessed to the Pollock murder. Well done.'

'Thanks, Sir. We might have a fresh lead on the sister's disappearance too.'

He told Mallon of Pat Mossop's tentative identification of John Barry as Phoebe Pollock's gentleman friend.

'I detailed Mossop to do a check at DCR on Barry. He's at it now.'

Mallon nodded enthusiastically.

'That sounds promising. We might have got the wrong man in that fellow Rowan, the porter. But he's been up to no good anyway, lifting wallets.'

He turned to Boyle.

'Inspector, will you lead the arrest party for this fellow Barry?'

Swallow knew it was Mallon's way of trying to restore Boyle's bruised pride. By right, the arrest party should be led by Pat Mossop. Boyle swelled a little.

'Of coorse, Sir.'

Swallow guessed that Boyle could already see his name in the newspapers, maybe even being mentioned to the Commissioner as the arresting officer.

Mallon tapped Swallow's report.

'Bring me back to Grace Clinton and her statement last night. She confirms your suspicions about what her husband was at. Pillaging valuables off the Gessel estate and working some sort of fraud on the land transfers.'

'She genuinely doesn't seem to know the details,' Swallow said. 'Or who else was involved.'

'Inspector Boyle, anything else in from the searches at the bank and the Land Office?'

'Nothin' great that I know of, Sir. We checked through all the sales and transactions around the Gessel estate. The level of co-operation was good,' he said obsequiously. 'I s'pose that was because it was yerself that authorised th'operation and, of course, in the light of his Lordship's order.'

'You can pass on the warmth of the reception, Inspector,' Mallon said impatiently. 'Tell us what you learned.'

Boyle smoothed out his papers in front of him. 'We secured the documents relevant to the sale of the lands. There was a powerful lot o' paperwork, I don't mind tellin' ye.'

He tapped a pudgy finger to the file.

'Accordin' to the documents provided by the solicitors, Messrs Keogh, Sheridan and James, Mount Gessel estate comprised lands that totalled 1,280 acres, 60 square roods and 22 square perches. This was valued at £88 on average of per acre, makin' a total purchase price of £10,240, 10 shillings and 6 pence.'

'Now,' he licked his lips, 'this acreage was divided between 72 families, all former tenants of the estate, into an average farm size of 17 and seven tenths of an acre, with the largest holdin' at 38 acres and the smallest at just two and a half acres....'

Mallon raised a hand.

'We don't need to know the mathematics of who got every patch of grass. What we need to know is do the figures tally. Is there any sign of anything irregular?'

Boyle's shoulders slumped apologetically.

'Indeed, there's ne'er a sign of any irregularity, Sir. The acreage certified be the solicitor an' confirmed be the Land Office are the same. The value put on the land and th' amount drawn down be the Land Office from the Treasury all tally.'

'What about the files at the bank?' Mallon asked Feore.

'The bank figures match those on the property files, Sir,' Feore indicated to his notes.

'The bank paid over the sum of £10,240, 10 shillings and 6 pence to Lady Margaret Gessel on the fourteenth of August of last year. The draft is drawn on the government's Land Office account. Two days later, on August the sixteenth, the cheque was cleared and the sum was paid into her account at Barclay's Bank, Great Portland Street, in London.'

'That's disappointing,' Mallon looked crestfallen. 'Arthur Clinton and Ambrose Pollock were thieves and fences. But we're no closer to finding any conspiracy to defraud the Exchequer.'

'No proof, Sir,' Swallow said. 'But there's more to this than a law clerk with a gambling habit lifting a silver table service and a few Greek coins. We can't see the connection yet, but I'm sure it's there.'

'I agree. But we're still working on supposition and instinct, not evidence.'

'Where do ye want us to go from here, Sir?' 'Duck' Boyle asked glumly.

'Since we haven't found anything irregular in the handling of the sale, the next step might be to trawl through the other estates that Clinton handled,' Mallon said wearily. 'But that'd involve going back for more court orders. We mightn't get them, and it would take time.'

Swallow tried to strike an optimistic note.

'We've still got a couple of boxes of deeds to go through at Keogh, Sheridan and James. I'd like to finish the job anyway for the sake of completeness.'

Mallon stood.

'Very well, but we'll have to finish tonight. I'll report to the Commissioner and the Under-Secretary shortly and try to buy a bit more time. They'll not be overjoyed that we haven't found something conclusive.'

'It might be said we're at an impasse, Sir,' Boyle volunteered. 'It's a legal term, Sir. Impasse. From the French, I believe.'

Mallon glared at him. 'I'm most grateful for that, Inspector. It's very helpful.'

SIXTY-SEVEN

John Leonard Barry recognised only one of the three G-men who came through the door. It was the small Belfast detective called Mossop. But he had no doubts as to the professions of the other two, in particular the jowly fellow with the waddling gait who seemed to be in charge.

'Mr Barry?'

'Of course, what I can do for?'

'Duck' Boyle was the soul of discretion. 'Detective Inspector Boyle, G-Division. Have ye a quiet room we kin use for a chat?'

Barry took them into his office. Boyle drew the arrest warrant from his pocket.

'John Leonard Barry, I am arresting you on suspicion that you murdered one Phoebe Pollock on September 29th last, contrary to Common Law, at the Northern Hotel, North Wall, such premises being situated within the Dublin Metropolitan Police Area.'

Barry saw that one of the G-man had moved to block the door.

'Bloody ridiculous,' he said emphatically.

'You were there,' he told Mossop, 'you saw what happened.'

'You're not obliged to say annythin' unless you wish to do so,' Boyle droned on. 'But annythin' you do say will be written down and may be used in evidence. D'ye understand?'

'Ah Jesus, this is a joke,' Barry blustered. 'I'm sending for a solicitor.'

'Duck' Boyle raised a hand.

'Furthermore, Mr Barry, there's a warrant to search your accommodation. I'll have the keys, if ye please.'

He looked around the office. 'Take yer overcoat wid ye now and come quietly, like a sensible man. Me instructions are that yer not be handcuffed unless that's necessary. An' I trust ye won't make it so.'

Now, Barry sat in the Inspectors' Office at Exchange Court, with 'Duck' Boyle opposite. Pat Mossop sat to one side, a bound notebook on his knee, a pen in hand and an open ink-well on the table beside him. The G-men had been decent enough. They had brought him a mug of tea from the police canteen. But that was two hours ago, and the questioning by Boyle and Mossop showed no sign of relenting.

'Ye killed her,' Boyle said. 'Mebbe strangled her.'

'Killed? Strangled?' Barry echoed. 'Strangled? Like I told you, I never saw the woman.'

'There are witnesses who'll swear you were seen with her on a number of occasions in licensed premises,' Boyle stabbed at his notebook. 'Reliable witnesses.'

Most of them, he thought to himself, you wouldn't trust with the Lord's Prayer.

'They're mistaken, I tell you. It must have been someone else. Definitely not me.'

At some point in the mid-afternoon there was a knock on the door, and the other detective who had come to the hotel stuck his head in. Boyle left to speak with him. When he came back into the room five minutes later, his face was like thunder.

'Now, Mr Barry,' he threw his flabby weight back into the chair. 'It's time the gloves kem off here. I've been patient in th' extreme. But I'm goin' to be very blunt with ye now. If you stick to what you're sayin' you're goin' to end up swingin' off a rope above in Mountjoy. On t'other hand, if there were mitigatin' circumstances of some kind, a judge might be inclined to be merciful. Needless to say, th' attitude of the police would be important in that decision. Am I makin' meself perfectly clear?'

Barry sensed a rising panic. Was this bluff or was it time to come clean? He had played his fair share of poker during his time, but he found it impossible to get the measure this overweight fool.

When 'Duck' Boyle dropped the gold watch on the table, Barry knew it was time to start dealing.

'Ye'll recognise this item, I suppose,' Boyle intoned. 'And ye'll know, o' course, that me officers had to lift the floorboards in yer quarters to find it, along wid a variety of other trinkets ye had stashed away for safe keepin' no doubt.'

He lifted the watch and looked at it approvingly. 'A very nice time-piece, Mr Barry. Twenty-four carat gold case. Made in Switzerland, no less. That'd fetch a fair few pounds, I'll warrant.'

He turned it around.

'An' a very touchin' inscription here on the back. '*With Deep Affection from Phoebe to Leonard. An' a date as well. June 1ˢᵗ 1887.*'

He had not for a moment contemplated that they would discover his cache under the floorboards in his bedroom. He had burrowed out the space himself under the joists, taking away timber and plaster lath to hide the black metal box. Even if the boards themselves were lifted, it would not be visible from above.

'The lads is very good at that kind o' work, Mr Barry,' 'Duck' Boyle said, reading his unspoken thoughts. 'Years o' huntin' for Fenian guns and American dollars in the most unlikely places. Ye develop an instinct o' sorts, I suppose.'

'Duck' Boyle looked out of the window and started to whistle. Pat Mossop examined his fingernails.

Then John Leonard Barry decided to tell his story.

SIXTY-EIGHT

He had met Phoebe Pollock a year ago when he went to Lamb Alley to pawn a string of pearls and a gold pendant.

'You have to understand,' he told the G-men, 'sometimes guests at the hotel might... mislay or... forget small, personal items. The salary as general manager isn't generous, so you could say that these... well... stray items could be regarded as a bit of a windfall. I'd make every effort, of course, to return them to their rightful owners. But if it proved impossible to trace them, what am I supposed to do?'

'Indeed.' Boyle's tone was sarcastic.

But, Barry explained, he felt it was prudent to use pawnbroker shops in parts of the city that were some distance from the hotel.

'Phoebe just took a shine to me. That was good. I had to use a false name.'

That made sense, the G-men had to acknowledge. Otherwise the police, checking the books in due course, would figure out what was happening.

On his second visit, he told them, he charmed her, inviting her to the tearooms at the Imperial Hotel on Sackville Street.

She blushed and stammered, but said that her brother did not approve of such things. On his next visit he invited her to walk out with him in the Phoenix Park. She declined this invitation also, but she slipped a small square of folded paper into his hand, glancing nervously at the window, through which he could see her brother at work in his office.

It was an invitation to meet at 10 o'clock that evening. The designated spot was outside St Werburgh's Church, two minutes from Lamb Alley. When they met, she linked his arm and insisted that they must walk together. They walked for an hour along Lord Edward Street, Parliament

Street, across Essex Bridge and along the quays as far as the Four Courts. Then they crossed the river again at Church Street.

'They were bats, herself and the brother. He wouldn't let her spend a farthing. I think they were starving in that bloody house. The only clothes she had was what she could pick out of the pawn herself. He wouldn't let her leave the house. So she'd wait until he was gone to bed and then she'd slip out. On that first night she stopped outside the Brazen Head and said "Take me in there and buy me a drink." Jesus, I can tell you she lapped it up. Large gins, port wine, whiskey, she'd manage them all, no bother.'

'That's what we heard.' Boyle interjected.

'She was demented, you know? One minute she'd be telling me that she had conversations with God and his Blessed Mother. She was convinced her brother was tied up with some criminal gang, and she could hear them sometimes with him in his office.'

'Was your relationship... intimate?' Boyle asked.

'Ah come on, Inspector. Give me some credit.' He gave a little smirk. 'Besides, I'd have no shortage of offers elsewhere, if you know what I mean.'

Mossop's pen flew across the pages, dipping furiously in and out of the ink-well as he sought to keep pace with the narrative.

'You're not goin' to tell me that this went on for a year?' Boyle said. 'Wanderin' the streets be nights and then goin' drinkin.' What was in it fer yerself, apart from havin' a convenient place to drop off what I'll charitably call "lost property" from the hotel?'

'Well, that goes to the heart of the matter,' Barry said. 'She said she had money put away. I won't deny that I saw an opportunity. I thought I might end up as owning a small hotel some place. Maybe in Cork, that's my native place.'

'So you planned to take her money?'

'Ah, I'd have done the decent thing, Inspector. She'd have been Mrs John Leonard Barry.'

'Jesus, she'd have been fuckin' made up, wouldn't she?' Boyle sneered.

'It would have been a fair bargain,' Barry's voice rose in indignation. 'She'd have escaped from that madhouse. I'd have had to put up with her, mad and all. It wouldn't have been a picnic for me.'

'So,' Boyle lowered his tone. 'What happened at the hotel last Thursday?'

'Bloody unfortunate. She turned up there. She took a room and collared me on the stairs. She said she had taken all the money from the shop and she had it in the two cases.'

'Did she tell you what had happened?' Mossop asked.

'She was raving that her brother was murdered a week ago by someone and that she'd be blamed. She wanted me to go on the evening boat to Liverpool, but I couldn't just drop everything and go like that. I had wages to collect. Valuables to put together.'

'Did you think she'd killed the brother?' Boyle asked.

Barry shook his head.

'I don't think so. She said she'd been afraid to tell anyone or to go to the police. She was in a frightful state, I can tell you, when she got here. I don't think she was capable of telling anything but the truth.'

'Are you saying she stayed in the house with her dead brother over all those days?'

'It seems so, yes. Christ knows, it must have been dreadful. But her whole life was so bloody awful that she probably just wasn't able to deal with it.'

'Go on,' Boyle said.

'Then she brought out the poison and opened the bottle. She said she'd do for herself if I didn't leave with her. I got her to put the cork back on it, and I tried to reason with her. But she started to rave.'

For a few moments, the only sound was the scratching of the nib of Mossop's pen. Boyle pushed his face up to Barry's until they were only inches apart.

'So that's when you killed her?'

'Killed her? Of course I didn't kill her. She wrecked the room. But I calmed her down. I took her out the back way to the Amiens Street railway terminus and put her on the train for Belfast with her suitcase full of money. But I'm damned if I know where she is now.'

'She left another case behind.

'I persuaded her I needed some cash. The plan was I'd follow her to Belfast in a day or two, but by the time I got back the police had arrived. I didn't have an opportunity to get into the room to retrieve the second bag.'

'Or the money?'

'That too,' Barry said bitterly.

'Duck' Boyle was stumped. Barry's story had the ring of truth.

'I'd like you to sign a statement t'all this, Mr Barry,' he said wearily. 'Officer Mossop will type it. It'll take about half an hour.'

'And what happens to me? I've told the truth now. I'm not a saint. But for God's sake, you know I'm not a murderer.'

'You're not a saint and I'm not God, Mr Barry. The nearest thing to God I've ever come across is a judge. But for the present I think ye've avoided the prospect o' meetin wan o' them lads.'

He hauled himself from the chair.

'If ye'd be good enough to sign the statement, ye'll be free to go.'

THURSDAY OCTOBER 13TH, 1887

SIXTY-NINE

Harriet was working on a bundle of school copybooks in the parlour when Swallow got home.

'How did you get on with Pat Mossop?' he inquired.

'There were three members of the society, apart from myself. I'm afraid I can't claim to have vision, but each of the others does, I'm sure of it.'

'So what did those with vision tell you?' he asked wearily. 'Where is this woman and what will she have for breakfast tomorrow?'

She flung a copybook onto the table.

'You are absolutely infuriating… don't be so sarcastic. As it happens, they got very strong sensations in that house, especially in the upstairs rooms. But what a horrible, dirty place it is. How anybody could have lived there, I don't know.'

'I could have told you that.'

'Well, first, all of the members felt that the woman is alive and still in this world. She is in fear but she is alive.'

'That's good. Now where is she in this world? I don't suppose they got an address, did they?'

'I asked you not be sarcastic. In fact, one of the members visioned her very clearly. What she said is that she had travelled north, "… as far as the end of the land," she said. She saw her in a city, busy streets, "… with a hill looking down on it and a great harbour opening to the sea."'

'Jesus,' Swallow said. 'She's in bloody Belfast. Barry is telling the truth.'

'Barry?'

'He's the fellow we had as a suspect for her murder. He says she went to Belfast.'

Harriet gave a smug smile.

'Now, maybe you won't be so dismissive of what I tell you in the future. And you won't be so disrespectful to people like Willie Yeats.'

Swallow shook his head in disbelief.

'He could go far, that fellow, I agree.'

SEVENTY

The manager of the Shelbourne Hotel was in the foyer to greet John Mallon.

'It's hotel policy, of course, to co-operate fully with the authorities, Mr Mallon,' he fussed. 'But I would hope that any police business can be conducted unobtrusively. I wouldn't want our guests to be put out in any way, as you might imagine.'

'The guest I'm due to meet is here at the request of my authorities,' Mallon told him. 'The Under-Secretary chose to accommodate Lady Gessel at your hotel. If it's a problem, I dare say we can find an alternative for her without any difficulty.'

'Oh no, not at all, I assure you.'

Mallon looked unconvinced. 'Thank you. This is Detective Sergeant Swallow. I believe Lady Gessel is expecting us.'

'Yes, of course. And I have arranged a private room on the first floor where you may converse privately.'

He gestured to a bellboy.

'Take these gentlemen to the Windsor Room.'

The Windsor Room looked out over the Green. It was elegantly furnished with a suite of deep-piled sofas, a rosewood table and a set of six matching chairs.

'Might as well make ourselves comfortable,' Mallon grunted, lowering himself into the nearest sofa. Swallow took a seat beside him.

After four or five minutes, the door was opened by the manager, ushering in a woman who Swallow estimated to be around sixty years of age, though she moved with the ease of a much younger person.

'Lady Gessel, may I introduce Chief Superintendent Mallon... and his sergeant,' the manager clearly had forgotten Swallow's name.

'Lady Gessel,' Mallon said politely with a small nod. 'This is Sergeant Swallow.'

Margaret Gessel smiled. 'Mr Mallon, I've heard a lot about you.'

She turned to Swallow. 'Good morning, Sergeant Swallow. What an unusual name.'

'Yes Lady Gessel. It's French I think, probably Norman.'

The manager withdrew, and Margaret Gessel took the sofa opposite the two G-men. Her features were still striking, Swallow reflected. She had the fresh, supple skin of a woman who had taken care of herself. Her hair was grey, but thick and perfectly coiffed. Her eyes were bright, blue and curious.

When she folded her hands in her lap, Swallow saw that they were strong and bony. Hands that had done work, tamed horses and, it seemed, learned how to use firearms. He thought he could see the arthritis-like signs of a broken index finger.

'I'm sorry to learn what happened on Saturday night at your home, Lady Gessel,' Mallon started. 'A terrible experience for anyone, and especially for a woman on her own.'

She tossed her head.

'After twenty years of the Land Leaguers and their friends, a criminal type from the back lanes of London offers no threat to me, I can assure you, Mr Mallon.'

'Our colleagues at Great Scotland Yard believe that he intended to do you harm,' Swallow said. 'It's lucky that you were able to defend yourself so well.'

'You make your own luck, Sergeant. In this instance, it was the luck of a .32 Smith and Wesson five-shot revolver, plus the fact that I have a steady hand and a sharp eye.'

'Indeed,' Mallon said. 'Before we go any further, I'd like to express my appreciation of the fact that you've been willing to come to Dublin to assist us. Do you have any idea of why you might have been a target for harm?'

Her eyes flashed with anger.

'I can only imagine. The detective from Scotland Yard wasn't telling me much. He said that you would do that. Something about the sale of Mount Gessel, I understand.'

'That's correct, yes.'

'Well, I'm damned if I'm going to be threatened in my own home, Mr Mallon. And if there's anything I can do to bring the law down on whoever is behind the attack on me at this stage of my life, by heaven I'll do it. So, tell me what I can do.'

'We suspect there's been some serious irregularity in the sale of Mount Gessel, and perhaps in the sale of other properties.' Swallow said. 'But so far we haven't been able to identify it with precision. We suspect that at least one person has been murdered to cover this up. There may be more. Professional criminals were sent here from London to try to silence possible witnesses. The attack on you was probably an attempt to prevent you giving evidence as well.'

She seemed momentarily shaken, pausing to consider Swallow's words.

'Evidence? Evidence of what?'

'We don't know,' Mallon said. 'We hoped that, by going through what we know of the sale of your former property, you might be able to spot something that would point us in the right direction.'

'We've seized the papers relating to the sale and the redistribution from the solicitors' office here in Dublin,' Swallow said. 'We've worked our way through all the sales, and we don't seem to be able to find anything out of the ordinary.'

She raised her hands in a gesture of exasperation. 'I don't understand. Mount Gessel wasn't an especially big estate. We're talking about 950 acres divided among, what, seventy families? If there's an irregularity, as you call it, it should be easy enough to identify it.'

Swallow almost heard the click in his brain as he registered what Margaret Gessel had just said.

'I'm sorry Lady Gessel, how many acres did you say?'

'About 950. It was actually 952 and a few square perches.'

'You're sure of those figures Ma'am?'

She sighed impatiently.

'Of course I'm sure, Mr Swallow. If you handled the rent books and the accounts of an estate for twenty years like I did, you'd be sure too.'

'What's your point, Sergeant?' Mallon asked.

'The point is that all the documents I've seen indicate that the Mount Gessel estate comprised almost 1,200 acres.'

'Absolute nonsense,' Margaret Gessel said.

Swallow felt a delightful surge of comprehension.

'That's it,' he slapped the side of the sofa. 'That's how they've been doing it! God, the sheer simplicity of it. They overstate the size of the acreage to be transferred. The Treasury pays out for land that doesn't exist. The extra money is creamed off, and nobody's the wiser.'

Margaret Gessel was exasperated. 'I got my price. £45 an acre, that's what I was offered and that's what I got. So who are the "they" who are "creaming off money," as you put it?'

Mallon grimaced. 'I don't think we know the answer to that yet, but I can tell you we're a good deal closer to it than we were before we had this conversation.'

'And the other thing I can tell you,' Swallow added, 'is that there's got to be a few people involved in this.'

'I don't understand,' she said. 'Who's involved?'

'The scheme is simple,' Swallow explained. 'A couple of hundred fictitious acres were added to your property when the Treasury was asked to put up money for the purchase. To get away with that, it must have been necessary to put up false maps and false certificates. I believe it required the involvement of at least one dishonest lawyer or law clerk, maybe more than one. It probably involved a bank or banker. And it had to involve someone, or more than one person, in the administration.'

Margaret Gessel shook her head in disbelief. She reached to the bell-pull beside the sofa.

'I don't know about you gentlemen, but I need a very large sherry to cope with this. Will you join me?'

They both declined.

'I am not a young as I was, Sergeant, so I may have difficulty picking up details. So may I ask you explain to me how this is connected with the fact that the Gessel silver and my late husband's great uncle's collection of ancient coins are for sale in the shops in Dublin?'

'They were misappropriated by a dishonest law clerk engaged in the sale of your estate,' Swallow said. 'I believe the silver was sold or passed to Ambrose Pollock, a pawnbroker here in the city, who was a receiver of stolen goods. Somehow, someone else involved in the fraud heard about it. They knew their enterprise was at risk if these items were to find their way onto the open market.'

'I can see that.'

'So the person or persons engaged in the fraud decided to silence anybody who might have known about the theft of the silver and the coins,' Swallow said. 'The pawnbroker was murdered in his shop. Another woman who innocently bought some of the coins was attacked and might well have suffered the safe fate. It just happened that I came on the scene at her shop here in the city. And the attempt on your own life confirms the deadly intention of these people,' Mallon said.

'So what are you going to do, Mr Mallon? I certainly hope that these people can be brought to justice.'

'We'll need you to examine all the documents we have in relation to the transfer of the estate. And we'll need you to sign a statement that you never authorised the disposal of the silver or the coins to Pollock, the pawnbroker.'

'I'll certainly do that. I'll do anything within reason to get these... bastards.'

FRIDAY OCTOBER 14TH, 1887

SEVENTY-ONE

Margaret Gessel identified the last missing pieces of the jigsaw almost immediately she joined Swallow and Mossop in the Windsor Room the following morning.

Mossop had laid out the remaining deeds of transfer that she had not yet examined on the rosewood table. To Swallow's eye, there were fewer than a dozen to be checked. Margaret Gessel looked tired, he thought. She had put a lot of energy into her task yesterday. This morning she showed her years a little more, but she was energetic and keen to get on.

'Deed number seventy-one, Lady Gessel,' Mossop said, handing her the first of the documents, lightly tied with green ribbon. She undid the ribbon and peered at the papers.

'This is nonsense, a fabrication,' she exclaimed almost immediately, waving the deed. 'There's no such holding, no such tenant and no such purchaser.'

She spread it on the tabletop.

'Fifteen acres, two square perches and two square roods at Clonanish or someplace so called, to be allocated to Michael Bartley Fahy. There's no such person, never has been anywhere near Mount Gessel.'

'Are you sure?' Swallow asked. 'There might be some mistake.'

'Sergeant Swallow, do you think I don't know my tenants, each and every one of them? And the size of every holding on the Mount Gessel estate? Please don't insult my intelligence. This document is a fraud, a forgery.'

Within half an hour she had pronounced nine other deeds to be fraudulent. Mossop tallied the acreage of the fictitious holds.

'It's exactly 202 acres, Boss.'

'That's the difference between the size of the estate as you confirm it,' Swallow told her, 'and the land paid for by the Government.'

'I can damned well count too,' she snapped. 'I can see what's happened.'

An hour later, Swallow was with John Mallon in the Under-Secretary's office in the Upper Castle Yard.

The assembled cast was much the same as the previous meeting two days before. Smith Berry and Major Kelly sat against the wall, backs stiff against their chairs.

'It's simple, Sir,' Mallon told West Ridgeway. 'Brazen too, if I may say so. They simply added on fictitious holdings of land and submitted them for payment by the Treasury. Then they pocketed the difference. In this instance I reckon the profit would have been in the order of £9,000. And the question then is, if Clinton did it in the case of the Mount Gessel estate, did he do it in others?'

'It can't be as simple as that,' West Ridgeway said. 'There had to be checks on the transactions.'

'That's why we sent Inspector Boyle down at the Land Office, Sir,' Mallon replied. 'But somebody in the Treasury must have responsibility for checking these transactions against the survey maps and then certifying that all's in order. Clinton didn't act alone. This couldn't have done without inside help.'

'Have we any idea how many other estates this fellow Clinton handled?' Smith Berry asked.

'There's at least five others that I know he was involved in,' Swallow said. 'But we haven't gone near those files yet.'

'So it could be five times the amount?'

'It could be very much greater,' Mallon said. 'If there are other law firms where the same dodge is going on, this may be a much more widespread problem.'

West Ridgeway looked shocked. 'Are... you... serious, Mr Mallon?'

'We just don't know. Clinton was a follower, not a leader. I suspect we'll find that someone else, very much smarter and very much more manipulative, is behind all this.'

'What do you do next?' West Ridgeway asked.

'I need a warrant to seize the papers at the Treasury Office in the Custom House that relate to the sale of the Mount Gessel estate. We need to find who signed off there on the fictitious land sales.'

'You'll have it within the hour, Mr Mallon. In the meantime, nobody must know about this outside our group. We don't need a political crisis.'

'I understand, Sir.'

West Ridgeway steepled his fingers.

'This is now a matter of such grave importance that I believe it is time fully to brief the Chief Secretary, Mr Balfour and the government. I will seek a meeting with Mr Balfour immediately.'

'There have been certain other developments, by the way,' Mallon said.

'Tell me.'

'It's better that Detective Sergeant Swallow does that, Sir. He's closer to it.'

West Ridgeway looked interrogatively at Swallow.

'Sergeant?'

'We believe that we may have identified the person who murdered Pollock, the pawnbroker. My belief is that the murder is connected with this business. I'm just not sure how or why.'

'Who is the person you suspect? What are your suspicions based on, Sergeant?'

'Dr Lafeyre, the medical examiner, has provided us with significant clues in the form of finger-marks that were left at the scene. The finger-marks are those of Grace Clinton, widow of the late Arthur Clinton. She admits to having been there.'

'Finger-marks?' Kelly said. 'Preposterous. This is more of the bluff and flannel we get from G-Division.'

'I don't think so,' Swallow answered. 'We also have a confession. I think it was self-defence, but that's a matter for a court to decide.'

'First you told us it was his sister who killed him,' Kelly said mockingly. 'Now it's this Clinton woman. When will you make up your mind?'

'We make up our minds when we have all the information we need, Major Kelly. That might not be a process that you're especially familiar with, but it's how we do things in G-Division.'

SEVENTY-TWO

'Painting class?' Mallon asked.

Swallow and the G-Division chief had emerged from the Under-Secretary's office into the Upper Yard. 'You're going to your painting class?'

'It's always on Thursday afternoon. If you're agreeable, I'll be back by 5 o'clock. I thought it might be possible to get a couple of the lads at Exchange Court to execute the warrant at the Treasury Office. It's a matter of going through the files and picking up the relevant papers.'

'I suppose so,' Mallon said. 'You might detail Mick Feore to do it. He'd need a couple of good men with him. But he'd have a bit of diplomacy about him dealing with the civil servants down there. Check back in with my clerk when you're at finished your… painting class.'

He went to the crime sergeants' office and sent for Feore.

'Chief Mallon has a court order to enter the Land Office to seize all the papers relating to the sale of Mount Gessel. I want you to collect two or three men and execute it as soon as you can.'

'Sure, Boss, I can get a couple when the 2 o'clock shift comes in for duty. What do want me to do with the papers?'

'Bring them to Mr Mallon's office. His clerk will put them under lock and key.'

Swallow was apprehensive about meeting Katherine Greenberg for the first time since their encounter in London. He resolved that as far as he was concerned it would be business as usual.

She was there before him. She had settled in at her usual place and was laying out her materials. Swallow moved across to take the adjoining place as usual.

'Good afternoon, Katherine.'

She turned, smiling.

'I wasn't sure if you would be here. When did you get back from London?'

There was no trace of knowing in her tone. She might have been making an inquiry of a casual acquaintance or a commercial colleague just returned from a business visit.

'I took the late Sunday night crossing,' he said. 'And yourself?'

'I had some calls to make on Monday. I travelled on Monday evening.' She turned from her easel.

'Did your investigation in London succeed…with that man Shaftoe?'

'Shaftoe's dead,' he said simply. 'He was shot before he could lead us to his bosses.'

She seemed momentarily taken aback. Then he saw a hardening in her eyes.

'I'm sorry you didn't find out what you needed. But I'm glad that he's got what he deserved.'

'You could say that. But it's never a pleasant sight to see any man shot to death.'

There was an awkward, elongated silence as he laid out his brushes and colour box. He realised that he had not brought his own work in progress with him. Anyway, he reckoned, his attempts at capturing Charlie Vanucchi's flesh tones were so poor they were better not seen.

'You might have told me that the police were coming to the shop to take photographs,' she said. 'I thought you were in charge of the investigation.'

The tone was reproachful.

'I didn't know,' he answered truthfully. 'Dr Lafeyre was checking other aspects of the case.'

She did not need to know that Harry Lafeyre had identified her, even briefly, as a suspect in the murder of Ambrose Pollock.

The classroom was filling. Lily Grant's pupils were nothing if not enthusiastic. They eagerly scrutinised their neighbours' work or invited comments on their own. The air was filled with a hubbub of questions and comments. When Lily came in she had to call for silence more than once before she could make herself heard.

'Good afternoon, everybody. Today is going to be a little bit different. So far you've done all of your work indoors. But of course more artists are inspired by nature, and that means that they want to paint in the open where the light is different, very much stronger as a rule even than in the best studio.'

She waved a hand towards the windows.

'As you can see, it's a bright day. Not very warm, but there are clear skies and strong light. So I'm going to take you to the open outdoors and ask you to do some work for me on colours in the sunlight. You won't need to carry your easels because I've arranged with the porters to set up a dozen of them where we're going. Simply bring your books and your colour boxes. We're off to the Royal Hospital.'

It was a fifteen-minute walk from the Art School on Thomas Street to the spacious acres surrounding the Royal Hospital at Kilmainham. The class moved in crocodile formation, Lily leading the way. They turned off Thomas Street into Bow Lane, past Jonathan Swift's hospital for the mentally ill, before crossing the little River Cammock that flanked the Hospital grounds.

Approaching the end of Thomas Street, Swallow glanced upward at the window of his old room. Grant's was quiet, settling into the slow pace of the afternoon. Swallow wondered if Maria was upstairs. He saw Tom, the senior barman, in profile through the window, polishing glasses behind the counter.

Lily had clearly done this before. She bade a cheery 'good afternoon' to the red-coated pensioner in the sentry box at the gateway. Then she led her little battalion across the grass to the north side of the building, constructed on the order of King Charles II as a home for retired soldiers and sailors.

The afternoon sun came across the top of the building to flood the broad flight of steps leading to the North door. Two porters from the Art School were busy unloading easels from a hand cart and setting them up on the steps. One man dropped a side shelf from the handcart and put out jars of water to be used for dipping and washing the painters' brushes.

'Now,' Lily announced. 'You have a ready-made lecture theatre here with as fine a view as any artist can ask for.'

The pupils dispersed themselves on the stone steps. Below them, the ground fell away to the river, rising on the other bank to meet the wooded curtilage of the Phoenix Park.

Behind the trees, the Wellington monument stood like a great, shining sword that a giant might have plunged into the ground above the city. Brief puffs of blue-white steam formed in the air and then vanished, marking the progress of a train exiting from the King's Bridge terminus hidden below in the valley.

Swallow had kept to himself on the walk from the Art School, but now, by coincidence or otherwise, he found himself on the uppermost step, side by side with Katherine.

'I want you to look first at the greens,' Lily called to the class. 'Start with the grass here in the grounds and see which of the greens in your colour boxes might best match it. Then I want you to look across the valley at the greens and the yellows of the Phoenix Park, the different trees, the pastures and so on.'

There was much commotion as easels were adjusted and paint boxes were precariously balanced. Some pupils were dabbing colour down onto the paper almost immediately. Others seemed to be hesitant and unsure, watching the changing light in the sky and looking doubtfully at their materials.

'It's impossible to get any constant light,' Katherine said. There was a note of irritation in her voice. 'The sun comes in and out and changes everything. It's very confusing.'

'Sure,' Swallow said. 'What you'd imagine as a strong green looks washy when the sunlight hits it.'

'I think you'll have found that it's a lot more difficult to get your colours right when you're out here in the sunlight,' Lily told them. 'So don't just stick with your greens. Be experimental. It's autumn, after all. Try to mix with your browns, your yellows, your white, even your greys.'

After half an hour or so, Lily started her inspection of her pupils' work. She moved from one to the other, offering a suggestion here, giving a little praise there. To Swallow's eye, most of what had been done by the class was dreadful. When Lily passed behind him, appraising his own effort, she nodded curtly.

'It's easy to be dazzled, isn't it, Mr Swallow?'

They worked for an hour and a half. The sun arced behind the building and began to drop in the October sky. A chill came on the wind from the valley below. Lily gave the signal to finish and wash up.

A few pensioners from the Hospital had gathered to watch the class at its work. Two or three sat contentedly on a wooden bench a few yards away from the steps while their companions stood around. As the class finished, a couple of the elderly men wandered up to examine the painters' work.

'Oh, begod you've done terrible damage to the poor oul' Phoenix Park there,' one of them joked to Swallow, leaning forward crookedly to get a closer view of the painting.

'Sure ye have it in a shade o'colour that God nivvir invinted,' he cackled. 'Now, yer lady friend there, she's closer to hittin' the target.' He nodded towards Katherine's easel.

Swallow and the pensioner recognised each other simultaneously. The old man was a retired militia sergeant and a regular at Maria Walsh's public house. Swallow occasionally slipped him a quiet drink on the side.

'It's yerself, Misther Swalla'. Sure I didn't recognise ye outdoors. God, yer a man o'many talents, out here paintin' and the like.'

He turned to his companion. 'This gintleman happens to be a friend o'mine, an' him a G-man, a sergeant no less.'

The second pensioner looked impressed and made an instinctive salute.

'Yer gone lately from the Widda' Walsh's,' the old militia man said. 'Yer missed, ye know. Sure, the place isn't the same widdout ye.'

Swallow smiled. No doubt the odd free whiskey passed out across the bar had been appreciated.

'I'll tell ye somethin', Misther Swalla', if ye'll listen to me.' The old man tugged at Swallow's coat sleeve. 'Ye were well off where ye were above in Grant's.'

He saw Katherine's face instantly darken in annoyance.

'Ye should go back up there to the Widda' Walsh this evenin' and make up whatever differences yiz have. Take an ould fella's advice. Sure yiz made a grand pair. Didn't the whole o' the Liberties know it? Didn't the whole o' Dublin know it?'

SATURDAY OCTOBER 15TH, 1887

SEVENTY-THREE

From the content of the newsboys' billboards, Swallow reckoned that in all the circumstances it would be a good day for G-Division. The *Freeman's Journal* announced:

'WOMAN CHARGED WITH MURDER OF AMBROSE POLLOCK'

The Irish Times, usually more sceptical, seemed to be less certain of its ground, but it was still positive.

'LAMB ALLEY MYSTERY MAY BE NEAR TO SOLUTION'

It was the sort of good news that Mallon liked to bring to the Upper Yard. The police were on top of the situation, crime had been grasped by the throat and the citizenry could sleep easily again in their beds.

'Duck' Boyle was running the morning parade at Exchange Court. When Swallow arrived, the place was humming with good spirits. Every G-man knew it was a day when tails would be up, when even curmudgeons like Boyle would be in good humour.

'Good man, Swalla', great work there.' Boyle gushed. 'Sure, we're on the pig's back now.'

Swallow was surprised there was no report from Feore awaiting him in the crime sergeants' office. He assumed that Feore had executed the warrant to seize the Mount Gessel papers at the Treasury Office and that the material had been deposited, as he had instructed, with Chief Mallon's clerk. There was no report, though, and no sign of Feore.

The duty G-man from the public office stuck his head around the Parade Room door.

'The chief wanted you to check in with him as soon as you arrived, Sergeant.'

Swallow took the back door from Exchange Court and crossed the Lower Yard to Mallon's office. The clerk pointed to a chair.

'Sit down and don't move. Himself is up with the Assistant Under-Secretary. He said he'll send for you, and I'm not to let you out of me sight. Here, have a read of the rags.'

He tossed a *Freeman's Journal* and an *Irish Times* across the desk.

'Did you get a deposit of files from Mick Feore for the Chief?' he asked the clerk.

The man shook his head.

'Not this morning. Maybe it came in last night after I'd gone.'

That was odd, Swallow reckoned. He sensed that something was wrong. He would have to wait until he met Mallon to get an explanation. He had an hour to go through the newspapers. He had started into the classified ads in *The Irish Times* when a messenger arrived.

'Yer wanted up the Yard now, Sergeant.'

The group assembled at Smith Berry's office was smaller than that brought together on the previous day by West Ridgeway.

Smith Berry sat at the head of the table. Swallow thought that he looked as if he had eaten something disagreeable. His chief security adviser, Major Kelly, was to his right.

Kelly was squashing a heavy cigar into an ashtray in the centre of the table. Swallow registered his smug expression. Across from Kelly, the Chief Commissioner, Sir David Harrel, nervously folded and refolded a sheet of blotting-paper.

John Mallon sat halfway down the table with a face like a thunder-cloud, dark and angry.

'Sergeant Swallow. Sit, please.' The Assistant Under-Secretary struggled to form a joyless smile.'

'Thank you for joining us.'

'Thank you, Sir.'

The Assistant Under-Secretary coughed nervously.

'Now, Swallow, here's how it is. You've done excellent work on this matter. No doubt, no doubt whatsoever about that at all.'

He looked at the others as if seeking corroboration. Harrel nodded silently. Mallon continued to glare at all around him.

'Major Kelly has examined all of the papers from the Treasury Office relating to the sale of Mount Gessel estate, and several other properties handled by the late Mr Clinton,' Smith Berry continued.

'Major Kelly?' Swallow asked. 'How did that happen? I was under the impression that everything relating to Mount Gessel is in the hands of my officers?'

Smith Berry raised a hand.

'Please, Mr Swallow, I'll come to that. In each case, the sales and the values were signed off by one very senior individual who had been authorised to do so. This was fraud, embezzlement perhaps, on a grand scale, at the very heart of the administration. The Treasury Office, as you know, is the Holy Grail.'

'Well, it was pretty clear that Clinton could not have acted alone,' Swallow said. 'He needed help at the highest level.'

'Yes, that is why I've discussed these developments with the Chief Secretary. And the Chief Secretary, in turn, has consulted with his Cabinet colleagues in London.'

Swallow caught Mallon's eye. Smith Berry's invocation of the various high functionaries indicated that the stakes were rising.

'I believe that the... irregularities – shall we use that term? – that have come to light... have now been contained, and it is thanks to the excellent work of Mr Mallon and yourself. We have determined the extent of these irregularities, and I believe I can say with certainty that they will not recur.'

'I think you should speak plainly to Sergeant Swallow, Sir,' Mallon said wearily, 'with the greatest respect.'

The Assistant Under-Secretary appeared puzzled.

'Is there any more to say, Mr Mallon?'

Mallon's face was clouded with anger.

'Sergeant Swallow and his colleagues have put in weeks of work on this case. They've not seen their homes or their beds for days at a stretch. They've engaged in some of the most impressive police work that I've seen in my career.'

He paused to draw breath.

'Sergeant Swallow can speak for himself. But I know that he came to work this morning in the expectation that before the day grew old he would be making arrests, taking in the people who've been behind this business.'

There was silence. The Assistant Under-Secretary licked his lips nervously before he spoke.

'Yes, of course, Mr Mallon. I will explain what I can.'

He fixed his eyes somewhere on the ceiling.

'Mr Swallow, you are aware that the government's overriding objective at this time is to successfully conclude the transfer of properties across the country from the landowners to their tenants. The Cabinet is of the view that therein is the best prospect for peace and stability in the country and indeed for the entire kingdom.'

'I understand, Sir.'

'Therefore, nothing can be allowed to disrupt or interfere with this process, don't you see?'

'Yes, Sir, but surely....'

'If it were to become generally known that it had been corrupted, right up to the level of the Treasury Office, we might well have threats by Mr Parnell or by the leaders of the tenants' organisations to have nothing to do with it. Or indeed we might have a fit of nerves on the part of some of the bigger landowners who aren't yet fully convinced about what is on offer to them.'

'These are things beyond my remit,' Swallow said carefully.

He tried to catch Mallon's eye, but the chief was studiously staring at the tabletop in front of him.

'Yes. Well, we are relying on Mr Mallon's diplomatic skills to keep Mr Parnell happy on this. Meanwhile, the Chief Secretary and perhaps even the Lord Lieutenant will talk to some of the more influential leaders of the landowners. And the speediest of action will be taken to... shall we say... neutralise those elements within the administration that have been engaged in this corruption.'

Swallow felt a tightening in his chest as his anger rose. He knew exactly what he was being told. The case was being buried to suit the politics of the moment. He understood why Mallon looked furious.

He decided to play his own mischievous game.

'This is very good to hear, Sir. So you'll want me to act immediately. I can have the principal offenders in Kilmainham in a matter of hours. I'm expecting a report back from Detective Officer Feore. Last night he seized the relevant papers at the Treasury Office.'

Smith Berry flushed crimson.

'That is not how we intend to proceed from here, Sergeant. In the circumstances... the sensitivity... very great sensitivity... I have decided that any future steps in the matter will be taken out of the hands of G-Division and will be carried out by officers under Major Kelly's direction, reporting directly to me. Let me tell you furthermore that the papers seized under warrant by Detective Feore at the Treasury Office have been brought directly to me.'

Swallow saw a creamy grin spread across Kelly's face.

'Are you saying that someone superseded my orders to Detective Feore?'

'Yes. I did. And I have now passed the matter to Major Kelly.'

'Where's Feore then? I'll wring his bloody neck.'

Mallon intervened.

'It's not Mick Feore's fault. He received a direct order from Mr Smith Berry and I had to confirm it. I swore him to silence and told him to take today off as a rest day.'

Swallow could not contain himself any longer.

'One of my own men, taken away from my command and... subverted. And then you tell me that Major Kelly is taking over the case! He knows fuck all about this investigation, or any other. He's... as thick as pig shit in a bottle.'

'How dare you, Swallow!' Smith Berry shouted. 'The highest authorities... let me be blunt with you... want this business buried. No fuss. No charges. No publicity.'

'You mean that criminals who've defrauded the Treasury are going to go unpunished, Sir? This isn't just a matter of land and money; people have died. Lives have been lost. Other people's lives have been put in jeopardy.'

The Assistant Under-Secretary shifted uneasily in his chair.

'It's not that criminals will go unpunished, Sergeant. Oh no, far from it. The principal offender's career is blasted and he is disgraced. He will be offered a place in the Colonies that will reflect the odium to which he has been relegated. For a man of his former position I assure you he will be severely punished.'

'You're saying that there won't be any charges.'

'I am.'

Swallow was silent.

'I think I can say to you, Sergeant, that your zeal in these matters has not gone unnoticed,' Smith Berry said.

He wanted to shout back. He wanted to throw it in his face that he had no need of compliments. He had been zealous and successful in other high-profile investigations without any recognition or tangible reward.

'I have to abide by my authorities' decisions, Sir,' he said finally.

'There's one other matter, Sergeant, that needs to be dealt with.'

'What's that, Sir?'

'You have this fellow Darby in custody. The man you shot during the attempted raid at Greenberg's. I believe the best course of action is to return him to England.'

'I don't understand, Sir.'

'Think it through, Sergeant. If he comes to trial he will claim to have been working under government instructions. The whole business about the Mount Gessel fraud, the coins, the silver, it would all have to come out.'

'He had a knife to an innocent woman's throat in the shop. I don't doubt he'd have used it if he had to. I saw it.'

Smith Berry paused.

'I understand, of course, that you have a… certain affinity… with Miss Greenberg. That makes it more difficult for you. But it could also be embarrassing for the police, not to say problematic for yourself, if he were to allege that you shot him unnecessarily because of some… personal motive.'

Swallow's anger spilled out again.

'Personal motive!? For Christ's sake, I had a split second to decide. I acted as a good policeman should, in order to protect life and property. It had nothing to do with any so-called "personal motive". You should be giving me a bloody medal instead of threatening me.'

Smith Berry coloured in anger.

'You forget yourself again, Sergeant. How dare you speak to me in those terms?'

'Now,' he pointed to the door, 'I repeat, I'm aware of what you have done. Because of that I'm going to pretend that you haven't said what you just did or used the language you did. Go back to your duties and make sure that my directions in relation to Darby are complied with speedily.'

Mallon stood. He caught Swallow's eye.

'There appears to be nothing further that requires police attention here,' Mallon said. 'If that is so, Detective Sergeant Swallow and I will return to Exchange Court.'

Swallow recovered his self-control.

'May I request one item of information before I go?' he asked.

'What's that Sergeant?' Smith Berry asked cautiously.

'I'd like at least to know the identity of the chief organiser of this conspiracy. Who signed off on the imaginary land sales that the Treasury paid for?'

'No, Sergeant. It's restricted now. Only Major Kelly will need to know it. He will shortly proceed with his men to take that individual into custody and return him to London.'

'You know he has the blood of quite a few people his hands? Ambrose Pollock, Arthur Clinton, Teddy Shaftoe, just to name the ones we know about.'

'Yes. But I'm glad you didn't use the term "innocent people." All of them were involved in this criminal process.'

Swallow shook his head.

'Mr Smith Berry, the Crown doesn't deserve the loyalty that people like me give it. I do my job because I think this country needs order and peace and a bit more fair play. I just hope we're able to hold it together a bit longer.'

'We all have our orders to follow, Detective Sergeant.'

SEVENTY-FOUR

In the afternoon, he went with Mallon to visit Lady Margaret Gessel for the last time at the Shelbourne Hotel. West Ridgeway had arranged for her to be escorted by one of his officials to the evening sailing from Kingstown.

Swallow was still seething. Mallon had made an unsuccessful effort to soothe him.

'They have their own ways of sorting things out,' he said. 'They have ways of inflicting pain.'

'Maybe I'm old-fashioned,' Swallow's tone was bitter, 'but I relish the idea of a cold cell, hard labour and lousy food for the criminal, whatever class he comes from. They're protecting one of their own, I don't doubt it.'

Mallon did not dissent.

They sat in the Windsor Room looking out across the square. The trees were rapidly losing what was left of their foliage. Winter was tightening its grip on Dublin.

'I want to say thank you for your help, Lady Margaret,' Mallon said when she had joined them. 'It wouldn't have been possible to put the full picture together without your assistance.'

'You're very welcome, Mr Mallon. And you too, Mr Swallow. I hope you have enough to nail them all, whoever they are.'

'I think so.' He was vague. 'We got some of them. And we put a stop to their game.'

'Let me ask you a direct question, Mr Mallon.'

'Ma'am?'

'Is my husband's cousin, Sir Richard Gessel, involved in any way in the fraud?'

Swallow saw his boss tense.

'I can say that I have no knowledge of him being involved.'

Classic Mallon.

'Thank you, Mr Mallon. That is some slight relief.'

Later, Swallow took custody of Jack Darby at Mountjoy Prison to bring him to the mail packet at Kingstown.

'You're a lucky man, Darby,' Swallow said as the police side-car passed by the wide expanse of Sandymount Strand. 'If I had my way you'd be rotting in Maryborough for the next twenty years. Anyone who takes a knife to a woman shouldn't expect any mercy.'

Darby grinned.

'Way I 'eard it from one of the screws in that Kilmain'am place, you and the Jew girl are more than just casual acquaintances anyway.'

Swallow wanted to stop the car, take Darby out and kick him up and down the Strand.

'One more word like that and I'm bringing you back to Mountjoy you little cockney shite. And don't ask me about the charge; I'll think of something.'

There was silence for the next mile or so.

'Wot 'appened to Teddy?' Darby asked.

'Same as will probably happen to you,' Swallow said tersely. 'He got involved with people who were just as ruthless as himself, only smarter and better at it.'

At the Carlisle Pier, he opened Darby's handcuffs. The G-man was watched by the mill of passengers, some of them nodded in silent acknowledgement as Swallow marched his prisoner to the third-class gangway.

'Get on board,' Swallow said. 'And if I see your ugly face anywhere in this city again I'll put a fucking bullet through each of your eyes.'

Darby did not answer. He was staring open-mouthed past Swallow to where the first-class passengers were boarding the vessel on a separate gangway. His face registered puzzlement, then recognition of something or someone, then excitement.

He jabbed a pointing finger towards the first-class gangway.

'It's 'im... fack it. It's the fackin' toff wot set me an' Teddy up to do the robbery... there 'e goes, the facker.'

351

Swallow turned to follow Darby's line of sight.

He saw Major Kelly on the first-class gangway. Three heavily built members of his posse were around him. In between them, clearly a prisoner although not handcuffed, was George Weldon.

Weldon stared back at Swallow and Darby. Then he grinned and raised his hat in a mocking gesture as he boarded the mail boat.

SEVENTY-FIVE

When John Mallon declared he was going to a public house and that he wanted company, it was as rare as the sighting of a white blackbird.

'Come on,' he inclined his head towards the door. 'I want to get out of this place for a while. And I'm not drinking on my own. It's too dangerous.'

Swallow was unsure if Mallon was worried about the official consequences of going on a bender, or about compromising his security by going to a public house.

'Where do you want to go, Chief?'

Mallon had sent his clerk to fetch Swallow from the crime sergeants' office.

'We're going to the Brazen Head,' he said. 'At least you can put names on the criminals down there.'

They took a corner of the select bar, partly shielded from curious eyes by a wood and glass partition. Mallon ordered a large Tullamore for Swallow and a Bushmills for himself.

He took his first mouthful of the whiskey.

'The French have a phrase, *c'est la vie*. That's life.'

There was an edge of bitterness.

'We need the wisdom to know what we can change and the patience to endure what we can't.'

Swallow bit his tongue. He knew enough about patience and endurance.

'You're right, Sir. You have to be philosophical.'

'Aye, philosophical, that's the word. It'll be business as usual for the lawyers, the civil servants and the rest of them. And we're left with a great big nought after weeks of bloody effort.'

'Ah but it's great to know that the poor sloggers in the police can take credit for keeping the system going,' Swallow said sarcastically. 'The landlords get their money. The farmers get their land. There's peace in the streets. It'd make you proud.'

He drank from his Tullamore.

'What'll happen to Grace Clinton, Sir?'

'You couldn't be sure. I expect the Attorney General will have her tried for manslaughter. If she can plead self-defence she'll probably be let go. She'll do a few months in prison in the meantime.'

'There's nobody to contradict her,' Swallow said. 'The only witness is Phoebe Pollock. And God knows where she is or if we'll ever hear of her again.'

Mallon chuckled. 'If she's wise she'll keep going as far as she can while her money lasts. I'll tell you something interesting about her later.'

'Is there anything to be brought against Barry?'

'Probably not.' Mallon tossed back his drink. 'The likelihood is that he told the truth: he put her on the train to Belfast. He persuaded her to give him a few quid. Quite a few quid. But it's hard to see how we could put any criminal charge around that.'

'By the way,' he tapped his empty glass, 'it's your round.'

Swallow ordered the same again.

The first large Tullamore had warmed him and taken the edge of any sense of deference to his superior.

'Isn't it wrong, though? We're talking about a woman gone astray in the head and a poor bastard running a second-rate hotel who saw a chance to make a few bob. But the real robbers, the big fellows in the stripy pants and the top hats, are too big and too important to be touched. We're only a fucking joke, aren't we? And the law is another fucking joke.'

Mallon shrugged.

'You're an educated man, Swallow, you'll know the Latin saying, *salus populi suprema lex esto*. Let the good of the people be the highest law.'

'You mean the good of the top people. It's not the poor devils ploughing the fields or digging the roads.'

Swallow wondered if it was time to tell Mallon about the job offer from Jenkinson at Scotland Yard. He had turned it over in his mind many times in the past forty-eight hours. He was still unsure of what he would do. But he was not going to miss the opportunity to stick the offer under Mallon's nose. Maybe later, when they would each have had a few more drinks.

'I knew that fellow Weldon,' he told Mallon. 'I met him a few times with Harry Lafeyre. Smooth type. Very personable. He even took my former landlady, Mrs Walsh, to the theatre.'

'Imagine that,' Mallon said dryly.

Swallow guessed he was not telling Mallon anything he did not already know.

'There had to be somebody high up behind the land fraud,' he said. 'I thought it might be that Gessel fellow in the Prime Minister's office. He had the opportunity and the connections.'

'We can't say he wasn't involved,' Mallon mused. 'Weldon was the fellow who gave Shaftoe and Darby their orders. He must have picked up reports of the coins being sold around the city. And he knew there had to be someone, somewhere in the plan, who wasn't keeping to the rules. It wouldn't have taken him long to figure it was probably Arthur Clinton'

He sipped his Bushmills. 'But maybe he wasn't the top dog either.'

'Maybe. These fellows know how to work the system,' Swallow muttered.

'That's what we're paid for, Swallow, to keep the system running, for the people at the top and at the bottom.'

'Well, we do a pretty job of it for the crowd at the top anyway,' Swallow said, putting back a mouthful of Tullamore. 'And speaking for myself, I don't sense that's there any great feeling of gratitude for it.'

Mallon chuckled.

'I said I'd tell you something interesting about Phoebe. I had a visitor earlier, Mr John Leonard Barry. He wanted to show me a postcard he'd just got. From Belfast, posted yesterday, signed "Fondly, Phoebe." It asked him to travel there and to check into the Abercorn Hotel.'

'I don't believe it. She's in Belfast. The bloody visionaries were right.'

Mallon looked puzzled.

'Visionaries?'

'It's too complicated to explain. Forget I mentioned it.'

'You've had a grievance over not getting the step up to inspector ever since the Phoenix Park murders,' Mallon said when the drinks arrived. 'And you're entitled to that,'

'Good of you to say so, Sir,' Swallow said. The whiskey had not yet brought him to the point of open insolence.

'And it's bloody annoying to see people like Boyle moving ahead,' Mallon said. 'You know he's on the promotion list for superintendent?'

'Ha bloody ha,' Swallow said into his drink.

'It's an ill wind that doesn't blow a bit of good though.'

'What do you mean?'

'He'll go off into uniform somewhere. Rathmines or Kingstown. That'll leave a vacancy at inspector in G-Division.'

Swallow snorted. 'Yeah, a nice slot for some fucking mason or time-server with a brother in the Upper Yard.'

Mallon wagged a finger.

'Don't be so cynical. Like I said, it's an ill wind that doesn't blow some good. I was in with Smith Berry just before I came up to your office.'

'So?'

'So, I explained to him that if you hadn't cracked this case so early it would have blown up in public. The newspapers and the opposition and all the agitators would make hay on it. I told him we owed you a debt.'

'If you don't mind me saying so, it's been that way for a while, Chief,' Swallow said.

'I got you confirmed on the list for detective inspector. You'll be promoted just as soon as Boyle moves up.'

Against his expectations, Swallow felt oddly emotional. First he felt that he wanted to hit Mallon between the eyes. Then he felt he wanted to slap him on the back.

He heard himself say, 'It's about fucking time.'

That was what he thought. In fact, the words did not come out. Instead he looked at the two glasses, now empty again.

'It's my round, Chief.'

Mallon looked into his empty glass.

'You wouldn't have heard the news about Jenkinson at Scotland Yard, of course?'

Swallow had no idea what he was talking about.

'No, Sir.'

'Gone, as of last night. Resigned, I gather. They're bringing back Robbie Anderson to head the Special Irish Branch.'

'Was there a reason?' Swallow was wary. 'Anything... in particular?'

'I think he wanted out. He'd been at it a long time. I think he was just weary and worn out.'

He drank from his newly-filled whiskey tumbler.

'But it goes to show you, doesn't it? Here today, gone tomorrow. You wouldn't want to rely too much on what that kind of a fellow would be promising, would you?'

Epilogue

The pawn shop on the corner of Lamb Alley and Cornmarket remained closed. The windows at street level had been boarded up after a couple had been broken by late-night revellers. The constable who had been on special post there since the murder had been reallocated to beat duties.

There was word that a butcher from The Coombe was interested in putting in a new shop when the courts would have wound up the estate of the late Ambrose Pollock. For the present, though, the pawn shop remained eerily vacant, the boarded windows staring sightlessly at the twin churches of St Audeon across the street.

Swallow finished in Exchange Court just after 9 o'clock. He exited the detective office and turned past the City Hall for Castle Street. It was cold and dark. Soon it would be November.

Earlier, 'Duck' Boyle had visited him at the crime sergeants' office.

'Me last day here, Swalla'. I kem to shake yer hand and wish ye well before I go.'

Boyle had assembled his books and personal files in two large bundles that he placed on the desk beside the main door.

'I'm startin' in Rathmines on Monday. Ye'll be very welcome anytime yer in th'area. Of course, I'll be a busy man out there.'

Swallow answered with calculated ambiguity.

'Oh, as ever.'

'Everythin's in order in me own office. All reports up to date.'

He dropped a brown envelope on the desk in front of Swallow.

'You might want to have a squint at that yerself. The top copy's gone to the chief. But I slipped in an extra carbon so that copy you have there doesn't exist... officially, that is.'

Swallow reached out for the envelope.

'Ah, don't bother readin' it till I'm gone,' Boyle said. 'It's th' official report into that shootin' over at Greenberg's. The conclusion is that th' officer in question acted properly. No case t'answer. In fact, I'm sayin' he should be commended.'

Swallow offered to help him carry the books and files to the main steps, where an open car waited.

Boyle stepped up to the car.

'An' of course, I hear the word is that yer goin' to have a bit o' good news yerself soon. "Detective Inspector Joseph Swalla". It has a good ring to it.'

When Boyle had departed, Swallow returned to the office and closed down his own paperwork. Exchange Court would not be greatly diminished in its operational capacities by the departure of 'Duck' Boyle.

He reached the corner of Werburgh Street, where he would generally turn to make for Heytesbury Street and his rented house. On this day, though, he crossed the street under the shadow of Christ Church. He made his way along High Street and Cornmarket. The change of direction had been instinctive rather than rational. He was unsure what he was going to do. He refused even to think about it. After St Audoen's, he quickened his pace.

Someone said his name and bade him good night on Thomas Street. He recognised the beard and then the brown Franciscan habit.

'And where might you be going at this hour of the night, Sergeant?' Friar Lawrence asked. The tone was genial, solicitous.

'To tell you the truth, Father, I'm not entirely sure.'

The elderly friar chuckled.

'Ah, I'd say you're going in the right direction anyway.'

He pushed through the frosted glass doors of Grant's, breathing in the warm, smoky air of the select bar. The house was busy. There was noisy conversation and laughter coming from the snugs. A junior barman that he did not recognise was serving from behind the counter. At the end of the bar, Maria was talking to Tom, the senior man. He walked over to her.

Tom tactfully stepped away and busied himself rearranging glasses on the worktop behind the bar.

At first, Maria had looked startled. Then she smiled cautiously.

'Joe. It's a surprise to see you here… It's a nice surprise… that's what I mean.'

'It's nice to be here too.'

'Will you have… something?'

'No thanks… not here… not in the bar, that is. But you said if I ever needed supper or a late meal.…'

'Why yes, would you like to come up to the parlour?'

They made for the stairs that led to the first floor. Rain had started to spatter against the windows fronting onto Thomas Street. He breathed in the familiar scents of wood and furniture polish, cooking from Carrie's kitchen, wine and porter and turf fires.

'Yes,' he said. 'I think I'd like that very much.'

-The End-